"SO FAR AS I'M CONCERNED, SEX CAN BE ROWDY OR BRIMFUL OF MOONLIGHT: SO LONG AS IT'S SEX AND NOBODY'S GETTING HURT, I LIKE IT!"

THAT'S

DAVY

He's the child of a time so far in the future it looks like the past . . .

He's a youth as enamored of daring adventure as he is with the most pleasant of respites . . .

He's a young man who tells it all as it was—and is—with the greatest pride . . . and not the slightest inhibition!

SPICY . . . RACY . . . AND ROBUST

"A JOYOUS, BAWDY, ACHING MASTERPIECE BY ONE OF THE BEST AND WISEST STORY TELLERS OF OUR TIMES!"

—Peter S. Beagle
Author of
The Last Unicorn

Also by Edgar Pangborn:

COMPANY OF GLORY

GOOD NEIGHBORS & OTHER STRANGERS

A MIRROR FOR OBSERVERS

WEST OF THE SUN

WILDERNESS OF SPRING

THE TRIAL OF CALLISTA BLAKE

DAVY

Edgar Pangborn

A Del Rey Book

BALLANTINE BOOKS • NEW YORK

NOTE: The characters in this novel are fictitious in a limited sense—that is, they won't be born for several hundred years yet.

A Del Rey Book
Published by Ballantine Books

Library of Congress Catalog Card Number: 64-10349

ISBN 0-345-30702-X

This edition published by arrangement with St. Martin's Press

Manufactured in the United States of America

First U.S. Printing: December 1964
Fourth U.S. Printing: November 1982

First Canadian Printing: February 1965

Cover art by Boris Vallejo

to
All of Us
including
JUDY

1

I'm Davy, who was king for a time. King of the Fools, and that calls for wisdom.

It happened in 323, in Nuin, whose eastern boundary is a coastline on the great sea that in Old Time was called the Atlantic—the sea where now this ship winds her passage through gray or golden days and across the shoreless latitudes of night. It was in my native country Moha, and I no more than a boy, that I acquired my golden horn and began to learn its music. Then followed my years with Rumley's Ramblers into Katskil, Levannon, Bershar, Vairmant, Conicut and the Low Countries—years of growing, with some tasty girls and good friends and enough work. And when, no longer with the Ramblers, I came into Nuin, I must have been nearly a man, or the woman I met there, my brown-eyed Nickie with the elf-pointed ears, would not have desired me.

I learned my letters, or they called it learning them, at the school in Skoar, but actually I knew nothing of reading and writing until my time with the Ramblers, when Mam Laura Shaw lost patience with my ignorance and gave me the beginning of light. Being now twenty-eight and far advanced in heresy, and familiar with the fragments of Old-Time literature, I say to hell with the laws that forbid most Old-Time books or reserve them to the priests!

Somewhere I have picked up the impudence to attempt writing a book for you, conceiving you out of nothing as I must because of the ocean between us and the centuries that you people, if you exist, have known nothing of my part of the round world. I am convinced it is round.

My way of writing must follow an Old-Time style, I think, not the speech or writing of the present day. The few books made nowadays, barbarously printed on miserable paper and deserving no better, are a Church product, dreary beyond belief—sermons, proverb, moral tales. There is some ginger in the common speech, it's true, but it is restricted to a simplicity that renders it, on the whole, hellishly dull—let any man not a priest use a term that cannot be grasped by a drooling chowderhead, and eyes slip sidelong in suspicion, fingers make ready for the flung stone that has always been a fool's favorite means of putting himself on a level with the wise. And finally, English in the pattern of Old Time is the only language I could have in common with you who may exist and one day read this.

We are free men and women aboard this vessel, carrying no burden of cherished ignorance. In the country that drove us out they preen themselves on freedom of religion, which meant in practise, as it evidently did throughout Old Time, merely freedom for a little variety within the majority's religion—no true heretics wanted, although in the last century or so of Old Time they were not persecuted as they are today, because the dominant religion of that time, on that continent, was thinned down to a pallid reminiscence of its one-time hellfire glory. The Holy Murcan Church, and the small quackpot sects that it allows to exist, were certainly latent in Old Time, but so far as one can tell at this distance, Christianity in the America of what they called the 20th Century was hardly capable of scaring even the children. On this schooner there is freedom from religion, and in writing this book for you I shall require that freedom; if the thought offends you, take warning at this point and read some other book.

Our ship, our *Morning Star*, follows a design of Old Time, resembling no other vessel of our day except one experimental predecessor, the *Hawk*, burnt at her moorings four years ago in the war of 327 against the Cod Islands pirates. When the *Hawk* was built, men watched the placing of her timbers, saw the tall pine masts brought from Nuin's northern province of Hampsher, and they said she would sink on launching. She sailed bravely for months, before fire destroyed her off Provintown Island. Something in us remembers her, where her blackened bones must lie in the dark making a home for octopus or the great sea snakes. And we heard the same prophecy about the *Morning Star*. They saw her launched, the masts were stepped, the sails took hold of the sky, she went through her trials in Plimoth Bay like a lady walking on a lawn—they said she'd capsize at the first gale. Well, we have weathered more than one storm since we began our journey toward the sun's rising.

The world is round. I don't think you walk upsydown carrying your heads under your shoulders. If you do I'm wasting my time, for to understand the book I mean to write a man would need to have a head fastened on at the upper end of his neck, and use it now and then.

Our captain Sir Andrew Barr would also be damn surprised to find you walking upsydown, and so would my two best-loved, Nickie my wife and Dion Morgan Morganson lately Regent of Nuin—who are partly responsible for this book, by the way: they urged me into writing it and now watch me sweat. Captain Barr suggests further that anyone who seriously entertained that upsydown mahooha would almost certainly piss to windward.

There were enough maps and other items of scientific information at the secret library of the Heretics in Old City of Nuin to give us a fair picture of the world as it was some four hundred years ago and as it must be now. The rise in sea level, which seems to have been catastrophically rapid during the period when Old-Time civilization went phut, makes a liar out of any Old-Time map so far as coastlines are concerned. The wrath of the world's waters would have been responsible for many inland changes too—earthquake, landslip, erosion of high ground in the prolonged torrential rains that John Barth describes in his (forbidden) journal.

Well, of course it's the truth, the many kinds of truth in the old books that causes the Church to forbid most of them, and to describe all the Old-Time knowledge as "primitive legend." It won't do to have a picture of this earth so jarringly different from the one the Holy Murcan Church provides—not even in a society where hardly one

9

man in two dozen is literate enough to recognize his own name in writing. Too much truth, and too much ginger to suit the timid or the godly or the practical joes who make a good living helping the Church run the governments.

The earth is a sphere within empty space, and while the moon and the Midnight Star circle around it, it circles the sun. The sun also journeys—so the Old-Time learning tells me and I believe it—and the stars are faraway suns resembling our own, and the bright bodies we see to move are planets something like ours—except the Midnight Star. I think that swift-coursing gleam was one of the satellites sent aloft in Old Time, and this I find more wonderful than the Holy Murcan legend which makes it a star that fell from heaven as a reproach to man when Abraham died on the wheel. And I think the earth, moon, planets, sun and all the stars may be journeying, for a while or for eternity, but not, I dare say, with any consideration for our convenience—for we can if we like invent God and then explain his will for the guidance of humanity, but I would rather not.

Until I began it I never dreamed what a labor it is to write a book. ("Just write," says Dion, for the sake of seeing me sputter—he knows better. Nickie is more helpful: when I'm fed up with rhetoric I can catch her tawny-gold body and wrestle its darling warmth.) I try to keep in mind how much you don't know, how men can't often see beyond the woods and fields of their homelands, nor beyond the lies and true-tales they learned in growing, the moments of pain or delight that may seem to make a true-tale out of a lie, a vision, a fancy, or an error out of a truth as stubborn as a granite hill.

Whenever I get stung by an idea I've got to go on scratching as long as it smarts. My education, as I've already hinted, was delayed. At twenty-eight I believe my ignorance is expanding in a promising sort of way, but forgive me if at times I tell you less than I might or more than you wish. I reached fourteen as empty of learning as a mud-turkle though slightly less homely, being red-haired, small but limber with a natural-born goofy look, and well-hung.

The republic of Moha, where I was born in a whore-

10

house that was not one of the best, is a nation of small lonely farms and stockaded villages in the lake and forest and grassland country north of the Katskil Mountains and the rugged nation that bears the mountains' name. One day Katskil may conquer all Moha, I suppose. I was born in one of Moha's three cities, Skoar. It lies in a hollow of the hills almost on the line where the Katskil border ran at that time.

In Skoar life goes by the seasons and the Corn Market trade. Wilderness is a green flood washing up to the barrier of the city's rather poor stockade, except where the brush has been cleared to make the West and the Northeast Roads a little safer for their double streams of men, mule-wagons, soldiers, pilgrims, tinkers, wanderers.

There's a raw splendor to those roads, except when wartime makes folk more than ever afraid of travel and open places. In good times the roads reek of horse, ox-team, men, of the passage of chained bears and wolves brought for sale to the city baiting-pits; under sunshine and free winds the stink is nothing to trouble you. You may see anything on the go in the daytime. Maybe a great man, even a Governor, riding alone, or a holy character on a pilgrimage—you know it's that, most likely a journey to the marketplace in Nuber, where Abraham is believed to have died on the wheel, because the man is stark naked except for his crown of briers and the silver wheel hung at his neck. He never looks to left or right when people edge up close shyly touching his head or hands or testicles to share his sanctity and heal themselves of private troubles. Or it may be some crowd of street-singers and tumblers, with whiteface monkeys chittering on their shoulders and caged parrots quarking horny talk.

Once in a while you'll see the gay canvas-covered mule-wagons of a Rambler gang with sexy pictures and odd designs all over the sides, and you know that wherever they stop there'll be music, crazy entertainments, good ball-tickling sideshows, fortunetelling, fine honest swindling, and news from far places that a man can trust. Rumors come and go, and a Rambler considers it a duty to cheat you in a horsetrade or such-like slicker than a gyppo, but the Ramblers also take pride in bearing nothing but true-

11

tales from the distant lands, and the people know it, and value them for it so highly that few governments dare clamp down on their impudence, randiness, free-living ways. I know; I never forget I was with Rumley's Ramblers for the best years of my life before I found Nickie.

Another thing you might notice would be a fancy litter with drawn curtains, the bearers matched for height, moving in skillful broken step so that the expensive female stuff inside—might even be a Governor's personal whore —needn't stick her head out and blast the bearers for clumsy damned idle sumbitches. Or there might be a batch of slaves chained tandem being marched for sale at the Skoar market, or a drove of cattle for the slaughterhouse distracting the whole road with their loud stupidity and oneriness—those steers don't want to go, not anywhere, but the road pushes them along its gut, a mindless earthworm swallowing, spilling out at the anal end and reaching for more.

The roads are quiet at night. Brown tiger and black wolf may use them then—who's to say, unless it's a night-caught traveler who'll see nothing more afterward?

Farming is heartbreak work in Moha as everywhere. The stock gives birth to as many mues there as anywhere; the toll taken by the wild killers is high, the labor is sweat and disappointment grinding a man to old age in the forties, few farmers ever able to afford a slave. The people get along though, as I've seen human beings do in worse places than Moha. The climate is not as hot and malarial as Penn. There's trade in timber and saddle-horses; manufacture too, though it can't match the industry of Katskil or Nuin. A barrel-factory in Skoar turned out coffins as a sideline and prospered—Yankee ingenuity, they called it. They scrape along, the same poor snotty human race, all of a muddle and on the go, as they've always done and maybe always will until the sun sweats icicles, which won't be next Wednesday.

A maybe. Now that I know the books, I can't forget how this same human race must have survived the Years of Confusion by a narrow squeak, the merest happen-so.

The other two big centers of my homeland are Moha City and Kanhar, walled cities in the northwest on Moha

Water, a narrow arm of the sea. Eighteen-foot earthwork walls—that's enough to stop brown tiger's leap, and it makes Skoar with its puny twelve-foot log palisade a very cheap third. The great Kanhar wharves can take outriggers up to thirty tons—the big vessels, mostly from Levannon, that trade at all ports. Moha City is the capital, with the President's palace, and Kanhar the largest—twenty thousand not counting the slaves, who might make it twenty-five. Moha law reasons that if you count them like human beings you may end by treating them the same way, exposing a great democracy to revolution and ruin.

Now I think of it, every nation I know of except Nuber is a great democracy. The exception, Nuber the Holy City, is not really a nation anyway, just a few square miles of sanctified topsoil facing the Hudson Sea, enclosed on its other three sides by some of Katskil's mountains. It is the spiritual capital of the world, in other words the terrestrial site of that heavenly contraption the Holy Murcan Church. Nobody dwells there except important Church officials, most of them with living quarters in the mighty Nuber Cathedral, and about a thousand common folk to take care of their mundane needs, from sandal-thongs and toilet rags to fair wines and run-of-the-mill prosties. Katskil country doesn't produce fine wines nor highly skilled bed-athletes —they have to be imported, often from Penn.

Katskil itself is a kingdom. Nuin is a Commonwealth, with a hereditary Presidency of absolute powers. Levannon is a kingdom, but governed by a Board of Trade. Lomeda and the other Low Countries are ecclesiastical states, the boss panjandrum being called a Prince Cardinal. Rhode, Vairmant and Penn are republics; Conicut's a kingdom; Bershar is mostly a mess. But they're all great democracies, and I hope this will grow clearer to you one day when the ocean is less wet. Oh, and far south or southwest of Penn is a nation named Misipa which is an empire, but they admit no visitors,* living behind an earthwork wall that is

---

* Davy means, no northern visitors. They have some commerce with the region known in Old Time as South America. In 296 a handful of refugees from some Misipan political tempest reached Penn overland, and gave this and other information before they died of malaria, infected wounds and dysentery. They spoke an

13

said to run hundreds of miles through tropical jungle, and destroying all northern coastal shipping—by the use of gunpowder no less, tossed on the decks by clever catapult devices. Since the manufacture of gunpowder is most strictly forbidden by the Holy Murcan Church as a part of the Original Sin of Man, these Misipans are manifest heathens, so nobody goes there except by accident, nobody knows whether this empire is also a democracy, and to the best of my information nobody cares to the extent of a fart in a hurricane.

Fifty miles south of Kanhar lies Skoar. There I was born, in a house that, while not high-class, was no mere crib either. I saw it later, when old enough to be observant. I remember the red door, red curtains, brass phallus-lamps, the V-mark over the front door that meant it was licensed by the city government in accordance with the Church's famous Doctrine of Necessary Evils. What showed it wasn't high-class was that the girls could lounge on the front steps with thighs spread or a breast bulging out of a blouse, or strip at the windows hollering invitations. A high-class house generally shows only the V-mark, the red door, and an uncommon degree of outward peace and quiet—the well-heeled customers prefer it that way. I'm not over-fussy myself—so far as I'm concerned, sex can be rowdy or brimful of moonlight: so long as it's sex, and nobody's getting hurt, I like it.

In such houses, of whatever class, there's no time for kids. But children are scarce in this world and therefore prized. I was well-formed, nothing about me to suggest a mue, but as a whorehouse product I was a ward of the State, not eligible for private adoption. The policers took me from my mother, whoever she was, and put me in the Skoar orphanage. She would have got the payment usual in such cases, and would then have had to change her name

English so barbarous that there has been argument ever since over much that they tried to say. I learned of this by listening in as a small boy on semi-formal conversations between my grandfather President Dion II and the Penn ambassador Wilam Skoonmaker. My poor uncle, later Morgan III, held me in his lap while he took notes on Skoonmaker's stately talk and I admired his embroidered pants.

—Dion Morgan Morganson of Nuin.

14

and move to some other city, for the State preferred that wards of my sort should know nothing of their origin—I learned mine only through the accident of overhearing a blabbermouth priest at the orphanage when I was thought to be asleep.

I grew up at the orphanage until I was nine, the usual age for bonding out. As a bond-servant I still belonged to the State, which took three-fourths of my pay until I should be eighteen. Then, if all had gone well, the State would consider itself reimbursed, and I would become a freeman. This was the Welfare System.

At the orphanage nearly everything got done with patient sighs or silence. It was not crowded. The nuns and priests wouldn't stand for noise, but if we kept quiet there were few punishments. We were kept busy at easy tasks like sweeping, dusting, laundry, scrubbing floors, cutting and carrying firewood, washing dishes and pans, digging the vegetable patch, weeding and harvesting it, waiting on table which meant watching scum gather on the soup during Father Milsom's prayers, and emptying the sacerdotal chamberpots.

In spite of considerable care and kindness we grew up familiar with sickness and death. I recall a year when there were only five boys and eight girls, and work got tough—the average population was around twenty children. Our guardians suffered for us, praying extra hours, burning candles of the large economy size that combines worship with fumigation, bleeding us and giving us what's called vitamin soup which is catnip broth with powdered eggshell to stiffen the bones.

There was no schooling to speak of at the orphanage. In Moha schooling belonged to the years between the ninth and twelfth birthdays, except for the nobility and candidates for the priesthood, who had to sweat out a great deal more. Even slave children had to go through a bit of schooling: Moha was progressive that way. I well remember the district school on Cayuga Street, the weariness of effort that never found a real focus, and now and then a sense of something vital out of reach. And yet our school was very progressive. We had Projects. I made a birdhouse.

15

It wasn't much like the ones I'd made for fun, off in the woods on my lone, out of bark and vines and whittled sticks. The birds themselves were uneducated enough to like those. The one I made at the school with real bronze tools was lots prettier. You wouldn't want to hang it in a tree of course—you just don't do such things with a Project.

My bond-servant pay wasn't docked for school hours; a good law saw to that. All the same, compulsory progressive education is no joke, when it takes so much time out of your life that might have been spent at learning something.

The only child friend I remember from the orphanage time is Caron, who was nine when I was seven. She didn't grow up with me but was sent to the orphanage after her parents liquidated each other in a knife brawl. Only a few months and then she was bonded out, but in that time she loved me. She was quarrelsome with everyone else, constantly in trouble. Late at night, when the supervisor dozed off by the one candle, there'd be some flitting back and forth between the boys' and girls' sides of the dormitory, although the penalty for getting caught at sex games was twenty lashes and a day in the cellar. Caron came to me that way, slipping under my blanket bony and warm. We played our fumbling games, not very well; I remember better her talk, in a tiny voice that could not have been heard ten feet away. True-tales of the outer world, and make-believe, and often (this scared me) talk of what she meant to do to everyone in the institution except me—all the way from burning down the building to carving Father Milsom's nuts, if he had any. She must have been bonded out away from Skoar, I think. When I was bonded myself, still lonely for her two years later, I never won a clue to what had happened to her. I learned only that the lost do not often return in life as they do in the kindly little romances we can hear from the story-teller beggars at the street-corners for a coin or two.

Caron would be thirty now, if she's alive. Sometimes, even in bed with my Nickie, I recall our puppy squirming, the wild inconsequences of childhood thought, and imagine that if I saw her now I would know her.

I do remember one other, Sister Carnation, smelling of

16

crude soap and sweat, who mothered me and sang to me when I was very small. She was mountainously fat with deep-sunk humorous eyes, a light true voice. I was four when Father Milsom checked my whines of inquiry by saying Sister Carnation had walked with Abraham. So I was sick-jealous of Abraham till someone explained it was only a holy way of saying she had died.

I was bonded out as a yard-boy at the Bull-and-Iron tavern on Kurin Street, and worked at it till a month after my fourteenth birthday, which is where I mean to begin my story. Board at half price; after that and the State's three-fourths were taken out, I had two dollars a week left, and I supplemented the board unofficially too. Oat bread, stew, and whatever can be "uplifted" as Pa Rumley of Rumley's Ramblers used to say—a boy can grow on that. And the stew at the Bull-and-Iron was thicker and better than anything at the orphanage—more goat and less religion.

2

On a day of middle March a month after my fourteenth birthday I sneaked away from the Bull-and-Iron at first-light, goofing off. It had been a tough winter—smallpox, flu, everything but the lumpy plague. Snow fell in January an inch deep; I've seldom seen it so heavy. Now, winter being gone, I ached with the spring unrest, the waking dreams. I wanted and feared the night dreams in which some fantastic embrace short of completion would wake me with jetting of the seed. I knew a thousand ambitions that died of laziness; weariness of nothing-to-do while everything was yet to be done—most children call that boredom, and so did I, although childhood was receding then and not slowly. I saw the intolerant hours slip past,

17

each day befooled by a new maybe-tomorrow and no splendid thing coming down the road.

There was a frost in Febry* on my birthday; people said it was unusual. I recall seeing from my loft window that birthday morning a shaft of icicle clinging to the sign over the inn doorway—a noble sign, painted for Jon Robson by some journeyman artist who likely got bed and a meal out of it, along with the poverty talk Old Jon burped up on such occasions. (Only Jon Robson's daughter Emmia remembered it was my birthday, by the way; she slipped me a shiny silver dollar, and a sweet look for which I'd have traded all the dollars I owned, but as a bond-servant I could have been slapped in the stocks for having such a thought about a freeman's daughter.) The sign showed a red bull with tremendous horns, ballocks like a pair of church-bells; representing the iron was a bull-ring dart sticking out of his neck and he not minding it a bit. Mam Robson's idea likely. For a harmless old broad she got a surprising bang out of the bear-pit, bull-ring, atheist-burnings, public hangings. She said such entertainments were mor'l because they showed you how virtue triumphed in the end.

The wolves sharpnosed in close that winter. A pack of blacks wiped out a farm family at Wilton Village near Skoar, one of the families that risk dwelling outside the community stockade. Old Jon told every new guest the particulars of the massacre, to make good table-talk and to remind the customers how smart they were to come to a nice inn behind a city-type stockade—reasonable rates too. He might be still telling that yarn, and perhaps mentioning a redheaded yard-boy he once had who turned out to be a real snake in his bosom not fit to carry guts to a bear. Old Jon had connections in Wilton Village and knew the family the wolves killed. In any case he never kept his mouth shut more than a few minutes unless aristocracy was present: then, being a Mister himself, the lowest grade of nobility, he'd hold it shut, his blue damp

---

* Davy has asked Dion and me to ungoof the spelling here and there, but nobody could claim this one isn't an improvement.
—Miranda Nicoletta deMoha.

eyes studying their faces in his lifelong search for the best arses to kiss.

He wouldn't keep it shut when he slept. He and the Mam had their bedroom across the wagon-yard from my loft. In mid-winter with their windows closed tight against draft-devils I'd still hear Old Jon sleeping away like an un-greased wagon-wheel. Once in a great while I'd hear the Mam howling briefly during his bedwork. It's a good question how they managed it, a two-hundred-pound lard-bucket and a little dry stick.

In the dark of that March morning I fed the horses and mules, reasoning that someone else could get his character strengthened by shoveling. The tavern did own a pair of slaves for outside work. My only reason for ever cleaning the stable was that I like to see such jobs done right, but that morning I felt they could take the whole shibundle and shove it. It was a Friday anyway, so all work was sin-ful, unless you care to claim that shoveling is a work of piety, and I want you to think carefully about that.

I crept into the main kitchen, knowing my way around. Although a yard-boy, I practiced the habit of washing whenever I could, and so old Jon let me help at waiting on table, minding the taproom fire, fetching drinks. I was safe that morning: everybody would be fasting before church, comfortably, in bed. The slave Judd, boss of the kitchen, wasn't up yet, so his scullion helpers would also be dead to the world. If Judd had discovered me the worst he'd have done would have been to chase me a step or two on his gimp leg, praising God he hadn't a chance of catching me.

I located a peach pie. I'd skipped fasting and church a long time—not hard, for who notices a yard-boy?—and no lightning had clobbered me yet, though I'd been plainly taught that the humblest creatures are the special concern of God. In the storeroom I uplifted a loaf of oat bread and a chunk of bacon, and started thinking, Why not run away for good? Who would care?

Old Jon Robson would: squaring my bond would hurt in the pocketbook nerve. But then I'd never asked to have my life regarded as a market commodity.

Emmia might care. I worked on that as I stole down the morning emptiness of Kurin Street, true sunrise almost half

19

an hour away. I worked on it hard, being fourteen, maybe more active in the sentimentals than most downyskins of that age. I had myself killed by black wolf, and changed that to bandits because black wolf wouldn't leave enough bones. I felt we should provide bones. Somebody could fetch them back to show Emmia. "Here's all's left of poor Davy except his Katskil knife. He allowed he wanted you should have it, was anything to happen to him." But I'd never actually got around to saying that to anyone, and anyhow bandits wouldn't leave a good knife, rot them.

Emmia was sixteen, big and soft like her Da, only on her it looked good. She was a blue-eyed cushiony honeypot with a few more pounds than most girls have of everything except good sense. For a year my nights had been heated by undressing her in my fancy, all alone in my stable loft. The real Emmia occasionally had to bed down with important guests to maintain the reputation of the inn, but I wouldn't quite admit the fact to myself. Certainly I'd been hearing the old cunty yarns and jokes about innkeeper's daughters for years, but except for Caron lost in childhood Emmia was my first love. I did somehow avoid understanding that the darling quail was obliged to be a part-time whore.

I was gulping when I passed the town green. Pillory, whipping-post and stocks had become grayly visible, reminders of what could happen to a bond-servant who should get caught putting a hand on Emmia's dress, let alone under it. As I neared the place where I meant to get over the stockade, most of the flapdoodle about bones drained out of my head. I was thinking about running away for real.

Found and brought back, I could be declared a no-brand slave and sold by the State for a ten-year term. But that morning I was telling myself what they could do with such laws. I had the bacon and bread, my flint-and-steel and my luck charm, all in a shoulder-sack that was my rightful property. My knife, also honestly mine by purchase, hung sheathed on a belt under my shirt, and all the money I had saved in the winter, ten dollars, was knotted into my loin-rag—the bright coin that Emmia gave me tied off separately, never to be spent if I could help it. Up in the woods of North Mountain where I'd found a cave in my solitary wanderings of the year before, I had other things stored— an ash bow I had made, brass-tipped arrows, fishline, two genuine steel fish-hooks, and ten more dollars buried. The arrow-tips and fishline were cheap; it had taken a couple of weeks to save enough for those good fish-hooks, seeing how scarce and precious steel is nowadays.

I scrabbled over the palisade logs while the sleepy guard was out of sight on his rounds, and took off up the mountainside. The Emmia who talked in my heart quit whimpering over bones. I thought of the actual soft-lipped girl who would surely want me to turn back and stick it out through my bond-period, although in the flesh I'd done nothing hotter than imagine her beside me on my pallet during those rather sad private games.

Climbing the steep ground away from the city, I decided I'd merely stay lost a day or two as I'd done other times. Then it had usually been my proper day off. Not always: I'd risked trouble before and blarneyed out of it. This time I'd stay until the bacon was gone, and work up some fancy whopmagullion to tell on my return, to soften the action of Old Jon's leather strap on my rump—not that he ever hurt much, for he lacked both muscle and active cruelty. The decision calmed me. When I was well into the cover of the big woods I climbed a maple to watch for sunrise.

From up there the roads out of Skoar were still shut away from sight by the forest. Skoar was insubstantial, a phantom city caught and hung in a veil of early light. I think I knew it was also a prosaic reality, a huddle of ten thousand human beings ready for another day of working, swindling, loafing, stepping on each other's faces or now and then trying not to.

Before reaching my maple I had heard the liquid inquiry of the first bird-calls. Now the sun-fire would soon be at the rim; the singers were wide awake, their music rippling back and forth across the top of the world. I heard a white-throat sparrow, who would not remain long on his way north. Robin and wood-thrush—could a morning begin without them? A cardinal shot past, ablaze. A pair of white parrots broke out of a sycamore to skim over the trees, and

I heard a wood-dove, and a wren exploded his small heart in a shower of rainbow notes.

I watched a pair of whiteface monkeys in a sweet gum nearby; they didn't mind me. The male put down his head so his wife could groom his neck. When she tired of it he grabbed her haunches and helped himself to a bit of love, a thank-you job acted out with his favorite tool. They sat then with their arms around each other, long black tails hanging, and he yawned at me: "Eee-ooo!" When I looked away from them the east was flaming.

Of a sudden I wanted to know: Where does it come from, the sun? How is it set afire for the day?

Understand, in those days I hadn't a scrap of decent learning. At school I'd toiled through two books, the speller and the Book of Prayers. At a Rambler entertainment when I was thirteen I'd picked up a sex pamphlet because I thought it had pictures, and would have bought a dream book if it hadn't cost a dollar. I knew of the Book of Abraham, called the one source of true religion, and was aware that common men are forbidden to read it lest they misunderstand. Books, say the priests, are all somewhat dangerous and had much to do with the Sin of Man in Old Time; they tempt men to think independently, which in itself implies a rejection of God's loving care. As for other types of learning—well, I considered Old Jon remarkably advanced in wisdom because he could keep accounts with the bead-board in the taproom.

I believed, as I'd been taught, that the world consisted of an area of land three thousand miles square, which was a garden where God and the angels walked freely among men performing miracles until about four hundred years ago when men sinned by lusting after forbidden knowledge and spoiled everything. Now we're working out the penance until Abraham the Spokesman of God, Advertiser of Salvation whose coming was foretold by the ancient prophet Jesus Christ sometimes called the Sponsor, Abraham born of the Virgin Cara in the wilderness during the Years of Confusion, slain for our sins on the wheel at Nuber in the thirty-seventh year of his life, shall return to earth and judge all souls, saving the few and consigning the many to everlasting fire.

I knew the present year was 317, dating from the birth of Abraham, and that all nations agreed on this date. I believed that on every side of that lump of land three thousand miles square the great sea spread to the rim of the world. But—what about that rim? The Book of Abraham, said the priests, does not say how far out it is—God doesn't wish men to know, that's why. When I heard that in school, naturally I shut up, but it bothered me.

All my doubts were young and tentative: new grass struggling up through the rotted trash of winter. I did think it remarkable how the lightning never roasted me no matter how I sinned. At the close of my last school year a whole week was devoted to Sin, Father Clance the principal giving it personal attention. The Scarlet Woman puzzled us: we knew whores painted their faces, but it did sound as if this one was red all over—I didn't get it. We knew what the good father meant by the Sin of Touching Yourself, though we called it jacking off; a few of the greener boys were upset to learn that if you did it your organs would turn blue and presently drop away; two fainted and one ran outside to vomit. Girls and boys had been separated that week, so I don't know what sacred information got rammed into the quail. I could see that I must be too altogether trifling for God to bother about me, since I'd been taught the technique at least four years earlier at the orphanage, wasn't even slightly blue, and still had everything. Father Clance was large and pale; he looked as if his stomach hurt and someone else was to blame. You felt that before blundering along and creating human beings male and female, God might in common decency have first consulted Father Clance.

The Church made it plain that everything connected with sex was sinful, hateful, dirty—even dreaming of a lay was called "pollution"—and also deserving of the utmost reverence. There were other inconsistencies, inevitable I suppose. The Church and its captive secular governments naturally wished the population might increase; with so many marriages sterile, mue-births coming nearly one in five, it's an empty world. But the Church is also committed to the belief—I don't understand its origins—that all pleasure is suspect and only the joyless can

23

be virtuous. Therefore the authorities do their best to encourage breeding while solemnly looking the other way. Something like a little show we used to put on when I was with Rumley's Ramblers: four couples munching a nobility-type dinner with slaves bowing in the baked meats, and those aristocrats jawed gravely about the weather, fashion, church affairs never cracking a smile—but the audience could see under the table, where a squirming of fingers and bared thighs and upper-class codpieces was wondrous to behold.

The mind of Father Clance could take that kind of inconsistency with no pain; not mine. Religion requires a specially cultivated deafness to contradiction which I'm too sinful to learn.

Of course at fourteen I understood that you agreed out loud with whatever the Church taught, or else. I watched my first atheist-burning after I started work at the Bull-and-Iron. The attraction was a man who'd been heard to tell his son that nobody was ever born of a virgin. I'm not clear how this made him an atheist, but knew better than to ask. In Moha the burnings were always part of the Spring Festival—children under nine were not required to attend.

From my maple I watched the birth and growing of the day. Unexpectedly I thought: What if someone were to sail as far as the rim?

It was too much. I shied away from the thought. I slid from my tree and climbed on through deep forest, where the heat of day is always moderate. I traveled slowly so as not to raise a sweat, for the smell drifts far and black wolf or brown tiger may get interested. Against black wolf I had my knife—he hates steel. Tiger is indifferent to knives —a flip of his paw will do—but he usually avoids mountain country to follow the grazers. He's said to respect arrows a little, and thrown spears and fire, though I've heard of his leaping a fire-circle to take a man.

I wasn't too concerned about those ancient enemies that morning. My perilous thought was generating others: Suppose *I* went to the rim, and saw the sun catch fire? . . .

In heavy woods at any time of day there's an uncertainty of twilight. Objects seemg more and less than real, when the light reaches them in a downflowing through the leaves. Part of night lingers. The question what is behind you may hold something more than fear. A good or desired being might walk there instead of danger, who's to know?

My cave on North Mountain was a crack in a cliff broadening inside to make a room four feet wide and twenty deep. The crack ran up into darkness but must have reached the outside, since a draft like the pull of a chimney kept the air fresh. Black wolf could have entered, even tiger though he would have found scant room to maneuver. I'd driven out copperheads when I found the cave, and had to watch against their return; sweeping with a branch for scorpions was another housekeeping routine. The approach was a narrow ledge that widened in front of the cave with enough earth to support some grass and then led on more steeply to the other end of the cliff. The cave was on the east face of the mountain, Skoar in the south shut away. I could build small fires at night, searching the glow for a boy's visions of places unexplored, faraway times and other selves.

That morning I first made sure of my bow and other gear. All there, but I felt a strangeness. I wet my nose to sharpen the scents; nothing wrong. When I found the cause, on the back wall where my glance must have gone at first unseeingly, I was not much wiser. A picture had been drawn by a point of soft red rock. It must have been done since my last visit, in November. It showed two faceless stick figures, with male parts. I'd heard of hunters' sign messages, but this said nothing of that sort. The figures merely stood there. One was in good human proportion, elbows and knees bent, fingers and toes carefully indicated. The other reached the same height but his arms were too long and his legs too short with no knee-crook. I found no tracks, nothing left behind in the cave and nothing stolen.

I gave it up. Someone had passed by since November, and left my gear untouched; no reason to think he meant me any harm. I made sure a horse-shoe hidden under a rock in the front of the cave was still in place, though I'd never heard of pictures being left around by witches or

25

any other supernaturals. I gathered fresh boughs to sleep on, and a mess of firewood, and lay out in the sun for daydreaming, naked except for my knife-belt. Without such free time now and then, how would we ever find new methods of protecting the moon from the grasshoppers? I didn't forget the picture, but I supposed the visitor was long gone. My thoughts sailed beyond the limits of day.

I thought of journeying.

The Hudson Sea, Moha Water, the Lorenta and Ontara Seas—I knew all those were branches of the great sea that divides the known world into islands. I knew that the Hudson Sea in many places is barely a mile wide, easy for small craft. And I knew that thirty-ton outriggers of Levannon sailed through Moha Water to the Ontara Sea, and then to Seal Harbor, on the Lorenta Sea, where most of our lamp-oil comes from. Seal Harbor is still Levannon soil, the ultimate tip of that great snaky-long country and the largest source of its wealth, the northernmost spot of civilization, if you can call a hell-hole like Seal Harbor civilized. (I was with Rumley's Ramblers, fifteen years old, when I saw it. Shag Donovan's bully-boys tried to grab one of our girls, something that wouldn't be attempted on a Rambler gang anywhere else in the world. We left three of his men dead and the rest thoughtful.) Beyond Seal Harbor those Levannon ships proceed down the Lorenta to the great sea, and south along lonely coasts to trade with the city-states of Main and then with the famous ports of Nuin—Newbury, Old City, Hannis, Land's End. That northern passage is long and bad, travelers said at the Bull-and-Iron. Fog may hide both shores, and they're the shores of red bear and brown tiger country not fit for man. All the same, that route was thought safer than the southern course down the Hudson Sea and along the Conicut coast, and Levannon ships laden with the manufactured goods of Nuin usually returned the northern way too, beating against contrary wind and current rather than risking a clash with the Cod Islands pirates. We've cleaned the pirates out now, but at that time their war canoes and lateen-rigged skimmers had the nations by the balls, and twisted.

26

Lazing on my ledge that morning, I thought: If the Levannon thirty-tonners make the north passage for trade, why can't they sail much further for curiosity? Sure I was ignorant. I'd never beheld even the Hudson Sea. I didn't know that curiosity is not common but sadly rare, and without experience how could I imagine the loneliness of open sea when land has become a memory and there's no mark to steer by unless someone aboard knows the mystery of guessing position by the stars? So I asked the morning sky: If nobody dares to sail out of sight of land, and if the Book of Abraham won't tell how far is the rim or what's beyond it, how can the priests claim to know?

Why can't there be other lands this side of the rim? How do they know there *is* a rim? Maybe the Book of Abraham did explain that much, if one were allowed to read it, but then what about the far side? There had to be one. And something beyond the far side. So what if *I* were to sail—east—

Nay, I thought—nay, Mudhead! But suppose I did travel to Levannon—that wasn't far—where a young man could sign on aboard a thirty-tonner?

Suppose for instance I started this morning, or at least tomorrow?

3

I thought of Emmia.

Once from the street I had glimpsed her at her window naked for bedtime. A thick old jinny-creeper grew to the second story of the inn where her bedroom was. Behind the leaves I saw her let down her red-brown hair to tumble over her shoulders, and she combed it watching herself in a mirror, then stood gazing out at the night a while. The next building had a blind wall where I stood. No

27

moonlight, or she would have seen me. Some impulse made her cup her left breast in her hand, blue eyes lowered, and I was bewitched to learn of the broad circle around the nipple, of her deep-curved waist, and the dark triangle just visible.

Naked women weren't news to me, though I'd never been close to one. Skoar had the peep-shows called movies, including penny-a-squint ones I could afford.* But that rosy marvel in the window was *Emmia,* not a picture nor a puppet nor a worn-out peep-show actress with an idiot dab of G-string and a face like a spilled laundry bag, but Emmia whom I saw each day at tasks around the tavern in her smock or slack-pants—mending, dusting, overseeing the slaves, candle-making, waiting on table, coming out to my territory to collect eggs or help feed the stock and milk the goats. Emmia was careful with her skirt, the Emmia I knew—once when the old slave Judd, not thinking, asked if she'd be so gracious to use the ladder and reach something down so to spare his gimp leg, she told her mother and had him whipped for bawdy insolence. This was Emmia, and in me, like stormy music, desire was awake.

Love? Oh, I called it so. I was a boy.

She drifted out of sight and her candle died. I remember I fell asleep that night exhausted, after the imaginary Emmia on my pallet had opened her thighs. It became a canopy bed: I was inheriting the inn and Old John's fortune for saving Emmia from a mad dog or runaway horse or whatever. His dying speech of blessing on our marriage would have made a skunk get religion.

I had not seen Emmia naked again, but the picture of

---

* They have the Church's grudging permission to exist, and rate a whole paragraph in the Church's celebrated Doctrine of Necessary Evils. This monument of shrewd piety is believed by the public to have been devised by the disciple Simon at the supposed founding of the Church in 44. Actually the document they call the original is on a type of parchment that was developed in Nuin, not Katskil, and only about 50 years ago. I examined it myself on a visit to Nuber. No scholar can say exactly when the Holy Murcan Church began to exist, but it cannot have been a functioning institution for more than 200 years.

—Dion M. M.

her at her window remained warm in me—(it still is). It was with me on my mountain ledge that morning as the time glided toward noon . . .

Ears and nose gave me the first warning. My hand shot to my knife before my eyes found my outrageous visitor on the upward slant of the cliffside path.

He smiled, or tried to.

His mouth was miserably small, in a broad flat hairless face. Dirty, grossly fat, reeking. His vast long arms and stub legs told me he must be the subject of that drawing. He did have knees: drooping fat-rolls concealed them; his lower legs were nearly as thick as his ugly short thighs. Almost no hair, and he wore nothing; a male, but what he had to prove it appeared against his fat no larger than what you'd see on a small boy. In spite of the short legs he stood as tall as I, around five feet five. His facial features—button nose, small mouth, little dark eyes in puffy fat-pockets—were merely ugly, not inhuman. He said in a gargling man's voice: "I go?"

I couldn't speak. Whatever appeared in my face made him no more terrified than he was already. He simply waited there, misery standing in the sun. A mue.

Everywhere the law of church and state says plainly: *A mue born of woman or beast shall not live.*

You hear tales. A woman, or even a father, may bribe a priest to conceal a mue-birth, hoping the mue will outgrow its evil. The penalty is death, but it happens.

Conicut is the only country where the civil law requires that the mother of a mue must also be destroyed. The Church is apt to give her the benefit of the doubt. Tradition says that demons bent on planting mue-seed may enter women in their sleep, or magic them into unnatural drowsiness; thus women may be assumed not guilty unless witnesses prove they copulated with the demon knowingly. A female animal bearing a mue is usually put out of the way mercifully, and the carcass exorcised and burned. The tolerant law also reminds us that demons can take the form of men in broad daylight, with such damnable skill that only priests can discover the fraud . . . Stories buzzed at the Bull-and-Iron about mues born in secret—single-eyed, tailed, purple-skinnned, legless, two-headed, her-

29

maphrodite, furred—that grow to maturity in hiding and haunt the wilderness.

Everywhere, it is the duty of a citizen to kill a mue on sight if possible, but to proceed with caution, because the monster's demon father may be lurking near.

He asked again: "I go?" Immense, well-formed on his soggy body, his arms could have torn a bull apart.

"No." That was my voice. Pure chicken—if I told him to go he might be angry.

"Boy-man-beautiful."

He meant me, damn it. For politeness I said: "I like the picture." He was bewildered. "Lines," I said, and pointed into my cave. "Good."

He understood—smiled anyway, drooling, wiping away the slop across his chest. "Come me. Show things."

I was to go with him and maybe meet his father?

I remembered hearing of a recent witch-scare over at Chengo, a town rather far west of Skoar. Children saw demons, they said. A ten-year-old girl said she had been coaxed into the woods by a bad woman and hidden where she was obliged to watch that woman and others of the town rushing around and playing push-push with man-shaped devils that had animal heads. She was about to be dragged out of hiding and presented to the coven when a cock crew and the revels ended. The girl would not swear the demons had flown off into the clouds, and folk got cross with her about that, since everyone knows it's what demons do, but she did name the women so that they could be burned.

I slipped on my clothes and said: "Wait!" I entered my cave motioning the mue to remain outside. I was shaking; he was too, out there in the sun. I thought he might run away, but he stayed, scared of his own courage like a human being—and that thought once lodged in my head would not leave it. What after all was wrong with him except his hideous short legs? Fatness—but that didn't make a mue, nor the ugly squinched-up features, nor even the hairlessness. I recalled seeing, at the public bath-house in Skoar, a dark-skinned man who had almost no pubic hair and only a trace of fuzz under his arms—no one thought anything of it. I thought: What if some of the mue-tales are lies? Did a being as human as this have to live as a monster in the wilderness just because his legs were too short? And hadn't I heard a thousand yarns on other subjects at the Bull-and-Iron that I *knew* to be bushwa, the tellers not expecting belief?

I cut my loaf of oat bread in half. I had some notion of taming him like a beast by feeding him. I wanted my luck-charm. Its cord had broken and I was keeping it in my sack till I could contrive another. I took up the sack—was I for Abraham's sake *going* somewhere?—and the hard lump of the charm through the cloth did comfort me.

They carve such junk for tourists in Penn, as I found out later in my travels. My mother—anyhow someone at the house where I was born—gave me this, for I was told it hung at my neck when I arrived at the orphanage and they let me keep it. I probably cut my first teeth on it. It is a body with two fronts, male and female; the two-faced head has a brass loop embedded so you can wear it on a string. The folded arms and sex parts are sketched in flat and unreal. No legs: the thighs run together in a blob flattened on the bottom so you can set it upright. How the little gods get by without a rump I don't know—maybe that's how you know they are gods. It used to fascinate Caron. She liked to hold it under our blanket, and said it meant we would always be together.

I took the half-loaf of oat bread to the mue. He didn't grab. His flat nostrils flared; like a dog's his gaze followed my fingers as I broke off a piece and ate it myself. Then he accepted the rest, and gnawed, slobbering with eagerness, though with his fat he could hardly have been going hungry, and it was soon finished. He said: "Come me?" He walked up the path and looked back. Like a smart dog.

I followed him.

Those stub legs pumped along pretty well. On a level he waddled; on rising slopes his hands pressed the ground for a speedy four-legged scramble. Downgrades bothered him; he followed a long slant where he could. He moved quietly as I'd learned to do in the woods, knew the country and must have been getting a living from it. He doubtless had no name.

A state ward, I had no last name. Just Davy.

Don't imagine that thing with the bread came from any grown-up goodness in me. At fourteen whatever goodness I had was growing in the dark, obscured by shabby and cruel confusions that were inside of me as well as in my world: ignorance and fear; contempt of others for my class, which I was expected to pass on down to the slave class while all concerned made big talk of democratic equality; the cheating and conniving I daily saw people do, and their excuses for it—hi-ho, can't be so wrong because look, even the nobility are bootlickers, pimps, swindlers, thieves, don't you know? That's ancient, I believe, that game of supposing you make yourself clean by pointing at the dirt on somebody else. No, I wasn't good or kind.

Since human beings make and choose their own ends, goodness can be an end in itself without supernatural gimmicks, but that idea never came into words for me until I heard the words in Nickie's voice. Yet I think that I did dimly understand, at fourteen, how if you want to be a good human being you have to work at it.

There was that early protest in my mind, that recognition of the mue's humanity. But as I walked on through the forest with him I was governed mainly by fear and a dirty kind of planning. Schooling and the tavern-tales had told me mues weren't like witches or spooks. Although the offspring of demons they couldn't vanish, float through walls, use spells or the evil eye. God, said the authorities, may not be thought of as allowing such powers to a miserable mue. A mue died when you stuck a knife in him, and it needn't have a silver point.

The law said when, not if. You must if you could; if not you must save yourself and bring word, so the mue can be hunted down by professionals with aid of a priest.

The leather of my knife-sheath brushed my skin at every step. I began to resent the mue, imagining his hellish father behind every tree, building up the resentment like a fool searching after an excuse for a quarrel.

We reached one of the mountain's flanking ridges, where old trees stood enormous, casting deep shade from their interlacing tops. They were mostly pine, that through the years had built up a carpet of silence. The mue disliked this region—on clear and level ground anything could overtake him. He padded on with worried side-glances, nothing about him to suggest a demon's protection.

They didn't say a demon *always* attended a mue . . .

I decided it would be best to kill him on flat ground, and watched a spot below his last rib on the left side. After the stab I could be instantly clear of his long reach while the blood drained out of him. I drew my knife, and lowered it in my sack, afraid he might turn before I was ready. He cleared his throat, and that angered me—what right could he have to do things the human way? Still, I felt there was no hurry. This level area stretched on far ahead; I'd better wait till I was steadier.

At the tavern I wouldn't brag. I'd maintain a noble calm, the Yard-Boy Who Killed A Mue.

They'd send me out with an escort to find the remains and verify my story. The skeleton would do, considering the leg-bones, and that's all we'd find, for in the time it took the mission to settle arguments and get going the carrion-ants, crows, vultures, small wild scavenger dogs would have done their wilderness housecleaning. Maybe I'd drop something near the body. My luck-charm—that would fix anyone who set out snickering at me behind his hand.

It came to me, as I caught the mue's foul smell, that this was no daydream. I might be questioned by the Mayor, even the Bishop of Skoar. The Kurin family, tops in the Skoar aristocracy, would hear of it. They could make me the same as rich, a bond-servant no more. Why, I would ride to Levannon on a bright roan that none but I dared handle, and with two attendants—well, three, one to dash ahead and make sure of a room for me at the next inn, where a maid-servant would undress me and bathe me, wait on me in bed if I wished. In Levannon I would *buy* a thirty-ton outrigger, and look at that green hat with a hawk's feather, and that shirt too, a marvel of Penn silk, green or maybe gold! As an adopted son of the nobility I could wear a loin-rag of what color I chose, but I'd be modest, I'd settle for freeman's white, so long as it was silk. I didn't think I wanted britches with a codpiece, a style just then coming into favor. Those I'd seen looked

33

clumsy, and the codpiece an unnecessary brag. Moose-hide moccasins I'd have, purtied up with ornaments of brass. I might start smoking, with a rich man's fancy for nicely cured marawan and the best pale tobacco from Conicut or Lomeda.

I fancied Old Jon Robson ashamed of all unkindness and anxious to crowd in on the glory. I would permit it. Clickety-clackety, he knew all along the boy had it in him.

Mam Robson might have a go at supplying me with a few ancestors. Already, when slightly pleased with me, she'd remarked that I sort of resembled a relative of hers who rose through the ranks to be a Captain in the Second Kanhar Regiment and married a baron's daughter—which showed, said she, that people with square chins and plenty of ear-lobe were the ones that got ahead in the world—this was one for Old Jon, who had several chins but none of them too clearly connected with his jawbone.

❋　❋　❋

Who can say what man might have visited the house where I was born?

I'm concerned about varieties of time: one reason why I stepped in here a moment behind the asterisks. You'd best get used to the idea that my brain-scratching—digression is the word some people would prefer—is not a suspension of action but a different kind of action, on a rather different time scale. Your much-abused amiable mind, all of a doodah over women and children and taxes and a certain almost needless worry of yours about whether you exist, may dislike the suggestion that more than one kind of time is allowable, but give it a go, will you? Meanwhile, on what we might call the asterisk time scale, you can't very well stop me if I choose to claim that Pappy was a grandee, some hightoned panjandrum traveling incognito through Skoar and planting me in an idle moment when he had a hasty hard on and a smidgin of loose change—why not? Well, later in the book I'll tell you why not, or why probably not. Don't rush me.

I used to hate my shadowy father in my early years. I was six when, since I had accidentally overheard talk of my origin, Father Milsom told me what parents are, and said my Da was undoubtedly just a whore's customer, and then added some dismally fit-for-six explanation of the word "whore" to complete the confusion. Yes, I hated my nameless father's guts; and yet when Caron first slid under my blanket I told her the President of Moha had visited Skoar in disguise, stopping off at the Mill Street house to make a baby—me. After that I felt better about the whole deal. Who wouldn't, with a President in the family? Caron —bless her—was quick to play along and devise generous plans full of arson and bloodshed for establishing my birthright.

A few nights later I learned that her mother, nine months before she was born, had a Passionate Affair with the Archbishop of Moha who also just happened to be passing by, and noticed her extreme beauty and sent litter-bearers after her so she could visit his residence in secret. Kay, so we had plans for Caron too, but were smart enough to keep all such enterprise under the blanket, where sometimes we called each other President and Presidentess, with frightful oaths never to speak of the matter in daytime.

If you find that anecdote funny, go to hell.

* * *

Walking on behind the mue, my overheated fancy also heard Emmia Robson: "Davy darling, what if *you'd* got hurt?" Maybe not "darling" but even "Spice," the love-name girls in Moha don't use unless they really mean come-try-something. "Nay, Spice," s's I, "it was nothing, and didn't I have to destroy the brute for your sake?"

I decided the conversation had better take place in her bedroom. She had let down her hair to cover the front of her, so my hands—gentle but still the hands that had rid the world of a dread monster—parted the softness to find the pink flower-tips. And here and now, walking behind him in the woods, all I had to do—

The mue stopped and faced me. He may have wanted to reassure me, or transmit some message beyond his powers of speech. I took my hand out of the sack, without

35

the knife. I couldn't do it, I knew, if he was looking at me. He said: "We go not—not—"

"Not far?"

"Is word." He was admiring—what a marvel to know all the words I did! "Bad thing come, I here, I here." He tapped his ponderous arm. "You—I—you—I—"

"We're all right," I said.

"We. We." He had used the word himself, but it appeared to disturb or puzzle him.

"We means you and I."

He nodded in his patch of leaf-dappled sunlight. Puzzled and thoughtful. Human. He grunted and smiled dimly and went on ahead.

I sheathed my knife and did not draw it again that day.

4

The region of great trees ended. As if sliding into dark water we entered a place where the master growth was wild grape; here day would always be a kind of evening. The slow violence of the vine had overcome a stand of maple and oak. Many of these were dead, upholding their murderers; others lived, winning sunlight enough to continue an existence of slavery.

Still I found an infinity of color and change. Some of the gleams in the vagueness above me were orchids. I glimpsed a blue and crimson parrot, and a tanager who was first a motionless ember and then a shooting-star. I heard a wood-dove lamenting—so it sounds, though I believe he cries for love.

The mue glanced up at the interlocking tangle and then at my legs and arms. "You not," he said, and showed what he meant by catching a grapevine loop and swarming up it until he was thirty feet above ground. He launched his bulk across a gap to grab another loop, and another. Many yards away, he shifted his grip with ease and returned. He was right, it wasn't for me. I'm clever in the trees, and slept in them once or twice before I found my cave, but my arms are merely human. He called: "You go ground?"

I went ground. The walking became nasty. He traveled ahead above a vile thicket—fallen branches, hardhack, blackberry, poison ivy, rotten logs where fire-ants would be ready with their split-second fury. Snake and scorpion could be here. The puffy-bodied black-and-gold orb-spiders, big as my big toe, had built many homes; their bite won't kill but makes you wish it had.

The mue held down his pace to accommodate me. A quarter-mile of this struggle brought me up to a network of catbrier and there I was stopped: ten-foot elastic stems in a mad basket-weave, tough as moose-tendon and cruel as weasel-teeth. Beyond, I saw what may have been the tallest tree in Moha, a tulip tree at least twelve feet through at the base. The grape had found it long ago and gone rioting up into the sunshine, but might not have killed the giant after another hundred years. My mue was up there, pointing to a vine-stem that dangled on my side of the briers and connected with the loops around the tree. I shinnied up and worked over; he grasped my foot and set it gently on a branch.

As soon as he was sure of my safety he climbed, and I followed for maybe another sixty feet. It was easy as a ladder. The tree's side-branches had become smaller, the vine-leaves thicker in the increase of sunlight, when we came to a mass of crossed wood and interwoven vine. Not an eagle's nest as I foolishly thought at first—no bird ever lifted sticks of that size—but a nest certainly, six feet across, built on a double crotch, woven as shrewdly as any willow basket in the Corn Market and lined with gray moss. The mue let himself into it and made room for me.

He talked to me.

I felt no sense of dreaming. Did you in childhood, as I did now and then with Caron, play the game of imaginary countries? You might decree that if you stepped through the gap in a forked tree-trunk you'd be entering a different

37

world. If then in the flesh you did step through you found you must continue to rely on make-believe, and I know that hurt. Suppose you had been met, in solid truth, on the other side of your tree-trunk, by a dragon, a blue chimera, a Cadillac,* an elf-girl all in greeen—?

"See you before," the mue said. So he must have watched me on other visits to North Mountain—me with my keen eyes and ears, studied by a monster and never guessing it! He would not have passed the human kind of judgment on the monkey tricks of a boy who thought himself alone; that consoling thought came to me after a while.

He told me of his life. Mere fragments of language to help him, worn down by years of speaking to no one but himself—I won't record much of the actual talk. He waved toward the northeast, where from our height the world was a green sea under the gold of afternoooon—he had been born somewhere off that way, if I understood him. He spoke of a journey of "ten sleeps," but I don't know what distance he might have covered in a day's travel. His mother, evidently a farm woman, had raised him in the woods. To him birth was a vagueness—"Began there," he said, and fumblingly tried to repeat what his mother had told him of birth, giving it up as soon as I showed I understood. Death he grasped, as an ending. "Mother's man stop live"—before he was born, I think he meant. Describing his mother, all he could say was "big, good." I guessed she would have been some stout farm woman who managed to hide her pregnancy in the first months, and perhaps her husband's death made matters simpler.

By law, every pregnancy must be reported immediately to civil and church authorities, no pregnant woman may be left alone after the fifth month, and a priest must be present at every birth to decide whether the child is normal and dispose of it if he considers it a mue. There are occasional breaches in the law—the Ramblers for instance,

---

* Anyone by paying a candle, a prayer and a dollar may enter the Murcan Museum in the cellar of the Cathedral at Old City and look at ancient fragments of automotive vehicles. In other words Davy knows perfectly well these mechanisms are not legendary, but must have his fun.

—Dion M. M.

always on the go, could evade it much more often than they do—but the law is there, carrying a heavy charge of religious as well as secular command.

This mue's mother had no help in raising him to some age between eight and ten except that of a big dog. It would have been one of the tall wolfhounds a farm family needs if it is to risk dwelling outside a stockade. The dog guarded the baby when the mother could not be with him, and grew old as he grew up.

*   *   *

We have two wolfhounds aboard the *Morning Star*, Dion's Roland and Roma. They are friendly enough now, but while Dion's mood was black with misery over what had happened in Nuin—our loss of the war, forced flight, certain destruction of nearly all the reforms begun while he was Regent and Nickie and I his unofficial counselors —no one dared go near them except Dion himself; not even Nickie nor Dion's bedmates Nora Severn and Greta Shawn. The dogs dislike the motion of the ship—Roland was seasick for two days—but keep alive on smoked meat and biscuit that nobody grudges them.

Yesterday evening at sundown Nickie was at the rail, for once looking behind us to that part of the horizon beyond which lie Nuin and the other lands, and Roland came to lean sentimentally against her hip. She touched his head; not with them, I watched the westerly breeze rumple his gray pelt and Nickie's luminous brown hair. It is cut short like a man's, but she's all woman these days, dressing in the few simple garments she has made for herself from the ship's store of cloth—necessity, since most of us came aboard with nothing but what we were wearing, that ugly day. Yesterday in the red-gold light she wore a blouse and skirt of the plainest brown Nuin linsey —all woman but in a mood not to be touched,* I thought, and so I did not go to her in spite of a hunger to take hold

* Matter of fact, dear, I was merely wondering if supper would stay down.

—Miranda Nic etc.

39

of her small waist and kiss her brown throat and shoulders. Roland, after winning her hand's casual recognition, stepped away and lay down on the deck not too near, adoring but keeping it to himself, waiting for her to look at him again if she would. He could be aware, as I am, how in spite of all pressures of male and female vanity, male and female foolishness, women are still people.

* * *

The mue's mother had taught him speech, now distorted by the years when he had small chance to make use of it. She taught him to win a living from the wilderness—hunting, snaring, brook-fishing with his hands, finding edible plants; how to stalk and, most important, how to hide. She taught him he must avoid all human beings, who would kill him on sight. I can't guess what sort of existence she imagined for his future; maybe she was able to avoid thinking of it. Nor can I guess what made him risk his life by approaching me, unless it was an overwhelming hunger for any sort of contact with what he knew to be his own breed.

At some time between his eighth and tenth years—"she come no more." He waited long. The dog was killed by a woods buffalo—little hellions they are, no more than half the size of tame cattle but frightfully strong and intelligent; we lost a man to one of them when I was with Rumley's Ramblers. The mue gave me most of that story in sign language, crying freely when he spoke of the dog's death and casually urinating through the floor of his nest.

When he felt that his mother must have died too, he made his journey of ten sleeps. I asked about years; he didn't understand. He had no way of telling me how often the world had cooled into the winter rains. He may have been twenty-five years old, when I saw him. During that journey a hunter sighted him and shot an arrow into him. "Come me sharp-stick man-beautiful." His fingers squeezed a remembered throat, he cried and belched and made a wet howling noise, his mouth spread open like a little wound. Then he studied me calmly to see if I understood, while a worm of fear stumbled down my back.

40

"Show now," he said, and lifted himself abruptly to descend the tree, all the way to the ground.

Inside the catbriers a floor of rocks surrounded the tree, making a circle six feet out from the base. It created a fortress for him; only a snake could penetrate those thorns. The rocks overlapped so neatly the brier did not force its way through; many layers must have been fitted together—yes, and painfully searched out, painfully brought along the grapevine path. He had a stone hammer here, a rock shaped into a chopper, a few other gidgets. He showed me these, not so trustingly, and indicated I should stand where I was while he got something from the other side of the tree-trunk.

I heard rocks cautiously moved. His hands appeared beyond the trunk, setting down a rose-colored slab; I knew it would be the marker-stone of some poor hideaway. He returned to me, carrying a thing whose like I have never seen elsewhere.

I thought at first it might be some oddly shaped trumpet such as hunters and the cavalry use, or a cornet like those I'd heard when Rambler gangs visited Skoar and set up their shows in the green. But this golden horn resembled those things only as a racing stallion resembles a plow-horse—both honorable creatures, but one is a devil-angel with the rainbow on his shoulders.

The large flared end, the two round coils and the straight sections of the pipe between bell and mouthpiece—oh, supposing we could cast such metal nowadays we'd still have no way of working it so perfectly into shape. I knew at once the instrument was of Old Time—it could not have been designed in ours—and I was afraid.

Ancient coins, knives, spoons, kitchenware that won't rust—such objects of the perished world are often turned up in plowing or found at the edge of ruins that wilderness has not quite covered, like those on the Moha shore of the Hudson Sea near the village of Albany that lead down into the water like a stairway abandoned by gods. If the Old-Time thing has a clear harmless function the rule is find-ers-keepers, if you can pay a priest to exorcise the evil and stamp the object with the holy wheel. Mam Robson owned a skillet of gray metal that never rusted, found by her grandfather in turning over a cornfield, handed on to her at her marriage. She never used it but liked to show it to the inn guests for an oh-ah, telling how her mother did cook with it and took no harm. Then Old Jon would snort in with the tale of its discovery as if he'd been there, while her sad face, unlike Emmia's round pretty one but rather like a Vairmant mule's, would be saying *he* was no jo to ever find *her* such a thing, not him, blessed miracle if he got up off his ass long enough to scratch . . . If the ancient thing is too weird the priest buries it,* where it can do no harm.

In the mue's hands the horn was a golden shining. I've seen true gold since then; it is much heavier, with a different feel. But I call this a golden horn because I did think of it so for a long time, and the name still suggests a kind of truth. If you're sure there's only one kind of truth, go on, shove, read some other book, get out of my hair.

Uneasily the mue let me take it. "Mother's man's thing she say." I felt better when I found the wheel-sign—some priest, some time, had prayed away the spooks. The horn gathered light out of that shady place, itself a sun. "She bring, say I to keep . . . You blow?" So at least he knew it was a thing for music.

I puffed my cheeks and tried—breath-noise and a mutter. The mue laughed and took it back hastily. "I show."

---

* Or if smart he marks it with the wheel-sign and sends it to one of the shops in the large cities that specialize in dudaddery for the sophisticated—that is, the suckers. One in Old City is famous for selling nothing the owner can't guarantee to be totally useless— Carrie's Auntic Shoppy, well I remember it. Because the Regent was expected to encourage commerce, I bought an Old-Time thing-amy there, a small cylinder of pale gray metal with a tapered end. That end has a tiny hole, out of which pops a wee metal whichit if you push the other end; push it again and the thing pops back. One of my philosophic advisers suggests it may have been used in the phallic worship that we assume was practised privately along with the public breast-belly-thigh cult of ancient America: I don't find this convincing. I believe you could use the gidget for goosing a donkey, but why wouldn't any Goddamn pointed stick do just as well? There is need for more research.

—Dion M. M.

His wretched mouth almost vanished in the cup, his cheeks firmed instead of puffing. I heard it speak.

I wonder if you know that voice in your part of the world? I will not try to describe it—I would not try to describe an icicle breaking sunshine into colored magic, nor to draw a picture of the wind. I know of only one place where words and music belong together, and that is song.

The mue pressed one of the valves and blew a different note, and then another. He blew a single note to each breath with no thought of combining them, no idea of rhythm or melody. Why, at the first sound my mind had overflowed with songs heard at the tavern, on the streets, at Rambler shows, and far back in the time when fat sweet Sister Carnation sang for me. To the poor mue, music was just notes indefinitely prolonged, unrelated. He could have blown that way all day and learned no more.

I tried to ask where it had come from; he shook his head. "Was it kept hidden?" Another headshake—how should he know? Questions from a world not his, that allowed him no gift but the cruel one of birth. "Did you use it to call your mother?" He looked empty-faced, as if there might be some such memory, none of my business, and he carried the horn back into hiding without answering.

I again saw his hands on that reddish rock, heard it set back in its former place, and knew I could find that place in ten seconds, and knew the golden horn must be mine.

It must be mine.

He returned smiling, comfortable now that his treasure was safe . . . I do claim one trace of honor: I did not again plan to kill him, nor even think of it except for one or two random moments. That's my scrap of virtue.

* * *

The lantern in our cabin is sputtering and my fingers are cramped. I need a fresh nib in my pen—we have plenty of bronze nibs, but I can't be extravagant. And I'd like a breath of air topside. Maybe I'll bother Captain Barr or Dion, or remind Nickie we haven't yet tried it in the

43

crow's-nest. The night is uneasy; northwest gusts are warm but appear to have a power behind them. The morning came in with an explosion of crimson, and all day long my ears have been tight with a promise of storm. The other colonists—we've lately been calling ourselves that—are edgy with it. At the noon meal Adna-Lee Jason broke out crying from no clear cause, explaining it with a mutter about homesickness and then said she didn't mean that. Maybe I'll just loaf at the bow, taste the weather my own way, and try to decide whether I mean to go on with this book . . .

I'm going on with it, anyway Nickie says I am. (It was fine in the crows'-nest. She got dizzy and bit my shoulder harder than she meant to, but a few minutes later she was daring me to try it up there again some time with a real wind blowing. Ayah, she can cook too.) I'm going on with my book but I dread the next few pages.

I could lie about what happened with the mue and me. We all lie about ourselves, trying to diddle the world with an image that's had all the warts rubbed off. But wouldn't it be the cruddy trick to begin a true-tale and back off into white-wash lying at the first tough spot? By writing at all I've made the warts your business—of course it's not quite fair, since I'll never know much about you or your Aunt Cassandra and her yellow tomcat with the bent ear. But hi-ho, or as I remember my Nickie saying on another occasion: "Better spare the mahooha, my love, my carroty monkey, my all, my this and that, my blue-eyed comforting long-handled bedwarmer, spare the mahooha and then we'll never run short of it."

* * *

When the mue and I were climbing up away from that rock floor, seeing the dirt on his back gave me my idea. I asked him: "Where is water?"

He pointed into the jungle. "I show drink."

"Wash too."

"Whash?" It wasn't his specialty. He might have known the word in childhood. You see my cleverness—start him really washing and he'd be away from home a long time.

44

"Water take off dirt," I said.

"Dirt?"

I rubbed a speck off my wrist, and indicated some of his personal topsoil. "Water-take-off is wash. Wash is good, make look good."

The great idea broke like a seal-oil lamp afire—*a* great idea, not quite mine. "Whash, be like you!"

I swung out along the grapevine, sick, not just from fear he'd kiss me in his delight. He followed, gobbling words I couldn't listen to, believing I could work a magic with water to make him man-beautiful. I never did, I never could have intended he should think that.

We traveled downhill, out of the ugly thicket and into clearer ground. I kept track of landmarks. When we reached the bank of a brook I made him understand we needed a pool; he led me through alders to a lovely still-ness of water under sun. I shed my clothes and slipped in. The mue watched in amazement—how could anyone do that?

I was sick with knowing what I was about to do; the with grins and simple words and a show of washing my-self to explain how it was done. He ventured in at last, beauty of the pool was wasted on me. But I beckoned him the big baby. It was nowhere deeper than three feet, but I dared not swim, thinking he might imitate me and be drowned. I now hated the thought of his coming to any harm through me except the one loss that, I kept telling myself, couldn't matter—what could he want of a golden horn? I helped him, guiding him to move in the water and keep his balance. I even started the scrubbing job on him myself.

Scared but willing, he went to work, snorting and splashing, getting the feel of it. Presently I let him see me look as if startled at the sun, to tell him I was thinking of time and the approach of evening dark. I said: "I must go back. You finish wash." I got out and dressed, waving him back, pointing to the dirt still on him. "Finish wash. I go but come back."

"Finish, I be—"

"Finish wash!" I said, and took off. He probably watched me out of sight. When the bushes hid me I was running and my sickness ran with me. Up the easy ground, into grapevine shadows and straight to his tree, up the vine, down behind the briers. I found the red rock at once and lifted it aside. The horn lay in a bed of gray-green moss. I took that too, as a wrapping for the horn inside my sack. I was up over the briers, and gone.

In no danger from the mue if I ever had been, I ran as fast as before, but now like an animal crazed by pursuit. A black wolf could have closed in on me with no effort.

Once or twice since then I have wished one had—before I knew Dion and the other friends I have today, the dearest being the wisest, my wife, my brown-eyed Nickie of the delicate hands.

5

Three nights ago—I was off watch—a hell of a gale swooped out of the northwest, and up went some of these pages like a mob of goosed goblins. Nickie grabbed the ones fluttering near the port-hole, and I grabbed Nickie. Then the cabin tilted steep as a barn roof, the lantern smoked viciously and went out, and we were piled up against our bunk hearing the sea beaten to frenzy. But our *Morning Star* bore down against the goaded waters; she righted herself and rushed away with arrogant steadiness into the dark.

Captain Barr had smelled danger and got us reefed down just enough, ready as a race-horse; he didn't bother calling up the off watch.

I remember that square dark block of man at Provintown Island in 327, for I was there when the *Hawk* burned at her moorings. We'd gone ashore to accept the pirates' surrender and take formal possession of all the Cod Islands in Nuin's name. The fire may have been started by a spark from the galley stove. Sir Andrew's face hardly shifted a muscle when the red horror rose out there and roared across her decks. Dying inside, he turned to us and remarked: "I think, gentlemen, we'd be well advised not to exaggerate our difficulties." When Sir Andrew Barr dies for the last time it will be with some stately comment like that, pronounced so cleanly you can hear each punctuation mark click into the right place. If the pirate boss, old Bally-John Doon, had nourished any notion of taking advantage of the fire it must have perished at those words; after the *Hawk*'s survivors swam ashore and were cared for the ceremony proceeded just as planned.

In 322, the first year of the Regency, Barr was already dreaming of a strong ship rigged entirely fore-and-aft. The dream grew out of a diagram in a magnificent book at the underground library of the secret society of the Heretics—an Old-Time dictionary. We have it on board. The front cover and some of the introductory pages are missing; the borders carry the scars of fire, and on the brittle sheet that now begins the book there's a brown stain. I think someone bled after rescuing it from a holy bonfire, but make up your own story. Sparked by the diagram, Barr searched out more information on Old-Time shipbuilding—all he could get—until through the Heretics he made contact with Dion and his conception was embodied in the building of the *Hawk,* and later the *Morning Star*.

When it was clear, in the last days of General Salter's rebellion, that we would probably lose the final battle for Old City, we divided the books with the brave handful of Heretics who elected to remain. And we did lose the battle, and fled aboard the *Morning Star*—suburbs ablaze, stench of hatred and terror in all the streets—a hard decision, I suppose harder for Dion than for the rest of us. The dictionary was almost necessary for us; I can't think of any one book that would give us more.

Those Heretics who remained were not all of them older people. A good number of the young stayed on, having some love and hope for Nuin in spite of everything. Theirs was the greater risk. We are only venturing on the unexplored; they dared to stay in a country that will again

47

be governed by men who believe themselves possessed of absolute truth.

Captain Barr trusts our spread of eager canvas as no landsman could, and knows the sea in something like the way I knew the wilderness when I was a boy. A relentless perfectionist, he calls the *Morning Star* a beginner's effort. It doesn't conceal his love for her, which I think exceeds any he ever felt for a woman. He never married, and won't bed with a girl who might demand permanence.

That evening when the storm cut loose Nickie and I weren't expecting the universe to turn upsydown, so we got caught bare-ass innocent. I don't think she minded, after prying my elbows loose from her knees.* Of course now that she's taken to signing her full name and title of nobility I can see there'll be no dull times ahead. (Dma. stands for "Domina", which is what you call a lady of the Nuin aristocracy, married or single.) Already I've learned that when I come back to this manuscript after any absence it's best to examine it, the way a dog searches himself after associating with mutts who may have a different entomological environment. I got "entomological" out of the Old-Time dictionary and I find it beautiful. It means buggy.

That wind blew until the following afternoon, shrill continuous wrath. On my watch I had the wheel. I'm happy then in any weather, overcoming the impulse of the wheel toward chaos, my own strength and its demand for order enough but only just enough, and under me a hundred tons of human creation straining forward against space and time. You may have your horses; I say there's no poem like a two-masted schooner, and I'll hope to ride a ship now and then until I am too old to grip the spokes, too dull of sight to read the impersonal assurance of a star.

That day of wind, Second Mate Ted Marsh had to transmit orders by waving his hands or bringing his mouth next to my ear. Few orders needed, though. We could do no more than run before it under jib and storm-sail, and so we did, taking no harm. Next morning the uproar was spent: we

---

* That was easy—all I had to do was give you a bust in the face.
—Dma. Miranda Nicoletta St. Clair-Levison de Moha.

were creeping, and a few hours later becalmed. We still are. The wind had spat us out into a quiet, and fog claimed us. It lies around us now, the ocean hushed as if we had come to a cessation of all endeavor, motion, seeking, a defeat of urgency by silence. The sea level is not what it was when our Old-Time maps were made. The earth has changed, and those who live on it. There's been no man sailing here since before the Years of Confusion.

Tonight our deck lanterns probe a few yards. From our cabin I hear fog-damp dripping off limp canvas. The animals are all quiet—chickens and sheep and cattle aslumber I suppose, and never a bray from Mr. Wilbraham penned aft with his two jennies who are expected to love him if anyone can; even the pigs have apparently knit up the ravell'd squeal of care. Nickie too has gone sweetly to sleep—truly asleep: she can't prevent a quiver of the black eyelashes when she's shamming.* She said a few hours ago that she doesn't feel oppressed by the fog but has a notion it might conceal something pleasant, an island for instance.

I intended when I began this book to tell events in the order they happened. But when I woke this morning in the fogbound hush I fell to brooding over the different varieties of time. My story belongs in four or five of them.

So does any story, but it seems to be a literary custom that one kind should dominate, the others being suppressed or taken for granted. I could do that, and you who may exist might be too cloth-headed or stubborn or to busy keeping the baby out of the molasses to feel anything missing, but I'd feel it.

There's the stream of happenings I picked up a little after my fourteenth birthday. Call that the mainstream if you like; and by the way, I shall have to make it flow a little faster soon, since I haven't the patience for a book seven or eight million words long. Besides, while it's possible you exist, if I confronted you with a book like that, you might weasel out of it by claiming you don't.

* Beast! No respect for Shakespeare. Classifies his wife with the rest of the livestock, no special privileges. Rips the veil from her most intimate deceptions. A beast. I'm going to walk home.

—Nick.

49

There's the story I live (pursued by footnotes) as this ship journeys toward you—unless the journey's already ended: I saw no hint of a wake when I was on deck, the sails hang spiritless, a chunk of driftwood lies in polished stillness only a trifle nearer the ship than it was an hour ago . . . You could hardly read that mainstream story without knowing something of this other: whatever I write is colored by living aboard the *Morning Star*— glimpse of a whale a week ago—the gull who followed us until he discovered with comic suddenness that he was the only one of his kind, and wheeled, and sped away westward—why, I wouldn't have begun this chapter here and now, in this way, if Nickie had not spoken a casual word or two night before last about the different kinds of tempest. She wasn't thinking of my book, only loafing with me in the aftermath of a love-storm, when she had been mirthful and sweetly savage (one of many aspects)— grabbing the skin of my chest with sharp nails as she rode astride of me, a spark-eyed devil-angel moaning, writhing, laughing, crying, proud of her love and her sex and her dancing brown breasts, all muscle and spice and tenderness. Quiet in the afterglow, her dark arm idle across me, she only said that no storm is like any other, no storm of wind and rain, or of war, or of the open sea, or of love. This book is part of my life, and so to me it matters that Nickie's drowsy words started a course of thought leading to Chapter Five in this place, at this time.

A third sort of time—well, I'm obliged to write some history, for if you exist you have only guesswork to tell you what's happened to my part of the world since the period we call the Years of Confusion. I think there must have been a similar period for you—my guesswork. Your nations were stricken by the same abortive idiotic nuclear war and probably by the same plagues. Your culture showed the same symptoms of a possible moral collapse, the same basic weariness of over-stimulation, the same decline of education and rise of illiteracy, above all the same dithering refusal to let ethics catch up with science. After the plagues, your people may not have turned against the very memory of their civilization in a sort of religious frenzy as ours apparently did, determined like spoiled brats

50

to bring down in the wreckage every bit of good along with the bad. They may not have, but I suspect they did. The best aspects of what some of us now call the "Golden Age" were clearly incomprehensible to the multitudes who lived then: they demanded of the age of reason that it give them more and more gimmicks or be damned to it. And they kept their religions alive as substitutes for thought, ready and eager to take over the moment reason should perish. I can't suppose you did much better on your side of the world, or you would possess ships that would have made contact with us already.

I keep wondering whether, over there, the spooky religion of Communism may not have slugged it out with its older brother Christianity in the ruins. Whichever won, the human individual would be the loser.

Ever notice that only individuals think? . . .

After the collapse, human beings evidently existed for some time in frightened dangerous bands while weeds prepared the way for the return of forest. Those bands were interested in nothing but survival, not always in that—so we're told by John Barth who saw the beginning of the Years of Confusion. He gives them that name in his fragment of a journal, which ends with an unfinished sentence in the year the Old-Time calendar called 1993. The Book of John Barth is of course totally forbidden in the nations we have left behind, possession of it meaning death "by special order"— that is, directly under supervision of the Church. We must make more copies as soon as we can set up our little press somewhere on land with a chance of renewing the paper supply.

Book-voices of Old Time tell me also of the vastly older ages, the millions of centuries extending back of the short flare which is human history to the beginning of the world. When I speak of even a small interval like a thousand years I can hardly grasp what I mean—but for that matter do I know what I mean by a minute? Yes—that is the part of eternity in which Nickie's heart asleep will beat sixty-five times, give or take a few, unless I touch her, and her pulse hastens perhaps because in sleep she remembers me.

By starting after my fourteenth birthday I made myself

responsible for yet another time, the deep-hidden years before then, the age no one quite recalls. Once improperly straying I looked up at the underside of a dark long table, myself surrounded by a forest of black-robed legs and big sandaled feet, by the unwashed smell—and there in a corner shadow a gray spider hung and twitched her web, disturbed by me or by the clash of plates, rumble and twitter of empty talk overhead . . .

Nickie is my age, twenty-eight, pregnant for the first time in our years of pleasure with each other. (What is time for a being in the womb who lives in time but can't yet know it?) She told me about it last night, when she was sure. Across the cabin from me, staring into the flame of a candle she held, Nickie said: "Davy, if it's a mue—?"

Touched with anger, I said: "We didn't bring the priest-written laws of that country with us." She watched me, Miranda Nicoletta lately a lady of Nuin, and I afraid—I shouldn't have said "that country" in the unthinking way I did, for Nickie has a natural remembering love of her homeland, and used to share her cousin Dion's visions for it. But then she smiled and set down the candle and came to me, and we were as near as we ever have been—considering the inveterate loneliness of the human self, that is very near. Love is a region where recognition is possible. Her way of moving when she is drowsy makes me think of the motion of full-grown grass under the fondling of wind, the bending with no brittleness, yielding without defeat, rising back to upright grace and selfhood after the passage of the unconquering air.

Captain Barr always calls her "Domina" because it sounds natural to him even out here where old formalities hold no force. Back in Nuin after he got his knighthood he could have addressed her as "Miranda," or "Nickie" for that matter, but he was born a freeman and recognition came late—not until Dion was Regent and searching for men of brains and character to replace the hordes of seventh cousins, professional brown-nosers and what not who swarmed into the state jobs under Dion's mentally incompetent uncle Morgan III. A respect for the older nobility is ingrained in Captain Barr, and in this instance it's not extravagant, considering the amount of dignity that

Funny-puss can pile on at will. Let's clear up that St. Clair-Levison thing, by the way. It merely means her pop's name was St. Clair and her mama's Levison, both being of the nobility or, as she is inclined to say, "nobs with knobs on", a peculiar expression. If Senator Jon Amadeus Lawson Marchette St. Clair, Tribune of the Commonwealth and Knight of the Order of the Massasoit, had married a commoner, which I can't imagine Buster doing under any circs, Nickie's last name would be just St. Clair.

The deMoha is largely imaginary, like a bridegroom's seventh round. I mean, when I became slightly important in Nuin, Dion felt I should possess a more decorative handle, as a social convenience. After kicking my intellect around the bush and coming up with nothing better than Wilberforce, I asked his help and he suggested deMoha. With which I am stuck. You should have seen how relieved and happy the Lower Classes felt about washing my linen and so on after I got thus labeled but not before: for a top-flight snob, give me a poor man every time. And since according to our notions (but not those of Nuin) Nickie and I are most sincerely married, she calls herself deMoha and you can't stop her. She claims I possess a natural nobility that remains in evidence with my clothes off, a rema'kable thing, and she has me so bewitched and bewattled that I naturally agree.

"Even with a light burning?" s's I.

"Or widout," s's she. Nuin people can pronounce *th* perfectly well, but often they don't bodda.

Now I suppose you want me to explain why Nuin is called a Commonwealth when it's been governed by a monarchy known as a Presidency, and a Senate with two left feet, for going on two hundred years. I don't know.

I had to hug Nickie awake this morning and tell her about varieties of time. She listened briefly, slid her hand over my mouth, and remarked: "One moment, my faun, my unusual chowderhead, my peculiar sweet-stuff so named because time is far, far too pressing to employ any such dad-gandered and long-syllabled and so deplorably erotic word as beloved, my singular and highly valued long-horned trouble-shooter, before we discuss anything that difficult we ought to wrestle (and don't worry about

53

the baby) to decide who has to go to the galley and fetch us breakfast in b—"I won. Only woman I ever heard of who's just as wonderful at it in the morning. So eventually she had to go fetch breakfast, and returned to our cabin with Dion trailing.

Not that she needed help in carrying the jerk meat and poor-jo biscuits, but I was pleased to see she'd loaded Dion down with a teapot and a jug of cranberry juice— we have to drink it, by his orders and Captain Barr's. We have other antiscorbutics, salt cabbage for instance and sauerkraut; these we face at mid-day and suppertime with what courage we can summon. I remained respectfully in bed, Nickie slid back under the blanket with me, so the late Regent of Nuin had no place for his highborn rump except the floor, or my built-in desk seat which was obscured by some of Nickie's clothes—anyhow the seat is too low for Dion's long legs. He said: "Mis'ble lazy crumbs. I've been fishing since dawn, working-type jo."

"That's nothing," I said. "I've been thinking."

"Catch anything, either of you?"

"Nay, Miranda—tied down the line and went back to sleep. Besides, Mr. Wilbraham was watching and it threw me off. Hate to have a donkey look over my shoulder."

I out with it, about varieties of time and story.

"Direct narrative's the main thing," Dion said.

"Why," said Nickie, "the story of the voyage is clearly the best, because I'm in it already. Won't be in the mainstream till he's struggled up to his eighteenth year."

Dion grunted, in one of his lost, abstracted moods. He is forty-three; our tested and satisfying friendship can bridge the gap of totally different birth and upbringing more easily than the gap of age—how could I ever quite know how the world looks to a man who's been in it fifteen years longer than I? . . . The darkness of his skin was a mark of distinction in Nuin. Morgan I, Morgan the Great who stirred up such a king-size gob of history two hundred years ago, is said to have been dark as a walnut. Nickie's a deep tan with a rosy flush. I never met any of the Nuin nobility as blond as I am, though some approach it—the Princess of Hannis was a blazing redhead. If I understood the old books a little better or if more of them

54

had survived the holy burnings, I suppose I could find the characteristics of the varied races of Old Time in modern people—an idle occupation, I'd say . . .

"You're both spooking up the wrong tree," I said, "because all the different kinds of time are important. My problem is how to go from one to another with that utter perfection of grace which my wife finds so characteristic of me." Captain Barr's cat, Mam Humphrey, walked in just then, tail up, very pregnant, and looking for a soft place to sleep out the morning; she jumped on our bunk, knowing a good thing. "Historical time for instance. You must admit there's a case to be made for history in moderation."

"Oh," Dion said, "I suppose it's useful material for stuffing textbooks. Lately we've lived rather more than a bellyful of it."

Nickie was getting maudlin, kissing Mam Humphrey's black and white head and mumbling something Dion didn't catch about two girls in the same fix. As it happened we didn't tell Dion of the pregnancy till later in the day.

"Still are," I suggested. "This voyage is history."

"And the fog still deep," Nickie said. "Oh—when I was getting the grub Jim Loman told me he saw a goldfinch skim by just when it was getting light. Do they migrate?"

"Some." I was remembering Moha. "Most stay the winter, anyway September's too early for migration."

"When the fog is gone," she said, "and the sun discovers us, let it be an island with none there but the birds and a few furry harmless things, the goldfinches no one could want to kill, the way they dip and rise, dip and rise —isn't that the rhythm of living by the way? A drop and then a lightness and a soaring? Nay, don't speak a word of my fancy unless you be liking it."

Dion said: "It could be the mainland of a nation with no kindness for strangers."

"Damn that prince," she said. "I set free a small thing too large for my own head, whang goes the arrow of his common sense and down comes my bird in flight that was all the time na' but an ambitious chicken."

"Why, I'm liking that goldfinch as much as thou, Mir-

55

anda, but I'm a thousand years older, the way I used to be the simulacrum of a ruler, and that means to contend with folly—compromise with it—after a while the heart sickens as thou knowest. Nothing strange about my uncle going mad. A good weak man, I think, gone into hiding, into a shell his mind built for him. What we saw—the fat thing on the floor drooling and masturbating with dolls, that was the shell. I suppose the good weak man died inside it after a while, the shell continuing to exist."

The thing had to be gelded, before the Church would allow it to go on existing in secret and agree to the polite fiction of "ill health" to spare the presidential family the disgrace of having produced a brain-mue—which could have caused a dangerous public uproar. The priest who castrated him told Dion that after the first shock, Morgan III seemed to recover a moment of clarity and said plainly: "Happy the man who can no longer beget rulers!"

"Hiding," Nickie asked, "from the follies he feared he might himself commit?"

"Something like that. As for me, I suppose I shall be something to frighten good Nuin children for centuries, as the Christians of Old Time used to rattle the bones of the Emperor Julian miscalled the Apostate."

"Write Nuin's history thyself," said Nickie, "outside of Nuin. How else could it be done anyway?—certainly not in the shadow of the Church."

"Why," said Dion, thinking it over—"why, I might do that . . ."

"We've thought we wanted to find mainland," I said, "but I can go along with Nick—why not an island? Does the Captain still say we're near what the map calls the Azores?"

"Yes. Of course our calculation of longitude is off—the best clocks already three minutes in disagreement. Made by the Timekeepers' Guild of Old City, best in the known world, and by Old-Time standards what are those craftsmen? Moderately fair beginners, gifted clodhoppers."

I began clacking then, instructing Dion for a while on the political management of an island colony of intelligent Heretics. I have that fault. In a different world—and if I didn't spend so much time more profitably, making music

56

and tumbling my rose-lipped girl, I think I might have become a respectable teacher of snotnoses.

Later this morning we were busy. Captain Barr ordered out the longboat to try towing the *Morning Star* clear of the fog, and we went on a snailpace for some hours. He quit the attempt when the men were tired, though the lead was still finding no bottom. He was sure he smelled land through the fog-damp, and I smelled it too. That land could rise sheer and sudden out of deep water. Tomorrow, if the fog gives us fifty yards or better of visibility, he may try the towing again.

The stillness troubles us. We listen for breakers or the slap of water against stone.

Nickie sleeps; I am suspended in my own mist of memory and reflection and ignorance. How truly is a man the master of his own course?

The unknown drives us. We could not know we were to lose the war in Nuin. How should I have known I would find and covet the golden horn? But within my small range of knowledge and understanding, driven by chance but still human, still brainy and passionate and stubborn and no more of a coward than my brothers, it's for me to say where I go.

Let others think for you and you throw away your opportunity of possessing your own life even within that limited range. You're then no longer a man but an ox in human shape, who doesn't understand that he might break the fence if he had the will. Early in our years together Nickie said to me: "Learn to love me by possessing thine own self, Davy, as I try to learn how to possess my own—I think there's no other way."

As men and not oxen, I suppose we are men with a candle in the dark. Close in the light with walls of certainty or authority, and it may seem brighter—look, friends, that's a reflection from prison walls, your light is no larger. I'll carry mine through the open night in my own hand.

6

I couldn't stop running with my golden horn till I'd rounded the east side of the mountain, passed the approach to my cave without thinking of it, and was looking down on the Skoar church spires. I collapsed on a log gulping for air.

The skin of my belly hurt. I found a patch of red and a puncture mark. I'd blundered through an orb-spider's web and only now would my body admit the pain. I'd been bitten before and knew what to expect. Hot needles were doing a jerky jig over my middle; my head ached, I'd soon have a fever, and then by tomorrow it wouldn't bother me much. I was enough of a child and a savage to marvel at God's letting me off so lightly.

I unwrapped the horn and raised it to my lips. How naturally it rested against me, my right hand at the valves! I imagined the ancient makers putting a guiding magic in it. They simply took thought for the shape of human body and arm, like a knife-maker providing for the human hand. Partly by accident, I must have firmed my lips and cheeks in almost the right way. It spoke for me. I thought of sunlight transformed to sound.

I returned it to the sack, scared. Not of the mue three miles away with the mountain between us, but of his demon father. Fevered already, I said aloud: "Well, fuck him, he don't exist no-way." Know what?—nothing happened.

Maybe that was the moment I began to understand what most grown people never learn, and did not even in the Golden Age, namely that words are not magic.

I said (silently this time) that it didn't matter. The horn was *mine*. I'd never see the mue again. I'd run away to Levannon, yes, but not by way of North Mountain.

The spider-bite set me vomiting, and I recalled some wiseacre saying the best treatment for orb-spider's bite was a plaster of mud and boy's urine. Loosening my loin-rag, I muttered: "A'n't no use account I a'n't a bejasus boy no more." And laughed some, and piddled on bare earth to make the plaster anyhow. I'm sure it was as good as anything the medicine priests do for the faithful—didn't kill me and made the pain no worse. I went on downhill to the edge of the forest near the stockade, to wait for dark and the change of guards.

A wide avenue, Stockade Street, ran all around the city just inside the palings; after the change the new guard would march a hundred paces down that street, and I would hear him go. That spring they were more alert than usual because of a rising buzz of war talk between Moha and Katskil; border towns take a beating in those affairs. At the end of his section he'd meet the next guard and bat the breeze if the corporal or sergeant wasn't around, and that would leave my favorite spot unwatched. Later on the guards would take longer breaks in safe corners, smoking tobacco or marawan and trading stiffeners,* but the first break would suit my needs. Meanwhile I had an hour to wait and spent it unwisely thinking too much about the mue, which made me wonder what sort of creature *I* was.

I knew of brain-mues, the most dreaded of all, who have a natural human form so that no one can guess their nature till their actions reveal it. Sooner or later they behave in a way folk call the mue-frenzy, or insanity. They may bark, fume, rush about like beasts, see what others do not, lapse (like Morgan III) into the behavior of an idiot child, or sit speechless and motionless for days on end. Or they may with the most reasonable manner speak and obviously believe outrageous nonsense, usually suspecting others of wickedness or conspiracy or supposing themselves to be famous important people—even Abraham, or God himself. When brain-mues reveal themselves this way they are given over to the priests for dis-

* Moha idiom. Davy means the type of anecdote known in Nuin as a "tickler" or, for some undecipherable reason, "smut."
—Dion M. M.

posal, like people who develop mysterious discolorations or lumps under the skin, since these are also considered to be the working-out of a mue-evil.

An Old-Time book we have on board describes "insane" people very differently, as sick people who may be treated and sometimes healed. This book uses the word "psychopathic" and mentions "insanity" or "craziness" as unsuitable popular terms. Ayah, and nowadays if you call a jo "crazy" you only mean he's odd, weird, full of mahooha, a long-john-in-summer, a quackpot. Our Old-Time book speaks of these people with no horror but with a kind of compassion that in the modern spook-ridden world human beings seldom show except to those who very closely resemble themselves.

Well, hunkered in the thicket outside the palisade, I knew nothing of books except as a dusty bewilderment of my schooltime, now past. I thought, with none to console me: Do brain-mues act as I've done? *No!* I said. But the idea lurked in shadow, a black wolf waiting.

Behind the palings a man with a fair tenor and a mandolin was singing "Swallow in the Chimbley," approaching down a side-street. Skoar folk had been humming that ever since a Rambler gang introduced it a few years before. It made me think of Emmia, less about my troubles.

Swallow in the chimbley,
  Oop hi derry O!
Swallow in the chimbley,
  Sally on my knee.
Swallow flying high,
Sally, don't you cry!
  Tumble up and tumble down and lie with me.

The evening was hot, heavy with the smell of wild hyacinth, so still I could hear that man hawk and spit after goofing the high note the way you expect a tenor to do if he's got more sass than education. I liked that.

You can't live thinking you're a brain-mue.

Swallow in the chimbley,
  Oop hi derry O!

Swallow in the chimbley,
  Sally jump free—
Left her smock behind,
Sally, don't you mind!
  Tumble up and tumble down and lie with me.

The singer was evidently the stockade guard's relief, for now I heard the ceremony of the change of guards. First the old guard hollered at the new to quit making like a Goddamn likkered-up tomcat and get the lead out of his butt. After that, the solemn clash of gear, and a brisk discussion of music, the rightness of the town clock, what the corporal would say, where the corporal could shove it, and a suggestion that the musical new guard do something in the way of sexual self-ministration which I don't think is possible, to which the singer replied that he couldn't account he was built like a bugle. I sneaked over to the base of the stockade, waiting out the ceremony. At last the new guard stomped off down the street on his first round—without his mandolin since he had to carry a javelin.

Swallow in the chimbley,
  Oop hi derry O!
Swallow in the chimbley,
  Sally cry "Eee!"
Catch her by the tail,
Happy little quail!
  Tumble up and tumble down and lie with me.

The spider-bite hampered me climbing the stockade, but I made it, the burden in my sack unharmed. I sneaked down Kurin Street to the Bull-and-Iron. Emmia's window was lit, though it wasn't yet her bedtime. When I reached the stable, damned if she wasn't there doing my work for me. She had finished watering the mules, and turned with a finger at her lips. "They think I'm in my room. Said I seen you at work and they took my word for it. I swear, Davy, this is the last time I cover up for you. Shame on you!"

"You didn't have to, Miss Emmia. I—"

" 'Didn't have to'—and me trying to save your backside a tanning! Moving away, Mister Independent?"

I squirmed my sack to the floor; my shirt sprung open and she saw the smeary bite. "Davy darling, whatever?" And here she comes in a warm rush, no more mad at all. "Oh dear, you got a fever too!"

"Orb-spider."

"Dumb crazy love, going off where them awful things be, if you was small enough to turn over my lap I'd give you a fever where you'd remember it." She went on so, sugary scolding that means only kindness and female bossiness.

When she stopped for breath I said: "I didn't goof off, Miss Emmia—thought it was my free day." Her soft hands fussing at my shirt and the bitten place were rousing me up so that I wondered if my loin-rag would hide the evidence.

"Now shed up, Davy, you didn't think never no such of a thing, the way you lie to me and everybody it's a caution to the saints, but I won't tell, I said I'd covered for you, only more fool me if I ever do it again, and you're lucky it's a Friday so you wasn't missed, and anyway—" There was this about Emmia: if you wished to say anything yourself you had to wait for the breath-pauses and work fast against the gentle stream that couldn't stop because it must get to the bottom of the hill and there was always more coming. "Now you go right straight up to your bed and I'll bring you a mint-leaf poultice for that 'ere because Ma says it's the best thing in the world for any kind of bite, bug-bite I mean, a snake is different of course, for that you've got to have a jolt of likker and a beezer-stone* but anyway—oh, poo, what did you put on it?" But she didn't wait to hear. "You take your lantern now, I won't need it, and straight up to bed with you, don't stand there fossicking around."

"Kay," I said, and tried to hoist my sack without her

---

* Any odd-shaped stone supposed to have medicinal powers, more often called vitamin-stone. I made quite a few for sale when I was with Rumley's Ramblers; rubbing with wet sand gives them a nice weathered look. My own footnote, by damn!

—D.

noticing it, but she could talky-talk and still be sharp.

"Merciful winds, what have you got there?"

"Nothin'."

"Nothin' he says and it pushing out the sack big as a house—Davy, listen, if you've latched onto something you shouldn't I can't cover *that* for you, it's a sin—"

"It's nothing!" I yelled that. "You gotta know everything, Miss Emmia, it's a chunk of wood I found so to carve you something for your name-day, 'f you gotta know ever' durn thing, if you gotta."

"O Davy, little Spice!" She grabbed me again, her face one big rose. I barely swung the sack out of the line of operations before I got kissed.

No one had kissed me since Caron. True, "little Spice" doesn't mean the same as just "Spice." But Emmia was keeping hold of me, her fragrant heat pressing—lordy, I hadn't even known a girl's nipples could grow firm enough to be felt through the clothes! But something was wrong with me; I was growing limp and scared, stomach fluttering, the spiderbite jumping. "Aw Davy, and I was scolding you so, and you sick with a bite you got account you was doing something for me—O Davy, I feel awful."

I dropped the sack and tightened my arms, learning her elastic softness. Her eyes opened wide in astonishment as if no such thought had ever touched her so far as I was concerned, and maybe it hadn't till she felt my hands growing a little courageous at her waist and hips.* "Why, Davy!" My hands relaxed too soon and she collected her wits. "You go up to bed now like I said, and I'll bring the poultice soon as I can sneak back out here."

I toiled up to the loft, the memory of her flesh printed on mine, reached my pallet without dropping the lantern, and hid my sack in the hay. I flung off my loin-rag but kept my shirt on because of a fever-chill. Under the blanket limp and shivering, I watched fantastic nothings ebb and

---

* I dunno, Davy. I may form a Sisterly Protective Order of Phemale Women, myself president as well as founder if the salary is right, for the constitutional purpose of taking you out somewhere and drowning you. After the historical event we'd hold commemorative meetings, and drink tea.

—Miranda Nicoletta.

flow in the darkness around the rafters of the loft, so far above my puddle of lantern-light. I smelled the lantern's rancid seal-oil, the dry hay, the sweat and manure of horses and mules below. I wished I dared show the golden horn to someone and tell my story. Who but Emmia? At that time she was my one friend.

The bond-servant caste is a sorry thing in Moha, squeezed from above and below. Slaves hated us for being slightly better off, the lifers not so sharply as the short-term slaves, who probably felt they weren't too different from us, a mere matter of conviction for minor crime instead of our accident of birth or bad fortune. Freemen despised us for the sake of looking down on someone—no real satisfaction in looking down on a slave. Emmia could have got into bad trouble by showing affection for me when any third person was present; I never expected her to, and that she should do so when we were alone was still a puzzle to me that night, in spite of all the lush daydreams I was in the habit of building on the fact—it just hadn't occurred to me yet (outside of daydreams) that there was anything about me a woman would actually love.

I must have heard the whole run of popular sayings: "All bond-servants steal a little"—"Give a b.s. an inch and he'll take a yard"—"A bond-wench may be a good lay but remember your whip!" All the old crud-talk that people seem to need to shore up their vanity and avoid the risk of looking honestly at themselves. In the same way, people said: "All slaves stink." They never asked: Who lets them have a basin to wash in or time to use it?

And in Moha you heard that no Katskil man should be trusted alone even with a sow. Conicut people tell you every other man in Lomeda is a fairy and the rest back-scuttlers. In Nuin I have heard: "It takes three Penn tradesmen to cheat a Levannon man, two Levannese to cheat a Vairmanter, and two Vairmanters have no trouble cheating the Devil." And so on and on, everything your neighbor's fault until some time maybe a million years from now when the human race runs out of dirt.

At school I heard the teacher-priests explain how race prejudice was one of the sins that persuaded God to destroy the world of Old Time and make men pass through the

Years of Confusion so there would be only one race with traces of all the old ones in it, and my opinion of God went up several notches. Inside, though, a somehow older boy who wasn't quite ready to show his head went on muttering that it was too nice and simple: if God was going to take that much trouble why couldn't he make modern people decent and kind in other ways?

Today I know it's a mere historical accident that has made us all fairly close to the same physical pattern in that part of the world. We are the descendants of a small handful of survivors, and they happened to include most of the races of Old Time. Anyone who deviates too far is still treated outrageously, if he escapes early destruction as a mue. In Conicut, with Rumley's Ramblers, I would have been uneasy about my red hair, if it hadn't been a strong gang that took care of its own.

Freeman boys, many from poor families living no better than I did, ran in street-gangs and wanted no part of a b.s., unless they could catch one alone, for fun. I could have made friends with a freeman boy, meeting him by himself, but the herd pattern is death on friendship. If the pack must come first—its rituals, cruelties, group make-believes and sham brotherhood—you have no time left for the individual spirit of another; no time, no courage, no recognition.

Against the danger of the street-gangs I had my Katskil knife, but I was so sharp at nipping out of sight whenever I saw more than three boys in a group that I'd never been obliged to use the steel in self-defense. Good thing too, for getting hanged would have interfered seriously with writing this book, and even if you don't exist I'd hate to see you suffer a deprivation like that.*

But even in fever common sense told me I could not show Emmia my golden horn and tell the story. She would never understand why I hadn't killed the mue. She would be demoralized by the mere thought of a mue existing near the city. Like most women she could scarcely bear the

* Notice he never pauses to consider how it feels to be married to an Irish bull. However, courage! Am *I* cowed by such a brute? Why, yes, now I think of it.

—Nickie.

sound of the word "mue"—she'd sooner have had a rat run up her leg.

Then for a while I think the fever sent my wits wandering out of the world.

* * *

While I wrote this morning the fog dissolved. Nickie called me on deck an hour ago—her face was wet—and pointed to the blur of green two or three miles southeast. As I was watching, a white bird circled down to the island. No smoke rises from it; the day is a quiet of blue and gold.

I'll make only this note of it for the present. We have a light westerly, and Captain Barr intends to circumnavigate, tacking as near the island as he safely can. We shall watch for harbors, stream outlets, reefs, beaches, any sign of habitation. Major note: Miranda Nicoletta is happy.

* * *

I was pulled awake by feeling another blanket being spread over me. Wool-soft it was and sweet with the girl-scent of Emmia—I mean her own, not the boughten perfume she sometimes used. She must have brought it from her own bed, and I a damned yard-boy not brave enough to kill a mue but low enough to steal from him.

Emmia was talking, of what I don't know; in the middle of the pleasant sound I spoke her name. She said: "Hush, Davy! How you do run on! Be the good jo and let me put on this poultice—don't squirm so!" Her voice was as kind as her hands that eased down the blankets and pressed a minty-smelling pad where my skin still hurt, some. The pain was no longer serious; I was pretending to be worse off than I was, to prolong her soft attentions. "What was you yattering about just now, Davy? Where the sun rises, you said, only it's night, you know it is, so maybe you was fevery the way I heard about a man had the smallpox and he thought he was tumbling off a hoss, so whoa he says, whoa, and falls out of bed for real and dead as anything the next day, the chill you know, come to think, that was Morton Sampson that married a connection of Ma's and used to live on Cayuga Street catacorny from the old schoolhouse . . ." I wondered if I could have spoken in my fever about the golden horn. She was coaxing my arms under the blanket. "Yes, you went running on, about traveling, merciful winds, I guess you must like to talk, I couldn't scarcely get a word in by the thin edge—oh, feel that sweat! Your fever's busted, Davy, and that's what they call a good sweat, you be all right now, only keep warm, boy, and you better get to sleep too."

I said: "If a man went far—"

"Ayah, that's just the way you was running on, only now you should get to sleep because like Ma says if a person don't get enough sleep the next day is ruint, see?" Resting a hand on the blanket, she was watching me not quite so directly. Her conversational brook went on, but I think already we had some of the special awkwardness a man and woman feel when each knows the other is thinking of the intercourse not yet shared. "I do marvel—where the sun rises, think of having such fancies when you be fevered, still it must be nice to travel, I always wished I could, like that friend of Pa's, I can't think of his name, anyway he went all the way to Humber Town—oh, who *was* it?—Peckham—I'll think of it in a minute, it wasn't Peckham no-way—why, Hamlet Parsons was who it was, remember?—Ham Parsons of course with the one gone eye account of an ax handle in the one I mean, all the way to Humber Town and come to think, that was just two summers ago because it was the same year we lost old White-Stocking from the bloat—what a nice old thing he was . . ."

It was restful, sleepy-making, like a brook, like a tree murmuring the wind, only bless her, Emmia wasn't built like a tree and her bark wasn't scratchy, not anywhere. In my half-sick drowsiness I wondered why I should feel afraid of Emmia when she was being so kind to me, bringing that blanket, sitting now so close that my right arm was cramped because it didn't dare sprawl across her lap. I suppose I knew myself to be two or more people, that common trouble. The Davy who wanted to be a gentle, loving (and safely blameless) friend—that's the only one who was afraid. The healthy jo who needed to grab her

67

and lock her loins till he could spend himself was not afraid of Emmia but only, in a practical way, of the world: he didn't want to be slammed into the pillory. What never occurred to me until years later was that all these inconsistent and troubling selves are real as soon as your mind has gone through the pain of giving them birth.

7

"Be you warm enough now?" I made some kind of noise. "You know, Davy, them fancies you get in a fever a'n't real dreams like, I mean not like the ones that tell your fortune if you go to sleep with a corncob under the pillow. You sure you be warm enough?"

"I wish you was always with me."

"What?"

"Wish you was with me. In my bed."

She didn't slap my face. I couldn't look at hers, but of a sudden she was lying on the pallet warm and close, her breath fluttering my hair. The blankets bunched thick between us. She was on my right arm so it couldn't slip around her. She held my left hand away. I had at least three times her strength and couldn't dream of using any of it. "Davy dear, mustn't—I mean we better not, only—" I kissed her to stop the talk. "You're being bad now, Davy." I kissed her ear and the silken hollow of her shoulder. I hadn't known it, but that was blowing on a fire. Her thigh slid over me and she was trembling, pushing against me through the blankets and presently whimpering: "It's a sin—Mother of Abraham, don't let me be so bad!" She thrust herself free and rolled away. I thought she would get up and leave me, but instead she lay on the bare floor rumpled and careless, her knees drawn up, her skirt fallen, hands pressed at her face.

For just that moment, her eyes not watching me, her secret place uncovered wanton and helpless for me, I was all man responding and could have taken her, never mind whether she was crying. Then my mind went idiot and yelped: If Mam Robson comes looking for her, or Old Jon? I heard her fainting voice. "Why'n't you do it to me?"

I flung the blankets away. The final cold killing thought arrived, not in words but a picture: a wooden frame on a tall column; holes in the frame for the offending bond-servant's neck, wrists and ankles; a clear space on the earth so that rocks and garbage could be readily cleared away after the thing in the pillory had become a mere lesson in morality too motionless to be entertaining.

Emmia's suffering face was turned to me. She knew I had been ready for her and now was not. She embraced me clumsily, trying to restore me with shaking ineffectual fingers. Maybe that was when she too remembered the law, for she suddenly dragged the blankets over me and stumbled away. I thought: It's all up with me—can I run?

But she was returning. Her wet face was not angry. She sat by me again, not too near, her smock tucked in at her knees. She groped for a handkerchief, found none, mopped her face on the blanket. "I wouldn't hurt you, Miss Emmia."

She stared dumbfounded, then laughed breathlessly. "*Oh* you poor sweet cloth-head! It's my fault, and now I suppose you think I'm one of these girls'll do it for anybody, not a mor'l to their name, honest I'm not like that, Davy, and when it's just you and me and us such good friends you don't have to call me *Miss* Emmia heavensake! Aw Davy, things sort of go to my head, I can't explain, you wouldn't know—"

At least she was talking again. My panic faded. The brook ran on, growing more restful by the minute.

* * *

Speaking of brooks—

I stopped writing a week ago, and resumed it this afternoon within sound of a tropic brook. The day has been filled with tasks of settlement on our island. We mean to

69

stay at least until those now in the womb are born, maybe longer. Maybe some will stay and others go on—I can't imagine Captain Barr letting the schooner ride too long at anchor . . . The brook runs by a shelter Nickie and I are sharing with Dion and three others while we work at more permanent buildings for the colony.

The island is small, roughly oval, its greatest length along the north-south axis, about ten miles. It must be within the region where the old map gives us a few dots named the Azores. We sailed around it that first day, then seeing no other land on the horizon we inched into the one harbor, a bay on the eastern shore. We anchored in five fathoms near a clean strand where a band of gray monkeys were picking over shells and finding something to eat—hermit crabs. We waited that day and night on board to learn of the tides—they are moderate—and watch for signs of human or other dangerous life.

No one slept much that night at the anchorage—a deep warm night, rest from the long strain and fears of voyaging, a full moon for lovers—high time for a night of music and drink and cheerful riot. There are forty of us—sixteen women, twenty-four men—and nearly all of us are young. We came ashore in the morning not too hung over, all eager except Mr. Wilbraham who never is.

The only wild things we've seen are the monkeys, a few goats, short-eared rabbits, a host of birds. On a walk around the island yesterday Jim Loman and I found tracks of pig, fox and wildcat, and we saw flying squirrels much like the gentle things I used to glimpse in the Moha woods. It must be that human beings haven't lived here since Old Time. We may find ruins in the interior.

On a knoll near the beach we've cleared away vegetation to make room for houses. The brook flowing by the base of the knoll originates a mile inland from the island's highest hill, about a thousand feet above sea level, we guess. Along the brook a tough reed-like grass grows in abundance; it might be good for paper-making as well as thatch. Our houses will be lightly constructed—thatched roofs on tall supports, the thatched walls coming only half-way to the line of the eaves, the kind of airy buildings I saw in Penn when I went there with Rumley's Ramblers in 320. They keep a kind of freshness even on the hottest day, and if hurricane comes—well, you haven't lost too much; you build again.

We wonder of course what snake is in this Eden.

* * *

Speaking of brooks—

Look, said Emmia's personal brook, what we almost did was a terrible sin because I was a Mere Boy and an awful sin anyhow, only we hadn't done anything so there *wasn't* any sin and all her fault too, but she'd just take it to God in prayer without having to confess it, and never would tell on me, wild horses wouldn't drag one word out of her, because mostly I was a good dear boy that couldn't help being born without no advantages, except for wildness and goofing off and like that, but when I corrected that I'd be a good man who everybody'd respect, see, only I must prove myself and remember that like her Ma said life wasn't all beer and skittles whatever skittles were, she'd always thought it was a funny word, well, life was hard work and responsibility and minding what wiser folk said, not only the priests but everybody who lived respectable because there was a right way and a wrong way just like her Ma said, and you must *not* be all the time goofing off the way other people had to cover up and so on because they kind of loved you and feed the plague-take-it old *mules*. I said I was sorry.

Well then, I did ought to feel just a *smidgin* of repentance about tonight, not because it was my fault, it wasn't, it wasn't, except maybe I shouldn't ought to've kissed her just *that* way, because boys ought to be kind of careful and try to stay pure and like reverent by not thinking too much about you-know-what, anyhow after my apprentice time I'd prob'ly marry some nice woman and everything would be nice, and by the way I mustn't feel bad about it not you-know standing up like, because she happened to know for a fact the same thing happened to lots of boys if they was just scared or not used to things, see, it didn't necessarily mean they had some enemy doing nasty things with a wax image, although of course if I was a full-growed

71

man it could be that and you had to be careful, anyhow it was all her fault like she'd said before. I said I was sorry.

She said she knew I was and it did me credit, and nobody would ever know, and as for the laws, why, they'd ought to take them mis'ble laws out and drown them, because bond-servant or no I was as good as anybody and she'd say it again, as good as *anybody*, more b' token she wouldn't let anyone hurt one hair of my head, ever, only what she meant about proving myself, well, see, I ought to go and do something difficult, she didn't mean anything wild or goofy, just something hard and well, like noble or something, so as to—so as to—

"Miss Emmia, I mean Emmia, I will, I mean it, cross my heart I will, like what frinstance?"

"Oh, you should choose it yourself, something you don't want to do but know you should, like going to church regular, only it don't have to be that, you ought to want to do that anyway. No, just something good and honest and difficult, the way I'll be proud of you, I'll be your inspiration like—no, you mustn't kiss me again, not ever until you be freeman, mind now I mean it."

She stood up away from me, smoothing her skirt, her eyes downcast, maybe crying again a little, but in the weak lantern-light I couldn't be sure. "I'll try, Emmia."

"I mean I want us to be good, Davy, like—like respectable people, nice people that get ahead and get asked to go places and stuff. That's what they mean, see, by fearing God and living in Abraham and like that, I mean there's a right way and a wrong way, I mean I—well, I a'n't always been too good, Davy, you wouldn't know." She was at the trap-door, setting down the lantern. She blew it out to leave for me at the head of the ladder. "You go to sleep now, Davy—little Spice." She was gone.

I could have run after her then, ready as ever I would be, no more sense than a jack-in-the-box, and no less. But I only went to the window, and saw her vague shape crossing the stable yard, and crawled back under the blankets into a dream-tormented sleep.

I was running—rather, a mush-footed staggering on legs too heavy and too short—through a house dimly like the Bull-and-Iron. It possessed a thousand rooms, each

72

containing something with a hint of memory: a three-legged stool the orphanage kids sat on when they were naughty; a ring Sister Carnation wore; a cloth doll; my luck-charm upright in one of the crimson slippers Caron wore when she first came to the orphanage—(they'd been swiftly taken away from her as a sinful vanity). In that house black wolf followed me, in no hurry—he could wait. His throat-noises resembled words: "Look at me! Look at me!" If I did, even once, he would have me. I went on—each room windowless, no sunrise place. The doors would not latch behind me. When I leaned against one, black wolf slobbered at the crack, and I said over my shoulder: "I'll give Caron my Katskil knife and she will do you something good and difficult." He shut up then, but I must still find Caron or my threat was empty, and it may be she went on ahead with one brown foot bare and my candle upright in the other crimson slipper, but I don't know, for I tripped and went down, knowing black wolf was about to snuff at my neck, then knowing I was awake on my pallet in the stable loft, but for a while I wasn't certain I was alone.

I was alone. I smelled the dry hay, and Emmia's scent—merely from her blanket. Late moonlight showed me the loft window. The spider-bite was a harmless itch and soreness. I found my sack and felt of the golden horn. It was not mine.

I knew what that action must be, good and honest and difficult. My horn must go back to an ugly creature who could make no use of it. Was that good? Well, it was difficult and honest. I could never tell of it to Emmia—unless maybe I dressed up the story—changed the mue to a hermit perhaps? Nay, when had I ever told the girl anything but the simplest every-day matters? Why, in my day-dreams. Then, sure, she never failed to respond wonderfully.

I would run away, scorned, abused, in danger of my life because Emmia had reported me to the authorities for not killing the mue. Then, let's see—would I fall prey to the policer dogs? Facing them, I would say—nope. Well, climb a tree, talk from there? Balls.

However, some far-off day I might revisit Skoar, a

73

scarred and sad-faced man disinclined to mention heroic action in the far-off wars of—Nuin? Conicut? Why wouldn't I captain an expedition that did away with the Cod Islands pirates? So in gratitude a friendly nation made me Governor of them balmy isles—

Kay, in those days how was I to know the Cods are a few lumps scattered through the waters off Nuin as if someone had flung gobs of wet sand out of a bucket?

Emmia, having sorrowfully blamed herself all these years, might recognize me, but alas—

A rat lolloping across an overhead beam scared the bejasus out of me. I slung on my clothes, and felt for the lump of my luck-charm in the sack. I must find another cord and wear it again the right way. I would cut a length of fishline for it when I got to my cave. I tried not to think of the horn. My moccasins went into the sack on top of it, and I settled my knife-belt.

Emmia's blanket mustn't be found here by somebody who'd say it proved we spent the night together under it. I crammed it on top of the moccasins and went down the ladder. Going away for real, I thought.

But Emmia mustn't be harmed, as she might be if the blanket merely turned up missing. All permanent property of the Bull-and-Iron seemed to be attached to Mam Robson by a God-damn mystic cord. Food in moderation you could steal, but let a blanket or candlestick or such-like walk with Abraham, and something wounded the Mam deep in her soul; she couldn't rest till she'd searched out the cause of the pain, all the better if she could drive Old Jon into a twittering frenzy while she did it.

I stood under Emmia's window studying the big jinnycreeper. The ancient stem was sturdy and should hold me. Old Jon and the Mam slept on the other side of the building. The rooms nearest Emmia's were for guests; below was a store-room. Only a reckless randy-john would climb up there. I climbed.

The vine gripped the bricks with ten thousand toes, bent and whispered but did not break. I clung with an arm over the sill. I'd carried the blanket up in my teeth and left my sack in deep shadow. I dropped the blanket inside the room that was rich with Emmia's fragrance. I heard a small puppy-moan that must mean sleep, maybe the nudging of a dream. She might wake, see my shadow and scream the house down. This was the shape my fear took that time. I was on the ground and jittering away down Kurin Street before I could stop trembling.

Sick-angry too because I had not gone to her bed, but I could dream up plentiful reasons for not going back *now*. They drove me on—over the stockade, up the mountain. But I would return, I told myself, after I restored the horn. I'd try to please her. Hell, I'd even go to church if there was no way to weasel out of it. And (said another self) I would get it in.

* * *

Dion has offered the colonists a name for the island—Neonarcheos. I think I like it. It is from Greek, a language already ancient and unspoken in the Golden Age. Dion is one of the few among the Heretics who studied that, and Latin. (The Church forbids to the public anything at all in a language not English—it could be sorcery.) He introduced me to the Greek and Latin authors in translation; I note that they also looked backward toward a Golden Age preceding what they called the Age of Iron . . .

Dion's name for this place says something I wanted said—new-old. It connects us somehow with the age when this island—and the others that must lie close over the horizon, all of different shape and smaller than they were before the ocean rose—was a Portuguese possession, whatever that may have meant to it; yes, and with a time far more remote, when civilization capable of recording itself was a new thing on earth, and this island was a speck of green in the blue inhabited, as when we found it, only by the birds and other shy things who live their entire lifetimes without either wisdom or malice.

* * *

When I climbed North Mountain again to return the horn I did not see true sunrise, for by the time it arrived I was in that big-tree region where the day before I might

75

so easily have killed my monster. I was not hurrying; reluctance made me feel as though the air itself had thickened to a barrier. I did not feel much afraid of the mue, though when I entered the tangle where his grapevine pathways ran I was looking upward too much, until certain timorous fancies were flooded out of me by a wrong smell—wolf smell.

I drew my knife, exasperated—must I be halted, distracted by a danger not connected with my errand? The scent was coming from dead ahead, where I had to go in order not to lose the marks of my passage of the day before. I was not far from the tulip tree. Knife ready, I made no effort to be quiet—if the wolf was lurking anywhere within a hundred yards he knew exactly where I was.

You can't look quite straight at black wolf even from the rail above the baiting-pit. Something about him pushes your gaze off true. I spoke of that once to Dion, who remarked that maybe we glimpse a fraction of our selves in him. My dear friend Sam Loomis, a gentle heart if ever there was one, used to claim he was sired by an irritated black wolf onto the cunt of a hurricane; in such nonsense talk he may have been saying something not entirely nonsense.

When a man hears black wolf's cold long cry in the dark, his heart does strain at its human boundaries. You, I, anyone. You know you won't go out there to hunt with him, quarrel with him over the bleeding meat, run down the glades of midnight with him and his diamond-eyed female, be a thing like him. But we are deep enough to contain the desire; it does not altogether sleep. All nights are resonant with the unspoken. Latent in our brains, our muscles, our sex, are all the harsh lusts that ever blazed. We are lightning and the avalanche, fire and the crushing storm.

That morning I found my black wolf quickly. She was below the grapevine that hung down outside the catbriers, and she was dead. An old bitch wolf—my knife prodded the huge scrawny carcass, six feet long from her snout to the base of her mangy tail. Scarred, foul, hair once black gone rusty with festered spots. When alive, for all her decay she could still have hamstrung a wild boar. But her neck was broken.

Lifting, poking with my knife—I could not have touched her with my hand and not puked—I proved to myself that her neck was broken. Doubt it if you like—you never saw my North Mountain mue and his arms. Her body was already losing stiffness, and a line of the midget yellow carrion ants had laid out their mysterious highway to her, so she must have been dead for several hours. The cover was too dense to admit the wings of crows or vultures, and it is said the small scavenger dogs of the wilderness will not touch black wolf's body. I rubbed away a bit of the ants' path and watched stupidly as they fiddled about restoring it. The dry blood on the rocks, the ground, the grape-stem, was not from the dead wolf, who had no wound but a broken neck.

I read the signs. She had ambushed the mue when he was near the vine. Bushes were flattened and torn; a heavy boulder had been jerked out of its earth-pocket. It would have happened the day before, perhaps when he came back from the pool. He could have been careless from distress, wondering why he had not changed to man-beautiful.

Or he might have lifted the rose-colored rock to find his treasure gone, and come storming out ready to attack the first thing that moved.

Either way, I was guilty.

Her mouth was agape, the teeth dry. I noticed one of the great stabbers in the lower jaw had broken off long before, leaving a blackened stump in a pus-pocket that must have caused her agony. I believe it had never occurred to me before that a black wolf like any other sentient thing could suffer. The other long tooth of the lower jaw was brown with dry blood.

I climbed the tulip tree. There were blood-smears all the way. I did not think the mue could have lost so much and still be living, but I called to him: "I've come back. I'm bringing it back to you. I took it but I'm bringing it back." I mounted a thick branch above his nest and compelled myself to look down. The yellow ants must have formed their column on the opposite side of the trunk, or surely I would have seen them sooner.

He was human. Knowing that, I was wondering for a

77

while how much of my schooling had been lies on top of lies.

I alone remember him. You may remember what I've written, a book-thing for leisure talk. But as I write this now I am the only one who even knows of him except Nickie and Dion, for I've never told any others, except one person who is dead, how it was that I won my golden horn.

8

I returned to my cliffside cave, and the day passed over me. Right or wrong, for good or evil, the golden horn was mine.

I recall a half-hour blazing with the knowledge that I, myself, redhead Davy, was *alive*. I had to throw off my clothes, pinch, slap, stare at every astonishing part of my hundred and fifteen pounds of sensitive beef. I slapped my palm on a sun-hot rock for the mere joy of being able to. I rolled on the grass, I ran up the ledge into the woods so that I might make love to a tree-trunk and cry a little. I flung a stone high, and laughed to hear it tumble far in the leaves.

I would not be going to Levannon on a spirited roan, with three attendants, and serving-maids spreading their knees for me at every inn. But I would go.

With my horn, I dared that day to learn a little. Humility came later: when I play nowadays I know I can only touch the fringes of an Old-Time art beside which the best music of our day is the chirping of sparrows. But before my lips grew sore that first day I did learn by trial and error how to find a melody I'd known since I was a child. I think "Londonderry Air" was the first music I knew, sung to me by dear fat Sister Carnation. Curiosity drove me on past ordinary fatigue. I found the notes; my ear told me I was playing them true.

Thanks to the great dictionary, I know that my horn is what was known in Old Time as a "French horn." The valve mechanism can be kept in repair by modern workmen—I had a little work done on it at Old City; the horn itself we could never duplicate in this age. I have been playing it now for about fourteen years, and I sometimes wonder if a horn-player of Old Time would consider me a promising beginner.

When I quit my studies that day in the woods, the afternoon was nearly spent. I made a belated meal from the left-over bacon and half-loaf of oat bread. Then I scooped a pocket in the earth rather far from my cave, and buried the sack there with my horn wrapped in the gray moss. Only memory marked the spot, for I knew I would be returning very soon. I was going away from Skoar; that, I felt now, was certain as sunrise. But this one night I must return to the city.

I had cut a length of fishline for my luck-charm, but found the cord unpleasantly rough at my neck, so again I put the charm in the sack, along with the horn. And forgot I had done so—you might remember that. Later, when it was important to me, to save me I couldn't recollect if I had put the charm in the sack or continued to wear it a while longer in spite of the chafing. If you exist, your memory has probably goofed you the same way. If you don't exist, why don't you give me a breakdown on that too?

Everything looked simpler to me that evening, when I had buried my horn. I was not daydreaming nor building my fortunes on a chip of the moon. I just wanted Emmia.

I hid again in the brush near the stockade, and after I heard the change of guards—they were late—I crept close to the palings and continued to wait, for I was sure I hadn't heard the new guard march down the street in the usual way. And I must have been more exhausted than I knew, for I fell stupidly asleep.

I'd never done it before in such a dangerous spot, and haven't since. But I did then. When I came to myself it was night, with a pallor of early moonlight in the east.

Now I had no way of guessing about the guard until I heard him, and waited another dreary while. A pig wandered along the avenue inside the stockade, passing private remarks to his gut about the low quality of the street garbage. Nobody shied a rock at him, as a guard would almost certainly have done to keep off dull times. Sick of waiting, I took a chance and climbed.

The guard let me scramble over and down on the city side. Then I heard his quick step behind me and a bang on the head toppled me. As I rolled over his expensive cowhide boot was churning my belly. "Where you from, bond-servant?" My gray loin-rag told him that about me—we were required to wear them, as slaves wear black ones and freemen white; only the nobility is allowed to wear a loin-rag or britches of interesting color.

"I work at the Bull-and-Iron. Lost my way."

"Likely tell. They never teach you to say 'sir'?" Lamplight from down the street showed me a tight skinny face set in the sour look that means a man won't heed anything you say because his mind was all made up about everything long ago when you weren't around. He fingered his club; his boot was hurting me. "Kay, let's see your pass."

Anyone entering or leaving Skoar at night had to have a pass with the stamp of the City Council, unless he was a uniformed soldier of the garrison, a priest, or a member of the upper nobility with a shoulder-tattoo to prove it. Of course freemen and the lower nobility—(Misters like Old Jon and such-like)—didn't go off down the roads after dark except in large armed groups with torchlight and foofaraw to keep off wolf and tiger, but there were enough of those traveling groups—caravans they're called—to keep the City Council happy stamping things. However—oh, in the spring after the weather settled to sweet starry nights, and hunting beasts were unlikely to come near human settlements because food was easy elsewhere, boys with their wenches would be slipping over the palisade all the time. Scare-screwing, the kids called it. I never heard of such parties getting killed and eaten, but maybe it does something for a girl if she can imagine that with a boy on top of her. And the guards were expected, almost officially, to look the other way, for as I wrote a while back, even the Church admits that breeding must be encouraged, especially among the working classes. On June mornings the grass just outside the stockade was apt to be squashed flat as a battlefield, which in a way it was.

"A'n't got a pass, sir. You know how it is."

"Don't give me that. You know everybody got to have a pass now, with a war on."

"War?" I'd grown so used to the yak about possible war with Katskil I'd given it no more heed than mosquito-buzz.

"Declared yesterday. Everyone knows about it."

"Not me, sir. Lost in the woods yesterday."

"Likely tell," he said, and we were back where we started. If war had been declared yesterday, wouldn't Emmia have spoken of it to me? Maybe she had, while my wits were wandering. "Kay, so wha'd you do at this 'ere wha'd you say the God-damn name of the place was?"

"Bull-and-Iron, sir. Yard-boy. You ask Mister Jon Robson. Mister. Member of the City Council too."

I didn't blame him for not being impressed. Misters are a nickel a pair. Even Esquires don't have the important shoulder-tattoo, and Esquire was the biggest Old Jon would ever get to be. The guard's foot rolled me from side to side, hurting and churning. "Hear tell they's lots of redheaded scum in Katskil. No pass. Doing a sneak-in. And bearin' down on this crap about Mister like I needed a sumbitch like you to teach me manners, little snotnose fart that a high wind'd blow away. Aw, even if you a'n't lyin' you got to be reamed out some. Take you to the Captain is what I got to do. By him, being Mister Jon Whosit's pansy a'n't helping you."

I called him a bald-assed son of a whore, and now that I look back on it I believe that was almost the wrong thing to say. "Give y'self away then, Katskil. You be a Katskil spy. No b.s. is going to talk thataway to a bejasus member of the city gov'ment. Git up!"

He had become an obstacle between me and Emmia, just that, hardly anything more. He'd told me to get up, but his foot was still grinding me. I grabbed it, heaved, and he went flying ass over brisket.

My beef does get underestimated because of my pidlin

81

size and natural-born goofy look. His brass helmet slammed the palings, a bone snapped in his neck, and when he spread out on the ground he was dead as ever a man needs to be.

No pulse at his throat; his head flopped when I shook him. I caught the death smell—the poor jo's bowels had let go. Not a soul near; shadows lay heavy, with only one dull lamp down the street. The noise of the helmet on the logs had been small. I could have climbed back over the stockade and been gone for good, but that's not what I did.

As I knelt staring at him the universe was still full to bursting with the hunger for Emmia that had drawn me back. There seemed to be some connection as I looked at the dead guard, my love-rod stiffening like a fool, as if he'd been a rival. Why, I'm no rutting stag that needs to crash horns into another male to make himself ready for the does. I wasn't heartless either. I recall thinking there'd be others—wife, children, friends—whose lives would be jolted by what I'd done. That pale brown fitfully illuminated thing beside my knee was a human hand, with dirty fingernails, an old scar in the crotch between thumb and forefinger; maybe it could play a mandolin once. But it was dead, dead as the mue, and I was alive and hot for Emmia.

I left him, not hating him at all, nor myself too much. Nor did I think once, as I stole across the city, of the Eye of God beholding every act, the way the church teaching had told me it does, and this seems curious to me, for at that time I was by no means free for any clear thinking.

Nobody was abroad now except the watch, a few idlers and drunks and fifty-cent prosties, all of whom I could avoid. In the more respectable region where the Bull-and-Iron stood there wasn't a cat stirring. The only light at the inn was in the tap room; I caught the drone of Old Jon talking along to some polite guest who likely wanted to go to bed. The moon was fairly high. I saw glints of light from it on the jinny-creeper leaves. I climbed softly, easily, and let myself over the sill.

The moonlight gave me faint shapes: a chair, a bit of angular darkness probably a table, and a pale motion near at hand—why, that was myself, my image in the wall mirror by this window. I watched the image slip off shirt and loin-rag and lay the knife-belt on them, and stand naked as if held fast by its own quietness. Emmia stirred then, murmuring, and I went to her.

My own shadow had been hiding her from the moon. As I moved, the light displayed her; she might have been glowing in the dark, her warmth like a touch as I bent over her and my hand made contact with tender silkiness. She was lying on her side, her back to me. The sheet was at her waist, pushed down because this night was heavy as the rose-season of summer.

My fingers brought the sheet gently further down, barely touching the swell of her hip. Lightly also I touched the dark mass of her hair on the pillow and the dim curves of her neck and shoulder, and I wondered how she could sleep when my ungentle heart was so quickly and heavily drumming. I let myself down on the bed. "Emmia, it's just me, Davy. I want you." My hand roved, astonished, for my liveliest imaginings could never have told me how soft is a girl's skin to a lover's fingers. "Don't be scared, Emmia—don't make no noise—it's Davy."

I felt no waking start, only a turning of her heat against my thigh, then answering pressure of her hand to tell me she was neither angry nor afraid. Later I wondered if she might not have been awake all the time, pretending sleep for a game or to see what I would do. Now she was staring up at me from the pillow and whispering: "Davy, you be such a bad boy, ba-ad—why, oh, why did you go away again today? All day? So wild and crazy-like, what'll I do about you at all?"—calm, soft talky-talk as if there was nothing remarkable about the two of us being on her bed naked as eggs in the middle of the night, my hand curling over her left breast and then straying downward bold as you please and she smiling.

Yes, and so much for last night's instructions on virtue and mustn't-kiss-me-again. Gone like late-staying oak leaves when the spring winds lose patience, for I was kissing her now for sure, tasting the sweet life of her lips and tongue and nibbling her neck and telling her there was a right way and a wrong way and this time we'd bejasus do it the right way because I was going to have it into her

83

come hell or hi-ho. And she whimpered: "*Ah* no!"—in a way that couldn't mean anything except: "What the devil would be stopping you?"—and twisted her loins away from me, only to remind me I must use a little strength in this game.

I was also driven to say: "Emmia, I did go off to do something difficult and honest—done it best I could, only it's a thing I can't tell you of, not ever, Spice. And I got to run away."

"Nay." I don't know if she heard anything truly except the "Spice." I was at her ear again, and kissing the funny tip of her breast, and then her mouth. "So bad, Davy!—so bad!" Her fingers wandered now and demanded, as mine did, and mine found the little tropic swamp where I'd presently go. "Spice yourself!" she panted. "Tiger-tom. I won't let you run away from me, Tiger-tom, won't let you."

"Not from you."

"You be all man now, Davy. Oh!"

I did want to say I loved her, or some such message, but speech was lost, for I was over her, clumsy and seeking, understanding for the first time the mimic violence that a loving heart can't allow to go beyond the bounds of tenderness. She who had maybe always understood it, resisted me enough so that I must hold her down, overcome her, until presently the hot sweaty struggle itself was binding us together, as closely as our lips were bound whenever our mouths met and clung in the strife. Then, no longer resisting, her hands helped and guided me toward the blind thrust that took me into her.

I could imagine myself her master then, while she was locked fast to me and groaning: "Davy, Davy, kill me, I'm dying, my lord, my love, you damn big beautiful Tiger-tom —keep on, oh, keep on!"—but all in a tiny voice, no outcry, mindful of our safety even when my world blew up in rainbow fire. So now I am fairly sure, years later, that in the first embrace I can't have satisfied her completely. Kindness Emmia possessed. I think that to some extent, that first time, she acted a part out of kindness, well enough so that a green boy could feel happy and proud, emperor of her shadowplace, a prince of love.

It's not true to say there's only one first time. My first

was Caron who understood what game the grown-ups played, and we played it the witless childhood way, maybe better than most tumbling whelps because in a more-than-childhood way we did honestly cherish each other as people. But you may come to the first time with another as though the past were swept aside and you the same as virgin, entering a garden so new that all flowers taken in the past seem to belong to young years, smaller passions. I don't suppose this could be true for the men who are driven in a mischancy race from one woman to the next, never staying long enough with one to learn anything except that she has—what a surprise!—the same pattern of organs as the last. Nor could it be true of the female collectors of scalps. But it's true for anyone like myself to whom women are people, and is probably true for a woman who can see a bedmate is a friend and a person, not just an enemy or a child substitute or a phallus with legs.

Emmia smoothed my hair. "Mustn't run away."

"Not from you," I said again.

"Hush then."

I was finding a clarity like what may come with the ending of a fever. The world receded, yet grew sharper in lucid small detail. The dead guard at the stockade, the gleam of my golden horn, the mue become food for the yellow ants—all keeenly lit, tiny, perfect, like objects seen in sunlight through the bottom of a drinking glass. In the same vision I could find the fact of Emmia herself, that big-thighed honeypot deep as a well and shallow as a ripple on a brook, whom I now loved unpossessively.

She whispered: "I know what made you a big lover all-a-sudden. Found you a woods-girl out wilderness-way, one of the you-know, Little Ones, and she must be purtier than I be, and put a spell onto you the way no girl can say no."

"Why, an elf-girl'd take one look and say poo."

"Nay—got a thing or two about you, Davy. Some time I'll tell you how I know you been next to an elf-girl." Emmia was laughing at the fancy, half-believing it too, for elves and such-like are real to Moha folk, as real as serious matters like witchcraft and astrology and the Church. "Nay, own up, Tiger-tom, and tell me what she did. Feed my boy one of them big pointy mushrooms that look like you-know-what?"

"Nay. Old witch-woman, terrible humly."

"Don't say such things, Davy! I was just fooling."

"Me too. Kay, tell me how you know."

"So what'll you do for me if I do? I know—scratch my back—ooh, lower—that's it, that's good—more . . . Kay, here's how I know: what happened to your luck-charm?"

My brain banged into that one head-on. I was sitting bolt upright, scared frantic. I knew I had cut that fishing cord, strung the charm on it, and worn it. And not touched it since—or had I? . . . That I did not remember, and could not . . . Had it worked loose when I climbed the jinny-creeper?—impossible: I'd gone up like a slow wisp of smoke. The stockade then?—no. I'd done that too with great caution; besides, the logs were set so close you couldn't shinny up—had to work your fingers into the cracks and your toes too, climbing with your body curving out; my chest wouldn't have touched the palings. But when the guard clouted me I'd fallen face down and rolled, and his foot came down on my middle. My charm must have been torn loose when he roughed me, and I too mad to notice. Presently I couldn't believe anything else.

"Davy, love, what'd I say? I was just—"

"Not you, Spice. I got to run away."

"Tell me." She wanted to pull me back down to her, taking it for granted my trouble was only a boy's fret, something a kiss would fix.

I told her. "So it must be back there, Emmia, in plain sight. Might as good've stayed to tell 'em I done it."

"O Davy! But maybe he—"

"Sumbitch is dead as shoe-leather." I must have been thinking till now that I could run or not as I pleased; now I felt sure it was run or be hanged. Sooner or later the policers would find out whose neck the charm belonged to . . . "Emmia, does your Pa know I took off today?"

"O Davy, I couldn't cover for you today—*I* didn't know you was gone. Ayah, Judd wanted you should take the mules out for to turn the vegetable patch—and found you gone—went and told my Da, and he said—my Da said

86

you better have a real fine entertaining pile of—well—I mean, he said—"

"Just tell me."

"I can't. He didn't mean it, he was just running off at the mouth."

"Just say it, Emmia."

"Said he'd turn in your name to the City Council."

"Ayah. To be slaved."

"Davy, love, he was just running off at the mouth."

"He meant it."

"No!" But I knew he'd meant it; I'd tried his patience too far at last. Having a bond-servant declared a slave for misconduct was too serious for even Old Jon to make flap-talk about it. "Look, Davy—they wouldn't know the charm was yourn, would they?"

"They'll find out." I was out of bed and hustling on my clothes. She came to me, distracted now and crying. "Emmia, is it a fact the war's started?"

"Why, I told you that last night!"

"Must have been while I was light-headed."

"You stupid thing, don't you ever listen to me?"

"Tell me again—no, don't. I got to go."

"Oh, it was that town off west—Seneca—Katskils went and occupied it and *then* declared war, a'n't that awful? There's a regiment of ourn coming to Skoar to see they don't try no such here—but I *told* you all that."

Maybe she had. "Emmia, I got to go."

"O Davy, all this time we been—don't go!" She clung to me, tears streaming. "I'll hide you." She wasn't thinking. "See, they'd never look for you here."

"Search the whole inn, every room."

"Then take me with you. Oh, you got to! I hate it here, Davy. It stinks."

"Abraham's mercy, keep your voice down!"

"I *hate* it. Home!" She was trembling all over. Her head swung away and she spat on the floor, a furious little girl. "That for home! Take me with you, Davy!"

"I can't. The wilderness—"

"Davy, look at me!" She stepped into moonlight, her hair wild and breasts heaving. "Look! A'n't I all yourn?—all this, and *this!* Didn't I give you everything?" Nay, I'll

87

never understand how people can speak of love as if it were a thing, and given—cut, sliced, measured. "Davy, don't leave me behind! I'll do anything you want—hunt—steal—"

She couldn't even have climbed the stockade.

"Emmia, I'll be sleeping in trees. Bandits—how could I fight off a bunch of them buggers? They'd have you spread-eagled in nothing flat. Tiger. Black wolf. Mues."

"M-m—"

"In the wilderness, yes, and don't ask me how I know, but those stories are true. I couldn't take care of you out there, Emmia."

"You mean you don't want me." I hitched on my knife-belt. "You wouldn't care if you've give' me a baby—men're all alike—Ma says—don't never want nothin' but put it in and then walk off. I despise you, Davy, I do despise you."

"Hush!"

"I won't, I hate you—screw *you*, did you think you was first or something? All right, now *call* me a whore!"

"Hush, darling, hush! They'll hear."

"I hate the whole mis'ble horny lot of you—you dirty lech, you *boy*—so proud of that stupid ugly thing and then all's you do is run off, damn you—"

I closed her mouth with mine, feeling her need of that, and pushed her back against the wall. Her fingers were tight in my hair, my knife annoying where it hung between us, but we were locked in the love-seizure again, I deep in her and not much caring if I hurt her a little. She responded as if she wanted to swallow me alive. By good fortune my mouth still held hers closed when she needed to scream. Exhausted afterward, and desperate to be gone, I said: "I'll come back for you when I can. I love you, Emmia."

"Yes, Davy, Spice, yes, when you can, when it's safe for you, dearest." And what I heard in her voice was mostly relief. In both our voices. "I'll wait for you," she said, believing it. "Always I'll love you," she said, believing it, which made it true at the time.

"I'll come back."

I've wondered how soon she understood we'd both been lying, mostly for decent reasons. Maybe she knew it as soon as I was climbing down the vine. Her face, like a faded moon, vanished from the window before I turned away down the street. Nothing in life had ever drawn me with such wondrous power as the unknown road ahead of me in the dark.

9

A thickening fog was turning moonlight to milkiness. As I passed the pillory in the green I said under my breath: "I had her twice, once in bed and once against the wall." Wonderful, as if no one had ever laid a woman before. True, the small sound of my own voice scared me, and I continued along the empty street in a more slinky style, like a cat retiring from a creamery under trimmed sail with a cargo in the hold. But I still felt proud, and knew also an unfamiliar charity toward the whole big fat world and everyone in it except maybe Father Clance.

As I passed the baiting-pit I heard the moan of a bear who'd soon be used up in the Spring Festival—odd how human beings often celebrate the good weather by hurting something. I could do the bear no good but I think he did me some, reminding me to taper off a mite on my encompassing love for all mankind, who if they caught me would clobber me as thoroughly as they'd clobbered him. I went on, alert again, to a black alley that would bring me out near the spot where I'd left the dead guard lying.

I felt unseen doorways. A lifeless thing slithered under my feet. Dog, pigling, cat—the Scavengers' Guild would dispose of whatever it was as soon as it annoyed the policers. In later years, when I was living with Nickie in Old City of Nuin where the poorest streets are kept clean, it would have made me angry. But I was Skoar bred and born: in Moha people below the aristocracy took scant pride in their way of living, claiming that dirt and decay held down the taxes—though I don't think the tax collector ever lived who couldn't see through a six-foot pile of rubble to the tender gleam of a hidden dime. When my foot slipped I merely grumbled: "Ah, call the Mourners!"

In Skoar that remark was so routine it hardly rated as a joke. The Mourners' Guild is a Moha specialty, a gang of professional singers and wailers who close in on a family that's had a mue-birth to create an uproar of the sacred type. The slave woman old Judd was required to live with bore a mue, a blotched eyeless thing—I saw it carried away wrapped in a rag. The caterwauling demanded by law went on two days. It would have been five for a freeman family, eight to ten for the upper nobility—and no one no matter how blue his blood could break away from the festivities more than just long enough to go to the backhouse and return. The object is to appease the spirit of the mue after the priest has disposed of the body, and to remind the survivors that we are all miserable sinners totally corrupt in the sight of God. It's called planned reverence.

The Guild could be hired for a normal funeral, but charged custom rates for that. At the burial of a mue in Moha, the family was obliged to pay the Guild only a nominal fee, hardly more than a seventh of a year's earnings, plus about the same amount for a casket the neighbors would consider adequate. For slaves like Judd the town itself met the expense of the Guild's fee and a nice basswood box, charging it off to community good will, one of the generous things that made a Moha citizen point with pride.

At the end of the alley I saw a flicker of torchlight by the stockade, distorted in the fog, and heard voices. They'd found him.

Policers, talking softly. I assumed they'd found my luck-charm too—luck, hell. I sneaked off the other way till the curve of Stockade Street blocked out their light; then I crossed to the palings and wriggled over. Unfamiliar with this section of the palisade, I tumbled into crackling brush. Dogs would have caught the noise, but the policers had none with them, yet.

A horned owl in the mountain woods was crying his noises of death and hunger. I heard a bull alligator roar, in a swamp that covered a few acres east of the city—old Thundergut was useful like the bear, reminding me I'd do well to pass through water and confuse the policer dogs. By daylight they'd have them around outside the stockade near where the guard had died, to cast for a scent, and they might follow mine as far as my cave. I must recover my horn and be long gone before then.

One brook ran between Skoar and my cave, a quick trivial stream. It would not kill the scent—on the way down I had merely stepped across it. To confuse the dogs I must find something better beyond the cave, in the morning. But tonight the brook might help me part way. It flowed under the stockade near where I was now, and out again into the alligator's swamp. I might follow it a mile upstream to a willow I knew I could identify in the dark, so I'd be that much further along at first-light.

I inched out of the brush and across a grassy area. The fog enforced a dismal slowness: in ten minutes I walked a thousand years, and heard the wet monotone of water when I had given up hope of it. A big frog ploshed from blackness to blackness unseen.

Struggling upstream, I imagined every danger crowding me. No alligators in shallow upland water, but there could be moccasin snakes. I could lose footing and brain myself. If black wolf caught my smell he could take me before I freed my knife. A swarm of mosquitos did find me.

In time the owl stopped hooting, and the alligator back there in the swamp must have caught up with what he wanted, for I ceased to hear him. When at last I no longer saw any milkiness of moonlight in the fog above me I knew I was under forest cover, where moonlight was always a some-time thing. Fog was still dense; I smelled it and felt the dampness on my flesh. My fingers constantly out exploring touched willow-leaves after another long while. I groped up the twigs to small branches, to larger, finally encountering one whose shape I remembered. Then I could climb, knowing the tree for a friend. High up, I took off my loin-rag, passed it around the trunk and knotted it at my midriff, the hell with comfort. Brown tiger is too heavy to climb.

I have seen him few times in my life, but I can observe the image behind closed eyes at any time, the vast tawny body cloudily striped with darker gold, fifteen feet from nose to tail-tip, paws broad as a chair-seat and eyes that send back firelight not green but red.

A passage in the Book of John Barth mentions a certain wild-eyed crank who, when the last Old-Time war was in the last phases of threatening, visited the zoos in several cities and turned loose some of the beasts at night, choosing only the most dangerous: cobras, African buffalo, Manchurian tigers. He sometimes murdered the night watchman or other attendant to steal the keys, and was finally killed himself, Barth says, by a gorilla he was releasing. He must have felt he was paying back the human race for this and that. Probably no beast ever disliked us as hotly as disgruntled members of our own breed.

Men hate and loathe black wolf, who in spite of his fearsome strength and shrewdness has some taint of the sneak and coward. I never heard anyone mention hating or loathing brown tiger, though when I was with Rumley's Ramblers I heard of a secret cult that worships him. Pa Rumley introduced me to one of them in Conicut, a friendly quackpot who let me listen in on one of their minor celebrations. They dabble in alchemy but apparently not witchcraft, and cook up a type of love potion for their own orgies that's said to work, though I never saw it proved. Mighty is he— so began their invocation—who walks like the mist at night, mighty indeed is the golden and well-intentioned one, the merciful and all-forgiving Eye of Fire! It was damned impressive, hearing people pray to a creature that actually existed: I enjoyed it, and was willing to overlook a few turns of expression that I felt to be slightly on the inaccurate side.

In my willow tree the mosquitos chewed me all to hell—

Do you mind a little more brain-scratching? The thought of mosquitos just now woke up the memory of a golden hot day in the pine-woods park outside Old City, a few years ago, when Nickie and I had an argument. She said mosquitos are brave, or they wouldn't return under slaps for a mere gulp of gore. I said they're stupid, because when the slap is clearly on the way they linger for one more swallow, and then they're too flat to enjoy it. They linger so's to gamble for glory, s's she. Stupid, s's I, or they'd wear armor over the soft spots like beetles, but they don't wear anything, and to show her what I meant by a soft spot I chewed her here and there. Flinging me down and pounding my head on the pine needles, she asked me did I mean those mosquitos were atchilly lewd and nude? I rolled her over. Look at 'em, s's I. Then she felt I should take her clothes off for the mor'l purpose of showing 'em how dreadful it is to be nude as a bug, and I thought she'd better do the same for me because we didn't want her being dreadful all alone if the going got tough. She also undertook to slap the ones that bit me whenever I was preoccupied with helping her to be dreadful, and I undertook vice versa which is interesting in itself. We agreed further to keep count of slaps, thus determining who the bugs thought had the richest flavor. In order to get undressed we'd been absentmindedly chasing each other around trees and over rocks and rolling about considerably, which takes time, and so had forgotten what the original argument was, but we thought the flavor thing might be it or anyhow just as good. When we were lying face to face engaged in some operation or other, I remembered the first argument, and what happened then *proved* that mosquitos are stupid: they felt that the time was favorable for unpunished biting, and this in itself was lucid thinking, but they never saw we each had a hand free to slap with.

Nickie of course is impossible to beat in any learned discussion on a high plane. She said, the little twirp, that those mosquitos were dying out of heroic generosity and devotion, because they saw how much we enjoyed slapping each other, and so yielded up their lives in altruism. This kind of good will, s's she, is a sign of the vast courage that goes with towering intellect. Look at Charlemagne, s's she, or some of those other Old-Time ninety-day wonders like St. George and his everloving cherry tree, or poor Julius Caesar dividing his gall in three parts so as not to offend his friends, Romans, countrymen and other types of etcetera.

Before I fell asleep in that willow my mind was troubled in another way, as it might have been by a glimpse of fire seen as redness on distant cloud. War. It was the knowledge, intruding on me now that I could rest with a trace of safety, that the Katskil war had become a fact, a thing darkly and truly happening.

People said there would always be war; they didn't say why. Of course as a child I could see what a grand thing it would be to perish gloriously, and first to rush about cracking the heads and spilling the guts of wicked joes who happened to be the Enemy. The army as represented by the garrison soldiers of Skoar wasn't exactly glorious, which may have given me some early doubts. The men were let out on pass in small groups; even the orphanage priests with all the power and authority of the Church behind them used to wince and fret when a knot of soldiers went roaring by in the street, skunk-drunk, howling dirt talk, pissing where they pleased, spoiling for rape or a free fight. The policers tried to keep up with them, steering them as quickly as possible into the cheap bars and cat-houses and then herding them back to their barracks ... I had heard of navies too, but never had seen anything to reduce their glory. Outrigger fleets, I heard tell, carrying built-in crossbows, fire-throwers, and captains who had a habit of dying on deck with words of immortal bravery. The fleets had born the brunt of the effort in a war sixty years earlier when, as our Moha teacher-priests put it, Moha reluctantly allowed Levannon her independence. Reluctantly allowed, my celebrated hinder parts!—Moha got the holy godelpus beaten out of her, and hanging on to the Levannon country would have been like a farmer in the west forty trying to keep in touch with an eastbound bull.

It was over my head in those years; now I realize how hard and patiently the Holy Murcan Church worked as an umpire in wartime. Being committed to a policy of loving-kindness (within reason of course) the Church took no part in war except to provide chaplains for the armed forces and facilities for the military type of prayer—which puts a slight strain on monotheism at times. Behind the scenes, however, the top brass of Church and State would be watching for a suitable moment when both sides were wearied out enough to negotiate. When that time came the Church would supervise, examine any treaty proposed, and approve it so long as it wasn't too openly hoggish. For the nations after all are not merely great democracies but Murcan democracies—that is, united in the faith though not in politics. The Church is fond of calling herself Mother Church, enjoying the role of skirted arbiter in the smeary bloody squabbles of her children (whom she didn't beget, but never mind that) and I guess she can truly claim to be the savior and protectress of modern civilization, such as it is.*

Since those days I have learned so much—from good stern Mam Laura of Rumley's Ramblers who made me solid with reading and writing, from Nickie above all, and from the years when Nickie and I were Dion's aides in his effort as Regent of Nuin to bring some enlightenment into the mental murk of his times—so much more than I ever learned in childhood that it is difficult to sort out what I knew then from later knowledge. It was in my boyhood, at the tavern, that I heard an old man, a traveler, describe the sack of Nassa in Levannon, a city notoriously sinful and a hatcher of heresies, in a war Levannon fought against Bershar soon after winning her independence from Moha. The Bershar hill-men laid siege to the city for fifty days. According to the teller of the tale, this was a case where the Church took sides almost openly, encouraging devout communities in other lands to send Bershar material support. It caused some angry heretical mutterings here and there. When Nassa surrendered at last, the survivors were disarmed, turned loose and hunted down like woodchucks

---

* According to a famous paragraph in the Doctrine of Necessary Evils, war is a periodic outlet for man's "natural" violence, unavoidable till the second coming of Abraham; thus it is a duty of the Church to allow a "limited amount" of violence, under proper control. It is interesting to note that this idea of the inevitability of violence was old in Old Time—not to say moldy—and the proponents of it were as well able then as now to overlook the history of some nations that had passed through many generations without war, to say nothing of the multitude of private lives that reject violence in favor of reason and charity.

—Dion M.M.

95

or rats, and then the whole city was set to the torch—"for the glory of God," as the Bershar commander put it. His remark was unpopular, especially in the Low Countries, where aid to Bershar had upped the taxes. Church dignitaries were greatly shocked at this "misinterpretation" of the ecclesiastical position, and the Prince Cardinal of Lomeda was obliged to come out on the steps of the Cathedral and be shocked in public before a grumbling crowd would quit and disperse.

When the war itself ended, the treaty specified that Nassa must never be rebuilt, and Levannon had to agree; it never had been. Our traveler could not recall what year the war was, but he said the pines where Nassa used to stand had grown better than twenty feet tall. And he said that the city of New Nassa, a few miles from the simple war memorial among the pines, was a much stronger town in the military as well as the economic sense—better command of the eastern road . . . Joking of course, Old Jon asked him: "Was you, sir, one of them terr'ble Nassa heretics, sir?" The traveler looked at him too long and unwinking, like an ancient turtle, and then laughed barely enough for politeness, without answering.

A regiment was coming to defend Skoar, Emmia had said. They'd use the Northeast Road—no other available except the West, and that must be busy if there had already been fighting in the Seneca region. It shouldn't matter to me, I thought, since I meant to avoid roads anyway until I was a long way from Skoar. My uneasiness subsided for lack of fuel and I drifted into a sort of sleep.

I woke in slowly lightening darkness, pulled from a warm riot with a girl who was not Caron but only a trifle bigger and older. I can't bring back much of her now except a red flower in the back of her dark hair that tickled my nose. She was singing; I kept whispering to her she better not, we better not do anything until Father Milsom fell back out of sight on the other side of the stockade. I was awake, my thighs gripping nothing but a branch. I ached, and I'll never see her again. They don't come back. Dion remarks it's just as well they don't, for if we hoped to find our unfinished dreams we'd be forever sleeping, and who'd cook breakfast?

Skoar, in fact everything of my fourteen years—(even Caron, even Sister Carnation)—seemed to me in that time of waking to have become like a mixed sound of voices behind me, farther and farther behind me on a road where I could do nothing but go forward.

The fog became swirls of gray replacing the night; I saw the shape of willow branches near my eyes. I wriggled down the tree in the milk-soft confusion and pushed on up the mountain, hungry, not much rested but clear in the head. The policers wouldn't like the fog, so I tried to, though it slowed me down. I arrived at my cave in half an hour, famished. I could spare no time to hunt. The fog was thinning away under the pressure of an invisible sun.

I dug up my money first—fifteen dollars altogether, it ought to help as soon as I came to any place where money mattered. At a moment when sunlight broke through the fog and edged the leaves with wet trembling gold, I had in my palm the shiny dollar Emmia had given me: it seemed not so very bright. After dropping it among my other coins I could hardly tell it from the rest. Then I recovered my sack, with the golden horn—and my luck-charm of course. Could I have known all the time that it was there, but needed some compelling reason for running away?—from Emmia? Skoar? From my boyhood self because I must have done with it?

A slim-witted wild hen came searching her breakfast of bugs barely ten yards off. My arrow lifted her head from her neck—she'd never miss it. I couldn't stop to make a cooking fire, but drank the blood and dressed her off, and ate the heart, liver and gizzard raw, wrapping the rest in burdock leaves for lunchtime. I recall I gave the luck-charm no credit, although in many ways I was still quite religious.

The nearest stream began at a spring on the mountain's northeast slope beyond my cave, a small loud brook with alders and brambles along the banks. I knew it ran two miles or so through the woods and then across the North-east Road at a little ford. I could follow it almost to the road and then use the road as a guide, glimpsing it now and then to check my position as I traveled east—toward Levannon.

The brook covered the bottom of a scratchy tunnel, a narrow green hell. Thinking of policer dogs, I had to try it. I stuffed my moccasins in the sack again, to save them. My bare feet winced at the thought of snakes, and took a beating on the stones.

Of course when the dogs lost the scent the men would use some brains, following the brook with the dogs searching both banks. At a break where the brambles gave way to common weeds, I stepped out and walked away, to make it look as if I had given up and started back toward Skoar. I passed within grabbing reach of a big oak but went beyond it, to a thicket where I messed around a little and peed on the leaves to keep the dogs amused. Then I backtracked and swung into the oak with care to leave no damaged twigs. From the oak, by risking one leap far above ground, I passed to another tree, and then from branch to branch all the way back to the brook.

They'd at least lose time beating their gums over it, maybe decide I was a demon and sit down and wait for a priest to come help them louse it up. But I stayed with the stream another half-mile, and when I left it I did so by the way of the trees again, proceeding through the branches to another great oak. There I climbed high, to study the land.

Clouds swarmed eastward playing dark games before the sun. Edgy weather, a petulant wind stirring the oak leaves with sultry insistence. A spring storm might be advancing.

The road was nearer than I thought. I saw a red gash less than half a mile to the east. It could only be red clay, where the road approached and crossed a rise of ground. Though the road was empty I heard an obscure and troubling sound that was no part of the forest noises. Turning my head to puzzle at it, I found I was staring down on what must be another section of the same road, startlingly near my oak, hardly fifty feet away, a spot where branches thinned out to reveal the red clay and some gravel. Confirming it, the unstable breeze brought me a whiff of horse-dung. Not fresh—this near part of the road was empty like the other, but I didn't like it, and clambered to a lower spot where I was better hidden. Whatever

98

the sound might mean it was fairly distant, a dry mutter not resembling either voices or a waterfall.

I cut off an end of my gray loin-rag and tied it around my head. I don't mind being red-haired, but it doesn't help you look like a piece of bark. While I was busied with that, a dot of life appeared on the distant road between me and the uneasy sky.

Even far off, a human being seldom looks like any other animal. In Penn, with the Ramblers, I've seen the flap-eared apes they call chimps, the chimpanzees of Old Time. I could always tell one of those from a man if I wasn't drunk or spiteful. The man I saw on the red clay road was too distant for me to be sure of anything but his humanity—that rather arrogant, rather fine human stance by which even a fool can defy the lightning with a hint of magnificence—and his alertness, his observant stillness under the intermittent sun.

10

That dot of man printed against the sky was studying the road. The noise ceased while he paused, then a tiny arm swung up and forward, and the uncertain sound resumed. Men must have used that signal from ancient days, when there's been good reason not to shout aloud: "Come ahead!"

He was followed at first by a few like himself in brown loin-rags and red-brown shirts, walking with the long stride of men used to extended journeys with light burdens. Advance scouts. The sound strengthened as the first horsemen appeared over the rise.

Feet of a mass of men and horses—having once heard the surge of it as I did that morning you'd never mistake it for anything else, whether the men are marching in rhythm or coming broken-step like the soldiers who followed that mounted detachment. This was no parade. They were coming to defend the city. I saw presently a group of men without spears surrounding a handsome motion of white, blue and gold—our Moha flag.

The advance scouts would not take much time to reach that near section of the road. I drew back all the way behind the tree-trunk, waiting. They were good—to tell of their passage I heard only a faint crunch of gravel. Then came the plop and shuffle of hoofs. I dared peek around the trunk as the cavalry went by; they'd leave it to the scouts and never think of looking upward. Thirty-six riders—a full-strength unit, I happened to know.

The horses were the breed of western Moha, mostly black or roan, with a few palominos like sunlight become flesh, all bred for grace and glory, maybe the best-looking children of my native land. Bershar is famous for horses too, by the way—mountain type, homely but steady in a crisis as these slimlegged beauties were not.

The horsemen were sleek young aristocrats. Owning their horses and gear, they'd feel they were doing the army a favor. They made a grand military picture. They wouldn't dream of riding any horses except the beautiful breed of western Moha—hell, I'd as soon send a green girl into battle. You can't trust them to stand, and if the rider loses control for an instant they go wild as the wind.

For most of the cavalry—the boys were that young—this would be the first war. Not so for the infantry—old faces there, furrowed by sword-work; hard-case types used to stinking rations and the rule of the bull-whip. Some were clods, others looked repulsively crafty—ex-slaves some of them, and some were petty criminals given a choice between slavery and infantry service. Any discipline they possessed had been banged into them from outside; they were men for the ugly labors, the uncelebrated dying. Except for the murders and rapes of their profession they had no pleasures but gambling, drink, cheap marawan, stealing, and whatever enjoyment can be wrung out of a fifty-cent prostitute or a complaisant drummer-boy. In their inarticulate heavy way I suppose they welcomed war and thus were good patriots. I'd say that building the infantry out of such trash was another Moha mistake—one that Katskil didn't make. An army of men able to think like human beings may be hard to handle, but it does win wars, so far as any army ever does.

A second mounted detachment appeared on the higher ground. That meant a second battalion—three companies, each of a hundred and fifty foot, plus the mounted unit of thirty-six. A Moha regiment consists of four such battalions. As it turned out, only two battalions were on the road—Emmia had heard it wrong, or some upholstered brass in Moha City decided that since Skoar was only a half-ass city with a twelve-foot stockade, why bother with more than half a regiment?

I watched the foot-sloggers down there. Some were marching with drooping heads—tired, hot, bored. Gnarled masks, two out of three pockmarked. From time to time I saw a dull mouth-gash turn sideways to shoot the juice of a ten-cent chaw. A twist of the wind brought me their reek, more disturbing than the sight of them. An army, however. On them, people said, depended our safety from the Katskil Terror. And, yes, there was a Katskil Terror. So far as any nation can be imagined to possess a personality, that presented by Katskil was iron-gutted, ambitious, stern. A political image of course, which means, largely a fantasy: the Katskil people themselves were and are of every sort, cruel, gentle, wise, silly, mixed-up average like the people of any nation.

I suspect the mere fact that their territory encloses Nuber the Holy City on three sides has inclined the nation (as a political fantasy imitating reality) toward a certain pious arrogance which the Church may privately deplore but will not openly condemn. Church decisions have been consistently pro-Katskil (within respectable limits) for so long now that no one expects anything else.

They streamed by below my oak tree, the sodden, witless, beaten faces. On the hill, a trumpet screamed.

Flights of arrows from both sides of the road had cut into our troops like a pair of scissors. Riders were toppling off their mounts, the horses going mad at once and plunging everywhere. No sound reached me yet but the trumpet cry.

101

The Katskil battalion in ambush had let half our line go by, then stabbed at the center. Moha's flank scouts must have merely skirted the edge of the woods; perhaps some idiot thought the forest too dense for an army to hide in it. Now that the trap was sprung, the Moha men doubling back to help—if they did—would have the hill to climb, and maybe the rush of a storm in their faces, for that fitful growing wind was a northeaster.

The trumpet blast echoed inside me—three short notes and a long. I knew it must be a recall of the first battalion that was passing below my tree. It halted them. I saw grotesque faces empty with shock. Someone started a yelping: "Skoar! To Skoar!" Noise swelled hideously on the name, and a furious young voice cut through it: "Get back up there! Move, you God damn pus-gutted slobs! You heard it. Move, move, you whoreson sumbitches, *move!*"

Up here—well, what was in it for them? Why, up there under blackening sky, men in dark green were pouring out of the woods and killing men in brown. I heard for the first time the shattering Katskil yell. And I saw our second battalion still marching over the rise—still in formation, poor yucks, stepping off a cliff in a dignified manner.

Yet there weren't so many of the dark green uniforms. No more had followed the first flood; plenty were already fallen—for make them angry or scared or merely startled like a herd of spooked cattle, and that Moha rabble could fight. Except at the initial surprise blow there can't have been much arrow work. Jammed there in the narrow gut of the road, both sides were forced to infighting, always a deadly business. I don't know how many brown shapes lay mingled with the green-shirted Katskil dead. The brown and red-brown melted at that distance into gory mud.

The flag of Moha reappeared, hurrying up the rise. At least the soldiers of the color guard weren't all of a whimper for the comfort of the city's stockade. To this day I wonder why a b.s. yard-boy on the run, with scant reason to love his native land, should have gulped tears of pride and awe at seeing how the Moha color guard knew where to go. A glory of white and blue and gold, it climbed the rise, that rag with no meaning except the fantasies men had woven into the fabric. A wave of green surged to meet it, a wave of men who just as dearly loved a rag of black and scarlet.

I saw that flag too, wrathful in the wind. Moha cavalry charged it; their horses fell pierced or hamstrung. Black and scarlet are colors of night and fire. That flag was glorious as ours, if there is such a thing as glory.

But down in my neighborhood was disgrace, nastiness of panic. I saw one flash of contrary action—one horseman galloped by toward the battle and in passing whipped the flat of his sword against a mouth that was howling: "To Skoar!" Only three riders followed him. Maybe the rest were out of my sight trying to stem the disorder of the infantry, the men who had come to defend the city and were now running for shelter inside it—a slow run, like the motion of men caught in momentum who must keep their legs moving or fall on their faces.

I took out my golden horn. Forty feet above them I blew the call that trumpet had sounded, three times.

I looked down. No one had located me. The sound would have seemed to be coming from all around them. They were not running now. I blew the call a fourth time, more quietly, as though the men of their own kind up the road had said in reasonable voices: "We are in trouble."

In the silence some cavalry boy dropped the words: "Kay, let's go take them!" They ran—the other way.

Moha won a dazzling victory that day, if there is such a thing as victory. I'm sure history calls it a victory, for the priests who turn out the little simple books for the schools must have recorded the piffling Moha-Katskil war of 317 —it didn't even last into the following year. Old woman history chewing her mishmash of truth and maybe-so beside the uncertain fire of today.

When I looked again at the distant rise I saw the color guard still cruelly pressed, no more than a dozen Moha men left around the standard-bearer. As the ring of defenders was cut even smaller it held shape in stubborn courage, a shine of steel within a dark green band. At the crest of the rise the demoralized cavalry was winning back some order. They might have been dangerous in a charge. Charging at what?—not at the nimble devils who slid in and out among them like green smoke. Here and

103

there riderless horses broke for the woods leaving man to his own sickening inventions.

But now came the cavalry of the first battalion returning up the hill roaring calamity, crashing first against the green band around the color guard and smashing it like a splintered wheel. The flag danced and moved up the rise. Then Moha's foot-soldiers—recovered, eager, their panic overcome by a simpler lust. My mind could hear their steel cuting through air and crushing flesh—for a minute or two I think I was shivering myself with my own insanity of pride. This was the accomplishment of my golden horn.

I watched a man in dark green flee for the forest cover with three Moha soldiers after him. One pursuer had lost his loin-rag and most of his shirt; distance made the naked man an insect—weedy, prancing high-kneed. A javelin caught the fugitive in the back. The naked jo and his companions slowly shoved steel into him as he lay motionless.

Since that day I have fought without disgracing myself in two wars, against the pirates in 327 and in the rebellion of this year, when we fought to defend Dion's reforms and were compelled to learn that the people will not and cannot benefit from any reforms unless they come gradually; I have never again taken my golden horn near the scene of war . . .

All Katskil men were now in retreat, and the flag of Moha already throbbed in beauty at the top of the rise. I saw no banner of black and scarlet; it must have gone with the retreat back into the woods. I saw no more sunlight. The fresh cavalry unit joined the broken one and their captains conferred under a gray sky. Only foot-soldiers were chasing the Katskil men into the woods. One cavalry captain was jerking his arms as if talking in wrath, or self-justification maybe. The other must have managed to strike flint and get a light to his pipe in spite of the dancing uneasiness of his horse, for I saw a tiny spook of gray float above his head.

A trumpet presently recalled the infantry—they could hardly have done much in the woods, where the Katskil men might regroup and make them sorry for it—and the Moha battalions were again in motion. Hardly more than twenty minutes could have passed since I saw that first scout. A skirmish, engaging less than a thousand Moha men, on the Katskil side perhaps four hundred.

The cause of the war was a dreary boundary dispute that had been kept alive one way or another for fifty years. So far as I can see, nations exist because of boundaries and not the other way around; the boundaries are drawn by people more or less like you and me and your Aunt Cassandra, and we like to think that as human beings we know enough not to sit down in wet paint bare-ass, or lift a porcupine by the tail, or hack the baby's head off to cure a teething pain. It's a curious thing; I can probably give you a perfect solution to any contradictions involved, next Wednesday, if I don't oversleep.

Words floated up to me from the road: "Did y' see the Katty I got, tall sumbitch with a beard? My God 'n' Abraham, don't look like they teach 'em to cover the gut aytall." Another voice was crying and petulant—the wounded were being carried by. A man wanted to see his daughter. They could bring her, he said—it was safe here, no stinking soldiers around—she was nine, she'd be wearing a brown smock her Ma made her—that voice faded out and another said: "My head hurts." Over and over, that also growing fainter, obscured by a shuffle of footsteps, clash of gear, other voices: "My head hurts—my head hurts . . ." They were gone, leaving the morning peaceful if there is such a thing as peace.

I had heard no noise of dogs behind me; now I was released from that and other fears. Skoar would be soon celebrating the entry of a glorious army, and never mind fugitive yard-boys. There'd be crowds, bonfires with kids dancing naked and shrieking, churches adrone with hymns of thanksgiving, taverns and whorehouses squaring off for a long night's work, policers busy with brawls and drunks and the quackpots who bounce out of their holes at the first whiff of excitement, and public speakers being trotted out of their stables—you know, with a rope at each side of the bit and a third handler in case the speaker should fumble at the happy task of ramming the splendid ma-hooha into the quivering public mind.

I studied the countryside, wishing the rain would arrive and lighten the air. Black dots were growing large like separated shreds of cloud. The crows were already on the scene; they would have been cynically watching from nearby. Other creatures would join them before long, the rats and wild yellow dogs and carrion ants.

A soldier who should have been dead reached upward and let his arm fall over his eyes. The motion, small to me as the stir of a fly's leg, caused a crow to flap away. I saw a snap of brilliance as light touched something on the moving hand, a ring or bracelet. He was like a sleeper who covers his eyes to preserve a dream. I thought: Man, turn over, why don't you? Turn *away* from the light if it hurts your eyes!

In the talk of the Moha men who passed below me I had heard no one speak of the horn call. Maybe each man supposed the music was for him alone.

It seemed to me I must go to that man whose arm had moved, or I would dream of him. I climbed down from my oak and walked boldly to the road. No danger. A red squirrel was already on a branch beside the road, watching me without scolding. I stepped out from the bushes and turned left, toward the battlefield, and reached it in a few minutes after only a few turnings of the road. The crow sentinels squawked word of me. I saw the lurching run and climb of one of the larger birds, red-necked and hideous, who circled so closely above me that I caught his stench and was almost fouled by a spatter of his muck.

The first man I passed wore dark green. He lay in the roadside ditch, face upturned and no-way angry. His bow was shorter and heavier than mine; it would be hard to bend but easy to carry in thick woods. I might have taken it but for a superstitious feeling that to do so would put me on a level with the vultures. I felt absurdly that all the dead were delaying me, as if they could wish to speak. A wart-nosed Moha veteran, for one, his gashed neck so twisted that although he lay belly-down his spiritless eyes appeared to watch me—why, alive he'd have had nothing to say to me, more than a snarl to get off the sidewalk if he noticed my gray loin-rag.

The man whose arm had moved lay as before, but he was dead. Maybe he had been all the time, the motion only one of those aimless things that occur after death. That sparkle on his hand was a ring, ruby-colored glass. Knowing him dead, I was free to be afraid again. The Katskil soldiers might not have fled far; slave gangs would come from Skoar to carry in the Moha dead. I crossed the rise and started down the other side intending to get back under the forest cover.

There had been some fighting on this side of the ridge; not much. I was halted by the sight of a small sandy-colored beast crouched at the edge of the road. A scavenger dog, large for his breed. They are said to be clever enough to follow an army on the march, as sometimes they follow brown tiger, and for the same reason. The dog, unaware of me, was watching something beyond a patch of bushes at my right. I had come quietly; his nose would have been already charged with the smell of human beings and their blood.

A little stream flowed from the woods into the ditch along the road. Toward this, from the thick bushes, a Katskil soldier was crawling, his bronze helmet slung over his arm. A thin gray-eyed boy, maybe seventeen. He was attempting to pull himself along by his arms, one leg helping. The other leg was gashed from hip to knee, and an arrow-shaft protruded from his left side.

The dog was a poor slinking thing, but it could kill a helpless man. The boy saw the brute suddenly and his face remained blank, curiously patient, shining with sweat. I set an arrow and as the dog whirled at the slight noise to face me I sunk it in his yellow chest. He leaped and tried to bite his flank and died.

The boy watched me, puzzled, when I said: "I'll get you the water." He let me take his helmet. It was hard for him to drink, his shaky hands no help. He rolled his head away and said: "I a'n't nothing to ransom—the old man ha'n't got a pot, never had." The effort of speech brought a stain of blood to his mouth.

"Will I lift you?"

He looked at the water, wanting it, and nodded. I felt the splash of the first rain-drops on my head. At the touch of my arm at his shoulder I saw it was too much for him. I spooned water in my hand, and he got down a little but

107

lost it in a sharp cough. The arrow may have pierced his stomach. He said: "Shouldn't've tried it."

I took the rag from my head and tried to close up the long wound in his thigh. The rag was not long nor wide enough; trying to fasten it was a nightmare frustration. A bang and roll of near thunder almost covered what the soldier was saying: "Let it be. Be you Moha, that red thatch?"

They have an odd speech in Katskil. I had heard it at the inn, though not much in the last two years when the war jitters were building up. They drawl in a pinch-nose way, leave out half their *r*s and any syllable that doesn't happen to suit them.

I told him: "I got no country."

"Ayah? You be'n't with us, I know ever' damn fool bum in the b'talion including myself."

"I'm alone. Running away."

"I get it." The rain came then in a sudden and ponderous rush, soaking us, hammering my back. I leaned over him; at least my shirt could keep the downpour from battering his face. "Ran away once myself—tried to, I mean." He seemed to want to talk. "Pa caught me filling a sack, believe me I got no forrader. He wa'n't for me going into the A'my neither, said it was all no consequence. You killed that yalla dog real neat."

"Damn scavenger."

"Jackalaws we call 'em down home. Handle a bow real good."

"I been in the woods a lot."

"Tell by the way you walk." His voice was reaching me with difficulty through the roar of water around us. "Running away. That 'ere gray—your ballock-rag—that mean bond-servant? Does in my country."

"Uhha."

"Look, boy, don't let it bug you. I want to tell you, don't let 'em tromp you or tell you where to go. They spit in your eye you spit back, see? . . . Nice country hereabouts, might be good corn land. Our outfit laid up all the night in the woods—under stren'th, the damn fool brass, the way they do things, one comp'ny split off yesterday for another job—hell with it. Wanted to say, I was noticing

108

what a pile of oaks you got around here. Means good corn land, ever' time. Last night was a real foggy sumbitch, wa'n't it?"

"I slept in a tree."

"Do tell. Raining now, a'n't it?" Both of us were drenched, the water bouncing a stream from a crease in his shirt where I couldn't shelter him, and pelting on his legs. But he was really asking, not sure of the world, his eyes losing me, finding me again.

"It's raining some," I said. "Listen, I'm going to get you deeper in the woods where won't nobody search, understand? Stay by while you heal up. Then you can come along."

"Sure enough?" I think he was seeing it, as I was trying to—the journeying, friendship, new places. We'd go together; we'd have women, amusement, something always happening. Above all, the journeying.

I said: "We'd get along all right."

"Sure. Sure we will."

I never learned his name. His face smoothed out completely and I had to let him lie back on the earth.

11

I remember the rain. Not long after my friend was dead, it slackened to a dull beating on the earth. I could not hope to scratch a grave in the tree roots and wet clay. In any case I have never liked the thought of burying the dead, unless it might be done as they do in Penn, marking the place with nothing but a grapevine; and taking the wine-harvest in later years with no sense of trespass or disrespect. If that can't be, maybe burning is best. Does it matter?—all the world's a graveyard, a procreants' bed, and a cradle.

I slipped away from the road into the bushes, sure now that there'd be no pursuit by men and dogs. In the dripping woods, however, I still moved softly. I was guessing my northeast direction accurately, for I had been on my way more than an hour when, off to my right where it ought to be, I heard a racket of hoofs galloping on wet road-mud, swelling loud, dying away into little taps like the noise a child can make by flipping a stick along a picket fence. A dispatch rider, probably, bound for Skoar. After that I heard only the diminishing sober discourse of the rain.

I grew hungry, but wanted a fire for my hen—raw chicken is discouraging. The morning was spent by the time I located a good spot. An oak had blown over against a slope years before, its root cluster jutting out aslant and catching a gradual drift of leaves, thus creating a roof of sorts. From the pocket of earth where roots had once grown, rains had dug out a drainage gully. I grubbed under the surface of the forest floor and found tindery stuff to start a blaze in the shelter of that overhang. Soon the fire was comforting me while my hen browned on a green ash spit. I hung my shirt and loin-rag on an oak-root near the warmth, and squatted naked letting the harmless rain sluice off my back. For a while, except to keep track of my cooking hen, I can't have been thinking at all. Rain lulls you out of alertness like someone talking on and on, explaining too much.

The men came quietly. I was aware of them only an instant before the thin one said: "Don't pull that knife, Jackson. We don't mean you no ha'm." His voice was firm but weary, like his long face under a bloody dark green rag.

"Don't be scared," said the other man, a moon-faced giant. "Matter-fact I been called by the blessed Abraham not to do no hurt to no man, also—"

The thin man said: "Hold up the mill, will you, whiles I talk to the boy? Jackson, the dang thing of it is, we'd like a snip of that 'ere, bein' stinkin' hungry is all."

He was about fifty, gray and quiet. The rag on his head gave the hollows under his smoky blue eyes a greenish tinge. Long grooves bracketed his mouth and nose. His

110

dark green shirt lacked a section where his head bandage must have been torn out; a hunting knife at his belt very much like mine appeared to be his only weapon. His belt was broad like a sash, with fold-over parts that would be useful for carrying small things. His lean legs sticking out of a shabby green loin-rag were dark and bunchy as bundles of harness leather.

The other man also wore the wreck of a Katskil army uniform; some kind of belt and rope-soled sandals. He carried a sword in a sheath of brass, a worthless thing in the woods. Both had at their belts long and rather flat canteens made of bronze that would have held about a quart.

Stupid as you can get, I said: "Where you from?"

The thin man gave me a good smile, dry and friendly. "Points south, Jackson. Will you share the meat with a man that fit your country yesterday and got a hole in his head, and a big old jo that looks fit to scare the children but don't want to fight no more?"

"Kay," I said. They weren't crowding me; I almost wanted to share it. "Yesterday? Be'n't you from that fight down the road by Skoar?"

"Nay. When was it?"

"Couple-three hours gone. I was up a tree."

"Couldn't think of a finer place with a fuckin' war goin' on."

"You Katskils done an ambush and got beat off."

He slapped his leg, mixed satisfaction and disgust. "God damn, I prophesied it. Could've told the brass, that's what you get for splitting the b'talion. Comes to me though, the meat-heads never asked me." He squatted on his heels beside me, giving my hen the gloomiest gaze any chicken ever got and no fault of its own. The moon-face jo stood apart, watching me. "I feel bad about this, Jackson, If'n it was just me and my large friend standin' over theah in the rain so bungfull of the milk of human kindness a man can't see where he'd squeeze in no more nourishment no-way—"

"Now, Sam," said the big man. "Now, Sam—"

But Sam liked to talk, and went on regardless, in his slow-drawly Katskil voice, amusement and sadness exchanging places the way clouds play games with the sun: "If it was only him and me and you, Jackson, we might make out, but the dad-gandered almighty thing of it is, we got one other mouth to consider which's got itself a bumped knee but still suffers if it don't eat good. You think that 'ere little-ass bird could do a fourway split?"

"Well, sure," I said—"two leg-hunks and two half-bosoms and ever'body arise from the God-damn table a mite hungry is good for you as the fella says—where's the fourth?"

"Off into the brush a piece."

"See like I told you, Sam? Boy's got an open nature full of divine grace and things. What's y' name, Red?"

"Davy."

"Davy what?"

"Just Davy. Orphanage. Bonded out at nine."

"Now we got no wish to betrouble you, but maybe you a'n't bound back wheah you come from?"

Sam said :"That's his business, Jackson."

"I know," said the moon-faced man. "I a'n't pushin' the boy for no answer, but it's a fair question."

"I don't mind," I said. "I'm on the run, ayah."

"Nor I don't blame you," says Moon-face. "Noticed that 'ere gray ballock-rag hangin' there right away, and what I've hearn about the way they'll always do the dirty on a b.s. in Moha, it's a national disgrace. You keep y' chin up, boy, and trust in God. That's the way to live, understand? Just keep y' chin up and y' bowels open, and trust in God."

"You let him snow you, Jackson, you'll start thinkin' they don't treat bond-servants like shit in Katskil too."

"Sam, Sam Loomis, some-way I got to break you of that 'ere cussin' and blasphemin'. A'n't no fitten type talk for a young boy to hear." Sam just looked at me; I felt he was laughing up a storm inside of him and nobody'd ever know it except himself and me. The big jo went on kindly: "Now, boy Davy, you mustn't think I'm claimin' I a'n't no sinner no more, that'd be an awful vanity, though I do claim a lot of stuff's been purified out'n me like a refiner's fire and things, but anyway—my name's Jedro Sever, call me Jed if you want, we're all democraticals here I hope,

112

and sinner though I be I fear God and go by his holy laws, and right now I says unto you lo, I says, bond-servant or no, you be just as much a man and citizen in the sight of God as I be, y' hear?"

More casual, Sam asked: "Things got tough?"

"You could say so." Then somehow I was blurting it right out: "An awful accident happened. I killed a man accidental, but nobody'd ever believe it was so, anyhow not the policers." I suppose I might have held it in if I hadn't taken them for deserters, on the run as I was and not concerned about Moha laws.

Jedro Sever said: "A'n't no such of a thing as an accident in the sight of God, Davy. You mean, it happened without *you* intending it. God's got his great and glorious reasons that a'n't for such as us to look into. If'n you be truthful about it not being intended, why, no sin theah."

Sam was looking into me with a cool thoughtfulness I'd never seen in anyone, man or women. I don't know how long it was before he let me off that hook—my hen was well browned, smelling just right, and the rain had slackened to a mere drizzle. "I'm taking your word," Sam said at last. "Don't never make me sorry I done it."

"I will not," I said. And I don't think I ever did. The confidence between Sam and me was a part of my life that was never spoiled. In the times that followed I often lost patience with him, and he with me, but—suppose I say it this way: we never gave up on each other. "Ayah," I said, "I run off, and I'd be a sure thing for hanging was I caught and took back to Skoar. Kindly avoid hanging whenever I can see my way to it, that's how I am."

"Whenever," said Jed, unhappy. "Look, boy, if you was ever once—"

"Joke, Jackson. Boy's joking."

"Oh, I get it." Jed laughed uncomfortably, the way you might if you accidentally interrupted someone taking a leak. "You know the country round heah, boy Davy?"

"Never come thisaway this far before. We're near the Northeast Road. Skoar's off west, five-six miles."

Sam said: "I was through these pa'ts yeahs ago, in peacetime—Humber Town, Skoar, Seneca, Chengo."

"Katskil border's a few miles south," I said.

"Ayah," said Jed, "but we be'n't bound thataway. Understand, in the sight of God we be'n't deserters. Me, I labor in the vineyard like on a mission, and old Sam Loomis theah, why, he a'n't no sinful man ay-tall, spite of his bad talk. One day God's grace is going to bust onto him like a refiner's fire and things. I mean he merely lost his outfit in a scrimmage like anyone might. Same outfit I was with—I left sooner, bein' called by the good Lord."

"Ayah," Sam said. "I lost track of my comp'ny in the woods after a little trouble yesterday, up the road ten mile. What the A'my does with deserters, Jackson—I mean with people it thinks is deserters—well, what they do, they string 'em to a tree for bow and arrow practise, and then so't of leave 'em. Saves a burial detail. Got my head busted and was knocked out a while, comp'ny gone when I come to, I don't blame 'em for thinking I was a deader, but I don't believe I got the patience to explain it all, was I to see 'em again. One comp'ny was detached from the b'talion, idea was to make a little show up the road, delay you Mohas and make you think it was all we had in the area. Then the main b'talion hiding down this-away could clobber you. Cute idea."

"The Mohas a'n't no army of mine. Got no country."

"Know what you mean," said Sam, watching me. "I'm a loner by trade . . . Well, them no'th Moha apple-knockers, excuse the expression, came along nine hours late, after whoring it up around Humber Town likely, so after they brushed us off they squatted down to camp for the night. I should know, having damn nigh walked into 'em in the dark. Must've been rested and happy by the time the b'talion jumped 'em this mo'ning. We didn't do too good?"

"Not too. Mohas was too many. Two to one or more."

"Boy's a gentleman," said Sam, and rested his wounded head on his knees. "Ayah, the brass gets fanciful and the men get dead." I'd spotted Sam Loomis for a woodsman; he had my habit of quick side-glances. He wouldn't be caught unready by the unexpected stir of a branch or slither of questing life along the ground. Jed might be; his eyes did not look alert. Baldness had thinned even Jed's eyebrows to pale wisps; it gave him the look of a great startled baby. "Jackson, that little-ass bird's near done."

114

As I took it away from the flame he added: "Maybe better slip on y' ballock-rag, account that other'n off in the brush —I just damn-all f'got to mention it—well, see, she happens to be a female woman." Then glancing up at Jed Sever's disapproving mass, he said: "Moves around real peart for a young boy, don't he?"

When I had my rags on Jed called off thinly into the wet woods: "Oh, Vilet!"

"Don't fret," Sam said to me under his breath—"I wouldn't done it to you only she's broad in the mind as well as in the beam."

Limping out of a nearby thicket, the woman said: "I hearn that, Sam." She gave him the small half of a grin, and the rest of us a challenging stare from under thick brows black as ink. Her dark green linsey smock left her knees bare, and the left one was bruised but not badly. She was anywhere in the thirties, a short slab-sided big-muscled wench with no waist to speak of, but someway you didn't miss it. Even with the slight limp she had a solid animal grace and sureness. She didn't like being wet as a mushrat. "I did oughta ream y' out, Sam, talking thataway about a tender blossom like me, hunnert and thirty pounds and all of it wildcat."

"A'n't she the sha'p little thing?" said Jed, and I saw he'd gone all mush-mind and lover-dreamy.

"Ayah," she sighed—"sha'p as an old shovel beat out onto the rocks ten-twenty yeahs." She slipped off a shoulder-sack something like mine, and tried to wring some of the water from her smock and pull it clear of her crotch and meaty thighs. "You men be lucky, them Goddamn loose shirts and stuff."

"Vilet!" No longer dreamy, Jed spoke like a stern grandfather. "None of that cussing! We been into that."

"Aw, Jed!" Her look at him was cocky, affectionate, submissive too. "You'd cuss, I bet, if'n you couldn't tell y' clo'es from y' hide."

"No I wouldn't." He stared her down, solemn as a church. "And 'hide'—that a'n't a nice word neither."

"Aw, Jed!" She squeezed water from her black hair. It was short, and shaggy as if she'd hacked it off with a knife, the way soldiers do if there's no barber in the outfit. She

115

dropped into a squat beside me and gave my leg a ringing slap with a square brown paw. "Your name's Davy, ha? Hiya, Davy, and how they hangin', lover-pup?"

"Vilet dear," says Jed, mighty patient, "we been into all that. No more cussing, no more lewd talk."

"Aw, Jed, I'm sorry, anyhow I didn't mean it like lewd, just friendly." Her eyes, dark greenish gray with a hint of golden flecks, were uncommonly lovely, set in the frame of her beefy homeliness, violets in rough ground. "I mean, Jed, things keep slippin' my mind and poppin' out." She pulled her wet smock out from her big breasts and winked at me, head turned so that Jed wouldn't see it, but she meant her words too; she wasn't fighting him. "You gotta be patient, Jed, you gotta leave me come unto Abraham kind of a gradual sort of a way, like I gotta creep before I walk, see?"

"I know, Vilet. I know, dear."

I cut the hen as fairly as I could and passed it around, and was about to start gnawing when Jed dipped his head and mumbled through a grace, mercifully short. Sam and I began eating right afterward, but Jed said: "Vilet, I was listenin' whiles I prayed, nor I didn't hear you none."

It's a fact: among the true religioners, if a priest is present, people keep quiet while he says the grace right, but if there's no priest everyone is expected to say it at the same time, leaving it up to God to analyze the uproar and sort out the faithful from the hippy critics. Of course, Jed hadn't heard Sam or me either, but our souls evidently weren't his concern, or else he felt they were too much of a job for him. Vilet's soul was different. She said: "Aw, Jed, I was just—I mean, I thank thee, O Lord, for this my daily bread and—"

"No, dear. Bread means real bread, so then if it's chicken it's best you say chicken, understand?"

"For this my—Jed, chicken don't *come* daily."

"Oh—well, kay, you can leave out the daily."

"For this my chicken and command—"

"Commend."

"Commend myself to thy service in Abraham's beloved name—kay?"

"Kay," said Jed.

After the meal Vilet limped off to hunt up more fire-wood. I wished that while she was busy I could ask who she was and how she came to be with us, but Jed had been observing the luck-charm at my neck, and asked me about it.

I said: "It's just a puny old luck-charm."

"Nay, boy Davy, it's a truth-maker. I seen one just like it at Kingstone, belonged to an old wise-woman. This is the spitn-image of it, bound to have the same power. Nobody can look on it and tell a lie—fact. Le' me hold it a minute and show you. Now, look this little man or this little woman right in the face and see if you be able to lie."

Deadpanning, I said: "The moon shines black."

"How about that?" said Vilet, dumping an armload of dead sticks. "How about that, Jed o' boy o' boy?"

"Why, I got him." Jed laughed, pleased. "Other side of the moon's got to be black, or we'd see the shine of it reflected onto the curtain of night, big white patch moving the way the moon does, stands to reason. But all's we see is the holes prepared in the curtain to let through the light of heaven, and a few of them dots that move different, so they must be little chips, sparklers like, that God took off of the moon to brighten things up. See?"

Drowsily admiring, Sam murmured: "Bugger me blind!"

"Sam, I got to ask you not to use them foul expressions in the presence of a pure-minded boy and a misfortunate woman-soul that's trying to find her way into the kingdom of ev'lasting righteousness, more b' token I won't put up with no more sack-religion, I purely won't."

Sam told him he was sorry, in a way that suggested he was used to saying it, and more or less meaning it every time. Good people like Jed would find things dull, I guess, if they couldn't arrange to get hurt fairly often. As for the luck-charm—well, Jed was much older than me, forty-plus, and a hell of a lot bigger as well as full of divine grace. I did think if I took another try at making extra work for the shovels I wouldn't be stopped by any dab of clay. But Jed was so proud and happy to have taught me something useful and surprising, I hadn't the heart to spoil it. Maybe I couldn't have anyway. Whatever mahooha I offered, he could have produced some gentle explanation

117

to prove I hadn't told a lie—working it along easy and patient, pushing and crowding Lady Truth around and around the bush till sooner or later the mis'ble old wench had to come crawling out where he wanted her, whimpering and yattering, legs asprawl and vine-leaves a-twitching in her poor scragged-up hair. "Well," I said, "I never did know it had no such power. It was give' me when I was born, and people have talked me considerable guck since them days, nothing no-way stopping 'em."

"You just never caught on to the way of usin' it," he said. He still held the image facing me, and asked me as if casually: "It was a true-for-sure accident, that thing you told about?"

Sam Loomis stood up tall and said: "Hellfire and damnation! We take his word and then go doubting it?"

Behind me I could hear Vilet quit breathing. Jed might be forty pounds heavier, but Sam wasn't anyone you'd try to take, head-wound or no. Jed said at last, mighty soft: "I meant no ha'm, Sam. If my words done ha'm, I'm sorry."

"Don't ask my pa'don. Ask his'n."

"It's all right," I said. "No harm done."

"I do ask y' pa'don, boy Davy." Nobody could have asked it more nicely, either.

"It's all right," I said. "It don't matter."

As Jed smiled and gave me back the clay image, I noticed his hand was unsteady, and I felt, in one of those indescribable flashes which resemble knowledge, that he was not afraid of Sam at all, but of himself. He asked, maybe just for the sake of speaking: "Was you bound anywheah special when we come onto you, boy Davy?"

"Levannon's where I want to go."

"Why—them's no better'n heretics over yonder."

Sam asked: "You ever bejasus been theah?"

"Sure I have and wouldn't go again at all."

"Got to cross Levannon if you and Vilet be goin' to Vairmant like you say."

"Ayah," Jed sighed, "but just to cross it."

They were still edgy. I said: "I dunno—all's I ever hearn of Levannon was hear-tell."

"Some pa'ts may be respectable," Jed allowed. "But

118

them quackpots! Snatch y' sleeve, bend y' ear. You hear the Church figgers if the quackpot religioners all drift into Levannon that makes it nicer for the rest of us, but I dunno, it don't seem right. Grammites, Franklinites, that's what religious liberty has brung 'em to in Levannon. No better'n a sink-hole of atheism."

I said: "Never hearn tell of Franklinites."

"Nay? Oh, they busted away from the New Romans in Conicut—New Romans are strong theah, you know. The Mother Church tol'ates 'em so long as they don't go building meeting-places and stuff—I mean, you got to have religious liberty within reason, just so it don't lead to heresy and things. Franklinites—well, I dunno . . ."

Sam said: "Franklinite a'gument sta'ted up about St. Franklin's name not being Benjamin and the durn gold standard not being wropped around him when he was buried but around some other educated saint of the same name. My wife's mother knowed all about it, and she'd testify on the subject till a man dropped dead. One of 'em carried lightning into his umbreller, I disremember which one."

"The Benjamin one," said Jed, all friendly again. "Anyhow them Franklinites did stir up a terrible commotion in Conicut, disgraceful—riots, what-not, finally made like persecuted and petitioned Mother Church to let 'em do an exodus or like that into Levannon, which she done it, and theah they be to this day. Awful thing."

"Wife's mother was a Grammite. Good woman according to her lights."

"Didn't go for to hurt y' feelings, Sam."

"Didn't. According to *her* lights I said. But when it come to my wife, why, I said to her, 'Jackson,' I said, 'you can be a Grammite like your respected maternal pair'nt and prophesy the end of the world till your own ass flies up,' I said, 'and bites this 'ere left one,' I said, '*or* you can be my good wife, but you can't do both, Jackson,' I said, 'account I a'n't about to put up with it.' Horned it out'n her too, so't of."

"Why," said Vilet, "you mean old billy ram!"

"Naw, Jackson baby, that a'n't meanness, that's just good sense, that is. All's I mean, she was a lickin' good

119

church-woman ever after, real saint, never had a mite of trouble with her that day fo'th. About religion, I mean. Did have a few other faults such as talky-talking fit to wear the han'le off a solid silver thundermug, which is why I j'ined the A'my so to get a smidgin of peace and quiet, but a real saint, understand, no trouble with her at all, no sir. Not about religion."

"Amen," says Vilet, and glanced up quick at Jed to make sure she'd said the right thing.

12

We spent the early afternoon in that place, drying out, getting acquainted. I again said something about Levannon and the great ships, the thirty-ton outriggers that dare to sail to the ports of Nuin by the northern route. And Jed Sever was troubled again, though not this time about religion.

"The sea's a devil's life, boy Davy. I know—I had a taste of it. Signed on with a fishing fleet out of Kingstone, at seventeen. I was big as I am now—too big to listen to my Da, that was the sin of it—but when I got back by the grace of God 'n' Abraham I weighed no more'n a hund'd and twenty pounds. We sailed south beyond the Black Rock Islands, wheah the Hudson Sea opens out into the big water—oh, Mother Cara have pity, that's a lonesome place, the Black Rocks! They say a great city stood theah in Old Time, and that's ha'd to understand. As for the big water beyond, oh, it's a hund'd thousand mile of nothing, boy Davy, nothing at all. We was gone seven months, op'rating from a camp wheah we smoked the fish, a mis'ble empty spit of land, sand dunes, dab or two of low hills, no shelter if'n the wind's wrong. Long Island it's called, pa't of Levannon and they's a few small villages at the western end within sight of the Black Rocks; any nation's free to use the eastern end—sand—seldom a living thing except the gulls. Men get to hating each other, such ventures. Twenty-five of us at the beginning, mostly sinners. Five dead, one murdered in a brawl, and mind you, the comp'ny expects to lose that many, expects it. We never saw a new face only when the comp'ny's freight vessel brung firewood and took back the smoked cod and mackle. And on our sailings—ah, sometimes we was a couple-three hours full out of sight of land! That's an awful thing. You be in God's hand, amen, still it's a terr'ble test of y' faith. Can't do it ay-tall without a compass, some call it a lodestone. Comp'ny owned one that was made in Old Time, and we had three men in the crew considered fit to han'le it and keep watch lest God should weary of holding the little iron true to the no'th for our sakes out of his ev'lasting mercy."

Vilet sighed. "Hoy, I bet them three was the real panjandrums of the outfit, wasn't they?"

"You don't understand these things, woman. Man's han'ling a holy object, y' own life depending on it, stands to reason you treat him respectful. Ayah, boy Davy, that's the blind side of nothing when you're out of sight of land. You work in skiffs, maybe six-seven hours labor with the big nets, and mustn't leave the main outrigger out of sight for that's wheah the compass is—come a sudden fog or a great wide wind, what then?—needn't ask. And when the last net comes in, then it's fight y' way back over the cruel water to make camp, get the fish smoked before they spile. To this day I can't abide the stink of fish, any fish, couldn't if I was sta'ving. It's a judgment onto me for a sinful youth. The sea's not for men, boy Davy. Le' me tell you—when I came home at last, sick and punied-out though I was I had me a woman-hunger fit to drive a man hag-wild, and—well, I won't go into that now, but on my first night back in Kingstone I succumbed to the urging of the evil one, and I got *robbed,* ever' penny of my seven months' pay. A judgment."

Sam said to the fire: "You claim God would gut a man just for heavin' it into a chunk of nooky?"

"Language! Nay, why was I robbed, if it wa'n't a judgment? Answer me that! Ah, Sam, I pray for the time when scoffing will pass from you. You harken to me, boy Davy: at sea you be a *slave,* no other word. A devil's life. Work, work, work till you drop, then comes the old chief's boot in y' ribs, and sea-law says he's got the right. I wish ever' vessel ever built was to the bottom of the deep this day moment. I do. You listen to me: it stands to reason, if'n God meant men to float he'd've give us fins."

We got moving soon after that, to look for a location where we might spend the night in better safety. I learned a few things from Sam as I walked with him, out of hearing of Jed and Vilet. Jed, he told me, was short-sighted, objects twenty feet away from him not much more than a blur, and he was sensitive about it, regarding it as another punishment dealt out to him by the Lord. I couldn't see Jed as any kind of sinner, let alone a big one, but Jed firmly believed the Lord had it in for him—testing him to be sure and maybe friendly at heart, but tough all the same, never giving him a break without taking away something else or reminding him of the Day of Judgment. The poor jo could hardly turn his head to spit or square off by a tree-trunk to take a leak, without the Lord's jolting him up about something he'd done wrong ten days ago, or ten years. Unfair, I thought, and unreasonable—but if that was the way Jed and God wanted it, Sam and I weren't about to butt in with our ten cents worth of suggestions.

* * *

In Old Time it was possible to help people with poor vision, by grinding glass into lenses that let them see almost normally. Another lost art, gone down the drain of ignorance in the Years of Confusion; recovered, however, and brought with us to the island.

At Old City, in the underground workshops adjoining the Heretics' secret library, there's been a man at work some thirty years on problems of lens-making; he still is, if he's alive and undiscovered by the victorious legions of God. Arn Bronstein was his name originally, but he elected to adopt the first name Baruch after reading the life of an Old-Time philosopher who also inflamed his

122

eyes grinding lenses, and who built a curious bridge of reasoning to carry him a remarkable distance beyond the bumbling Christianity and Judaism of his day. Our Baruch could have sailed with us; it was his own decision not to. When Dion was trying to persuade him to join the group who would sail with the *Morning Star* if we should lose the battle for Old City, he said: "No, I will stay where there's enough civilization, never mind its quality, so that a man can achieve obscurity." "Obscurity's all very well," said Dion—"do you want the obscurity of grinding spectacles for people who can't wear them without being burned for witchcraft?" Not answering that, having very likely not listened to it, Baruch asked: "And what facilities do you provide for contemplation aboard your—hoo, your beautiful *Morning Star?*" He asked that, crouching in the doorway of his musty workshop and blinking pink angry eyes at Dion as if he hated him; crying and swearing, Dion called him a fool, which appeared to gratify him.

Baruch was past fifty when the rebellion began. He said his manuscripts and optical gear made a load too heavy to carry, and he would have no one else burdened with it if you please. I remember him so, in the doorway, stoop-shouldered, shrunken, tortured eyes winking and watering, garments haphazard rags although he had money for good clothes, saying this and plainly meaning instead that he would not trust others, heedless ham-handed blunderers, to carry a load so precious. Then—ready to reject instantly any show of affection—he gave Dion a small book bound by himself, painfully handwritten by himself, a labor of pure love. It contains everything that Baruch knew and could tell of lens-making, so that granted the brains and patience (we have them) we can duplicate the practical part of the work at any time.

Many times since that day of retreat it has disturbed me to think of a lens-maker afflicted with something like blindness; of a man with a love for humanity who can't stand the sight, sound, touch of human beings near him. I can imagine nothing more ridiculous or insulting than "feeling sorry" for Baruch; I suppose his rejection of communication is the thing that wounds.

* * *

We killed a stag that afternoon. I saw him in a clump of birches and let fly my arrow for a neck shot. He went down and Sam was beside him at once, the knife swift and merciful in the throat. Jed was generously admiring. Vilet watched us, me cocky and proud, Sam still-faced with his reddened knife waiting for the carcass to bleed out, and I saw a waking of lust in her, her eyes dilated, lips a little swollen. If Jed had not been there, present but not really sharing the heart of the excitement, I could imagine her inviting Sam to spread her on the ground. There was that in her smoldering gaze at him—and at me, who after all had shot the arrow. But Jed was there, and in a few minutes we were busy cutting what meat we could carry, the heated moment gone.

We camped for that night in a ravine that must have been a good ten miles from Skoar, but still fairly near the Northeast Road—once or twice we heard horsemen. We made a temporary fireplace of rocks for cooking, below the rim of the ravine, where the blaze could not be seen from the road. When Jed and Vilet took their turn at gathering wood, leaving Sam and me alone, he answered a question before I spoke it: "A camp-follower they call 'em, Jackson. Means she's been whorin' it for a living, puttin' out for any jo in the comp'ny that had a dollar. She's good at it, too— I been in there a few times, never a dull moment. She was doing all right—the men treated her nice, got her food free, no pimp or modom riding her, chance to save up her cash for a rainy day. Every comp'ny's got one—I dunno how 'tis in the Moha army. Our boys always make a real doll out'n the comp'ny whore. It's natural—only female thing they got to love, and so on . . . Well, old Jed he kindly got religion, or he'd always had it, but I mean it so't of rifted up on him, anyway he decided God didn't wish him to stay in the A'my when there was a war on and a real chance he might be expected to hurt somebody. And it seems God told him to take Vilet along on his way out. He says it was God."

"So who else would talk thataway?"

124

Sam gave me one of his long cool stares, checked on the distance of Jed and Vilet off in the brush, and went on with the story: "It come to a head yesterday after we holed up near the road waiting for the Mohas. I blundered onto Jed and her in the bushes, supposed they was just fixing up for a quick piece, but it wasn't that. Jed he was lit up with the holy spirit or whatever, asked me to stick around and bear witness. He was explaining to Vilet how God wants her to give up the sinful life and love the Lord, along with him who's intending to lead hencefo'th a life of mercy and purity. Damn, he's already so gentle and good-hearted and mush-headed you wouldn't think there was room in him for enough sin to stuff a pisswilly walnut, but he don't think so. Got a conscience like a bull bison, that man, stompin' on him all the time. Well, looked to me like Vilet got a bang-up conversion, and when old Jed cut loose with this 'ere repent-leave-all-and-foller-me, why, bedam if she didn't, she did bedam . . . Jed he wanted I should come along too. I didn't estimate I was no-way called. He allowed they'd stay close by for a day or two and pray for me, and if'n I changed my mind I could sneak away from the outfit and make screek-owl noises three at a time till they j'ined up with me. Kay, s's I, and they took off. Dunno how they ever got by our sentries, him that clumsy with his poor eyesight, but Vilet's sharp in the woods, got him by some-way. Hadn't no intention of going with 'em, Jackson—I'm a loner by trade—but then I got my head hurt in that skirmish and the comp'ny took off without me. Real lost for a while. Damn nigh blundered into the Mohas like I told you. Bypassed 'em and come on down along the road—wrong way too, didn't realize I was headed for Skoar till daylight. Did the screek-owl thing a few times not expecting anything, but Vilet heard and answered, and we got connected. Know a rema'kable thing?—they got it fixed they'll go all the way to Vairmant and cut a fa'm out'n the wilderness which shall be lo, a temple in the lorn waste land and like that. A'n't bound thataway myself but bless 'em, s's I, hope they do."

"I notice you be calling 'em Jed and Vilet instead of Jackson."

"Oh, that. Wa'n't speakin' to 'em direct."

125

"I see. Like hell I see."

Sam put his hand on my head and pushed down—not hard, but I was sitting on the ground the next moment. He rumpled my thatch; all I could do about that was laugh and feel good. "Jackson," he said, "if you wasn't a big serious brain just like me I wouldn't betrouble myself to explain it. You see, in this world a man's got to piss up some kind of a whirlwind or nobody knows he's there. Now, me bein' mean, ugly, common's an old dry bull-turd in an upland medder, if I didn't do something a mite extra-onery—well, tell me, an old dry bull-turd, what does *it* do?"

"Just kindly sets there onto the grass."

"That's right! That's prezactly what it does. You never knowed a bull-turd, anyway not an old dry one, to get up on its hind legs and call people Jackson as if it didn't know their right names, nor you never will. So now I've answered your question fair and honest, what the hell you got into that sack? Been achin' about it all afternoon."

I might have told him the full story then about my golden horn—I did months later, when we happened to be alone—but Jed and Vilet were coming back. It wasn't for them somehow—there was all the trouble of explaining why I hadn't killed the mue, other difficulties. Jed heard Sam's question, however, and when he saw me reluctant and unhappy he gave me a little talk about how since the Lord had thrown us together we must try to be all for one and one for all, which meant sharing everything and not having secrets from each other. So it would be *spiritually* good for me to tell about what I had in my sack, not that he supposed for one minute it was anything I didn't ought to have, but—ayah, and meanwhile old Sam is standing off there not doing a thing to get off the hook, just minding the fire and spitting the venison on sticks to grill, and now and then casting me a blank look which might mean: Go ahead, *be* a bull-turd!

"Jed," I said, "would you hold this image again, the way I can look at it whiles I talk?"

"Why, sure!" He was startled and mighty pleased. Vilet sat down by me, her chunky hand on my back. Affection was her natural way, going along with the bouncy sex

126

though not the same thing. She liked to touch and nudge and kiss, make known her body's warm presence without any fuss, just as at another time she might say, merely by pouting her mouth or rolling her hip, "Let's have one!"

"Here's the true-tale," I said, looking at the clay image, "about how I come to kill that man accidental." You know, my pesky clay god-thing did bother me a bit at first. But I had meant to tell this part straight anyhow, about climbing back over the Skoar stockade and tangling with that guard. And when I continued, leaving out all mention of Emmia and saying I'd gone back over the stockade into the woods right away when I knew the guard was dead—oh, Mudface raised no objections.

"Poor Davy," said Vilet, and tickled me just below my loin-rag where Jed didn't see her hand. "Right back to the woods, huh? Didn't you have no girl in Skoar, lover-pup?"

"Well, I did so't of, only—"

"What you mean so't of? I wouldn't give the sweat off a hoppergrass's ass for a *so't* of a girl, Davy."

"Well, I meant *kind* of. But le' me tell you what happened in the woods that afternoon, before I accidental killed that jo. You people ever meet a hermit?"

"Ayah, once," Jed said. "Hillside cave outside of Kingstone, done his artful healin' by layin' on of hands."

"That's just the kind of hermit I mean," I said—"woodland type. I'd been goofing off, hadn't no right to quit work that day. Anyway I found this old hermit. All he had was a grass lean-to, no cave. Hadn't been real holy he'd been et up long before, wouldn't you think?"

"The Lord protects his own, alley-loo. That one at Kingstone's cave wa'n't nothing. Kept goats in it."

Sam asked: "Didn't it smell some?"

"Little bit," said Jed. "You take a hermit, he's got to overlook some things in God's service."

All right, but the hell with his hermit, I had to get them interested in mine. "This'n was terrible old and strange. When I first seen him it upsottled me so I almost stepped on a big rattler. But he seen it, told me not to move and made the sign of the wheel, and lo!"

"Lo what?"

"Well, I mean it just lo slid away, no harm done. Old

127

hermit he said it was a manifestation, account the serpent represented cussing, my greatest fault—which he couldn't've knowed except by second sight, because I hadn't done no sort of cussing there, you can believe."

It got Jed, the way I meant it to. "Praise the Lord, that's exactly how those things happen! You was led, you was *meant* to meet that holy man. Go on, son!"

"Well . . . He wasn't only old, he was a-dying."

"Oh, think of that!" says Vilet. "The poor old s—the poor old hermit!"

"Ayah. He looked that peaceful I wouldn't've ever guessed, but he told me. He said: 'I'm about to pass on, boy Davy'—nay-nay, there's another thing, he knowed my name like that, without my telling him. I was some flabberjastered and that's a fact. I b'lieve it was another manifestation."

"I do believe it was. Go on, Davy!"

"Well, he said I was the first to come by in a long time and do him a kindness, only shit—I mean goodness—I hadn't done nothing but set by and listen. He said to dig under his lean-to, showed me where, take what I found there and keep it by me all my life. Said it was an Old-Time relic and he knowed the evil was all prayed out'n it account he'd done it himself." I remember I was scared at the fine and healthy dimensions of that particular whifferoo —spooked enough to make my voice wobble. Jed and Vilet attributed it to reverence—if there's a difference. "Old hermit said God had guided me to it, meant the Old-Time thing for me if'n I'd learn to you-know, quit cussing and so on."

"Praise his name! And you was guided to us too, the way we'll all help you to quit and never cuss no more. So what happened then?"

"Then he—died."

"You was actu'ly present at the holy passing on?"

"Ayah. He blessed me, told me again where to dig, and then died—uh—in my arms." I gazed off into the deep woods, sober and brave, and did a gulp. After all, it was the first time I'd ever killed a hermit. "So—so then I fixed up a hardscrabble grave for him, and—" I stopped, suddenly sick, remembering the rain and a true happening.

But presently—in such a thing the mind sometimes appears to use no time at all—I felt that the soldier (who lived now in me and nowhere else) would be pleased to laugh along with me in there behind my eyes at my damnfool hermit, and why not? So I was able to go on with hardly a break: "Took what I found there and came away, was all."

I showed them my horn then, but dared not blow it so near the road. Jed and Vilet were too much in awe of it to touch it, but Sam held it in his hands, and said after a while: "A young man could make music with that."

Later while we were eating, I asked: "In the battalion—not your company but the men who'd've been in that fight I saw this morning—do you remember a jo, maybe seventeen or so, dark hair, gray eyes, real soft-spoken?"

"Maybe ten-twenty such," Sam said, and Jed mumbled something to the same effect. "Don't know his name?"

"No. Found him after the fighting was over, and we talked some. Nothing I could do for him."

Vilet asked: "He was hurt bad? Died?"

"Ayah. I never learned his name."

"Did he die in the Church?" Jed asked.

"We didn't talk about religion." Jed looked sad and shocked; I didn't understand at once. "I never did learn his name."

"Jackson," Sam said, and tossed me another chunk of venison, not saying anything just then that would make a demand on me. Later, when night had closed down and Sam and I were taking the first watch, I did understand what Jed had meant by his question, and childhood teaching was another burden of darkness.

A member of the Holy Murcan Church must make in his dying moments what the priests call a confession of faith, if he can speak at all, or he goes to hell forever. Should he forget because of pain or sickness, others present must remind him. I had been taught that much, like all children; why had it never entered my head when the soldier was dying? I had doubts, true, including doubts about hell, but—what if there *was* a hell? Everyone else took it for granted . . .

Sam and I had a small fire going, and the wall of the

ravine at our backs. Even with Sam near me, I had hated to see Jed and Vilet disappear in the little brush lean-to we'd flung together, though I knew they were no further off and probably not asleep. I began to see my gray-eyed friend twisting in the tar-pits, the brain boiling in his skull as Father Clance had so lovingly described; and he was crying out to me: "Why didn't you help?"

In marshy ground somewhere the low thunder of frogs was so continuous it had become a part of silence; the peepers were shrilling, and the big owls sounding off from time to time. When the moon rose at last it was reddened by a haze we had noticed at sundown, perhaps the smoke from distant occasions of war. Then I found myself up to my ears and over my head in the question: *How does anyone know?*

Who ever went down to the seventh level of hell and *saw* them hanging up adulterers by the scrotum, so that Father Clance, rolling his eyes and sweating and sighing, could later explain for us just how it was done? *How did he know?*

In lesser matters, hadn't I seen people win satisfaction and power over others just from knowing or pretending to know what those others didn't? Merciful winds, hadn't I just worked that same kind of swindle with my damned hermit?

Could anyone prove to me that the whole hell-and-heaven thing wasn't one big fraud? I may have started at that or fidgeted. Sam's whisper came: "What's the matter?"

The moon had shifted to whiteness, and his face was clear. I knew he wouldn't harm me or be angry, but I was still timid with my question: "Sam, be there people that don't believe in hell?"

"Jackson, you sure that's the question you want to ask? I got no wisdom on such things."

Of course, a question wasn't the thing; it was only a way of keeping myself off the griddle and putting him on it. "I mean, Sam, I kindly don't believe in it myself no more."

"Seen plenty hell on earth," he said after a while. "But that wa'n't what you meant."

"No."

"Well, the Church kind—I've noticed the only ones that

130

act like they want to believe it are the ones that see 'emselves safe-elected for heaven. Take old Jed theah, he don't get no bang out'n hell. Believes all right, but kindly arranges with himself not to think about it. Doubts, Jackson?"

"Ayah."

He was silent long enough to make me a little afraid again. "Me, I guess I've always had 'em . . . You a'n't scared I might talk to a priest?"

"How do you know *I* wouldn't?"

"I b'lieve I just know it, Jackson. Anyhow if I was you, sooner'n eat my heart out thinking that 'ere soldier's frying account of words that didn't get said, why, I'd undertake to wonder if the priests didn't invent the whole damned shibundle."

So he trusted me that much, and I could no longer have any doubt that Sam and I were both tremendous heretics and no help for it. I remember thinking: *If they was to burn Sam they got to burn me along-with.* And wishing I could say something like that aloud. But then it occurred to me that since he evidently knew so many of my thoughts without even trying, he wouldn't be likely to miss that one.

13

What I've so far written about happened in a few days of mid-March. By mid-June we were only a few miles further on, for we found a place so pleasant that we holed up there for three months. Sam's head-wound finished healing there, after a troublesome infection. We loafed, and I struggled through the first stages of learning to play my golden horn. We talked long, and made a thousand plans, and I was growing up.

The place was a cool deep cliffside cave something like

the one I had on North Mountain, but this one was low in the rock wall, fourteen feet above level ground. We had no view of distances from it, but looked into lowland forest as into a vast and quiet room. Shade from the mid-day sun, and no settlement near enough to trouble us. To study the surrounding country all we needed to do was climb a nearby sentinel pine and look away. From that height I never caught sight of man except wisps of smoke from a little lonesome village six miles east of us. The Northeast Road was two miles the other side of that village, and the name of the village we never learned. It wasn't Wilton Village—we'd slipped by that before we happened on our cave.

The only access to our hideaway was a drooping oak branch—difficult for Jed—and the only resident we had to disturb was a fat porcupine whom we hit on the head and ate because that was simpler than educating him not to come back and snuggle up to us where we were asleep.

For two weeks Sam was in bad shape from the infection, feverish and tormented by headaches. Jed cared for him wonderfully, better at it than Vilet or me, and even let Sam cuss all he liked. Vilet and I were the food-winners while Sam was sick, and Vilet searched out wild plants to make some healing mixtures for him. Her mother had been a mountain yarb-woman in southern Katskil, Vilet said, and a midwife too. She was full of stories about the old woman, and told them best when Jed wasn't around. Sam was pretty patient with her yarb mixtures, but after a while he did get a look when he saw her coming like a man who thinks that the next tree to go over in the storm will take the roof along with it. Then toward the end of his bad time, when she'd landed him with a potion which she admitted herself would prob'ly hoist the hide off a bear and him running, Sam said: "Jackson, it a'n't that I mind having my gizzard hit by lightning all twistyways, and I suppose I could get used to the feelin' I'm about to give birth to a three-horned giasticutus—what I can't no-way endure, Jackson, is the trompling."

"Trompling?" says Vilet.

"Ayah. Ayah. Them microbes and box-terriers that go rushin' along my gut tryin' to get the hell away from your remedies. You can't blame 'em, see, the way they set their feet down, only I can't stand it, Jackson, and so if you please I'll just arrange not to be sick no more."

* * *

We have been living slightly more than a month on the island Neonarcheos. The *Morning Star* sailed two days ago, to search the region east of us where other islands appear on the old map. Captain Barr intends to make no more than a two-day voyage and then return. He took only eight men, enough to handle the schooner.

We are not calling Dion Governor, not yet, because he rather clearly doesn't wish it. Still we all find it natural that important decisions—such as sending or not sending Captain Barr on this voyage—should be made mostly by Dion, and before long I think most of the colonists will want it formalized. We shall require something in the nature of a constitution, small though our group is, and written laws.

Back in Nuin and those other lands, the season will be chilling toward the winter rainy season; here we notice hardly any change. We have erected twelve simple houses; the brookside grass makes good thatch, though we must wait for heavy rains to test it. Seven of the buildings are on the knoll, spaced so that all have a view of the beach and the little bay, and one of the seven is Nickie's and mine. There's another on the beach, three along the creek, and Adna-Lee Jason with Ted Marsh and Dane Gregory have chosen to build their house away up on the hill where our stream originates. That's a love-alliance that began in Old City long before we sailed; they need it as Nickie and I need our more ordinary kind of marriage, and Adna-Lee has been happy lately as I never knew her to be in the old days.

Aboard the *Morning Star* we all learned a little of what it must have been like to dwell in the jammed cities and suburbs of the last days of Old Time. I was just now re-reading an ugly passage in the Book of John Barth: "Our statesmen periodically discover the basic purpose of war. They are, poor little gods, like farmers in a fix: if you have thirty hogs and only one small daily bucket of swill—?

133

And so the finality, the apocalyptic unreason, the shared suicide of nuclear war is for them the most God-damned *embarrassing* thing. Their one time-tested population control is all spoiled." A few paragraphs further on he remarks in passing that of course birth control had been a practical solution since the 19th century, except that the godly made rational application of it impossible even late in the 20th when the time was running out. What would he make of our present state, the reverse of the dismal population problem of his day?

I dare say no civilization ever completely dies. There's at least the stream of physical inheritance, and perhaps some word spoken a thousand years ago can exert unrecognizable power over what you do tomorrow morning. So long as one book survives anywhere—any book, any pitiful handful of pages preserved somehow, buried, locked away in vault or cave—Old Time is not dead. But neither can any civilization return with anything of its former quality. Fragments we may reclaim, memory holds more than we know, there's a resonance of ancient times in any talk of father to son. But the world of Old Time cannot live again as it was, nor should we dream of it.

* * *

Vilet often came along with me for hunting and fishing while Jed stayed behind to look after Sam. The first day that happened I felt an agreement between us, at first unspoken, created by occasional touches and glances, for instance when she was walking a few yards ahead of me in good forest silence, and turned to look at me over her shoulder, unsmiling. I think Vilet enjoyed being spooked by other people's mysteries now and then, like my hermit whopmagullion, but she wasn't one to make mysteries herself. That moment on the trail she might as well have said in words: "I could be caught with a little running."

Work came first, and we had luck with it that day, nailing a couple of fat bunnies and then locating a good fishing pool about a mile from our cave. There was a grassy bank, sunlight, and a quiet as though no man had troubled the place for centuries. We set out fish-lines, and when she

134

knelt on the grass to adjust hers, her arm slid around my thighs. "You've had a girl once or twice, I b'lieve."

"How d' you know?"

"Way you look at me." The next moment she was solid on her feet and pulling her ragged smock off over her head. "Time you *really* learned something," she said. "I a'n't young nor I a'n't purty, but I know how." Naked with not a bit of softness (you would have thought), cocky and smiling a little and moving her hips to bother me, she was a grand piece of woman. "Off with them rags, Lover-pup," she said, "and come take me. You'll have to work for it."

I worked for it, wrestling her at first with all my strength and getting no breaks at all until the struggle had warmed her up into real enjoyment. Then of a sudden she was kissing and fondling instead of fighting me off, laughing under her breath and using a few horny words I didn't know at that time; presently her hands were gripping her knees, I was in her standing, joyfully stallionizing it with not a thought in my head to interfere. When I was spent she flung me a punch in the shoulder and then hugged me. "Lover-pup, you're good." What I'd had with Emmia seemed long ago and far away.

We had other times, not so very many, for there were other sides to Vilet: moods of heavy melancholy, of a kind of self-punishing despair; the religious side, that belonged to Jed and was forever shadowing the rest of her life. Often (she told me once) she dreamed that she was in the act of selling her soul to the Devil, and he in the shape of a great gray rock about to topple over and crush her. She couldn't always be the good randy wrestling-partner when we had privacy and opportunity, but occasionally at such times she did feel like talking to me. It was a time like that, at the fishing pool again and maybe a week after our first romp, that she told me things about her relation with Jed Sever. Whenever Jed was mentioned in his absence by Sam or me, I'd notice a kind of still warning in her kind blocky face, like an animal bracing itself to defend if necessary. She'd hear nothing in criticism of him. At the fishing pool, after we got a few for supper we took a dip in the water to wash off the heat of the day, but she warned me off from playing with her and I wasn't in form for it myself; we just

135

sat by the pool lazing and drying off, and she said: "I got it figgered out, Davy, the mor'ls of it I mean. Not telling Jed about what we been having, it a'n't a real sin account it might burden him with grief, and anyway I got so much sin in the past to work off, this'n's just a little one. He's so good, Davy, Jed is! He tells me I got to think back through earlier sins and make sure I truly repent 'em, because see, you can't fix 'em all with one big bang-up repentance, you got to take 'em one by one, he says. So, see, I'm kindly working up to the present time but a'n't got there yet. I mean, Sugar-piece, if I don't commit no more'n one sin a day, or say two at the most, and then repent say *three* sins of past time the same day, well, I mean, after-while you get caught up like. Only it's so't of a heartbreak thing, times, remembering 'em all. I'll be all right by the time we get to Vairmant. And Jed he says it's too much to try to give up sin all to oncet, too rough,* the Lord never intended it like."

I said: "Jed's awful good, a'n't he?"

"Oh, a saint!" And she went on about how generous he was, and thoughtful, and how he'd explained everything about the way to Abraham; when they got their little place in Vairmant they were going to have sinners in every day to hear the word, just everybody, any freeman that would come. Dear Vilet, she was out of her gloomy mood and all aglow from thinking of it, sitting there by the pool naked as a jaybird and patting my knee now and then but not trying to rouse me up because it wasn't our day for it. "Jed, see, he's got a great lot of sin-trouble too. 'Most every day he remembers something out'n the past that sets him back because it needs repentance. Like frinstance yesterday he recalled, when he was five, going-on six he'd just learned about fertilizer, see? So here's his Ma's bed of yalla nasturtiums she was so peart about, and he wanted to do something real generous, make 'em twice as big and purty right away, so he pees the hell all over 'em, specially a big

---

* I feel that Jed was entirely right about this. My own planned salvation involves getting in as much sin as possible in the next 70 years, so that what I give up at age 98 will *amount* to something.

—Nick.

136

old gran'daddy nasturtium that's sticking up kindly impident—well, I mean, by the time he sees it a'n't turning out just right it's too late, he can't stop till he's emptied out." Vilet was crying a little as well as laughing. "So the bed's real swamped, petals flat on the ground, and he don't tell, it gets blamed on the dog and he dasn't tell."

"Oh," I said, "that sumbitchin' nasturtium was purely askin' for it."

"Ai-yah, I laughed too when he told me, and so'd he, just a mite, still it's ser'ous, Davy, because it kindly ties in with a real sin he done when he was nine, poor jo. He done it to the little neighbor girl and his Ma caught 'em into the berry patch. The girl she just larruped on the backside and sent her home bawling, but she didn't whip Jed. He says it's how he knows his Ma was the greatest saint that ever lived, for all she done was weep and tell him he'd broke her heart after all she done givin' him birth in pain and tryin' to raise him up to something. And so ever since he a'n't never put it into a woman, except once."

"He what? He never?"

"Except once. That God-damn Kingstone whore he talks about, after his God-damn fishing trip . . . Well, anyway—anyway he's a saint now, and all's he ever wants me to do is take my smock off and tromple him a little and call him bad names—he says it purifies him and so it's bound to be pleasing in the sight of God, like the whipping, only he a'n't had me do that lately, not since we come away from the A'my." She sighed and stopped crying. "He's so kind, Davy! And he always knows how 't is for me too, so sometimes he like helps me with his hand or like that, he says that's just a *little* sin, and anyhow we're both getting stronger and stronger in the Lord all the time now. Calls me his little brand from the burning, and I know that's Book of Abraham language but you can see he means it—why, sometimes he can hold me in his arms all night long and never get a hard on, a'n't that ma'velous?"

Those weeks in the cave were also a good time for learning a little about the playing of my horn. I gave it at least an hour of each evening, from deep twilight into full dark. In daylight there was too much danger of a stray hunter hearing and approaching unseen. After twilight not even bandits are likely to stir away from camp, in the Moha woods. I studied my horn, and I took part in our making of plans.

There was my plan about Levannon and the ships, but when I learned that even Sam was unhappy at the notion of my signing on aboard a ship, I shut my mouth about it, and though it didn't perish it remained in silence.

There was Jed's and Vilet's plan about the Vairmant farm. They were sure about the sinners but they kept altering the rest of the livestock. Vilet held out one long rainy day for goats while Jed stood up for chickens, and it began in fun but he wound up bothered and ended the discussion by saying goats were too lascivious, a word Vilet didn't know so it shut her up.

Sam, when he was well again, was more concerned about immediate plans. We wouldn't be able to go anywhere, he pointed out, so long as we had to travel in beat-up Katskil uniforms, a smock of the same dark green, and the gray loin-rag of a Moha bond-servant. He claimed he could see two good ways of acquiring suitable garments, both dishonest, and one honest way that wouldn't work and was fairly sure to get at least one of us jailed or hanged.

"Dishonesty," said Jed, "is a sin, Sam, and you don't need me to tell you so. What's the honest way?"

"One of us go to the nearest village and buy some clo'es. Got to walk in naked is all. Be had up for indecent explosion right off. I don't recommend it."

"I could say I lost 'em some place," Jed suggested. It was like him to take it for granted he ought to be the one to stick his neck out and get it chopped off. "I think I could justify that to my Maker as a white lie."

"But maybe not to the storekeeper," said Sam. "Anyhow you don't look like the type jo that would get deprived of his ga'ments casual-like—you be too big and important. And me, I look too mean."

"Maybe I say I lost 'em into a whirlwind."

"What whirlwind, Jackson?"

"A 'maginary one. I just say it blowed down the road a piece."

Sam sighed and looked at Vilet and she looked at me and I looked at my navel and nobody said anything.

"Well," says Jed, "I could hang leaves around my middle and make like lost in the woods, like."

Sam said: "I couldn't no-way justify pickin' innocent leaves for no such purpose."

"Look," I said, "it'd have to be me, acoount you don't none of you talk like Moha . . ."

"Sam, boy," said Vilet, "just purely for cur'osity and the sake of argument, which so't of dishonest ways was you in mind of?"

"Might hold up a pa'ty on the road and take what we require, but Jackson theah don't hold with vi'lence, me neither. Somebody'd get hurt or they'd run tell policer. Another way, one or two of us could shadow-foot it into some village or outlyin' fa'm and so't of steal something."

"Stealing's a sin," said Jed, and we sat around all quiet and sad, and I blew a few notes on my horn since it was getting dark. "Anyhow," said Jed, "I don't understand how a person could go and steal clothes off of a person without no vi'lence. I mean you got to think about human nature, specially women and like that."

Sam said gently: "So't of general workin' rule, Jackson, the way you steal clo'es, you steal 'em when there a'n't nobody in 'em, like in a shop or onto a clo'esline."

I said: "Why'n't we do that and leave a dollar to make it square?"

Well, they all gazed at me in a sandbagged style, the way grown-ups will gaze at something down there that just doesn't seem possible, and then I could see them get happier and happier, more and more mellow, till they looked like three saints bungfull of salvation and pie.

14

We set out next morning for that village six miles away near
the Northeast Road—Sam, Vilet and I. We reasoned, and
Jed agreed, that temporary sinners on a clothes-stealing expedition would need to be able to move fast and with good
eyesight. Besides, we needed to have someone minding the
cave and watching our gear. Besideser, he'd been working
hard since before sun-up praying good luck into a dollar
Vilet provided, because he said that if we left a genuine
good-luck dollar to pay for the clothes it would cut the
sin down to nearly nothing, and so he'd earned his rest.

I'd scouted the village two or three times on my lone. It
was a poor grubby thing with a ramshackle stockade closing in twenty or thirty acres, and so little cleared area outside it that I knew the people must live mostly by hunting
and fishing, plus maybe a few handcrafts for trade. A cart-
track connected it to the Northeast Road, but there was no
road on the back-country side. I'd located three outlying
houses with fair-sized gardens, two on the north-east side
and one by the back gate which probably belonged to the
man such villages call the Guide.

We halted on a tree-covered hillside where we could
watch that house by the back gate, for it did have an interesting clothesline, and as we watched, a thin wench in a
yellow smock came out and added a basketful of things to
what was already hanging there.

In a village like that, the Guide counts for more than
anyone except the head priest and the mayor. The Guide
bosses any work that has to do with the wilderness, arranges any large hunting and fishing parties, usually leading them himself, keeps track of seasonal and weather
signs, distributes whatever the group hunting and fishing

brings in, and takes a handsome cut of everything. In a mean small village like this he'd be appointed by the head priest and mayor together; in a baronial village—there aren't many in eastern Moha—he'd be a sales-manager (sometimes called vassal) of the baron himself, and fixed for life. In either case a village Guide is nobody to fool with, and here we were proposing to rob this one's everloving clothesline.

We watched from our hillside more than half an hour, watching not only the house but a big dog-kennel at the side. After that girl who hung up the clothes went back inside, we didn't see a soul stirring. Nor a dog. From the nature of a Guide's job, he's away from home a good deal. So are his dogs. And on the line was a huge white smock —it would cut up into three or four loin-rags. Other stuff too, a smallish yellow smock like the one the girl had been wearing, and a whole bunch of lesser items—towels, brown loin-rags. We couldn't pass it up.

Woodland cover ended a hundred yards from the house and a corn patch began; this was June, the young corn tall enough to conceal a man on all fours. That had to be me, for I was small and not wearing Katskil green, and if I got caught I'd at least have a chance to blarney out of it with a Moha accent. We worked down from the hillside through the woods, and I left Sam and Vilet at the forest edge, promising to whistle if I needed help. I crawled down between the corn-rows, sighting on that yellow smock like a target.* Late sunny morning was drawing into noon.

I was at the end of the corn-row when I caught a hint of women's voices in the house, faint, not the clack of visiting housewives. The clothesline hung between a post and the corner of the house, which was low and rambling and well made, with small windows barred against wolf and tiger and the sneak-bandits who haunt lonely country. I would have to cross a small yard in line with some of the windows. The main door of the house was facing me, and at my right, not more than two hundred feet away, stood the back gate of the village stockade. Beyond the clothesline

* That's my Davy. What other shape would get him started?
—Nick.

141

post I noticed a side door, toward the village, which probably belonged to the kitchen since a neat herb-garden grew just outside. I ducked across the yard, just then realizing that we hadn't contrived a cover for my red thatch. Nobody challenged me, and at the corner of the house where the clothesline was fastened I was nicely hidden from the windows. I was clawing the yellow smock off the line when the stockade gate creaked open.

A gray-haired woman came through, turning with her hand on the gate to instruct someone inside in a manner he'd remember; she'd evidently caught the gate guard snatching forty winks. The pause gave me a chance. I was into that yellow smock and had a towel twisted around my hair so fast I can't tell you how I did it. I'd gathered the remaining laundry into a wopse that hid more of me, by the time the dame ended her lecture and came on.

There'd been a flaw in my thinking: now that I'd become a winsome laundress it wouldn't look right if I just strolled off into the woods with the wash. I was obliged to take the stuff into the house. Beastly damp. If the gray-haired woman was nearsighted and preoccupied she might take me for the proper owner of that yellow smock, so on my way into the kitchen I tried to give my rump a gentle womanly twitch. I can't believe it was very attractive—wrong type rump.

The kitchen was big, cool, blessedly empty. Leaving the village alone, that elderly woman couldn't be coming anywhere but here. Probably visiting—the large white smock couldn't belong to her, designed for someone shaped like a beer-barrel with two full-grown watermelons attached.

Voices came from the next room, where the front door was. One woman, who must have gone to the window right after I'd crossed the yard, said: "It's her, Ma."

Ma replied: "Kay, you know what to do."

Not much in that, but it chilled me. The young voice was whiny, half-scared; Ma's tone was high, hoarse and breathy, telling me that she owned the big white smock and liked to eat. I remembered hearing it said that country folk like to use the kitchen door, and I smokefooted into a storeroom with my bundle of wash, eased the door shut and got my eye to the keyhole in time to see Yellow-Smock

142

and Ma come in. That store-room should have had access to the outside, but it didn't—only one high barred window. I was trapped.

Ma was not only ruggedly fat but six feet tall, her dress an ankle-length job of dead black, with expensive cowhide slippers showing at the bottom. Her hair was done up inside a purple turban, and bone ornaments swung at her ears. I still think the man of that house was the village Guide, sober and responsible as they have to be: there was hunter's gear hung in that store-room, and the location of the house was traditional for a Guide's dwelling. Maybe when the man was at home the fat woman was a model housewife, her black gown and turban stashed away where he wouldn't stumble on them. Dressed this way, she had to be a wise woman, and not the legal kind but the kind people sneak to for love philtres, abortions, poisons.

She set a crystal globe on the table, such as I'd heard of gyppos and Ramblers using in their fortune-telling, and plumped down there with her back to my keyhole, but not before I got a look at her face. Small cruel eyes, clever and quick-moving. Her beaky nose had stayed sharp while the rest of her face grew bloated in pale fat.

After that glimpse, her flat-faced daughter slinking by impressed me as a near approach to nothing. Going to the door to meet the gray-haired woman, whose knock I heard, she looked flat all over, as if during her growing up—she was somewhere in the twenties—her mother had sat on her most of the time. Her whispery greeting to the gray-haired woman was rehearsed and phony: "Peace unto you, Mam Byers! My mother is already in communication with your dear one."

"Oh. Am I late?" Mam Byers spoke like a lady.

"Nay. Time is illusion."

"Yes," said Mam Byers, and added emptily: "How nice you look, Lurette!"

"Thank you," said the flat-faced twirp, keeping it on a high plane. "Be seated."

The fat woman had not turned her head. She sat motionless, a great bulging buzzard, giving me a view of the back of her fat neck, offering no greeting even when Mam Byers sat down at the table. I saw the lady's face then, lean, hag-

143

gard, haunted. The fat woman said: "Look in the deeps!"

Lurette closed the outer door against daylight and drew heavy curtains at the windows. She placed candles beside the crystal, and brought a burning splinter from the hearth in the next room to light them. Then she drifted off behind Mam Byers, watching for signals I think. I've never seen anyone who looked so much like a witless tool, as if she had given up trying to be a person and become a stick that her Ma used to poke things with.

"Look in the deeps! What do you see?"

"I see what I've seen before, Mam Zena, the bird trying to escape from a closed room."

"Thy mother's spirit."

"Oh, I believe," said Mam Byers. "I believe. I may have told you—when she was dying she wanted me to kiss her. The only thing she asked—have I told you?"

"Peace, Mam Byers!" She sighed, the great hag, and rested her enormous arms on the table, where I saw her fat sharp-pointed fingers curled like the legs of a spider. "What does the poor bird do today, my dear?"

"Oh, the same—beating at the windows. It was the cancer—the smell—you understand, don't you? I couldn't kiss her. I pretended. She knew I was pretending . . ." Mam Byers had set down her expensive leather purse. I knew a poor village like this would have no more than one or two aristocratic families, and she would belong to one of them; it did her no good in dealing with these bloodsuckers. "Is it possible, Mam Zena? Can you truly bring her, so that I could speak to her?—oh, it was so long ago!"

"All things are possible, if one has faith," said Mam Zena, and Lurette was leaning over Mam Byers, stroking her shoulder and the back of her neck, speaking some words I couldn't catch in her whiny whisper.

"Oh!" said Mam Byers—"I meant to give you this before." And she started taking silver coins from her purse, but her hands shook, and presently she shoved the purse into Lurette's hands and seemed relieved to let go of it.

"Take it away, Lurette," said Mam Zena. "I cannot touch money." Lurette carried the purse away to a side-table, and I saw her cringe at what must have been a

144

burny-burn look from Ma. "Take my hands, my dear, and now we must wait, and pray a little."

That was evidently a signal for Lurette, who slipped out of the room and was gone a few minutes. She returned silently, coming only as far as the doorway behind Mam Byers to set down a dish of smoking incense which stunk up the place in no time. Lurette on that errand was naked except for a slimpsy pair of underpants, in the middle of a costume change I guessed; as she disappeared again I noticed that she looked flatter than ever in the nude.

It's worth remembering that Mam Zena and her whelp could easily have burned if this sort of thing was proved on them—the Church doesn't put up with that kind of competition. But I dare say there's no undertaking so dangerous, ridiculous, cruel or nasty but what plenty of goons are ready to have a go at it for a few dollars.

I got annoyed, and I suppose a little overcharged with teen-age hell; besides, I had to get away with my load of wash. Lurette was obviously going to perform as the spirit of Mam Byers' mother; being the opposition candidate was the only thing I could see that might have a future. I freed my knife from under that yellow smock, and put on the big white one over it. It must have cleared Mam Zena's ankles; on me it swept the floor with considerable dignity, even after I cinched it up with one of the white loin-rags. This left me a pair of bosom-sacks out front which were fine for a lot more laundry. Of course I was a little over-balanced —more a 20th Century style as I look back on it now— and my red hair poking up through and around the towel I'd tied over it probably struck a false note, and there could have been a couple-three other things inconsistent with feminine charm at its best. In spite of being dressed for the part, I didn't *feel* matronly. So almost right away I gave up any idea of being the quiet type, and finding some tomato sauce on the shelves I splashed a gob of it over the front of the white smock, and more on my knife. I wouldn't be Mam Byers' mother after all, but just some well-nourished lady who'd died sudden and still resented it.

Back at my keyhole I saw Lurette about to float in with filmy stuff hung all around her. You could make out a mouth painted large, a pair of eyes, not much more.

145

Hypnotized in the smoky darkness, wanting to believe, Mam Byers would see anything those frauds wanted her to see. That was proved right away, for Lurette entered before I had my nerve screwed up to act. Mam Byers—poor soul, she couldn't stay at the table as Mam Zena told her to, but jumped up and held out her arms. It somehow gave me the push I needed. I cut loose with "Murder! Murder!" and sailed in waving my gory blade.

Mam Zena rose like a bull out of a mud wallow, knocking over the table and candles, but it was Lurette who screamed in panic, and I went for her first, snatching hold of the drifting white stuff and tripping her so she hit the floor with a fine solid thud. Then I yanked back the window curtains, and when Mam Zena came for me—she had guts—I nipped behind her and started jabbing her in the rump, just enough to keep her active. "Run!" I said, and quoted something nice I recalled from Father Clance's teaching: "Flee from the wrath to come!"

She fled. I don't suppose anyone could stick around for that kind of goosing. She couldn't run for the village, not in a purple turban and black gown. She plunged away into the next room, and I had to let her go—also get out before she returned with some better weapon than mine. But meanwhile Lurette had scrambled up, and she did dart outside for the village, bare-ass, with no more sense than a spooked pullet. She was screeching "Murder! Rape! Fire!" I never did find out which one she thought it was.

I shoved the purse into Mam Byers' wobbling hands. At least she had seen Lurette unveiled; more than that I couldn't wait to do. I think she was cursing me as I ran out. Anyone is likely to be cursed for smashing a make-believe.

I went down those corn rows to the woods about as fast as I've ever covered the ground, still brandishing my tomato-killer without knowing it. Sam said later that if he hadn't known me real well he'd've been worried about my condition, but as it was he just wondered why so much feminine influence didn't do more to bring out the softer side of my nature. Vilet said she loved me too.

On the way back to the cave, after I'd told them the whole amazing story of my girlhood, I stopped in my

146

tracks. "Balls of the prophet!" I said—"I still got that dollar."

"Oh snummy!" says Vilet, and Sam looked grave. We sat down on a log to reason it out. "It'd be a sin if you'd meant to keep it, but you just forgot, didn't you, Spice?"

"Ayah. Stracted like."

"Sure," she said. "Still I suppose we got to ask Jed what's the mor'l thing to do."

Sam said: "Jackson, I'm half-way wishful we wouldn't do that. I think it'd be mor'lly good for us to solve this 'ere by our lone. Frinstance, could young Jackson, or you, so't of go on keeping it without meaning to?—naw, naw, sorry, I can see that wouldn't be just right. More the kind of thing I'd do myself, being a loner by trade."

"Of course," Vilet said, "them people was frauds and cheats—oh my gah!" She jumped up, spilling part of the loot she'd been carrying and brushing her worn old green smock as if she'd sat down on fire-ants. "What if that old bag put a witchment onto the clo'es?"

"Nay, Jackson, I b'lieve she couldn't at this distance. Besides, them spirit-maker frauds a'n't real witches. Know what?—they be more so't of quackpot religioners, and you know how Jed feels about such-like. He wouldn't want no dollar going to support heresy, now would he?"

"That's a fact," said Vilet. She was brushing the dirt off the clothes she'd flung away and folding them back into a nice bundle, her hands knowing and sensitive with the cloth. She had a good deal of faith in Sam's judgment when Jed and God weren't around.

"And look at it thisaway too," Sam said; "young Jackson heah has been under a bad strain—nay, I don't mean about was he a boy or a girl, I think we got that clear enough, he's as much a boy as any other jackass with balls, but what I mean, he done good work back theah, savin' a poor lady from sin and folly whiles we was just resting our ass in the brush. I won't say his hair has turned white from the exper'ence, because it ha'n't, but my reasoning is, he's *earned* that 'ere lucky dollar—a'n't that so, Jackson?"

"Ayah," said Vilet. "Ayah, that's so."

"Kay. But now, old Jed, he lives on what we got to call a higher mor'l plane—right, Jackson?"

"That's right," said Vilet.

"So if we was to tell a bang-up white lie about our boy leavin' the dollar theah, it'd spare Jed sorrow, right?"

"It would do that," Vilet said. "Still—"

"It'd keep the wheels of progress greased, *I* think."

"Ayah," said Vilet. "Ayah, that's so."

"Account of when you live on a higher mor'l plane, Jackson, you got no *time* to figger where ever' God-damn dollar went—if the Lord don't keep you hopping the unrighteous will."

"Well," said Vilet—"well, I guess you're right . . ."

We stayed at our cave hideaway a few weeks more, while Vilet fixed up clothes for us. She carried a little sewing-kit, and I never tired of watching her skill with it. Scissors, thimble, a few needles and a spool or two of wool thread; that was it, but Vilet could clutter up the landscape with marvels in a way I've seldom seen surpassed. The huge white smock provided three good freeman's white loin-rags for us and part of a shirt for Jed; then Vilet was able to cobble up the rest of that shirt and two more for Sam and me out of the remainder of poor Miss Davy's wash. That done, she cussed and sweated some, remodeling the yellow smock for herself, asking the woods and sky why in hell Lurette couldn't at least have grown a pair of hips. She dissected it, however, and added whatsits here and there; when she was done, it fit her cute as buttons.

We went on making plans. It seems to be a human necessity, a way of writing your name on a blank wall that may not be there. I can't very well condemn it, for even nowadays I'm always after doing it myself. We planned we'd go a few miles beyond that village and then strike out boldly on the Northeast Road. I with my real Moha accent would do most of the talking, we planned, but we'd all need to be rehearsed in a good story.

Jed and Vilet, we decided, had better be man and wife —they would be truly anyhow when they got to Vairmant. We four were all quite different in looks, but Vilet claimed she could see a kind of resemblance between Sam's face and mine, and was so positive about it I began to see it myself in spite of the obvious differences—Sam stringy and tall with a thin nose, I stocky and short with a puggy one. "It's mouth and forehead," Vilet said, "and the eyes, some. Davy is blue-eyed but it's a darkish blue, and yourn mightn't look too different, Sam, if you was redheaded."

"Got called Sandy when I was young," he said. "It wa'n't never a real red. If I was a real red-top like young Jackson, likely I could've busted my head through stone walls some better'n I have, last thirty-odd yeahs."

"Now, Sam," said Jed, "it don't seem to me, honest it don't, that God'd give a man the power to put his head through a stone wall except in a manner of speaking, like. Unless of course the wall was crumbly, or—"

"It was a manner of speaking," said Sam.

After kicking it around a good deal, we worked it out that Sam would be my uncle and Vilet's cousin. Jed had a brother in Vairmant who'd just recently died—born in Vairmant himself but moved away when young to Chengo off in western Moha. This brother bequeathed Jed the family farm and we were all going there to work it together. As for me, my parents died of smallpox when I was a baby, and my dear uncle took me in, being a bachelor himself, in fact a loner by trade. When my Pa and Ma died we were living in Katskil, although originally a Moha family, from Kanhar, an important family, damn it.

"I dunno," said Jed. "It don't seem just right."

"A manner of speaking, Jackson. Besides, I didn't mean them hightoned Loomises from Kanhar was aristocrats— just a solid freeman family with a few Misters. Like my own Uncle Jeshurun—Kanhar Town Council give him a Mister, and why? Account the taxes he paid on the old brewery is why, the way it was in the family couple-three generations—"

"Wine is a mocker," said Jed. "I don't want you should go imagining things like breweries."

"Damn-gabble it, man," Sam said, "I'm merely telling you what they done, no use telling a story like this'n if it don't sound like facts. *I* didn't start the durn brewery, more b' token if you ever hear tell of making wine in a brewery I want to know. It was great-gran'ther sta'ted it, understand, and she run along like a beaut till my Uncle Jeshurun, him with the wooden leg, took to drinking up the profits."

Jed studied away at it, not happy.

"You mean he done that too in a manner of speaking?"

"He sure as hell did."

"I mean, it just don't seem to me, Sam, that people are going to believe it. About drinking up a whole brewery. He couldn't do it."

"I can see you didn't know my Uncle Jeshurun. Leg was hollow, Jackson. Old sumbitch'd fill it up at the brewery after a long drunken work-day, take it home and get plastered, carry on like crazy all night long. He didn't just die neither, not my Uncle Jeshurun. He blowed. Leanin' over to blow out a candle, forgot whichaway to blow being drunk at the time, or rather he was never sober. Breathed in 'stead of out, all that alcohol in him went whoom—Jesus and Abraham, Mister, not enough left of the old pot-walloper to swear by. Piece of his old wooden leg come down into a cow pasture a mile away. Killed a calf. My Aunt Clotilda said it was a judgment—onto my uncle, I mean. Still, if it hadn't happened he might've had to leave town."

15

We started the day after the clothes were finished; we may all have been afraid of coming to like that cave too much. At least Sam and I felt—without ever saying so—that we would always be in some way on the move; and for Jed and Vilet the farm in Vairmant colored the future with the warmth of a lamp.

It's odd how little thought we gave the war, after being out of touch with the world more than three months. We wondered, and made some idle talk of it, but until we were on the move again, and the days were flowing out of June into the golden immensity of midsummer, we felt no urgent need to learn what the armies had done while we were so much at peace. They could have passed and repassed on the Northeast Road, Skoar could have fallen, we'd never have known it.

The border wars of that time and place were a far cry from what I saw and experienced of war later on in Nuin. In the Moha-Katskil war of 317 I don't suppose there were ever more than two thousand men involved in a battle: mostly feinting and maneuvering, armies shoving for position along the few important roads, avoiding the wilderness as much as they could; the forest ambush those Katskil men tried outside Skoar was unusual. As it happened, I saw no more of that particular war. It was settled by negotiation in September. Katskil ceded a trifling port and a few square miles of ground on the Hudson Sea in return for the town of Seneca and a thirty-mile strip of territory that gave them a long-desired access to the Ontara Sea. Brian VI of Katskil had other smart reasons for demanding those treaty terms—I didn't appreciate this until long later, when I was with Dion in Nuin and getting my own inside view of high-level politics. That thirty-mile strip cut off Moha from any land approach to the western wilderness; so if that unknown, probably rich region is ever tapped by land routes it will be a matter between Katskil and Penn—Moha needn't bother.

When we left our cave I was concerned with the more ancient war of human beings against other creatures who desire to hold a place on earth. I felt, superstitiously, that we had been having it too easy. In our hunting and fishing while we stayed at the cave we'd encountered nothing more dangerous than a few snakes. Once a puma started out of the brush ahead of Vilet and me and took off in almost comic terror. One night we smelled a bear, who might have got troublesome if he could have climbed after our supplies. It was only a black of course, as we knew from the prints we found in the morning. The great red bear is so scarce in southern Moha one never really expects to see him. North of Moha Water he is plentiful enough, one of the chief reasons why that great triangle of mountain country bounded by Moha Water and the Lorenta Sea remains mostly unexplored.

I find it strange, in reading Old-Time books, to notice

what unconcern the people of that age felt about wild beasts, who were scarce and timid then, overwhelmed by human power and crowding and incredible weapons. Man in that time truly seemed to be master of the earth. In our day, a few hundred years later, I suppose he's still the most intelligent animal at large, even still likely to succeed if he ever learns how to quit cutting his brother's throat, but he is under a slight cloud. We might become masters of the world again, but perhaps we ought to watch out for a certain cleverness I've noticed in the forepaws of rats and mice and squirrels. If they'd develop speech and start using a few easy tools, say knives and clubs, it wouldn't be long before they were explaining the will of God and rigging elections.

Gunpowder is forbidden by law and religion,* and this may be just as well, since guns to make use of it are forbidden also by lack of steel, lack of a technology capable of designing and making them, and nowadays by a lack of belief that such instruments ever existed. Since a vast amount of fiction was produced in Old Time, it is wonderful how the Church today can explain away anything unwelcome in the surviving fragments of the old literature by calling it fiction.

We had to remember that some bandit gangs were said to roam the wilderness, though eastern Moha did not have too bad a reputation that way—southern Katskil is lousy with them. Such outlaw gangs care nothing for laws or national boundaries; they live off the wilderness, and now and then take a toll from the villagers. Hardy souls—they kill off their old people, rumor says, and admit new members only after savage ordeals. The gangs are small—in Moha or Nuin you never hear of one attacking a town of

* The prohibition appears thus in the Book of Universal Law, 19th edition (the latest I believe) published at Nuber in 322: "It is and shall be utterly and forever forbidden on pain of death by whatever method the Ecclesiastical Court of the district shall decide, to manufacture, describe, discuss, create any written reference to, or in any manner whatsoever make use of the substance vulgarly known as Gunpowder, or any other substance that may by competent authorities of the Church be reasonably suspected of containing atoms."

—Dion M. M.

any importance, or a large caravan,† even for hit-and-run raids. The Cod Islands pirates are popularly supposed to have started from a bandit gang that got clever with small war vessels and then almost grew into a nation. In Conicut I heard the tale of a whole army battalion routed by a couple of dozen bandits who decided the soldiers were encroaching. The story was set in the rather distant past; the begging street-corner storytellers preferred a version in which the bandits had trained teams of black wolves to help them, under the command of a most unusual character named Robin or Robert Hoode.

I knew some unhappy moments when we went away from the cave for good that morning. For one thing I saw few opportunities ahead for playing with Vilet; with the feeling of losing her, I even imagined a little that I was in love with her—her common sense would have taken care of that if I had spoken of it; since I didn't, my own brains were obliged to handle it, and did so moderately well. Leaving the cave was in many other ways a good-bye—

I know: so is any moment. What happened to the jo who was breathing with your lungs five minutes ago?—or don't you care?

We spent most of the day in cautious travel through the woods, until we could be sure we were well beyond the village that had been so good as to furnish us with respectable clothes. I did wish I might have learned what happened there when Lurette crashed in shrieking about rape and fire, but I never shall know, so what the hell, write that story yourself if you're man enough. Then we altered our course, and came out on the Northeast Road at a place where it was climbing a considerable rise, the longer and steeper part still ahead of us. The sun stood behind us in the west; everything lay in a hot bright hush. We saw a few lines of smoke here and there in the south, distant villages. Nothing was moving on the road as we stepped out there in our good clothes—white freeman's

---

† Any group of travelers who follow the roads and keep together for safety is called a caravan. The word seems to have been used a little differently in Old Time.

—Dion M. M.

153

loin-rags, decent brown shirts, Vilet in the remodeled yellow smock. And we heard nothing—no voice, no creak of cart-wheels, no sound of cattle or horse or man. On the other side of the rise ahead of us there could be anything.

Jed asked: "What day is it?"

Bedam if we knew. I said Thursday, but Jed wasn't sure, and started fretting that he might have let a Friday morning go by without special prayers. He was for having them then and there by the roadside, but I said: "Wait, and hush the clack a minute—I want to listen."

I wanted something more than listening. I motioned them to stay where they were, and stepped a short way up the road to get clear of the human smell and study the breeze. Even then I wasn't sure.

I wished something human might join us, but the hot afternoon was quiet as a sleep. It happens Jed was right —the day was a Friday, the day God is said to have rested from the labors of creation, when all but the most necessary travel is forbidden or at least frowned on. And the war was still a fact, discouraging travel, though nothing in the summer air could make you think of it. Finally, it was late enough in the day so that any sensible traveler would be thinking of supper-time behind stockade walls.

When I rejoined the others Sam asked me carefully: "Did you catch it?"

"I think so." I saw Jed didn't understand. "We best move right on, keep close together till we come to a settlement. I think I smell tiger."

How steep was that sunny slope, how very long! I wanted us to climb it quietly, and Sam urged that too, but Jed thought best to pray, and when Sam asked him to avoid making noise and save his breath, Jed merely looked forgiving and went on praying, no help for it.

The road approached the illusion of an ending at open sky. You may see that, wherever a road mounts a hill, and you think of a drop into nothing or of sudden dying. If I could return to that strip of road today and travel it without alarm, without the faint ammoniac reek of the thing that was somewhere near us unheard, I suppose it would seem an ordinary climb. It was not so steep that a single ox couldn't have hauled a heavy cart to the summit—I dare say that was the standard of adequate road-building in most parts of Moha. Yet whenever the smell seemed to strengthen, or I imagined some hint of tawny motion among the trees at my left, I felt like a wingless bug climbing a wall.

Nor was that piece of road so very long, really—a quarter-mile perhaps, or less. The sun was not noticeably lower when we reached the crest of the rise—we did reach it, all four of us alive—and looked down, and saw a thing that might save us from the tiger, or might not.

We saw a stockaded village, the walls fairly well made, and it stood boldly at the edge of the road, no hideaway wilderness thing but civilized, respectable, important in its own right. It lay far enough below us in the valley so that we could see all but the north end of it, which was hidden by forest growth coming close to the stockade. We saw behind the palings a graceful church spire, the usual design of an upright bar rising from the wheel, and an orderly array of rooftops, including those of quite a few two-story dwellings. Next to the road, on our side, was a generous area of cleared land, with corn-patches, and black spots that showed where they maintained guard-fires at night to keep the deer, bison, woods buffalo and small creatures from ruining their plantings. Far down, yes, nearly half a mile, and for much of that distance, until we reached the corn planting, there would still be trees and brush creating a mystery at our left.

As we began the descent, Jed Sever would not look to either side of the road, not into the trees nor away into the lovely sunshine and green slopes of the southern side. He trusted instinct to place his feet for him, and looked upward toward his God, asking forgiveness for the sins of all of us. He was asking also that if the beast should strike it might take him first and not one of his friends—for he, though an even more wretched sinner perhaps beyond hope of salvation, was nevertheless more prepared in his mind for judgment and the wrath to come. "And if it be thy will," he said, "let their sins be upon me, Abraham chosen of God, Spokesman, Redeemer, and not upon them, but let 'em be washed clean in my blood* forever and ever amen."

Jed also tried to motion poor Vilet away from him to the other, probably safer side of the road, walking himself nearest to the forest cover, the sweat pouring from his forehead like tears. His big hands swung idle with no look of readiness for sword-work.

I can remember the distress his prayer gave me, in spite of my own fear and alertness. It seemed to me, especially in my new and bewildering acquaintance with heresy, that if there was one thing above all I could let no one else carry for me, it was my sins. Today I can discover no sin in anything except cruelty and its variations, and this for reasons that have nothing to do with religion, but on that day I was yet a long way from such opinions.

As we continued down the other side of that hill, the tiger scent diminished. I think it was some shift in the barely perceptible currents of the air. He was present but he did not strike. We moved on down the road—passing the forest cover at our left, reaching the corn plantings, passing them, approaching the open region and the village gate, and he did not strike.

From within the village came the sweet jangling of triple bells. Often they are made of the best bronze from Katskil or Penn—the Church can afford it—and the makers try to cast each group so that it will sound a major triad with the fifth in the bass. The third, struck last, floats in the high treble toward a tranquillity resembling peace, and the overtones play with a hundred rainbows. These village bells were announcing five o'clock: *"Time to quit work and pray and have supper."*

---

* The Holy Murcan Church apparently adopted the fantasy of vicarious atonement from Old-Time Christianity with one curious modification. According to the modern creed, any saintly man, not only Christ or Abraham, can take on himself the sins of others if the Lord agrees to the deal. Like modern believers, the Christians of Old Time seem never to have felt anything repellent or atrocious in the doctrine that a man could get a free ride into heaven on the suffering and death of another. The parallel to primitive god-killing rituals was of course noted only by scholars.
—Dion M. M.

156

Jed's prayers ended rather flatly. I still glanced behind me as often as I had done when we had the trees at our left, but the tiger did not strike, not then. I did not see him, not then.

The main gate of such a village is usually open during daylight hours so long as a guard is present, but not on Fridays, when it's considered best to keep folk within God's easy reach. So that day the ponderous log gate was shut, but I looked through a chink in the log slabs and saw the guard in his grass-thatched shelter, not asleep but mighty restful, sprawled on his cot with a leg hooked over a raised knee and his policer cap let down over his eyes. He bounced up fast enough when I hollered: "Hoy!"

Well, there are some things you do and say when approaching a strange village, and some you don't. I'd goofed in my usual rapid way, too rapid for Sam or Vilet to stop me, as I knew when the guard came swaggering with his javelin up and ready. I whispered to Sam: "Make like a Mister, think you could?"

He nodded, and was in front of me by the time the guard got the gate open and started bawling me out for disturbing the Friday peace—no manners—what ailed me anyhow?

Sam said: "My man, I apologize for my nephew's hasty speech. I am Mister Samuel Loomis of Kanhar, more recently of Chengo, and the lady is my cousin. This is her husband, Mister Jedro Sever, also late of Chengo but a legal resident of Manster, Vairmant—you may address her as Mam Sever when apologizing for your own bad manners." Sam had hitched his shirt slightly so that the hilt of his sheathed knife was visible, and he was rubbing a horny old thumb back and forth across the end of the bone knife-hilt, and looking down at that thumb along his thin nose, not as if he gave a damn, just sad and patient and thoughtful.

"Mam, I—Mam Sever, I—Mam, I—"

That could have gone on a long time. Sam cut it short by asking delicately: "Is the apology satisfactory, Cousin? And Jackson?"

"Oh, quait," says Vilet, hamming it some but not too much, and I mumbled my own snooty graciousness, and

Sam flipped him a two-bit to quiet the pain. Sam had startled me as badly as he had the guard—I'd never guessed he knew how to talk in that hightoned way. Maybe Dion could have found fault with it, but not I. He put me in mind of what I'd imagined about some of the fine old historical characters I'd learned of in school, in what they called a Summary of Old-Time History. Honest, Sam was just as cool and grand and you-be-damned as the best of them—Socrates, Julius Caesar, Charlemagne, or that splendid short-tempered sumbitch, I'll think of his name in a minute, who r'ared up and whipped the Barons and Danes and Romans and things out of merry England and clear across the Delaware before he was satisfied to let them go —Magnum Carter, that's who it was.

"Well, man," said Sam, "can we find anything in this village in the nature of decent accommodations?"

"Oh yes, sir, the Black Prince tavern will have nice rooms, I know the people and—"

"How far is Humber Town from here?"

"About ten miles, sir. Oughta be a coach from Skoar going through to Humber Town tomorrow—once a week, Saturdays, and always stops here of course, though with the war and all—"

"Ayah, the rest of our caravan is waiting on that coach at the last village where we stopped, some piddlepot hole in the ground, I didn't trouble to learn its name."

"Perkunsvil," said the guard with solemn pleasure. In a jerkwater village you can hardly go wrong by blackening the reputation of neighboring dumps.

"I guess. We got tired waiting for it. What town is this?"

"This is East Perkunsvil."

"Nice location. There's tiger up yonder, by the way— see many hereabout as a rule?"

"What! No, sir, that can't hardly be."

Jed spoke for the first time, and reprovingly: "Why not, man? Brown tiger's like unto the flame of God that burneth where it will."

The guard bowed, the way you'd better do at hearing anything with a holy sound, but he was stubborn. "Sir, I can tell you, brown tiger never comes anear this town. We don't ask God's reasons for the special mercy, it's just so."

I've noticed every village needs a unique source of pride. It may be a claim that nobody in the village ever had smallpox, or all babies are born with dark hair, or the local wise woman's aphrodisiacs are the aphrodizziest within forty miles—no matter what, so long as it provides a mark of distinction. In East Perkunsvil I suppose tiger hadn't come over the stockade within the memory of the oldest inhabitant, so the village was sure God had arranged that he never would. Sam bowed nicely and said: "You be rema'kably favored, doubtless a manifestation."

"Yes, sir, it may well be." He was downright friendly now as well as respectful. "Yes, sir, lived here all my life, and that's twenty-six years, never even seen the beast."

Vilet said: "Look up yonder then!"

Now chance never plays into *my* hands that way. If I'd said that, the brute would have been well out of sight before any head turned. And I guess Vilet had never got many breaks of that kind either, for later when we four were settled in our rooms at the Black Prince she had to go over it three or four times, and each time it put her in a warm sweet glow: " 'Lookit up yonder then!' I says, right smackdab on the very *second* I says it, and wasn't his o' face just like a fish and you a-squeezin' it to get the hook out?—oh snummy!" And she'd bounce and slap her leg and tell it again.

I must have turned when she spoke as quickly as the others, yet I felt as if my head were moving against a resistance, unready to behold a thing that all my life I had feared and in some way desired to behold. Smelling the beast on the road, I had known him from catching that smell once before in the hill country west of Skoar. It's ranker than puma smell, seems to hang heavier in the air. At that earlier time it had seemed just not quite right for puma, and I had climbed a tree and spent a long night there shivering, smelling him and thinking I did but not once hearing or seeing him. In the morning I'd wobbled down and found his enormous pugs in a bare spot of earth, deep, as if he might have stood there some time observing me through the dark, old Eye-of-Fire, and maybe thinking: *Well, let's wait till Red gets a mite bigger and fatter ...*

159

Now, I saw him.

A short way down from the crest of the hill we had descended lay a high flat-topped rock, thirty feet from the road on the open side, across from the forest. The top was slightly tilted, away from the road, so that when we walked past, it had looked like a simple edge, nothing to tell of the slanting platform. Had he watched us go by, or only just now arrived there? Maybe he had been not hungry, or restrained by the fact there were four of us. Maybe he knew my bow meant danger. I imagined him amusing himself with false starts, quivering his hindquarters, playing and enjoying the cat-game of delayed decision and finally for his own reasons allowing us to proceed. Now, following his immediate whim, he stood tall, and I saw him in remote dark gold against the deepening midsummer sky.

He gazed down toward us, or more likely beyond us. He must have known or sensed that the distance was too great for the flight of an arrow from my bow, if he was experienced in such things. He turned on his high rock with no haste at all, flowingly, to stare in another direction, off to the south across the valley, perhaps indifferently observing the smoke of other human places.

He sat down and raised a curled paw to his mouth to lick it and rub it comfortably over the top of his head. Then he washed his flank, and up went a hind leg catstyle so he could lean down and nuzzle his privates. He lost balance comically because of the slope of the rock, righted himself with a comedian's ease, and lay down and rolled with his feet in the air. And when he tired of that he yawned, and jumped down, and strolled across the road into the woods, and for a while he was gone.

16

That was the first time I had seen the inside of a village. Since then I've seen more than I can plainly remember, for when I was with Rumley's Ramblers we visited one after another throughout Levannon, Bershar, Conicut, Katskil, more than a year in Penn; the atmosphere and the people may vary a great deal, but the general pattern is much the same in all the nations. Wherever you find them, such villages are designed for one fundamental purpose, to give a small human community a bit of safety in a world where our breed is no longer numerous, not rich and sleek as in Old Time, not wise, and not very brave.

They are usually laid out in a square, in some location where a stream crosses fairly level ground. The drinking water comes from the upstream end, and the rest of the stream is regarded as a sewer—saves digging. Main Street, running down the midline of the village, will be rather wide and ordinarily straight, so that when you enter by the front gate you look all the way to the one in the rear; the other streets will be narrow except for the area, not always called a street, formed by a cleared space just inside the stockade. Often a green occupies the center of the village facing Main Street, with the usual equipment— bandstand, whipping post, stocks, pillory and maybe a nice wading pool for the children. You'll notice one block of houses better than the rest—bigger yards, maybe flower-beds along with the necessary vegetable patch, even a slave hut out back next the privy demonstrating that the family owns a servant or two instead of renting them out from the slave barracks on the downstream side of town. On that downstream side, beside the barracks, you can find what the people sometimes call the "factory," really a warehouse, for the village industries—home weaving, baskets, cabinet-work or whatever. The policer station will be on that side, and the jail, the public stable, the legal whorehouse, blacksmith shop, probably the baiting-pit if the village can afford to maintain one; and there will be several blocks on that side where the houses sag together in dejection, the drunks would rather sleep it off in their front yards than indoors, being independent free-men, and if any pigs from the prosperous neighborhood go hunting garbage on that side of town they prefer to travel in pairs.

In between those extremes stand the middle-class blocks, where the ideal is a harking back to Old Time, with all the houses exactly alike, all yards and gardens exactly alike, all the privies exactly alike with small cres-cent windows of precisely the same size emitting the same flavor of socially significant togetherness.

Now that I'd made Sam a Mister in my hasty way, he couldn't get out of it, and figured he might as well r'ar back and enjoy it. He was still carrying himself like God's favorite adviser when we blew in at the Black Prince. As a result, the weedy ancient in charge of the flea-bag fawned all over us, charging twice the normal rate for two of his best rooms which would have done credit to a hog farm anywhere; Sam wanted to bargain, but was afraid it might damage the picture of ourselves as slightly im-portant nobs. He said later that this was a considerable grief to him, descended as he was from a long line of il-lustrious chicken-thieves. He caught up on the bargaining later, with Rumley's Ramblers. I've heard Pa Rumley say that Sam could have bargained the beard off a prophet, and he meant Jeremiar himself, which was near-about the finest praise Pa Rumley could give any man. You know how attached prophets get to their beards, and Jeremiar was a vigorous type, who worked up such a thriving trade in woe and lamentations that the opposition finally crowded him into an ark and sent him down-river among the bull-rushers to get rid of him.

A group of pilgrims from up north had already got the very best rooms at the Black Prince, overlooking Main Street; our two were second best, I guess, each with a slit

162

of window looking north; I would have hated to see the worst. Beside the rickety cots they called beds the walls displayed dark smears telling of collisions between the human race and one of its closest, sincerest admirers. And over all things like a saintly benediction lay the smell of cabbage.

In a bedbug, so far as I understand him, there is not a trace of mirth or loving-kindness. Even their admiration for humanity is based on deep-seated greed. They have intellect, to be sure—how else would they know the exact moment when you're about to fall asleep, and select that moment for a stab? Dion says bugs go by instinct. I asked him: "What's instinct?" He said: "Oh, you go to hell!" Then Nickie flung in the statement that when you do something p'ison clever without a notion of what it's all about, that's instinct. But I still think they have intellect, and they probably brood too much until it curdles their dispositions, for note this: I never met a bug who showed me a trace of liking or respect, no matter what I'd done for him. Contempt is what they show, contempt. I've known a bug to stare me in the eye with my gore dripping from his jaws, and anyone could tell from his vinegary face that he was comparing me with other meals in the past and finding fault with everything—too salt, too gamy, needing more sass, something. He wouldn't have complimented me if I'd spiced my ass and put butter on it. So I contemptify 'em right back. I hate bugs. Damn a bug.

The vital philosophic point I'm trying to ram home through the fog of your incomprehension is this: If the human race should perish completely, what would become of the bedbug? I'm sorry I cursed them. We must return good for evil, it says here.

In the evolutionary sense, they must have grown up with us, and now they can't get along without us. Fleas are all right. Fleas don't need us. They'd eat anything, even a tax-collector. But the bedbug is our dependent, our responsibility. We made him what he is. He cries to us: "Strive on, lest we too perish!" Let us therefore*—

* I put him to bed, Nickie—he'll be all right in the morning.

—Dion.

* * *

I was about to digress anyway, before I began to notice how the fermented essence of an attractive grape that grows wild here on the island Neonarcheos has a curious side-effect, namely intoxication. According to the best information I can get together, that was last night; this is the following morning, somewhat late—any time now I expect to begin thinking that I shall live.

Captain Barr returned yesterday, which made it one of the days we celebrate, after sailing futher than he had intended. He was driven partly, he says, by a reluctance to believe what he was finding out.

There's no longer any doubt that this island where we have settled is the smallest and most westerly of the archipelago that in Old Times was named the Azores. The islands—smaller and differently shaped of course because of the rise in sea level—are all accounted for where the old map says they should be. And nowhere in all the group could Captain Barr discover any token of humanity. Goats, wild sheep, monkeys; on one island the men glimpsed a pack of what looked like wild brown dogs chasing a deer. Birds were everywhere, and in a bay where the *Morning Star* anchored, enormous sea snakes were playing in the shallow water, creatures I can't find described in any of the old books. Never a human figure, never any smoke against the sky. In the night hours at anchor, never a light on land, nor any sound but insects and frogs and night birds, and the talk of breakers on the sand. In the best natural harbors, jungle grows to the water's edge, hiding the debris of whatever men might have built there in Old Time.

Our ancient map shows shipping and air lines converging at this obvious way-station between Europe and the Americas. We know there had to be developed harbors, airports, towns.

No bomb would have fallen here in what John Barth calls the "one-day explosion." Very few fell anywhere, he says, and those were later called "accidents" by the surviving governments—he adds that the obliteration of twenty-odd million New Yorkers and Muscovites could perhaps be considered a "fairly major accident." Perhaps in these islands destruction came from the plagues that followed the war. John Barth wonders in his pages how many of the plagues were directly man-made and how many the result of viral or bacterial mutations, and comes to the reasonable conclusion that nobody can ever know. Or it may have been, here in the islands, the longer, quiet, almost orderly extinction of sterility, natural deaths exceeding the scanty births, in a population so long used to being taken care of by advanced technology that it could no longer look after itself, until eventually, somewhere, an old person died among the weeds with no one to scratch out a grave.

After all, in our own homelands, many non-human species died out from one cause or another. I have never seen a bluebird.

*　　*　　*

Those pilgrims were a pleasant crowd, in the care of a gentle willowy priest. He had long yellow hair that would be ready for a bath any day, and a homely mild face. His nose appeared to taper in the wrong direction because the tip was small and the space between his milky blue eyes quite wide, so the total effect was mousy. I liked him. When a man's wearing a floor-length shapeless priest's robe it's hard to tell whether he's tiptoeing, but Father Fay did seem to be, anyway there was a tittupy up-and-downness in his walk, and a flowing lift of his pretty white hands at each step, and most of the time a bright mousy deliberating smile. The pilgrims all respected him, even including the ten-year-old boy Jerry, who gave Father Fay a bad time not from any disrespect but just because ten-year-olds are like that.

I noticed Jerry even before we'd entered the Black Prince. The pilgrims were coming away from the church as we approached the inn, an orderly line with Father Fay doodle-diddling along at the head of it, and Jerry had somehow managed to get down at the tail without his Pa or Ma noticing. So what does he do but fall further back and cut monkeyshines in his pretty white Pilgrim's robe, a wavy warplume sticking up at the back of his head that the angels themselves couldn't comb flat. First he sticks out his rear and goes humping along imitating a poor old lady who's one of the pilgrims; then he straightens, and hikes his robe all the way to his navel, and proceeds bare-ass in a fine rendering of Father Fay's tiptoe, with a heavenly smile gleaming among the freckles and his little pecker flipping up at every step like a tiny flag in the wind. Terrible sacrilege, but I remember even Jed couldn't help chuckling.

They were bound for Nuber the Holy City, like almost every pilgrim group you were likely to meet west of the Hudson Sea; their all-white garments along with Father Fay's black would identify them as far off as you could see them, and no soldiers of either side would dare trouble them.

After Sam and I turned in and tried to settle ourselves for sleeping, as Jed and Vilet were doing in their room, I heard Jerry getting a bath. His Ma had evidently insisted on the inn help's bringing up a tin tub and water, just for that purpose. He was enjoying it, and raising all kinds of hell, roaring and splashing and making damn-fool remarks —you'd have thought the poor lady was trying to wash a bandit king. Then Pa came up from downstairs; there was a moment's fearful quiet, a fine solid whack on a wet backside, and from there on Jerry was being an awful good boy.

But as for Sam and me, after the first few attempts at sleep the cots were simply too war-torn and bloody for any use. We gave up and spread well-shaken blankets on the floor, hoping the hostile forces would lose enough time searching to give us a little rest.

The scent of tiger must have been thick in the air that night before we heard him roar. The heavy midsummer dark was trilling and jangling with the noise of insects and frogs, but I heard few other voices—no fox or wildcat was sending any messages abroad. At the inn, with other thick smells around me, I could not pick out the tiger's reek, but I felt his presence. I saw him repeatedly as he had looked on his rock in the late sunlight, and I knew he was out there in the dark, perhaps not far away.

166

When he did speak at last, even the insect noises briefly hushed, as if each witless clamoring thing had winced in the shell of a tiny body feeling a *What-was-that?*

His roar is blunt, short, harsh. It does not seem very loud, but has intense carrying power. It is never prolonged and he does not soon repeat it. Maybe he roars in order to frighten the game into a betraying shudder. The roar is too all-penetrating, too deep in the bass, too much a pain and quivering in your own marrow, to give you a true knowledge of his location. When I heard him that night he could have been half a mile away, or in the village itself strolling down one of the black streets in massive calm and readiness to destroy. I stole to the window, silently as though even inside this building a noise of my own could endanger me. Sam's voice came out of the dark: "Sounds like the old sumbitch a'n't too far off." I heard him shift and brace up on his elbow, listening to the night as I was.

The tiger did not speak again, but in the next room beyond the closed door I heard Vilet suddenly say: "Oh, Jed! Oh—oh—" and there was the rhythmic squeak of a cot, and a thumping as a wooden frame beat against the wall; for a moment or two I also heard Jed groan like a slave under the lash, and Sam said under his breath: "I'll be damned."

It was soon quiet again in there, at least no sound penetrated the doorway. Sam came over to the window and presently murmured: "Cur'ous—I didn't think he could."

"Just once, Vilet told me. Just once, with that Kingstone whore he talks about so often."

"Ayah, told me the same." I felt him watching me kindly and speculatively through the dark. Then he was leaning out the window, his dimly starlit face gazing down at the lightless village. "Little cunt been taking care of you, Jackson?"

"Ayah." I suppose my dull embarrassment was a result of orphanage training, a mixture of sour prudery and piety, that sticky mess with which the human race so often tars and feathers its children.

Sam and I could hear a child crying, away off somewhere in the village, probably frightened by the tiger's roar; it was a persistent helpless whimpering that a wom-

167

an's tired and kindly voice was trying to soothe. I heard her say—somewhere, bodiless, as if the words hung in the dark—"Ai-yah, now, he can't get you, baby . . ."

Getting dressed in the morning, it occurred to me, as I had suspected during dinner the night before—fast-breaking Friday dinner after sundown—that it wasn't all fluff and candy, being advanced from a bond-servant yard-boy, the lowest object above a slave, to the nephew of a long-legged Mister. I'd achieved this wonder myself, sure, but remembering that was small comfort. There are heavy penalties for impersonating an aristocrat, as heavy as the penalties on a bond-servant for wearing a freeman's white loin-rag. I had to burble to Sam about the remarkable powers of a plain white rag, but he was more interested in the practical side than in the dad-gandered almighty philosophy of it. "It comes to me, Jackson, you got to watch some of the God-damn *little* things, like not picking your nose nor wiping it so loud on the back of your hand, at least not whiles you be eating. Occurred to me last night at supper, but I didn't want to say anything with them pilgrims chomping away right at our elbows."

"Well," I said, "I had a snuffle and besides, I've seen gentlemen do that, at the Bull-and-Iron."

"There's an old saying, rank got its privileges, but a Mister's nephew a'n't all that important, Jackson. And another thing—language. Frinstance, when they brang in that God-forgotten smoked codfish last night, which smelt as if a whole pile of moldy ancestors had sudden-like gone illegitimate, why, an aristocrat would've told 'em to take it away, sure, and he'd've said something real brisk that they'd long remember, *but*—with a gang of holy pilgrims at the next table, Jackson, he wouldn't r'ar back and holler: 'Who shit all over my plate?' He just wouldn't, Jackson."

"Sorry," I said, sulky—I hadn't slept much. "I didn't know pilgrims didn't have to."

"It a'n't that, Jackson. In fact I b'lieve they do, in a manner of speaking. But the dad-gandered almighty thing of it is, you got to consider your influence on the young, the plague-take-it young. You take that 'ere young Jerry. Next time his Ma tells him to eat something he don't fancy, ask yourself what he's going to do and say—if his Da a'n't within hearing. Just ask yourself."

"See what you mean. A'n't he a pisser, though!"

"Ayah." But I couldn't sidetrack Sam when he was feeling educational. "And you take farting, Jackson. Common people like what you and me really be, we don't pay it no mind, or we laugh or something, but if you're going to be the nephew of a Mister you got to do a little different. If you let a noisy one go, you don't say: 'Hoy, how about that?' No, sir, you're supposed to get a sadful-dreamy look onto y' face, and study the others present as if you'd just never imagined they could *do* such a rude thing."

Vilet and Jed came into our room then, and Sam let up on me. Jed looked all wrong, dark under the eyes as if he hadn't slept, with a tremor in his big clumsy hands, and so Vilet of course was troubled about him. Sam was inquiring politely about the bugs on their side of the wall when Jed, not listening, crashed into it saying: "I prayed all night, but the word of God is withheld."

Vilet said: "Now, Jed—" fondling his arm while he just stood there, two hundred pounds of gloom, a great harmless bull somehow beat-out, no fight in him.

"I'd ought to leave y' company," Jed said—"a hopeless sinner like I be." He sat on my cot heavily and wearily; I remember seeing him look down and appear dimly surprised to find his hand resting on my sack, on the bulge of the golden horn, and he lifted the hand away as if it weren't right for him to touch a thing that had come from a holy hermit. "And the Lord said: I will spew thee out of my mouth—'s what he said, it's somewhere in the book. And that a'n't all—"

"Now, Jed, honey thing—"

"Nay, hesh, woman. I got to call to y' mind what the disciple Simon said: The Lord spoke but I turned aside. Remember? It's what he said after he'd denied Abraham and the Spokesman a-dyin', a-hangin' on the wheel in the Nuber marketplace. 'And they brought Simon to the marketplace—' that's how it goes, remember?—'to the marketplace, and Simon said: I do not know this man. And they questioned him again, but he said: I do not know this man.' And then you remember, afterward, when Simon was

169

put to the rack in the Nuber prison, he said them other words I mentioned: The Lord spoke but I turned aside. I'm like that, friends. The Lord spoke but I turned aside. The lighning'll find you too if I'm with you when it strikes. I don't wish to leave you, the way you been good to me and us real friends right along, but it's what I ought to do, and—"

"Well, you a'n't *about* to," said Vilet, crying—"you a'n't about to account we won't let you, not me or Sam or Davy neither."

"I a'n't fit," Jed mourned. "Wallowing in sin."

"Well you *didn't* then," said Vilet. "All's you done was put it in a couple minutes, and I loved it, I don't care what you say, a holy man like you does it, it *can't* be no sin, it a'n't fair, anyway if it was sin it's me that oughta burn—"

"Oh, hesh, woman! Your sins'll be forgiven unto you account your heart is innocent, but me I got the whole God-given knowledge of good and evil, for me there a'n't no excuse no-way."

"Well, come on down to breakfast before you make up your mind about things."

"Oh, I can't eat anything."

Still crying, Vilet said: "God damn it, you come on downstairs and eat breakfast!"

17

The pilgrims were already at breakfast, bacon and eggs no less, and thanks to the savings Vilet carried in her shoulder-sack, we were able to afford the same. She insisted on it too, with Jed in mind, for she subscribed to a theory very popular among the female sect, that ninety per cent of male grief originates in an empty stomach.

The dining-room at the Black Prince was so small you

could have spat across it, and by the look of the walls many former guests had. There were only five tables. The doddery innkeeper had a couple-three slaves for kitchen help but evidently didn't trust them to wait on table, and did it himself. Recalling the good-smelling, orderly, spacious Bull-and-Iron made it easy for me to despise this tavern, just like an aristocrat.

The Bull-and-Iron, now, was a fine brick building at least a hundred years old. The story was there'd been a lot more clear land around it when it was built, and Old Jon's father had sold off most of it for a big profit after the new stockade went up to accommodate the city's expansion, and land values rose. The Bull-and-Iron had fifteen guest bedrooms upstairs, no less, not counting the one for Old Jon and the Mam, nor Emmia's where I'd left my childhood. Downstairs, there was that grand kitchen with two store-rooms and a fine cellar, and the taproom, and the big dining-room with oak ceiling-beams fourteen inches wide and charcoal-black, and tables to seat thirty people without crowding. Maybe I remember the cool taproom best of all, and the artwork above the bar, a real hand-painted picture just full of people in weird clothes, some riding astraddle of railroad trains and others herding automobiles or shooting off bombs, but all sort of gathered around in worship of a thundering great nude with huge eyes and the most tremendous boobs, like a shelf under her chin. She sat there with her legs crossed showing all her immense white teeth and being adored, so you knew it was a representation of the Old-Time pagan festival of St. Bra. The painting carried the Church's wheel-mark of approval, or Old Jon couldn't have displayed it. The Church doesn't object to art-work of that type in the proper place, so long as it's decent and reverent and shows up Old Time as a seething sink of scabrous iniquity.

But the Black Prince at East Perkunsvil—hell, the only mural was a spot in the dining-room wall the size of my head where plaster had fallen and nobody'd ever possessed enough alimentary tubing to replace it. The only respectable mural, I mean. They had the other kind of course in the privy out back. One of our Old-Time books mentions some of that kind found in the excavated ruins of Pompeii: the style hasn't changed a bit.

There were seven of the pilgrims, the usual number because it's thought to be lucky—Abraham had seven disciples—there are seven days in the week—and so forth. East of the Hudson Sea, pilgrim bands often head for places less sacred than Nuber, usually shrines that mark where Abraham is said to have visited and preached, and those groups, especially in Nuin, are larger, often lively and full of fun. Itinerant students join them for mischief and company, and a crowd like that can stir up a really joyous commotion on the roads. The band at the Black Prince was different—unmistakably a religion-first company, all except Jerry, and from the look of his parents you got the impression that he would take some holiness aboard when they got to Nuber, or else. The other pilgrims of the group have become almost faceless for me in memory—three women and one man. One of the women was young and quite pretty, but all that comes back is an impression of timidity and a very white face; I think one of the two older women was her mother, or aunt.

"The ruins belonging to the Old-Time city named Albany, which we saw a few days ago, near the modern village of that name," said Father Fay, "are the last we shall behold on our way to Nuber." He was doing all right with the bacon too, for such a gentle man. "This region we are now traversing is said to have been mostly farm-land in ancient pagan times, so no great monuments are to be expected." Father Fay's baritone was rich, smooth, surprisingly strong; it made me think of warm honey dripping on a muffin, and when I looked again, bugger me blind if they didn't *have* muffins, real corn muffins, and fresh out of the oven, for I saw the vapor rise when Jerry opened one up and slapped the butter to it. "The truly mountainous territory of Katskil was left in ancient days, as now, more or less in its natural state."

"I've often wondered, sir," said Jerry's father, "what is the source of Katskil's prosperity. One doesn't expect to see wealth in a mountain country."

Sam murmured to me: "Levannon—tell by his accent."

"It's their southern provinces," said Father Fay. "Rich

farming land south of the mountains, all the way to the mouth of the great Delaware River, which I believe marks the entire boundary between Katskil and Penn . . . My conscience troubles me. I fear I may have neglected to point out some of the more instructive features of the Albany ruins, for I am always deeply moved by the sad splendor—" Jerry was full of squirm, and watching me in a weird warm pop-eyed way—"and also the dignity to be sure, of the antique ruined architecture seen at low tide —ah, and by moonlight too!"

"Ma," said Jerry.

"We were fortunate to have moonlight. One feels often the guidance of a heavenly power, on these pilgrimages."

"Ma!"

"That door over there—you know perfectly well—"

"Naw, I don't have to. I want—"

"Jerry, the Father was speaking."

"It's all right, Mam Jonas," said Father Fay with practiced patience. "What does the boy want?"

"Ma, I don't want my muffin." (Why would he?—he'd already had two, one when nobody was looking except me.) "Can I give it to him over there?"

Damned if he didn't mean me. I felt my face get as red as my hair, but that subsided. I half-understood the little devil wasn't just being a gracious prince favoring a humble subject: he actually liked my looks, and was drawn to me in one of those fantastic surges of childhood feeling.

"Why," said Father Fay, "Mam Jonas, this is the beginning I spoke of, blossoming of a truly Murcan spirit." And Father Fay sent me a wink in a helpless manner, an open request to play along while Jerry got it out of his system.

The introduction of official sanctity embarrassed Jerry and cramped his style, but he brought over the muffin very prettily anyhow, as the whole gathering blinked at us. Ever wake up in a cow pasture and discover that the critters have formed a ring around you and stand there gazing and gazing, chewing and chewing, as if you'd put them in mind of something, they can't think what but it'll come to 'em in a minute? I took the muffin and did my best thank-you, and Jerry retired, face blazing, speechless. The pilgrim lady who I'm certain was somebody's aunt said: "Aw, isn't

173

that sweet!" Jerry and I could then exchange glances of genuine sympathy because it wasn't practical to murder her.

"In viewing such ruins," said Father Fay, "and *especially* by moonlight, one feels always, one says to oneself, ah, had it only been God's will that they should be a little wiser, a little readier to heed the warnings. Such marvelous structures, such godless, evil beings!"

"Father Fay," said the pretty white-faced young woman, "is it true they made those great buildings with the flat tops out there in the water for—uh—human sacrifices?"

"Well, Claudia, of course you must understand the buildings were not then submerged."

"Oh yes, I know, but—uh—did they—"

"One is unhappily forced to that conclusion, my dear Claudia. Often indeed—" I think he sighed there and had another muffin; I'd finished mine under Sam's stern and reverent eye—"often those buildings are no mere squares or oblongs but have the definite shape of the cross, which we know to have been the symbol for human sacrifice in ancient times. It is saddening, yes, but we can find reassurance in the thought that there is now a Church—" he made the sign of the wheel on his breast, so we all did— "which can undertake the true study of history in the light of God's word and modern historical science, so that its communicants need not bear the burden of old sins and tragedies and the dreadful follies of the past . . ."

Out in the hazy hot morning, perhaps still within the forest shadows but certainly very near our weak man-made stockade, the tiger roared.

Everyone in the dining-room—except Jed, I think— looked first at Sam Loomis when that shattering voice outside struck at our marrow. They were probably not even aware of doing it, and surely had no conscious idea that he could protect them; they simply turned like children to the strongest adult present in the emergency. Even Vilet; even Father Fay.

Sam stood up and finished his breakfast tea. "If'n it's all right with you," he said, to a spot of air between Father Fay and the doddery inn-keeper, "I'll step out for a look-around." I don't suppose they were asking even that much of him, so far as they knew. He strolled to the door and stepped outside.

I said—to whom I don't know, maybe Vilet—"My bow's upstairs." Jed was standing then, ponderously, and he shook his head at me. I don't think he had once spoken since we came down to breakfast. I couldn't wait to understand him but darted up to our room. When I returned with my bow and arrow-quiver, they were all milling around a little. I saw Jed talking to Father Fay in an undertone, the priest listening in a distracted, unbelieving way, watching his pilgrim flock also and shaking his head. I couldn't hear what Jed was saying. Jerry was at the front window, his mother hanging on to him or he would have been outdoors. Father Fay frowned at my bow as I slipped past him and Jed, but did not speak nor try to stop me when I ducked out after Sam.

Sam was just standing out there in the sunny and dusty street with a few others. I saw occasional wind-devils rise and whirl and die as a sultry breeze hurried by on no good errand.

The elderly village priest—I heard one of the villagers call him Father Delune—had come out of the rectory by his little church, and was in the street craning his neck to look up at the bell-tower. He called—to us, I guess, since we were nearest—"Yan Vigo's going up for a look-out. We don't want too many in the street. It may be illusion." His voice was good, windy and amiable and edged with fear under control. "They should stay within and pray it be illusion." Sam nodded, but he was watching me. At that moment a weedy boy climbed out through a louvered window of the bell-tower and hauled himself up astraddle of the wheel-symbol, a good ten feet in diameter, out of which the spire rose. He would have been some thirty feet above ground, and could probably see over the stockade on all sides of the village. I remember thinking Yan had it pretty good.

When I reached Sam I knew he wanted to send me back inside. But I had brought my bow; he would not wound me that way. He just said: "Hear what I do, Jackson?"

I did hear it, from near the gate, where the guard who had admitted us the day before was again posted. He was in light military armor today, helmet, bronze breastplate, leather guards on thighs and crotch—all no particular use against tiger except to the extent that it made him feel better. He was carrying a heavy spear instead of a javelin —that did make sense—and his honest hands transmitted to the spear-head a tremor as if he were in the peak hours of a malaria; but he was staying at his post. The sound Sam meant was a light clicking or chopping noise, combined with blasts of soft snuffling breath like a giant's bellows working on invisible fire. You've probably noticed some little house-cat quivering her jaws on nothing when she sees a bird fly overhead out of reach or light on a high branch and scold her; along with the jaw motion there's a small hoarse cry, a kind of exasperated explosion not quite spitting or snarling, simple frustration, tension of the thing she would do if the bird could be grasped. But this noise outside the stockade gate was more than fifty feet away from Sam and me, and I heard it plainly.

The gate guard called: "I can see the shadow of him through the cracks!"

Sam said: "Jackson, you—suppose you go tell them people to stay inside."

I moved back uncertainly toward the inn doorway as Father Delune walked soberly by us to the gate. I had to stop, look back, learn what the priest meant to do. He stood right against the logs, praying, his arms spread out as if to protect the whole village with his dumpy old body, and his voice rang musically in the hot street. The breeze that clearly brought me the words also brought the smell of tiger. "If therefore thou art a servant of Satan, whether beast or witch or wizard in beastly form, we conjure thee depart in the name of Abraham, of the Holy Virgin Mother Cara, in the name of Saint Andrew of the West whose village this is, in the name of all the saints and powers that inhabit the daylight, depart, depart, depart! But if a servant of God, if thou art sent to exact a penance and all but one of us unknowing, then grant us a sign, servant of God, that we may know the sinner. Or if it must be, then come among us, servant of God, and his will be done! Amen!"

Yan Vigo's voice floated down with a break in it: "He goin' away!—maybe." His pointing arm followed the motion of the tiger who had evidently come from near the palings into the range of Yan's vision. "Standing out in the road, Father! It's a male, an old male."

"Depart! In the name of Abraham, depart!"

"Got a dark spot on the left, Father, like the one come onto Hannaburg last year . . . Just standing there."

Then—so much for my errand—Jed came out of the inn, and Father Fay with him, and though I mumbled something neither seemed aware of me. Vilet was back in the entrance staring after Jed, and the white clothes of the pilgrims made a shifting cloud behind her. Father Fay spoke plainly then: "No, my son, I cannot consent, cannot bless such a thing, and you must not interfere with the duty of my flock, which is to pray." Then all the pilgrims —Jerry and his father and mother, and the white-faced girl, and the old people, were coming out in the street, and rather than be stopped by me I think they would have walked through me if I hadn't stepped aside.

"Father," said Jed, "if you will not, then I must ask this other man of God." And he walked up to the gate, to Father Delune, passing Sam as if he didn't know him.

Vilet called to me: "Davy, he don't hear a thing I say. Don't let him do it, Davy!" Do what?—I didn't know. I felt as if we were all moving about in a fog, no one hearing the others—if little Jerry over there in his white robe quit his vague grinning and said something to me, I'd only see his mouth open, I'd hear nothing except the echo of the tiger's roar and that wet chopping of teeth.

Yan Vigo shouted down again: "He goin' west side. Can't see—Caton's house cuts me off." For that boy up there on the church tower it was probably the biggest day in a dull life; you could hear the fun in him like dance music the other side of a door. I was near enough myself to childish thinking to read the envy in Jerry too as he looked up at the tower.

Father Delune came away from the gate, listening to Jed. For a few minutes we made an aimless huddle there in the street—Father Delune, Sam, Jed, myself, and a nameless man from down the street. I saw no one who suggested an active hunter, let alone a Guide. I could look down the entire length of Main Street to its far end, where a smaller gate faced the wilderness. The Guide's house should be outside that.

Jed was suddenly on his knees to Father Delune. "It must be so, Father! Give me your blessing to go out theah and bring him onto me, so to spare the village, and take away my own burden of sin. I won't be afeared no-way if I can go with your blessing."

Sam said harshly: "You be no more a sinner than any other man hereabouts."

But Father Delune checked him with a crinkled hand, raised to ask the rest of us to be still and let him think. "It's not fitting," he said. "I never heard of such an action, it's not in reason. There may be sinful pride in it—my dear son, who art thou?"

"Jed Sever's my name, a grievous sinner all my life, and who's to say I a'n't brung the tiger onto the village account of me? Father, bless my going out to him. I want to die in the hope of forgiveness at the throne of Abraham."

"Nay, but—why, we all sin, from the moment of birth, but I can't think thou'st been so—so—" and Father Delune looked curiously, anxiously at Sam, even at me, wanting some kind of support from us I think, but hardly knowing what we could give nor how to ask for it. "Sin, Jed Sever—it writes itself in the face, one may say. You strangers, you be friends of this man?"

"My cousin by marriage," said Sam, "and a good heart, the best, Father, but over-zealous. His conscience—"

"You don't understand," said Jed. "Don't heed him, Father. He can't see the sin in my heart. The beast won't go till I do. I know that, I feel it."

"Why," said Father Delune—"he may have gone a'-ready, and no need of all this."

"Where's your Guide, sir?" Sam asked.

"Away. Three-day hunt with our best men."

The tiger roared, somewhere beyond the jumble of old houses on the west side of the village. I heard a rattling, a dull vibration, a crunch of cracking wood. Sam shouted up to the church tower: "Is he in, boy?"

"Nah." Yan Vigo's voice had gone high as a girl's. "Think he caught a claw in the bindings and something bust, but it a'n't down." Vigo meant the fastenings that held the stockade logs; they were leather thongs that had been bound there wet and allowed to dry, shrinking to a tight fastening. Only prosperous cities can afford iron bolts or wire. "He's circling around to the back gate."

"Father, bless me and let me go!"

I screwed up my own courage to speak: "Father, I'm a dead shot with this bow. May I try from one of the roofs?"

"No, son, no. Wound him and he'll destroy the village entirely."

That wasn't true and I knew it. A tiger is only a great cat. A cat suddenly hurt will run and not fight at all unless cornered or unable to use his legs. But I also knew it was useless to instruct a priest. I saw Father Fay's pilgrims kneeling together in the street, in front of the church. In spite of common sense I made one more try: "Father, I promise you, I could place one of these in his eye, I've practiced on knotholes at fifty yards—"

It only annoyed him. "Impossible. And what if the tiger is a messenger of God? I'll hear no more of that." He asked Sam: "Is this your son?"

"My nephew, and like a son. It's no empty brag, Father. I've seen him nail a—"

"I said I'd hear no more of that! Take the boy's arrows, sir, and keep them till this is over."

Sam had to take them, I had to yield them, both of us with blank faces. The pilgrims were singing.

The hymn was "Rock of Ages," which is from Old Time, a commonplace hymn that has survived the centuries when a limitless literature of better music perished. Jerry's voice amazed me, incredibly clear and sweet—well, I had never heard a trained boy soprano, and never did again until I came to Old City of Nuin, where the Cathedral trains them. At the second verse I heard someone behind me singing too—Vilet, my good warm Vilet still crying but singing through the sick snuffles and more or less on pitch. I couldn't sing, nor did Sam, who stood near me holding the arrows loosely in the hand nearest me.

Down at the far end of the street, above the rear gate which stood as high as the rest of the palisade, about eight feet, down there in the shimmering heat of summer morning we understood there was a face watching our human

179

uncertainties, tawny-pale, terrible and splendid. Across the light gold there were streaks of darker gold, as though between him and ourselves some defensive obstruction still cast the shadow of its bars—and to his eyes, some shadow on our faces too?

We had known it would come; maybe we had all known it would find us, in our various ways, unready. The pilgrims were all aware of that face at the end of the street, I think, but their music did not falter. Vilet stopped singing, however; I saw Jed lift her hand gently away from his arm, and then he was moving a step or two down the long street. At that moment the tiger's face dropped out of view.

"He's gone," Vilet said. "See, Jed—he's gone, I tell you." She must have known as we all did that the tiger had not gone. Jed did not look now like a man crazily determined to rush into danger. He was smiling, with some sort of pleasure. He had gone only a little way beyond the kneeling, singing pilgrims. Father Delune was praying silently, his old hands laced together below his chin; I think he was watching Jed, but did nothing to detain him.

Nor could I, nor Sam. We were all in a way paralyzed, alone, not hearing each other, watching the empty spot at the end of the street, the blind gray-brown of weathered logs and tropic green of forest beyond. Jed's face was pouring sweat as it had done the day before on the road. A tremor shook his hands and legs as if the earth were vibrating under him, yet he was going on, slowly, as one sometimes journeys in the sorrowful or terrifying or seeming-ludicrous adventures of a dream.

The tiger soared in an arc like the flight of an arrow, over the gate and into the village.

The tiger paused for a second, his eyes surveying, calculating lines of attack and retreat, measuring with a cat's wonderful swift cleverness. Jed made no pause but walked on clumsy and brave, disregarding or not hearing the two priests who now called after him in horror to come back. Jed was holding his arms spread wide, as Father Delune had done when praying at the front gate, but Jed seemed more like a man groping for direction in the dark.

The tiger ran flowingly toward us along the hot street, not in a charge at first, but a rapid trotting run with head

180

high, like a kitten advancing in sheer play, mimic attack. I suppose he could not have expected to see a human being walk toward him with those queer forbidding outspread arms. He rose on his hind legs in front of Jed and tapped at him with one paw. The motion seemed light, playful, downright absurd. It sent Jed's massive body twisting and plunging across the street to crash against the gatepost of a house and lie there at the foot of it disembowelled, in a gush of blood.

The tiger did charge then, a tearing rush so swift that there was time to hear a woman scream only once; then I saw the green fire of his eyes blazing full on us while his teeth fumbled an instant and closed in Jerry's back. Jerry's mother screamed again and lunged at the beast with little helpless hands. A swing of his head evaded her without effort. He was trotting off down the street the way he had come, head high again, Jerry's body in his jaws seeming no bigger than a sparrow's. He was over the gate and into the wilderness, the woman silent but tearing her pilgrim's gown to slash at her breasts and then beat her fists in the dust of the road.

I had snatched one of the arrows from Sam's hand. I remember having it on the string when the tiger was running away down the street, and a black thing crashing against me which was Father Delune snatching my arm so that the arrow flew useless over the rooftops. He may have been right to do it.

Moments later Sam and Father Fay and I were with Vilet, who was fumbling at Jed's body as if there were some way she could make it live. "Mam Sever," Father Fay said, and shook her shoulder, and glanced back at the other woman who needed him—but Father Delune and the older pilgrim women were helping Jerry's mother into the church. "Mam Sever, you must think of yourself."

She crouched on her heels glaring up at us. "You could've stopped him, the lot of you. You, Davy, I *told* you to stop him! Oh, what am I saying?"

"Likely we are all to blame," said Father Fay. "But come away now. Let me talk to you."

Sam's hand on my shoulder was taking me away too. We were in some partly enclosed place, the doorway of a shop I think, and Sam was talking to me, bewildering me more than ever, for it was something about Skoar. He shook me to get me out of my daze. "Davy, will you listen once? I'm saying it was just near-about fifteen years past, and one of them so't of average places—"

"You said 'Davy.' "

"Ayah, one of them medium places, not fancy but I mean, not so bad neither, can't fetch back the name of the street—Grain—no—"

Part of me must have been understanding him, for I know I said: "Mill Street?"

"Why, that was it. A redhead, sweet and—nice, someway, nothing like them beat-up—"

"So God damn you, you flang her a little something for your piece and walked out, that what you mean?"

"Davy, a man at such a place—I mean, you don't anyhow get acquainted before you're obliged to go, nor the girl she don't want to know you, come to that. And still and all, maybe you get to know as much as you do in some marriages, I wouldn't wonder." He would not either let go my shoulders or look at me, only staring over my head, waiting for me. "I been married—still am, come to that. Wife down Katskil way that damn-nigh talked me to death. But the little redhead at that Skoar place—I mean, half an hour of one night and then it's 'On your way, fella!' —and me with never a notion I could've left a package behind. Which maybe I didn't, Davy, we wouldn't ever know for sure. But I was thinking, I'd like for it to be so."

"I dunno why I spoke to you like that."

"Still sore?"

"No." I have never cried since that morning, but I'm inclined to think that, once in a great while, tears are useful to the young. "No. I a'n't sore."

"So supposing I am your Da—is it all right?"

"Yes."

18

The January rains fall more steadily here on the island
Neonarcheos than any we remember. For two weeks we
have been unable to work at clearing new ground. Nickie
is uncomfortable in pregnancy and so is Dion—I mean
that like me he is trying to give birth to a book, setting
down what he can recall of the history of Nuin before it
fades or becomes distorted in his mind. We do have paper
now: the brookside reeds yield a course product to our
primitive methods that takes our lamp-black ink reasonably well.

From lamp-black my mind jumps to lamps and lamp-oil.
When the casks of seal oil we brought in the *Morning Star*
have been exhausted we'll have no more. We can worry
away at native vegetable oils and waxes, and when our
sheep have increased there will be tallow to renew the supply of candles. Lambing time in a couple of months will be
a major event. Of course, Nickie and I seldom object to
going to bed early.

Lamps, candles, animal husbandry—we have enough
problems on that level to keep our people busy a hundred
years, if there's that much time. There may not be. We
needn't suppose that because we were the first in centuries
to sail the great sea, our enemies won't follow—soon, perhaps. They have as much courage of the simple kind as we
have, or they couldn't have won the war of the rebellion in
spite of their superior numbers. True, it called for the
imagination of Sir Andrew Barr, the knowledge in old
books forbidden, the orders and protection of Dion as
Regent of the richest and strongest of the nations, and the
labor of many hands, to create the schooner *Hawk* and
later the *Morning Star*. Salter's victorious army had no

such vessels to send in pursuit of us, no men capable of handling them. However, given the spark, they might build something capable of venturing out, if the Church would relax her prohibitions.

We carried with us all designs and working drawings made by our own people. The lower grade workmen had at first only a dim idea of what sort of ship they were engaged in building, but some of them will remember details, and all of them will talk if Salter wants them to. The Holy Murcan Church, up to now, has hogtied itself in this matter, committed to the doctrine that it is morally wrong, offensive to God, to sail out of sight of the land except by what fishermen call the relay system—one vessel holding in sight another which keeps the land within view. Even Dion could not have safely ordered such a ship as the *Hawk* without explaining to the churchmen that it was needed to overawe the Cod Islands pirates, and would never sail beyond those islands. And the *Morning Star*, he told them, was needed as a replacement—well—hm-ha— an insurance against a possible regrouping by those Satanic men.

It's not merely that it would annoy the Almighty to see a man damn-fool enough to fall off the edge of a flat earth; there's the larger doctrine, that any important kind of curiosity is wrong, a doctrine all religions of the past have been obliged to uphold as the only practical defense against skepticism. Still, theological obstacles are notoriously movable: if the Church knew we were safely ashore out here, a handful of escaped Heretics living in hard work and happiness on islands that could be valuable, I am certain that God's blessing on a punitive expedition could be almost instantly arranged.

Our military intelligence learned beyond a doubt that ex-pirates from the Cod Islands were scattered through Salter's army. They don't know big ships but they know the sea; in the old days before 327, when we had to knock them apart as a nation, their lateen-rigged skimmers may have ventured farther than we suppose. They could handle a large vessel for Salter if he ever managed to build one.

The Cod Islands people—the pirates and their women and slaves and followers—worshiped Satan, the old dark horned god of witchcraft ancient and modern. I'm sure they still do secretly. Likely they considered Old Horny a logical opponent of the existing order of things which they had no reason to love—besides, orgies are fun. The fact that Dion as Regent refused to permit wholesale burning of the Cod Islands people after the pirates' surrender was one of the most serious grievances the hostile section of the Nuin public, as well as the Church, held against him. The islands were taken over by respectable fishermen's guilds and added to the province of Hannis; the rank and file of outlaws and exiles and their women and children were allowed to disperse under a general amnesty. Since we hoped to abolish slavery altogether in Nuin and weren't inclined to set up a mess of new jails, I don't know what else in logic we could have done. I remember warning Dion that most of the pirates were not going to be grateful more than five minutes, and that the Church wasn't about to recognize any kind of mercy except its own. He knew that, but went ahead anyhow—and I suppose Nickie and I would have given him hell if he had changed his mind as a result of our cautions. Four years later, there the jolly pirates were, in Salter's army of the rebellion, ready and eager to fight on the Church's side against the man who had saved them from broiling by that same Church.

Incidentally I think Dion's insistence on amnesty instead of vengeance was the first occasion in modern times when a secular ruler has held out against Church pressure and got away with it for as long as four years. In the days of Morgan the Great the question didn't arise. Morgan was all for the Church, which was new then itself as a definite organization; he was an enthusiast, a warrior for God who could be just as happy converting a human brain as smashing it with a broadax, depending I guess on whether it showed any tendency to talk back.

And after a while, the Church may not find itself altogether happy with the Morgan dynasty ended and Erman Salter President. Salter will cancel the preliminary work we did toward getting rid of slavery; he will destroy our small beginning in the development of secular schools, and there'll be no more sacrilegious talk of relaxing the prohibitions on Old-Time books and learning. But after those matters are dealt with, the honeymoon between Salter and the Church is likely to peter out. Salter is power-hungry, and that is a disease which grows to a climax of disaster as certainly as a cancer. He respects the Church only for the material strength it derives from its power over men's minds, not for religious reasons and assuredly not for any temporal good the Church may do—(I as one of its sincerest enemies will admit that it does quite a lot). Salter is a practical man in the saddest sense of that term: a man to whom all art is nonsense, all beauty irrelevant, all charity weakness, all love an illusion to be exploited, and all philosophical questions bushwa. I know these things about him, because the fellow tried to get at Dion through me, quite soon after a humorous chance had swept Nickie and me into the presidential orbit and made us important. Salter was quite frank about the quality of his mind while he still believed I had a price. He has no convictions, religious, agnostic, atheist or any other—the religious mask is simply one of many to be worn at convenience. When his kind rules, as it sometimes did in Old Time also—sleep on your knife!

Nay, fair enough—some morning a few years from now we may see on the western ocean the approach of a small clumsy sail . . .

Yesterday afternoon Dion wandered in out of the rain with Nora Severn and told us he didn't want to be Governor. We've heard this before, and it makes certain kinds of sense, yet most of us hope he can be talked out of his reluctance. We've been kicking around a number of political ideas since at our last general assembly five were chosen to write a tentative constitution as it was done in Old Time, looking toward a day when these islands may hold a population large enough to need the larger formalities.

"I'm disqualified," Dion said, "by the very fact that I did govern in Nuin. Autocrat over maybe a million people—absurd, isn't it, that any man could be in a position like that? I would try, here, and be afraid all the time of old habits rising inside me. Davy, that day eight years ago—when you and Funny-face were sort of swept into office—I think it's eight years, isn't it?—"

186

"May Day, 323," said Nickie, and laughed a little.

"Yes. That day, why do you suppose I was so eager to hang on to you after the Festival of Fools was over? Oh, Nickie turning up when I hadn't seen her for two years and I'd even thought she was dead—of course. The little twirp was always my favorite cousin. But there was something else in it. I'd begun to distrust myself already, though I'd been Regent less than a year . . ."

I remembered the day. I often do; there's a brightness in remembering. Nickie and I were twenty, then. We had been living in Old City for two years—obscurely, because Nickie had run away from her family and couldn't bear the thought of being recognized, knowing the attempts that would be made to draw her back, and how such fuss and uproar would interfere with the work to which she was giving herself body and spirit. Her work was underground, with the Heretics, important and dangerous. Mine, for money-making, was in a furniture factory—Sam Loomis had taught me all he could of joinery when we were with Rumley's Ramblers—and my other work was to learn, to read the forbidden books under the guidance of Nickie and the Heretics who accepted me because of her, to grow up with a wider understanding of the world I had to live in. She took over, my sweet pepperpot wife, where my substitute mother Mam Laura of the Ramblers had to leave off. Well, but that day, the 29th of April, eve of the Festival of Fools which makes a joyous twenty-four hours of madness for Nuin folk before the gentler delights of May Day—that day Nickie and I were careless. It was the gaiety throughout the city, the reckless delicious urgency of a clear evening of spring, when the sky was piled high with violet-tinted clouds, and there were the street singers, and the flower-girls carried everywhere the scent of lilac.

We said we'd only go for a short walk, and keep away from the celebration and foolishness. But straying, pausing at a tavern where the beer was rather too good—oh, before long we were asking each other what harm it could do if we merely went for a few minutes to the Palace Square to hear the singing, and maybe watch from a safe place when the King and Queen of the Fools were chosen. And yet Nickie has told me since then that all along she had a

187

premonition we were going to be much more scatterbrained than that. I remember how as we drifted toward that part of town, Nickie was trying to determine how accurately she could steer my walking by bumping me with her hip, neither of us using hands or arms, and we arrived at Palace Square in that style—honestly not drunk, just happy.

The custom is perhaps a hundred years old, that at some time on the eve of the Festival of Fools—nobody knows the moment exactly, but it comes between sundown and ten o'clock—a boy on a white horse will ride through Palace Square with a jingly cap on his head and carrying a long whip that has a soft silken tassel at the end. He cavorts around the square sassing the crowd and being pelted with flowers; at last he flicks his whip at one man and one woman, choosing them to be King and Queen of the Fools for the next twenty-four hours. They're hustled up to a throne that stands waiting on the steps of the presidential palace, and the President himself comes out to crown them. He kneels to them, with considerable ritual, not all of it comic. The custom of washing the feet of the King and Queen had gone obsolete in Dion's time, but—

It happened to Nickie and me. I ought to have foreseen it. The crowd was large, the light failing, nevertheless my lady's face must have stood out among the other pretty girls in the crowd like a diamond among glass ornaments; I was obviously her companion, and I have red hair. The boy on his white horse bore down on us, making the crowd give way so that his whip could reach us. Then the people were closing in, laughing, kind, noisy-drunk and heavy-handed, carrying us up to the throne on their shoulders. And the Regent, Dion Morgan Morganson of Nuin, appeared in his fancy dress, and seeing Nickie—frightened I know she was, rumpled by the crowd's well-meant horse-play, staring straight in front of her—Dion went pale to the lips. Presently he was ordering one of the attendants to bring the silver basin that had formerly been used in this ceremony—I too ignorant to know this was unexpected—and he washed our feet although it had not been part of the ritual for thirty years.

"And distrusting myself," said Dion—speaking here in our airy shelter on the island Neonarcheos, his arm around

188

his lovely bedmate Nora Severn, and hearing as I did how a sea wind was wavering through the warm rain—"distrusting myself, I needed you, Miranda. Later on—" he said this with something more than courtesy—"I found out I needed Davy too, and the cockeyed useful way the little devil has of looking at things and speaking out."

I was aware, on that eve of the Festival of Fools, that Dion had loved my woman before ever I knew her. It was years before, actually, for he was fifteen when she was born. Her mother Serena St. Clair-Levison was Dion's first cousin. He was often with the family, and used to carry the baby around before she could walk. Her first clear word, spoken when he was swinging her up to the ceiling, was Di-yon . . . I could not have avoided knowing it, hearing him speak her name in a helpless, explosive way, there on the steps of the presidential palace when he was holding her little brown foot in his hands. It is not, today, the love of a very young man for a child, since Nickie is not a child. It is the love of friends, and on his side, more than that. We have been able to speak of it a little, the three of us; we do not when Nora Severn is with us, though she knows of it. It is not something that could be solved by a three-marriage, as Adna-Lee Jason and her lovers have done. Dion and I are are both too possessive, and Nickie is certain that for us it would not be the answer. Nay then, how much of our human complexity is our own fault!

"I think," said Nora Severn, "that a man who knows the old dangers of autocracy, watches for them in himself—why isn't such a man better as a governor than one who might have less self-knowledge? Not that I'm urging it—you're more fun as a private citizen."

She was wearing nothing but a little skirt, like most of our girls. Blonde and delicious, you wouldn't think to look at Nora almost naked that she's an expert weaver and spinner, so deft and imaginative that some of the older women have asked her for instruction. At work, she never spends a second of waste motion, though every thin steady finger seems to possess an independent life. She is trying sculpture too, claiming to be no good at it, and has searched the island for usable clay.

"Some of the time back yonder," Dion said, "I'm afraid

189

I *liked* being His Excellency by grace of God and the Senate Regent in Our Very Present Emergency—hoo boy! The emergency was good for eight years and would still be perking if we hadn't been kicked out. I think the term 'emergency' originally meant 'until His Excellency Morgan the Third by grace of God and the Senate President of the Commonwealth shall have the gracious goodness to cork off.' But then time spun on and on, and it came to mean 'that period extending from the time your Excellency got away with it until such time as your Excellency can by grace of God and the Senate be safely booted the hell out . . .'"

* * *

We were obliged to stay in East Perkunsvil until after Jed's funeral. But for Vilet we'd have been forced to do a sneakout, for Sam and I between us hadn't anything like the money needed for the expected religious performances, yet we were thought to be aristocrats and loaded with it—dear Jed, he would have explained it was a punishment on us for lying to the guard that evening. No doubt religion had to be invented for such gentle and simple minds, and perhaps they can't get along without it any more than I can get along with it. Vilet had enough salted away in her sack to meet the expenses, and now—why, now Vilet was a pilgrim and didn't want money.

She rejoined us that frightful morning after a long private session with Father Fay, and gave Sam what Father Delune had told her would be the cost of a good ceremony, our humble way of showing God that we understood and loved Jed for the martyr he was. She told us then how Father Fay had accepted her as a pilgrim, with the prospect that she might some day become sufficiently purified to take the veil. Maybe only Father Fay could have given Vilet that much comfort and saved her, as I hope he did, for the human race. In the same degree, maybe no one but Father Delune could have helped me so nicely along the path of heresy. I wanted to suggest to him that if God was all-knowing he might be able to catch on without our blowing everything on a church performance, and, if he was

190

really all-knowing, how about asking him what the hell good Jed's martyrdom did to anyone, beginning with Jerry? I said nothing at all of course, mindful of Sam's neck as well as my own, but my religious feeling ended just about then. I have never missed it.

I felt Vilet's quiet when she talked to us after that time with Father Fay; quiet and distance, yet she didn't seem a stranger. I had never understood the hidden existence of a nun in her, cool dim sister to the warm lovable wrestling-partner who'd opened her good flesh to me many times. The nun was in charge now, staring somewhat blindly out of the face of a woman who had in the last few hours aged twenty years. I don't think she asked Sam and me what we meant to do. She lost track of her words now and then, as if following some discourse in another room. Father Fay may have given her a penance-shirt to wear—her smock looked ridgy and she moved carefully like one in physical pain. Her left eye was blinking in a tic I'd never seen before. The pilgrims were conducting a private prayer-meeting of initiation for her soon—after which, she told us, she must not so much as speak to any male except Father Fay until the penitential part of her pilgrimage was done. Leaving us, she kissed me on both cheeks and told me to be a good boy.

I saw her once again, dressed in white with the other pilgrims, at the funeral two days later. If she knew where we were sitting she thought best not to look our way . . . It seems to me now that I loved her a great deal, maybe as much as I loved Caron who is probably dead.

* * *

I remember now a decree I pronounced from that throne on the steps of the presidential palace. The evening was wearing on; they'd brought us a musky wine that went to our heads. I decreed that everyone without exception must immediately live happily ever afterward; somehow I could think of no more fitting decree from a King of the Fools.

19

After the funeral—dismal enough it was, and our Jed would have thought it finer than he deserved—Sam and I didn't wait for the coach that might go by on Saturday, but decided to chance it on foot at least as far as Humber Town.

In East Perkunsvil after the disaster I heard virtually no talk about the tiger, and not even a sidelong mention of his possible return. The village Guide brought back his hunting party the next day—sorry, angry men they were when they heard the news—and in the afternoon men went out to cultivate the corn patches with no protection but a couple of bowmen. That night also, men were outside minding watchfires, not against tiger but just to keep the grazing creatures away from the corn. Hunters and old wives and other founts of absolute wisdom agree that unless old or sickly, a tiger will attack a particular village only once in a season, and then move on. It could even be true, though I doubt it.

The senseless, accidental quality of the event was what shook and overwhelmed me, I think. Sam stood by me; we didn't talk much; he was just there, letting me be alone with myself in his presence. Nickie is the only other I've known who can do that.* When the funeral was over and we were on the road again, I was beginning to understand how if there is any order, meaning or purpose in the human condition, human beings must make it themselves.

We made an early morning start. On such a summer

---

* I will praise my love for the honey of his words—honest, Spice, it's simply a matter of keeping one's mouth shut in a pleasant tone of voice.

—Nick.

morning, a west wind running along the hills and the sun not quite risen, a freshness everywhere, a ripple of birds' music, a glimpse of a whitetail deer slipping into the daytime secrecy of the forest, the warmth of the present and the surging life of your own blood make up the whole aspect of truth—how else could it be?

Humber Town is a busy and ambitious place, too small for a city, too large for a village—say about six or seven thousand population and, to use a quaint local expression, growing all the time. On the road Sam and I chewed over a few plans but settled nothing. I still desired Levannon, and the ships. But I had been noticing how often a plan is a scribble on the wind. Sam allowed that, to keep us going, he might look up some journeyman carpentry or mason work—he knew both trades—in Humber Town. He agreed it would be safest to move over into Levannon, if there still was a war going on- by the time we reached Albany on the Hudson Sea. At East Perkunsvil the only war news they had was whispery rumors about a battle at Chengo in the west, and another on the Hudson coast a little north of Kingstone, barely outside Katskil territory.

Sam and I had not spoken at all of the relation that might exist between us. But as we were coming up to the gates of Humber Town I said: "If'n you want to be my Da and I want it thataway, it maybe don't matter if I was or wa'n't out'n the actual seed?"

"Why, that's about the way I had it lined up to myself, Davy," he said. He'd been calling me Jackson as usual that morning. "We might leave it at that . . ."

The gate guard was happy about something, which made him show uncommonly good manners for a policer. As he let us in I heard the brisk tinkle and thrill of a mandolin somewhere. Then a drum was warming up oom-ta-ta oom-ta-ta, and a flute and a pretty sharp cornet jumped in, not quarreling at all, with the "Irish Washerwoman." It was happening out of sight around a curve of the main street, not far away. Wherever the Washerwoman came from, and I believe it was Old Time, she's a grand durable quail and always welcome. "There they go!" the guard said to us, and I saw his feet were interested, and so were mine. "Best

193

damn gang ever was here. You be strangers to Humber Town?"

"I was by, yeahs ago. Sam Loomis, and this 'ere's my boy Jackson—Jackson David Loomis. Who be they, sounding off?"

"Rumley's Ramblers."

"Ayah?" said Sam. "Well, that cornet's got a power into it, but he don't blow as good as my boy . . ."

A small idle crowd was already lounging at the rail fence that bordered the town green, though no special show was going on and it was only mid-morning, when most of the townfolk would be at work. The musicians had drifted together and tuned up to amuse themselves, that was all. But nobody with ears and eyes would just walk by, not with Bonnie Sharpe cross-legged on the grass tickling her mandolin, and Minna Selig with her banjo, and Stud Dabney teasing his drum to funny stuff with his white head stuck out over it and his squabby body in a kind of crouch, like a snowy owl about to fly away. Little Joe Dulin was there too tweedling his flute, and big Tom Blaine stood back of him—far back, following a rule of his own, for Tom always insisted he couldn't make his cornet cough up a decent tone unless there was a plug of *good* tobacco stuffing a hole where a couple of teeth were long gone, which meant spitting at the end of near-about every bar; and he couldn't spit good, he claimed, unless he was free to swing his head real liberal and fair warning to the world. Uhha, Tom was there in all his glory, as Sam and I joined the other loafers to rest our feet on the rails—Long Tom Blaine pointing his crazy cornet at the sky, a man drinking music and turning his head quick as a cat to spit and drink again. Hoy, so I'm running on ahead of myself and don't care. These were people I soon began to know and love; when I touched my pen their names came tumbling out.

The green was large and nicely designed—everything appeared spacious and rather different in Humber Town, or else I'm remembering it better than it was because that was where a good time of my life began, my time with Rumley's Ramblers. The wagons made a neat square within the green; I saw the big randy pictures and strong colors all over the canvas tops and sides, and the well-fed heavy-muscled mules tethered out where they could find shade and space to move about without bothering anyone.

Rumley's was a good-sized gang, with four of the large covered mule-wagons and two of the ordinary kind for hauling gear and supplies. The covered wagons—nothing like the rattletrap vans the gyppos use—are for the gang to dwell in whether they're on the move or in camp. One long covered wagon can provide cubby-hole quarters for more than eight people with their possessions, and you won't be too cramped so long as the clothes and things—dudery, to use the Rambler word—are properly stashed away. It's a thing you learn, and once you do, why, it's rather like living on shipboard and is not a bad way to live at all.

The musicians had polished off the Washerwoman by the time Sam and I got there. The girl with the mandolin was strumming aimlessly; the other had put down her banjo, and when she caught my eye and maybe Sam's her hand went up to her black curls in that feminine hair-fixing motion which goes back to the time when (Old-Time science says) we were living in unsanitary caves and women had to pay attention to the hairdo so that the mammoth-bones they got hit with would bounce gracefully. Minna Selig was a charming bundle, but then so was Bonnie Sharpe. For some time—near six months as I remember —I could hardly focus on one without being suddenly hornswoggled by the other. They planned it that way.

The flute-player and the cornet man strolled a little way off and settled down with a deck of cards. I saw a tall broad-shouldered gray-headed woman, barefoot and dressed in a faded blue smock, come out to sit on the let-down back step of one of the big covered wagons and smoke a clay pipe in solid comfort. The white-haired drummer, the snowy owl, had quit his music too but stayed by the girls, flat on his back with an ancient flopperoo of a farmer's straw hat over his face and his drumsticks weighting it down in case a sudden wind should rise and find him disinclined to move. Stud Dabney was tremendous at that sort of thing: Pa Rumley called him the original God-damned inventor of peace and quiet. He

195

devoted such enormous thought to working out new ways of being restful that it sometimes made him dreadfully tired, but he claimed this was in a good cause, and he'd keep it up b' Jesus 'n' Abraham, no matter if it wore him out into an early grave. He was sixty-eight.

That gray-haired woman on the wagon-steps had caught my attention about as strongly as the girls. It was her calm, I think. She'd done her morning chores and was enjoying the lazy break, but it was more than that. She spread calm around her, as other people may spread atmospheres of uneasiness or lust or whatever. Well, after I had known the lady quite a while—two years later, I think, when I was past sixteen—Mam Laura remarked to me that she thought her even disposition was partly a result of her trade of fortune-telling. "You can't," she said, "predict anything downright awful to the yucks, that's obvious—bad for business even if they could take it, which they can't. But I've got an old yen after truth inside me, Davy, same as your father has. So while I dream up sugartits of prophecy to happify the yucks and send 'em away imagining they amount to something, I'm thinking to myself about the actual happenings likely to come upon 'em—and upon me, merciful winds!—this side of death. It's sobering, calming, Davy. Including the *small* happenings—I mean the ten million little everyday samenesses that leave you weathered after a while like an old rock, like me, like an old rock in sandy winds. Ai-yah, and after such thinking inside of me while I prophesy, I'm beat but sort of cleaned out too, peaceful, feel like acting nice to people for a change and mostly keeping my shirt on. Philosophy's what it is, Davy —nay, and there's another advantage of Rambler life (which I prophesy you'll not be living all your days—you have a complicated future, love, too complicated for an old woman) and that is, a Rambler woman at my age (never mind what that is) can afford a smidgin of philosophy, the way I believe a woman can't if she's running the house and trying to fathom where romance went to and what in thunderuption ails her teener daughters . . ." She was spreading calm around her that first morning I saw her, smoking her pipe and studying everyone within her view but not seeming to.

I fidgeted against the fence rail and said: "Sam, for honest—how good do I blow that horn?"

"All I can do about music is like it. Can't even no-way sing. You blow it, to me it sounds good."

" 'Greensleeves', frinstance?"

The mandolin girl had a floppy lock of brown hair that tumbled over her eyes; kay, but the banjo girl had big full lips that started you thinking right away—well, "thinking" is the word I wrote there and I hate to scratch it out. The mandolin girl was still plinking a little, but mostly they were whisper-giggling together now, and I got the notion I was being analyzed.

"Ayah, 'Greensleeves' goes good," Sam said. "Ramblers —well, they're touchy people, you hear tell. Might be a wrong tell—never talked to any myself. Prideful, that's for sure, and smart, and full of guts. Folk say they're always ready for a fight but they never start one, and that's good if it's true. They take them big slow wagons into lone places no ordinary caravan woud ever go, and I've hearn tell of bandits tackling a Rambler outfit now and then, but never did hear of the bandits getting the best of it. Every Rambler boss got a silver token that gets him across any national boundary without no fuss, did you know that?"

"No, that a fact? Hoy, that means if we was with these people we could go smack over into Levannon, wouldn't have to steal no boat and dodge the customs and so on?"

He caught my arm and swung me back and forth a little, so I'd keep my mouth shut while he thought. "Jackson, you been contemplating stealing a vessel for to cross the Hudson Sea and similar such-likes?"

"Oh," I said, "maybe I done some thinking that a'n't so big of a much. But is that a fact, Sam? They could get us across if they was a-mind to?"

"They wouldn't do it smuggling style—lose their token if they did. I've hearn tell they never do that."

"But they could maybe take us into the gang?"

He looked pretty sober, and let go my arm. "Wouldn't be a one to say they couldn't—you anyway. You got this music thing, and kind of a way with you."

"Well hell, I wouldn't go with 'em unless you did."

He spread out his big clever hands on the fence rail,

more than ever quiet and full of reflection, studying all we could see of the Ramblers' layout. One of the plain wagons was parked, blocked up with its open rear toward the fence, near where the girls were loafing, and several large boxes stood in it; that would be the selling wagon, I knew from Rambler shows I'd seen at Skoar—they'd have a pitch going there by afternoon, with cure-all medicines and considerable junk, some of it good: I'd bought my fine Katskil knife from a Rambler trader. Another wagon, a covered one, stood facing a wide roped-off area of ground, and it had an open side; that would be the theater. "In that case," said Sam, and I felt he was as nearly happy as either of us could be with East Perkunsvil so short a way in the past—"in that case I believe you might give it a go, Jackson, for I think I see my way clear to go along."

"What you got in mind?"

"Terr'ble question, Jackson, always—nay, if I'm a-mind to squeeze, worm or weasel my way into some place where I a'n't expected, I most generally do. Wait a shake." I'd been about to clamber over the fence before my nerve gave out, but just then a new man came in sight around the wagon where the gray-haired woman was sitting, and leaned against the back step to pass the time of day with her.

He wasn't actualy big—not as tall as Sam—but managed to seem so, partly with the help of a thick black shag of beard that grew half-way down his chest. The black tangle matching it on his head hadn't been cut for two or three months, but I noticed the man had his vanities: his brown shirt and white loin-rag were clean and fresh, and his hairy legs wound up in a pair of moose-hide moccasins as wonderful as any I ever saw, for their gilt ornaments were nudes, and the antics he could make those golden girls perform just by wiggling his toes would have stirred up the juices of youth in the dustiest Egyptian mummy and I mean a married one.

Sam said: "I get a feeling that's their boss-man, Jackson. Look him over. Try and imagine him getting mad about something."

I swung myself over the fence. Once over, I felt everyone watching me—the girls, the card-players, even the white-haired man from under his straw hat, and the black-bearded boss-man whose voice was still going on in a mild rumble like a thunder-roll ten miles away. "Da," I said— Sam smiled quickly, wincingly as if all pleasure were partly pain, and I dare say it is—"Da, I can imagine it, but I can't no-way express it."

"Uhha. Well, you hearn tell about the hazy old fa'mer that got so nearsighted he set out to milk a bull?"

"And so then?"

"So nothing, Jackson, nothing special except they do say he a'n't come down yet, not to this day."

I had to go over then, or not at all. My good white loin-rag helped, but crossing the immense twenty yards between me and the musicians, my knees quivered, and my hands too, as I lifted out the golden horn and let the sunlight touch it; however, the way their faces gleamed with interest and excitement at seeing the horn cleared away my jitters and left me free to be another friendly human being myself. I said: "Can I make some music with you?"

The kitten with the dangerous lock of hair on her forehead and the quail with the bedroom lips were suddenly all business and no mockery. Music was serious. Bonnie asked: "Wherever was that made? Isn't it Old-Time?"

"Yes. I a'n't had it long. I can only play a few airs."

"Bass range?"

"Nay, seems best in the middle—I know there's notes on both sides I can't play yet."

Somebody said: "Boy 'pears to be honest." I'd felt all along I was being watched from under that straw hat.

The girls paid Stud no attention. "What airs do you know?" Minna Selig asked, and I learned she possessed a bedroom voice too, but right now she was all business, like Bonnie.

"Well," I said—"well, 'Greensleeves'—'Londonderry Air'—" Minna's soft-voiced gut-string banjo immediately sang me a few small chords, and I went wandering into "Greensleeves" with of course not the dimmest notion of what key I was using, or of harmony, or of how to adapt myself to another performer. All I had was the melody, and a natural feeling for the horn, and some guts and a whole lot of good will, and a keen ear, and a tremendous admiration for the way the neat black-haired girl sat there cross-legged with her banjo and her bedroom thighs. Then right away Bonnie's mandolin arrived, laughing and crying silver-voiced; her big gray eyes played games with me— that didn't distract her from the music, for she could slay a man with those things and never need to give a moment's thought—and her racing fingers gave my playing a translucent trembling background all the way through to what I supposed was the end.

The white-haired drummer had swung his arm to beckon a friend or two. People were coming out of the wagons. The flute-player and the cornet man had given up their card-game and were just standing by, listening, thinking it over. So well was the horn responding to me, for a minute I was in danger of thinking it was my playing that drew them and not the Old-Time magic of the horn itself. When I play nowadays that may be true; it can't have been true that day, though even sweet sharp Bonnie said later on that I did better than any ignoramus had a right to.

When I had (I thought) finished the melody, Minna's hand pressed my arm to check any foolishness, and away went Bonnie's mandolin shimmering and heartbreaking to find the melody on the other side of the clouds transfigured by a tempo twice as fast and dancing in the sun. Someone behind me had brought a guitar, which now was chuckling agreeably about the fun Bonnie was having up there. And Minna was intently humming three notes very close to my ear, just audible to me, and whispering: "Play those on your thing real soft when she goes to singing. Trust your ear how and when to play 'em. We'll goof some but let's try."

Do you know, we didn't goof, much? I was ready when Bonnie's light soprano soared, and Minna unexpectedly came through with a contralto smooth as cream. Well, those girls were good and double good. They'd been making music together since they were Rambler babies, besides having a rare sort of friendship that no man could ever break up. I never knew whether they were bed-lovers. Pa Rumley was a little down on such variations, I suppose a hangover of the usual religious clobbering in childhood, so it was a question you didn't ask. If they were, it didn't turn them against the male half: I had both saying oh-stop-don't stop after a while, and they were both all the more delicious for not taking me too seriously, since we were not, as people call it, in love.

When Bonnie sang a second verse of "Greensleeves" I heard something more happen along with that guitar. Intent on making my horn do what I hoped they wanted, I felt the addition only as a flowing, sustaining chordal murmur, almost remote although I knew the singers were standing quite close behind me. All our best were there—Nell Grafton and Chet Spender and handsome Billy Truro, the only tenor I ever heard of who could also play Romeo and skin mules. And for the down-in-the-cellar thunder-pumping bass we had Pa Rumley himself.

Bonnie wasn't playing while she sang, but holding her mandolin away, her other hand on my shoulder bedam —never mind, Minna had one on my knee, and some of that was to make a romantic picture for the crowd that was increasing out there in the road, but most of it was real. Bonnie somewhere had learned to sing without too much distorting the charm of her rounded, heart-shaped face—well, with nice teeth, ravishing complexion and brilliant eyes, who'd care if she did have to let the daylight in on her tonsils for some of the big notes? And by the prettiest accident, that day she was wearing a green blouse with long sleeves—you'd have thought the whole show had been planned a month in advance, and I'm sure the yucks believed it was.

When the song was done, and she'd waved and blown a kiss to the crowd, which was stomping and clapping, even a few of them snuffling—why, didn't she grab my shirt to pull me on my feet? "C'm' on, kid!" she said—"they love you too."

There was a dizzying pleasure in it, not spoiled by my knowledge that most of the excitement was for Bonnie and ought to be. Yes, I liked it, and I was growing up, I wasn't too demarbleized—

* * *

Nickie and Dion still quarrel occasionally about correcting the places where I goof the spelling. I can't interfere much, because I did ask them to, away back when I started this book. The last time I heard them beating away at it was very recently, in fact only a few minutes ago, I can't think why. I had dozed off in the sunshine or appeared to, and I heard Nickie ask Dion how he could be sure I hadn't meant to write it that way. "Can't," he admitted, "and even if I could, why should *I* be elected to defend the mother tongue against the assaults of a redheaded songbird, politician, hornplayer and drunken sailor? Hasn't she been raped by experts for centuries past counting, ever since Chaucer made such a bitched-up mess of trying to spell her, and doesn't she still perk?"

"A heartless, mean and lazy brute," said Nickie. "I hate you, Di-yon, the way you can't even come to the aid of Euterpe who lieth bleeding in the dust."

"Euterpe—who she?"

"What! You calling me a twirp?"

"No, but—"

"I 'stinctly heard you say 'You twirp!' "

"Miranda—Euterpe was not the God-damn Muse of Spelling."

"Oh, that's right. That was Melpomene."

"Sorry-sorry, she was the Muse of Tragedy."

"So all right! So English spelling always was a tragedy, so what other girl could handle it, so don't give me all that back talk or you'll wake up Davy."

I'd just perfected a theory of the origins of English spelling, so I woke up officially to share it with them. You see, there was this ancient gandyshank in the dawn of history who had a nagging wife and an acid stomach and chilblains, but English hadn't been invented, which left him in the demarvelizing position of being unable to cuss. However, the people in charge of politics had passed a revelation to make the alphabet and then chopped it into sticky chunks and passed them around so there'd be enough letters for everybody; so when the old jo's wife yakked or his feet hurt or his convictions rifted up on him, he'd snatch the alphabet chunks and heave them at the side of a cliff, the only form of cussing adapted to those early days. Centuries later some scholar with a large punkin head and very small bowels of compassion discovered the cliff and invented English right off whiz-pop just like that. But by then all the combinations a decent man would spell had washed off in the rain or the crows had et them.

Nickie asked: "How'd old Cliffbottom's wife come to nag and yak so if English hadn't been invented?"

Not a bit demongrelized, I told my wife: "She was slightly ahead of her time."

20

While "Greensleeves" was still being applauded I heard the black-beard rumble at us: "Put the lid on, kids. They look ripe for Mother." And as I was wishing I had a clue to what he meant, he said to me carelessly, pleasantly—I might have been underfoot for years and he so used to me he hardly saw me—"Stick around, Red."

I gulped and nodded. He slouched over to that wagon that held the boxes. The banjo girl pulled me down to sit beside her again and slid a friendly arm around me. "That's Pa Rumley," she said. "Next time he speaks to you you say 'Uhha, Pa.' 'S the way he wants to hear it is all. And don't worry, I think he likes you. I'm Minna Selig, so what's your name, dear?"

Hoy! That was demortalizing if you like. I found out soon enough that Rambler people call each other "dear" all the time, and it doesn't necessarily mean sweethearting, but I didn't know it then, and she knew I didn't. Close to my other ear, the little devil with the mandolin said: "And don't worry, I think Minna likes you. I'm Bonnie Sharpe, so tell *me* your name too—dear."

"Davy," says I.

"Oh, we think that's nice, don't we, Minna?"

Yes, they really worked me over. Well, but for the girls and their mild mischief and warmth and good humor, the end of "Greensleeves" might have been the end of my courage: I might have gathered the rags of my dignity around my shoulders and fled back over the fence with no more word even to Sam about what I wanted most in the world, which was to be accepted by these people and stay with them on their travels as long as they'd have me.

Pa Rumley standing in the back of that wagon flung up his arms. "Friends, I hadn't meant for to give you this here message of good tidings till later in the day, but you being drawed by our music—and our kids love you for the nice hand you give 'em—why, I'll take it as a sign to speak a few words, and you pass 'em on to your dear ones. Open up that gate and gether round, for lo, I bring hope to the sick and lorn and suffering—draw nigh!"

It was a pleasant custom in practically all villages and middle-sized towns that had no bigger park, to lend the Ramblers the town green for the duration of their stay, as a camp-site and show area; townfolk wouldn't normally intrude unless specially invited. I'd broken the rule. I think the reason why the girls said nothing about it was my natural-born goofy look, which often does wonders for me. The yucks opened the gate now at Pa Rumley's invitation, and drifted in, shy, and with the yuck's invariable anxiety to watch out against swindling—much good it does him. There were twenty-odd men and half again as many women gathered around the wagon, aggressively dough-faced, wanting to be convinced of something, it didn't much matter what. I saw Sam had strolled in with them. He stayed in the rear; when he caught my eye over a flock of bonnets and broad straw hats he shook his head slightly, which I took to mean that he had something cooking I'd better not disturb.

"There you are, friends, step right close!" A man would give a lot to own a voice like Pa Rumley's, big as a church bell but able to go soft as a little boy whispering in the dark. "This here is going to be a blessed day you'll long remember. You seem to me like fine intelligent souls, responsible citizens, men and women who've kept the fear of God in their hearts and evermore prayed and done their share. That's what I'll say to myself whenever I think of Humber Town, and good Mayor Bunwick who let us have these fine accommodations, and done so much for us—no sir, folks, Ramblers don't forget, never believe it if you hear they do. My friendship with your Mayor Bunwick, and the Progress Club, and the Ladies' Murcan Temperance Union—this is a memory I'm about to cherish all my days." As for Bunwick, the old fart certainly wasn't there at that time in the morning, but a number of his ratty cousins undoubtedly were, to say nothing of the ladies—besides, Pa always said that if you set out to kiss an ass you might just as well kiss it good. "Now, friends, you must have seen how this world is a vale of tears and mis'ry. O Lord, Lord, don't Death on his white charger go day and night raging and stomping up and down amongst our midst?—well, gentlemen hark! Why, it might be there a'n't a one of you except the children, God bless 'em, and maybe even some of them, that a'n't been bereavered already by the grim reaper. And sickness—yes, I'm a-mind to talk to you about the *common* sorrows, them that must come soon or late to one and all. They a'n't fancy things— step in a little closer now, will you?—oh no, nobody makes up stories about 'em, nor sad songs, but I say to you a man laid low by sickness, he's gone, folks, just as sure as a hero done to death in battle for his b'loved fatherland, amen, it's a fact."

He gave them time to look around at each other wise and serious and agree that it was so. "Friends, I tell you there do be some sorrows that can't never at all be healed except in the ev'loving hand of God and by the tooth of time that heals the blows of fate and dries up the tears of the wayworn, and gently leads, and allows the grass to grow green over lo, these many wounds. But concerning the grief of common sicknesses—now there, friends, I got a message for you.

"Forty-seven years ago, in a little village in the hills of Vairmant green and far away, there lived a woman, simple, humble, Godfearing, mild, like it might've been any one of the lovely companions and helpmeets I see before me right now in this good town—where I got to admit I a'n't yet beheld a member of the tender sex that a'n't lovely to behold." (There were just two good-looking women in that whole expanse of landscape and I was sitting between them.) "That's a fact, no flattery, gentlemen hark! Well, this gentle woman in Vairmant of whom I speak was bereavered of her good man in her middle years, and thereafter she devoted the remainder of a long and blessed life to the healing of the sick. Even her name was humble. Evangeline Amanda Spinkton was her name, and I want you should remember that name, for it's a name you'll come to bless with every breath you drawr. Some do say, and I believe it, that Mother Spinkton—ah yes, so a grateful world calls her now!—had in her veins the mystic Injun blood of Old Time. That's as may be, but there's no doubt at all the dear angels of the Lord guided her in her lifelong endeavor, her search after them essences of healing that the Lord in his infinite wisdom and mercy has placed obscurely in the simple yarbs that do dwell in the whispering woods or the sunkissed fields or along the gently murmuring streams—"

That gives you his style anyway. Pa never let anyone else handle the pitch for Mother Spinkton; even if he was down sick in bed and too mis'ble to live he'd r'ar up out of it to take care of that. He said he reverenced her too much to let any mere God-damn crumb-bum piddlebrained assistant lay a mortal hand on her sacred hide. He claimed also that he could taste and smell a crowd with a special knack nobody else possessed—except his grandfather of course, dead going on forty years—and this knack always told him right off whether to use gently murmuring streams or dark murmuring caverns. Either one might work all right—oh sure, it would *work,* he'd say, and spit over the footboard between the mules if he was driving, which he liked to do—it'd work, but the g.m.s. yucks are the common type, and the dark caverns type is different, that's all, and it's the mark of a real artist to be able to spot that difference and govern yourself accordingly. Long Tom Blaine used to give him an argument about it when the weather was right—Tom said yucks are yucks and that's it.

Pa Rumley blathered on, not exactly *claiming* that God and Abraham and all the angels had worked together showing gentle Mother Spinkton how to construct her

206

Home Remedy, the Only Sovran Cure for All Mortal Complainders of Man or Beast—but you were sort of left of a breathing exercise—he did it because he couldn't bear doing much more than what a musician would call a scale or a breathing exercise—he did it because he couldn't bear to let any crowd get away from him, any time, without selling it something. After five or ten minutes more of Mother Spinkton's character and biography, he squared away for a brisk analysis of a dozen or more diseases, and he was so tender and hopeful and horrible about it—hell, nobody could beat him at that; he'd have you locating so many simpletons* throughout your anatomy you simply couldn't spare the time to die from more than half of them. He'd wind up that section with a horde of widows and orphans at the grave, which Mother Spinkton might have prevented same had they but of knowed—come one, come all! Well, it called for an effort—Mother was one whole dollar a bottle. But did she sell?

Yes.

It's a matter of sober fact that she was a bird, and I do know, because Pa believed in her himself or appeared to, and had no more mercy on us than he had on the public. If you got sick and admitted it, you drank Mother Spinkton or faced Pa's displeasure, and we loved him too much for that.

It was Mother's unpredictable nature that made it impossible to get the best of her. Mother Spinkton could tear into anything at all—epizootic, measles, impotence, broken ribs, cold in the head—and if she couldn't cure it she wouldn't try, she'd just start up such a brush fire somewhere else in you that it didn't matter. Dab some of her on a mortal wound and you would, naturally, want to die, but she'd keep you that interested you couldn't manage it, for the sheer excitement of wondering how much she was going to hurt next, and where. Of course it might turn out to be an entirely different kettle of shoes of another color, but I'm trying to analyze the psychology of it.

Pa's own belief in her was a puzzle to me, but I state it

_____
* Out to lunch.

—N. & D.

for a fact. I've watched him making up a fresh batch according to the secret formula he'd worked out himself, just as careful and hopeful and bright-eyed and bushy-tailed as an Old-Time physicist with a brand new bang. And then by damn he'd drink some. I don't know—sow-bugs, horseradish, hot peppers, raw corn likker, tar, mara-wan, rattlesnake's urine, chicken's gall-bladder and about a dozen more mysterious yarbs and animal parts, usually including goat's testicles. Those last were hard to get unless we happened to be near the right kind of farm at the right moment, and Pa did allow they weren't absolutely essential, but he said they gave her a distinctive Tone that he was partial to himself. Tone was important. He'd drunk her with and without that Tone, he said, and it was possible that for the yucks it didn't really matter, because the first swallow was calculated to lift any yuck directly out of the studious frame of mind—still, if you cared, Tone was important. Pa Rumley liked to discuss vintages too. I never became that expert. All I could tell was that in some vintages Mother Spinkton wouldn't much more than stink out a town hall, but in her best years she was well able to clear a ten-acre field of everything movable, including the mules.

That morning in Humber Town, when Pa had wound up his spiel and was about to start passing out bottles with Tom Blaine wrapping up and collecting coin, along comes a hardcase old rip pushing through the crowd snorting and moaning with a hand to his chest and his long scrawny face all puckered up in the wildest sort of misery, so that I had to goggle twice and swallow before convincing myself that this antique calamity was my own Da, Sam Loomis, acting half again as large as life and rarin' to go.

"You theah! You talk of healing'? I'm comin' forward, but there a'n't no hope for me, not the way *my* mis'ry's been ground into me by a life of sin. Ah, Lord, Lord, f'give a mean horr'ble old man and let 'm die, can't you?"

"Why, friend!" Pa Rumley responded—"the Lord f'gives many a sinner. Come for'd and speak your mind!" He was a little uneasy. He told us later he wasn't sure he'd seen Sam and me talking together, at the fence.

Sam, that old scoundrel—my Da, mind you—said:

"Praise him evermore, but le' me lay my burdens down!"

"Let the poor soul come for'd there, good people—he's a sick man, I can see. Make room, please!" They did, maybe as much from pity as because Sam might have something catching. He did look just about finished—coughing, staggering, fetching up against the backboard of the wagon and letting Tom Blaine support him. If I hadn't seen that head-shake signal I'd have been over there lickety-doodah, and maybe spoiled things. "Comes on me sudden sometimes," he said, which took care of any critics who might have noticed him with me before the music, steady and hard as nails. "Real sudden!"—and with his face turned away from the crowd he sent Pa a wink.

After that you'd have thought they'd practised it for years. I whispered to the nearest ear, which happened to be Minna Selig's: "That's my Da."

"Ayah? Did see you together."

Bonnie said: "A'n't he a pisser!"

I near-about busted with pride.

Pa Rumley was leaning down to him, a soft angelic smile slathered over what you could see of his face outside the black foam of beard. His voice was globs of maple syrup out of a jug. "Don't despair, man—nay, and think of the joy in heaven over the one sinner that repenteth. Now then, where at is this pain?"

"Well, it's a chest mis'ry all kind of wropped up with a zig-zag mortification."

"Ayah, ayah. It hurts a mite cross-ways when you breathe?"

"O Lord, I mean!"

"Ayah. Now, sir, I can read a man's heart, and I says to you lo, about this sin, it's already near-about washed away in repentance, and all you need is to fix up the chest mis'ry so to make straight the pathway for the holy spirit and things—only you got to be careful of course."

Tom Blaine was right there with a bottle of Mother Spinkton, a look of gladness, and the father and mother of a wooden spoon. I have never understood, myself, how ordinary maple wood could hold together under the charring and shriveling effect Mother always had, but there's nothing I can do except tell history the way it happened. Bedam if those two old hellions didn't jaw it back and forth another five minutes, with Tom holding the spoon, before Sam would let himself be talked into swallowing some. They were taking a chance, *I* think: if the old lady had eaten her way through the spoon while they talked, the crowd might have lynched the pack of us.

Sam took it at last, and for a few seconds things were pretty quiet. Well, often you don't feel anything right away except the knowledge that the world has come to an end. Sam of course had been brought up on raw corn likker and fried food and religion; all the same, I don't believe anything in a person's past could actually prepare him for Mother Spinkton. He got her down, and when his features sort of rejoined each other so that he was recognizable again, I thought I heard him murmur: "This happened to *me!*" It was all right: any yucks who overheard him probably thought he was looking at the *nice* kind of eternity. Then as soon as he could move, he turned his head so that the yucks might observe the glow of beatitude or whatever spreading over him, and said: "Ah, praise his name, I can breathe again!"

Well, sure, a man's bound to feel a surrounding glory at finding himself still able to breathe after a shot of Mother Spinkton. But the yucks hadn't tried any of her yet, so I guess they didn't quite understand what he meant. "I was nigh unto death," says the old rip, "but here I be!" And they all pushed in around him then, wanting to touch and fondle the man who'd been snatched from the grave, even tromple him flat in pure friendliness.

Pa Rumley hopped off the wagon. He and Tom pried Sam loose from the public; then Tom went to work selling bottles—for a few minutes he was passing them out about as fast as he could handle them—and Pa Rumley walked the sick man over to that wagon where the gray-haired woman was still sitting smoking her pipe and enjoying everything. I trailed along, and the girls stuck with me.

It's hard to believe how much space you can find in one of those long covered wagons. The inverted-U frames supporting the canvas has cross-bars usually of hornbeam, just above head-height, and a light wicker-work platform rests on the cross-bars, making a sort of attic for storing light stuff. Those cross-bars also carry hanging partitions for the cubbyhole compartments that run along both sides of the wagon with a single-file walkway between. Up in front there's an area without sleeping compartments, just canvas walls with usually a window on each side. For laughs, we always called that area the front room.

That was where Pa Rumley took us now, to the front room of this wagon, which was the one with his own living-quarters. Because it was the headquarters wagon, the front room was nearly twice the size of those in the others, and had *bookshelves,* a thing I had never seen nor imagined. This wagon had only four sleeping spaces, two double and two single: singles for Mam Laura and old Will Moon who usually drove the mules, a double for Stud Dabney and his wife, and a double for Pa Rumley with whatever woman was sharing his bunk. Pa swept us in there—Bonnie, Minna, Sam and me. Mam Laura came in last with her clay pipe and sat cross-legged as limberly as the girls. I never heard of Ramblers owning a chair—you sat on the floor, or you lay, or sprawled, suit yourself. In that headquarters room, the whole ten-by-twelve floor was covered by a red bear pelt that was the pride of our hearts. Pa didn't say anything until the gray-haired woman had settled herself; then he just looked at her and grunted.

She puffed her pipe till it went out, and rubbed the bowl of it against her thin nose. Studying Sam she was, and he met the stare, and I had the feeling they were exchanging messages that did them good and were none of our business. Though grayer, she was slightly the younger, I believe. At last she said: "From the no'th of Katskil, be'n't you?"

"Ayah. A'n't had word of the war lately."

"Oh, that. It'll be over in a couple-three months. Rambler life attract you, maybe?"

"Might, allowin' for the fact I'm a loner by trade."

"Did a good job as a volunteer shill out there. Don't know that I ever saw that done before."

"So't of come over me all-a-sudden like, the way I wouldn't want you to think my boy's the only talented one in the family."

"You be his Da then?"

"Ai-yah, that's a special story," Sam said, "nor I wouldn't be a one to tell it without his leave."

She looked at me then, and I felt the kindness in her, and I told the story, finding it not hard to do. Bonnie and Minna had quieted down, anyway I guess they wouldn't have carried on the game of dividing me down the middle directly under her eye. I told the story straight, feeling no need to change or soften it. When I was finished Sam said: "He must be my boy. He don't *lack* my oneriness, you see—just a'n't quite growed up to it yet."

"Be *you*," Mam Laura asked me, "a loner by trade?"

"Likely I must be," I said, "the way when my Da makes that remark it rings a bell in me. But I like people."

"So does your Da," Mam Laura said—"did you think he didn't, Davy? Nay, I sometimes wonder if loners aren't the only ones who do." I was beginning to notice how she spoke rather differently from the rest of us. I couldn't have explained the difference at that time; I did feel that her way of using words was better than any I'd heard before, and wished for the knack of speaking that way myself. "You truly want to join up with us, Davy, the uncommon way we live that's never a safe thing, often lonely, hard, tiresome, dangerous?"

"Yes," I told her. "Yes!"

"Enough to suffer a little schooling in consequence?"

I had no notion what sort of schooling she meant—while I was knocking off my life story I'd already told her I knew all about how to handle mules. But I said: "Yes, I do—honest, I'd do *anything!*"

Pa Rumley laughed at that, gargling it in his beard, but Mam Laura aimed her smile mostly at the universe and not at me. "Hoy, Laura," Pa said, "didn't I keep telling you I'd raise a big old God-damn scholar for you somewheres, to squeeze the good out'n them books that've been wearing down the mule-power on this wagon all these years? Maybe I've even raised you more'n one. Be *you* a man for the books, Sam Loomis?"

My father looked away through one of the little windows—honest glass they were, sewed cleverly into slots in the canvas so that no wind would dislodge them or force the rain through. For a moment or two he looked older and grayer, my father, than ever before; if there was mirth hidden in his craggy face I couldn't find it. "That wasn't my fortune, Pa Rumley," he said. "I tried once to win me a little learning after my young years were long gone—nay, but it don't matter. If the lady will teach my boy, I'll answer for it he'll mind the lessons and get the good of it."

Pa Rumley got up and tapped Sam's shoulder and nodded at me. "He blows that horn pretty good too," he said. "Well—stick around. You're lucky—gentlemen hark! Yes sir, it just so happens you hit me at a lucky time: I got over the shock of being born a good while ago, more b' token I a'n't dead yet. Best time to tackle a man, understand?—somewhere in there betwix birth and death. If the sumbitch won't give you a decent answer then he never will."

21

We did stick around—four years.

Pa Rumley was a sharp-minded observant man, sober; drunk, he was still a good critic of himself, unless he passed a certain point of drinking that he could not always recognize, and tumbled into a black well of despair —then he had no judgment in his darkness, and someone had to stand by and drink with him till he dropped in his tracks. Except during those very rare crises, his sadness always had around it a nimbus of mirth, just as his loudest laughter carried the overtones of grief. True for all of us, but in him it was more obvious, as though the emotional raw stuff that nature, playing safe, doles out to most of us by the teaspoonful, had been sloshed into Pa Rumley with a bucket.

Pa used to claim that he'd fought and toiled and connived to make himself boss-man of the best God-damn gang in the world for the simple reason that he was at heart a benefactor of the God-damn yuman race, which without him would likely drop dead of its own boredom and meanness and hard luck and general shitty stupidity. And it's a fact, when you got down to cases he really didn't seem to have a thing in the world against yumanity except that he never would pronounce the plague-take-it thing with an aitch.

He had a long, thick-bridged nose that spread at the tip into a double knob. The whole organ had been slammed into at some time in the faraway past, so that when I knew him it aimed more or less at his right shoulder. He said it was no battle that bent it, more likely somebody sat on it when he was young. He asserted that in fact he never did fight except now and then with a club, which was why he never got licked. However, when I saw him personally lay out Shag Donovan who thought he was boss of Seal Harbor, Pa used no club except the knobby side of his fist, and all two hundred pounds of Shag went softly to sleep. (I was a bit helpful in that Seal Harbor thing, being fifteen and on the quarrelsome side for a while, a temporary trait, a sort of growing pain.) Another time, I heard Pa say that his nose took that starboard slant from having to keep alert and sniffing for the righteous, who generally come up on a man from behind.

It was a good commanding nose anyway, and useful to the gang because it told of his mood: so long as it stayed red or sunset pink there was nothing much to worry about, but if it went white while Pa was still sober, the wise thing to do was to keep out of sight and hope for the best, supposing you had anything on your conscience. His eyes were important signals too, small and black and restless. Just contrary to his nose, they went bloodshot when he was on the warpath—but of course if you were near enough to notice the swollen veins you wouldn't benefit by running.

I never knew him to clobber anyone who hadn't, according to Pa's lights, earned it. Anyone who did received the quick tranquillizing sensation of a tall building falling on him, and when he dug himself out from under that, always amazingly undamaged, he could do as Pa said, God damn it, or quit. In all my time with Rumley's no one left voluntarily until I did, and when I did it was no fault of Pa or myself: I left with his friendship and good wishes. If I could ever meet him again—idle remark, with all the sea between us and no prospect that any of us will ever turn again toward our native countries—it would be an occasion for affectionate talk and some long drinks. He'd be crowding seventy, now I think of it—and yet, he seemed so durable, it wouldn't surprise me to learn that the gang is still Rumley's Ramblers, still traveling somewhere and himself still the law and all the prophets.

He never got rough with the women, except for the love-roughness he must have provided when he took one as a partner for a night or a week or whatever length of time suited both. Now and then I've heard them wailing musically from the cubby-hole in his wagon—laughing the next instant or shouting wild talk with scant breath the way a woman won't do unless she's truly kindled. And I've seen them come out of there looking mighty rumpled, but never discontented.

Pa Rumley didn't talk about his cot-work—those who do often haven't done it of course—but some of the women did, to me no less, after I'd been with the gang a good while and developed a habit of listening, a thing almost unheard of in the teens. Minna Selig especially, three or four years older than I, was all hell on analyzing her feelings, for some odd time-passing fun she got out of it. I recall one occasion when she couldn't rest until she'd stacked up my performance (her word) against Pa's, detail by detail. I liked that quail, but that was one occasion when I wished she'd shut up—after all, I'd never claimed to be that good! Bonnie Sharpe could let in the daylight on Minna's intellect with a poke or two, but I didn't have the knack. When Bonnie wasn't around, Minna would go after a joke or a light remark as if it were a school problem, and everything else must wait till she'd explained it back to you and sorted out all its unreasonable aspects. I don't mean she was grim, she just got her kicks out of it, some way; I think the sweet kid got as much pleasure out of such operations as a dumb creep like me gets out of

215

laughing. It was Pa Rumley's singleness of purpose, she explained, that made him better in bed than a boy—*"Not* meaning for to hurt y' feelings, Davy, it's just something an older man learns, I guess. Pa's like a rock, see, I mean even his *face* gets hard, smooth, cold almost, like he a'n't hearing you no more at all, and you know you can do anything—holler, fight, struggle as much as you want, there's no danger you'll get away. Why, the wagon could catch afire and he wouldn't stop till he'd have it, right there." (I said: "You mean it's like being screwed by a mountain?" She wasn't listening.) "Now you, Davy, you be mostly too polite," said that nice Rambler quail instructing an ex-yard-boy. "And this might surprise you but it's a fact, Davy, a woman don't like too much of that." I says: "No?" "No," she says—"in fact it might surprise you, but a woman don't always mean exactly what she says—I know, it's real surprising." I said: "Sure enough?"

She said sure enough, and went on explaining it in the very friendliest way, I remember, while I said uhha and ayah and think-of-that-now—you know, being polite because it's my nature—while we were hearing also the loud lazy screak of the wagon-wheels and the country sounds outside. I was seventeen at the time of that conversation, if my memory hasn't goofed, and the countryside would have been the almost tropic splendor of southern Penn. It comes back to me with the musky sweetness of scuppernong grape in the air along with Minna's fragrance, and I lying politely on her bunk with a leg slid conveniently under her hot and sweaty little bare brown tail, waiting (politely) until the never-hurrying wagon should provide just the right amount of jolt to swing us back into action. I knew Minna was right of course, and what she said doubtless had some effect, or I'd have heard other complaints about politeness later on, and I can't recollect that I ever did.

Pa had never married. A Rambler boss seldom does. It's traditional that he should remain available to soothe the restless, arbitrate quarrels, comfort the widow, instruct the young, and pacify all concerned by procedures not very convenient for a married man.

He was wondrous patient with the children, the small ones anyway; until they were seven or eight years old he scarcely tried to comb them out of his hair. There were seven when Sam and I arrived, a better showing than most gangs could make—seven children, twelve women, fifteen men, so Sam and I brought the gang total up to thirty-six. Three more children were born during my four years with Rumley's. The oldest child was Nell Grafton's boy Jack, ten when I first saw him; his father Rex Grafton had gone blind with cataracts near the time of Jack's birth, and had taught himself harness-making, basketry, other skills. Jack was a handsome hellion born for trouble. Nell, that big sweet woman, mothered the whole gang and looked after her proud sharp husband in a way that sheltered his raw nerves and yet steered him away from self-pity, but her own wild boy she couldn't control. Once or twice I tried to beat the cruel streak out of him, and that didn't work either.

The bearing of Rambler children presents a continual problem to the Holy Murcan Church. How can the authorities be sure that all pregnancies are reported, no woman left alone after the fifth month, every birth attended by a priest, with a group that's always on the go, in and out of the wilderness, over national boundaries without inspection, even excused from the taxes and other responsibilities that go along with settled residence and national citizenship? You're right—they can't. A Rambler is called—legally and with the consent of the Church because the Church can't help it—a citizen of the world.

The Church has made sporadic efforts to take over the Ramblers, invariably catching its tail in the crack. Every now and then some enterprising prelate gives birth to an idea he thinks is new. The Archbishop of Conicut had a go at it in 318, not very long before we made a circuit of that country and then headed for southern Katskil and Penn. He decreed that every Rambler gang passing through Conicut must have a priest as one of its members. Simple, s's he—how could they object, and why did nobody think of this before? Word got around before his law went into effect; when it did, every gang had left Conicut. Outside each important border post—in Lomeda,

217

and at Dambury in the south of Bershar, and Norrock which is Levannon's only real southern port, and even away over at Mystic on the border of Rhode—a Rambler gang set up camp within sight of Conicut customs officers, with whom they fraternized agreeably enough, but for three months no Rambler gang set foot on Conicut soil, and no Rambler boss took the trouble to explain why.

They were polite with all visitors, but in those encampments they put on no shows that would be visible from the Conicut side. No music, for music doesn't recognize boundaries. No selling to Conicut customers, and no passing on of news. The gangs just sat there. A three-month block was enough to rouse every town and village in the land to a dither of exasperation and protest—nay, they were still grumbling about the "Rambler Strike" months later when we passed by, and I wished we'd been in on the fun, but we were away the hell up in northern Levannon at the time. Often during the three months a few hand-picked, soft-spoken priests visited the encampments and offered themselves as members—temporary members, even members with limited privileges, anything to get the gangs back in the country before the public rioted. The hopeful fathers were regretfully told that the boss just hadn't quite made up his mind but would be happy to inform them when he did. I think now, looking on it with the historical background that Nickie and Dion have given me, that if the Church had tried to get tough with the Ramblers the thing could have caught fire in a religious war, with results totally unpredictable; but they were smart, and played it soft. Then at last the gang at Norrock—by pre-arrangement, and that's a story in itself, the way the Rambler newsrunners went flickering along the back roads and dim trails from gang to gang with few the wiser—did accept a nice wee priest as a temporary member, and set forth across the country.

They'd prepared for it. That was Bill (Lardpot) Shandy's gang. Pa Rumley knew Lardpot; he said the man did everything the way he ate, never by halves. Before they set out with the priest, the big sexy pictures on the wagons were painted over with gray—drab and sad. Wherever they stopped, as if for the usual entertainments, no music was offered, just hymns. No plays, no peep-shows. Instead of the account of news from distant places that a Rambler boss customarily provides at the start of every visit, the priest was invited to deliver a sermon. This really hurt, for as I've said, the Ramblers are the one source of news that the people can trust: nothing else in our timid, poverty-ridden, illiterate world takes the place of the newspapers of Old Time. In much less than three months all Conicut was bubbling with rumors—earthquakes in Katskil, atheist uprisings in Nuin, Vairmant overrun with revolutionaries, prophets and three-headed calvès. That priest, poor devil—Lardpot had purposely chosen a born innocent—did actually preach a sermon, twice, the second time to a loyal hard-core group of five elderly ladies; they couldn't hear very well, but were gratified to learn the Ramblers had abandoned their nasty ways in favor of nice family-type instruction.

A law that originates in the Church is, naturally, never going to be repealed.* But before Bill Shandy's gang reached the border of Rhode, the Archbishop announced at the Cathedral in New Haven that the wretched clerk who originally transmitted the archiepiscopal message had committed an odious blunder of omission, for which he was now doing a penance that would keep him occupied for a while—here they say the Archbishop smacked his lips and smole a somewhat secular smile. What the Archbishop really said—and if he hadn't been so busy looking after the spiritual welfare of his flock he'd have learned of the error and corrected it much sooner—what he *really* said was that any Rambler gang *which so desires* may accept a priest as a member etc. etc. Observe, please, said the Archbishop, how vast a difference may result from the presence or absence of three little words, and do try to govern yourselves accordingly, and praise the Lord, and be mindful what you say. So there was dancing in the

* Correction: the Universal Tithing Law, which took an annual dollar from every individual over sixteen, was repealed in 324. True, the Church replaced it with what they call the More Universal Tithing Law, costing everyone a buck and a half; but the first law was honestly repealed, no crud.

—Dion M. M.

streets. I don't see how the best of Archbishops could get much more etcetery than that.

So, in practise, the Rambler citizens of the world live mostly by what the Church, like an uneasy schoolmistress, calls the "honor system." This means that a Rambler boss must take over in his own person many of the functions of policer, priest and judge. He is expected to see to it that pregnancies are reported, even if the gang is likely to be a hundred miles away a few months later. He must make sure women are properly attended through the critical time. And if by chance a mue is born when the gang happens to be not within reach of a priest, the Rambler boss himself must take the knife in his own hand and be certain it penetrates the heart, and with his own eyes see the body buried under a sapling that has been bent over on itself to form the symbol of the wheel . . .

Rumley's other three wagons, except the theater wagon, each had enough compartments for a maximum of twelve people without obliging anyone to sleep in the "front room," which was thought to bring bad luck—Rambler people were full of small superstitions like that, singularly free from the large ones. Including the headquarters wagon, the top limit for the whole gang would have been forty-two. Some gangs have six wagons or even more; that's too big. Thirty-six people, the number after Sam and I joined, was comfortable, not so big that Pa couldn't keep track of all that went on, but big enough so that the toughest bandit outfit wouldn't attack us—Shag Donovan's boys weren't bandits but town toughs, a far stupider breed.

That first day in Humber Town, after accepting us into membership Pa Rumley took off to look after this and that, and I recall Bonnie Sharpe settled down with the back of her head against Mam Laura's knee making small music with her mandolin, which left no one but Minna to look after Sam and me.

Rambler life followed a rhythm like that, of swift and obvious shifts from tension to calm. Bonnie had clearly relished hearing my story and Mam Laura's questions and my Da's occasional remarks, her humorous girl's eyes huge and gray turning from one to another of us, never missing a thing. Then I was done, and Bonnie knew that

Minna would look after us if nobody else got around to it, so for Bonnie I suppose the universe comfortably narrowed down to a trifling section of the red bear-skin, the shiny mandolin strings, the light sounds of music she was making, the pleasure she took in her own healthy body and the warmth of Mam Laura's knee. A time of tension, a time of uncomplicated quiet with music in it—I learned that rhythm too, after a while. If Nickie had not also learned it I couldn't get along with her as I do—well, without it she'd be someone else, unrecognizable. Spare me from living with worthy souls whose bow of enthusiasm is never allowed to rest unstrung.

Minna Selig, as she took us over to one of the other wagons, was wearing under her black curls a cute frown of thoughtfulness—

It has just this moment occurred to me that some of you who may or may not exist may also actually be women. If so, you would insist on knowing what else Minna was wearing, this preoccupation with what the other quail have on being an ineradicable trait which I have never been able to beat out of a single one of you. Kay—dark cherry-red blouse and sloppy linsey pants, and moccasins like what we all wore—all except Pa, that is, who would have reamed out anyone he caught imitating his gilt nudes.

Minna found places for us, just by chance (she said) in the same wagon where she and Bonnie slept. A happy chance: I kept the same compartment all the four years. Bonnie went over to another wagon when she married Joe Dulin in 319, and Sam later moved in with Mam Laura, a courtship I'll tell about—but only a little, only the surface happenings, for that's all I know: there was a depth to it, naturalness, inevitability, which they would not have wanted to explain if they could, and whatever I wrote about it would be no better than half-educated guesswork.

Yes, I stayed with that place Minna picked for me, making a home for myself out of a hole four feet by eight by seven, learning how to live cramped in small ways but not in large—unless you want to say that we're all bound to be cramped in a moment of time that rarely reaches even a century, on a speck of stardust that's been precariously spinning in nothing for a mere pitiful three or four billion years. I was also learning how few important material possessions there are that can't be readily stowed in four-by-eight-by-seven, leaving room for yourself, and now and then for Minna.

22

I came to Levannon and the ships, and I did not sail.

What is it, this very certain destiny that overtakes all our visions, our most reasoned plans equally with our fantastic dreams? Maybe whenever we think of the future, as we must if we're to be human at all, the act is bound to include a something-too-much, as if with all due human absurdity we were expecting chance to alter its course at the impact of our noise. A boy imagined the great outriggers, the fine thirty-tonners bound east by the northern route; his mind saw their canvas tall, mighty, luminous in a golden haze. A young man in the late summer of 317, the least important member of a Rambler gang he'd never heard of a month earlier, came off the flat-bottomed ferry-sailer into the reeking port of Renslar in Levannon, helping old Will Moon wrangle the mules. I suppose he was possibly a quarter-inch taller than when he took hold of Emmia Robson in the way of love. When the two had cussed and coaxed the lead wagon up the ramp and out of the way off the dock—Pa Rumley having pups all over the place, roaring advice to which leathery Will paid no attention—Will called the young man's attention to the vessel in the next slip, with a jerk of his wizened brown chin and a directional squirt of tobacco juice, and shouted in the manner of the partly deaf: "Can you read, boy?"

"Ayah, I can read."

"Mam Laura been learnin' you the learnin', I hear tell?"

"I can read, Will."

"Well, read me the name of that old shitpot yonder."

"Why, that's the *Daisy Mae,* it says."

Poor graceless squabby thing, she smelled of spoiled onions as well as dead fish. She was fat amidships with a tubby blunt bow and a square stern, her single outrigger as ungainly as a wooden leg. The oar-benches had been rubbed to a polish by the aching buttocks of the slaves who were likely penned up somewhere in barracks at that moment waiting for the next ordeal. Nothing else about her had any shine; reefing down hid only some of the patches in her sail. Will shouted: "You any good guessing tonnage?"

"Never saw that kind of boat before."

He went roaring into laughter. " 'Boat' is good—hoy, they'd skin you for that! 'Ships' you gotta call 'em when they're that size. Come on, give a guess how big she is."

She looked ancient as well as puny, a salt-frosted gray, a color of loneliness and neglect. She rode high in the water, empty, sun-smitten; if a watchman was aboard he must have been lurking below, where you'd suppose the hot stench would have been past bearing. I imagined her to be some little cargo tub built for short hauls between ports of the Hudson Sea, likely to be abandoned soon or broken up for firewood. "She a'n't as far gone as she looks," Will said—"they'll be painting her before she goes out again, and you'd be surprised." A miserable dockside cur had been attracted by the flavor of her garbage but didn't quite dare jump down on her deck. He lifted a scarecrow leg against a dock stanchion, aiming poorly and spattering the ship's rail. With an empty hand Will Moon made a stone-throwing motion; the mutt scrabbled away in terror, tail clamped between his legs. I fancied the dreary old vessel sighing meekly at the indignity, too feeble to resent it. "Come on, Davy—give us a guess."

"Couple tons maybe?"

"You got things to learn," Will said, and cackled with delight—when I'm sixty maybe I'll be all hell on instructing the young too. "Things to learn, bub—why, old *Daisy Mae,* she won't go a ton under thirty-three . . ."

No, I never sailed aboard a Levannon ship, nor ever sped down the road on a bright roan with three attendants, expecting a serving wench at the next inn to bathe me and warm my bed with her willing loins. But I did go with Rumley's Ramblers through all the nations of the known world except Nuin where Pa Rumley had once run afoul of the law, and the Main city states that you can't reach by land without passing over Nuin's province of Hampsher. I lent a hand wrastling those mules on the Renslar dock, and the same evening I was in the entertainment with my horn, never missing one for four years—they loved me. That year we went north along the Lowland Road of Levannon.

It is the greatest road of modern history. Moha's Northeast Road that pointed my way out of Skoar is a fine thing, but a cowpath beside the Lowland Road. There are travelers who would tell you that the greatest of all is the Old Post Road from Old City of Nuin to Renslar: such is the cussedness of the human race when determined to argue passionately about something that can't be any way proved —their whole damn trouble is that always they know I'm right but won't admit it. The Lowland Road of Levannon is not just a road; it's a natural force and a way of living. It runs from Norrock on the great sea, the Atlantic, all the way north to the rich nastiness of Seal Harbor, a distance of three hundred and seventy-some miles. It not only holds the nation of Levannon together like the spinal column of a snake, but in a real sense that road *is* Levannon. You can hardly say whether the towns strung along it like vertebrae are served by it or exist in order to serve it.

Traveling north, you walk in the morning shadow of the beautiful green mountains at your right hand. You see at once why the many small but vigorous towns and villages are needed there. Alert and usually fortified, they are connected to the big Lowland Road by good secondary roads and trails, to protect the artery of trade and travel from bandits and other wild beasts. Levannon is never like Moha, sloppy and shiftless about its roads, the one great road and the many small ones—they mean too much. As for the great Lowland Road, the mountains are sure to be either a shield or a menace depending on who commands the heights; a mountain trail is a nervous sort of boundary. Levannon dreams of possessing both sides of the great range; to Vairmant and Bershar and Conicut the same dream is a nightmare, which they will hold off if they can—those three have had no wars among themselves for at least fifty years, too well aware that they might at any moment need to be allies . . .

I have always found it difficult to understand that the whole region of our known world was in Old Time a small part of a very great nation. The idea of a war over possession of what they called the Berkshires and the Green Mountains would have made the men of that time smile indulgently as at a child's nonsense: the wars they were concerned with were, materially, so much bigger! Ethically bigger?—I think not, except that they had it in their power to destroy the world completely and very nearly did so.

Well up in the northern country, the mountains become low hills and finally subside into the flat land along the south coast of the Lorenta Sea. Up there crouches Seal Harbor, a steaming corruption near the mouth of a river that is called the St. Francis as it was in Old Time.

Seal Harbor is frankly nothing but a mammoth try-works. The lamp-oil seal, sometimes called hairseal, breed by the thousands on barren islands far to the north, beyond where the Lorenta Sea spreads out into the Atlantic. Those islands are strung along the wilderness coast of what the old maps call Labrador; modern Levannese call it the Seal Shore. The animals must have taken advantage of man's decline in the Years of Confusion to increase enormously: Seal Harbor people tell of modern voyages of exploration that have been made north of the regular sealing grounds—it's just seal islands and more seal islands, they say, up to the point where you can travel no further because the men won't stand it. They call it Northern Terror and it's a thing beyond argument or reason—partly the cold, and furious wind, but most of all what they describe as the "madness of the sun."

But men can manage their business in the southern part of the breeding grounds, and luckily for men, the seal apparently never learn. Greatly daring, the slow outriggers specially built for the task pull out of Seal Harbor late in

225

March and creep down the Lorenta Sea hugging its dangerous northern coast, past the island still named Anticosti and through a strait the sailors nowadays call Belly Wheel. That was once Belle Isle and meant Beautiful Island, but if you tell a modern sealer so, he'll stare you down with the blubber-faced incomprehension of one of the poor beasts who make his living for him; if it annoys him enough, he may charge.

After passing through Belly Wheel they follow the coast northwest. It's tricky work I suppose: they don't dare either to let the cruel land out of sight or to drift too close and risk being caught in the tideways and currents and flung against it. They arrive at the breeding grounds with the winds of the great sea on their necks, and go ashore in small boats to do their butchery in haste, with clubs. They take only the blubber, and the best hides of the baby and yearling seal, leaving all carcasses where they lie to be dealt with by the vultures or swept away in high tide for the swarming sharks. If the voyage were not so tough for those clumsy vessels, and if men were more numerous, less superstitious and a little more brave, the seal would be extinct by now in spite of their massive numbers. The sealers have no least thought of husbandry or mercy, only of the quick dollar. All they can do is kill and kill and go on killing till the fat hulls of the cargo vessels are replete. This they do so that we may have light in the evening.

The untreated blubber is brought back in that state to Seal Harbor. I've heard that the townfolk know when the returning fleet has come within ten miles, from the rancid stink that heralds it even if there's no east wind blowing. It's a cause for rejoicing—after all it happens only once a year. Then comes a few weeks of work, after which the good citizens of Seal Harbor go back to the longer holiday of loafing, hunting, whoring, fishing, brawling—above all brawling—and picking each other's pockets until the next year's "fat weeks." During the trying and for days afterward unless a merciful wind arrives, the smoke from the blubber-works lays a black-purple cloud over the shabby city, and even hardened long-time inhabitants are sick. That's one of the main reasons why it is a city of scum, misfits, criminals, failures. No one wants to live there who could earn a living and be welcome somewhere else.

We journeyed north by rather slow stages in the closing days of 317, often spending more than a week in a village if we enjoyed the style of it. Pa Rumley's way was leisurely; I've heard him remark that if a thing wasn't still there by the time you arrived it likely wouldn't have been worth hurrying after. Not many Rambler gangs head north when winter's advancing: as we drifted along the Lowland Road, always with the grave splendor of the mountains at the right hand, the villages were happy to see us and bought well, being somewhat starved for entertainment and news. At a good-sized town named Sanasint we turned east, crossing over the border into the north end of Vairmant. We spent the winter months of December through March in a way most Rambler gangs wouldn't have cared to do, at a lonely camp of our own devising in a pocket of the Vairmant hills. May, Pa explained, was the time to hit Seal Harbor, when the oil buyers had come and gone, and the companies had paid off the workmen but there hadn't been time for all the money to settle into the pockets of a few gamblers and crooks; but that wasn't his main reason for holing up during the winter. He did that for about three months of every year—nay, we did it down in Penn too where there's hardly such a thing as winter—so that the grown-ups could loaf and mend harness while the young stuff, by Jesus and Abraham, would please to settle down and learn something. Two things, Pa said, were capable of taking some of the devil out of the young— birch and learning. Of the two, learning was best, in his opinion, even if it did smart considerably more.

Mam Laura concurred. Gentle and gently philosophic at most other times, capable of sitting in the same position for an hour doing nothing but smoke her pipe and gaze at the landscape, Mam Laura became a demon of energy in the presence of a student who showed some inclination to learn a little. Anything went then—snarling invective, language that would have made my Da blush (sometimes did), sarcasm, intense but thoughtful praise, a slap on the cheek—anything, all the way up to a kiss or one of the honey-and-walnut candies that she kept secretly in her

227

own compartment and that no one else knew how to make. Anything went, so long as she could hope it would help to fix a bit of truth in your mind where with luck you might not lose it.

She was born in Vairmant, south of the tranquil wilderness spot where we made our winter quarters that year. The name of her birth town was Lamoy, a hill town close to the Levannon border. Later, when we were journeying down through that part of the nation, we avoided the turn-off for Lamoy although it was a prosperous place and we might have done well there. Mam Laura had nothing against it, but she had made a complete break with childhood long ago and had no wish to attempt revisiting the past. She was the daughter of a schoolmaster; I could hardly hold my amazement when I learned that in Vairmant, though the Holy Murcan Church controls the schools of course, the teachers are not necessarily all priests. Mam Laura's father was secular, a scholar and visionary, who privately gave her an education far beyond anything he was allowed to impart to the other children of his school: he had a quackpot theory that within her life-time it might be possible for a woman not a nun to be permitted to teach—a weird thought for which he could have been booted out of the school and into the pillory. In her darker moods Mam Laura sometimes said that he was fortunate because he died rather young. In such moods also, she sometimes felt that his teaching and en-couragement had merely unfitted her for any world except the one that existed only in his mind.

I didn't always understand, in the days when I was struggling to win my way into the region of knowledge she opened up for me, how completely a giver Mam Laura was—well, what child ever does grasp the motives behind a teacher's thankless labors, or for that matter the value of the teaching itself? I dare say a child with that much in-sight would be a sort of monster. But now, when Nickie's twenty-ninth birthday and mine are behind us, it seems to me I do begin to understand Mam Laura and her teaching —now, when we are so much concerned for the child Nickie is carrying, so full of thoughts for the child's future

228

and so uncertain what manner of world that child will be
driven to explore.

*　　*　　*

This is late April on the island Neonarcheos. Lately I
have written only sporadically, often unwillingly, angry at
a compulsion that can drive an otherwise reasonably intelligent man both toward and away from the pen—ah,
who but a fantastic quackpot would ever write a book?
Likely you noticed how my method of storytelling altered,
a while back. That was partly because my mind is frightened and distracted—Nickie is not well.

She insists her daily and nightly pain and discomfort
are entirely natural for the seventh month of pregnancy.
The perils of that stately condition are vastly exaggerated,
she says—she's never lost a husband from it yet. The child
lives and moves, we know; often she wants me to feel
"him" kick.

But there is another genuine reason why I'm writing
about my time with the Ramblers in what may appear to
you a more hasty style—no detailed story now, merely a
touching of what I best remember. I have no inclination to
apologize. Your own worst fault, you know, is just the
opposite of haste: I mean this dreadful mewling uncertainty, this messing about never quite able to make up
your mind whether you exist; you ought to overcome it if
it's within your power. No apology, but a moderate effort
at explanation.

There was a story I was compelled to write, inwardly
compelled, no doubt by an obscure hope that in writing
it I would come to understand it better myself. That was
the story of a particular part of growing up (as far as an
experience so continuous can have any "parts"), the story
of a boy who came out of one condition into another and
a wider one, though perhaps even less than a quarter-inch
taller in the busy flesh. Now that story, I was surprised to
notice a while ago, I have completed. What happened to
me with the Ramblers happened to a far older boy; my
meeting with Nickie (which I shall tell you about before
long, I think) happened to a man. These are other stories,

maybe beyond my power to write, maybe not. However—because there was a voyage, because life is continuous as daylight between dawn and dark, because I was concerned with varieties of time, because I heard no objections from your Aunt Cassandra nor yet from her yellow tomcat with the bent ear—that original story of a boy's journey grew inseparably in, out of, over, under, through, around, by, with and for those other stories; which obliges me to complete them too—a little bit. (Ask your Aunt C. how it's possible to complete something "a little bit"—you would have to exist in order to analyze and enjoy a literary gidget like that one, and you're probably not up to it.) I don't suppose there's any need to explain where that boy's special story ended or partly ended, since it will be obvious almost immediately to a learned, compassionate, profoundly and generously perceptive scholar and gentleman—or quail—like yourself.

Merely notice and remember, if you wish, that for a good many pages now, and on to the end of the book whenever and wherever that may happen, we—I mean myself and you more or less with me, which after all comes fairly close to admitting you might exist—well, we are like people who have finished one day's journey, and find that here at the inn there's still some time for drinks and conversation before we sleep.

* * *

"Look at him there!" says Mam Laura—"only look at him sitting there with a redheaded face hung up perpendicularly forninst his brains, trying to tell me you mustn't split an infinitive! Mustn't, mustn't, mustn't, frig mustn't! Why, Davy? Why?"

"Well, that grammar book says—"

"Bugger the buggerly book!" she'd cry out. "I want to hear one stunk-up lonely reason *why* you mustn't!"

"To be honest, I can't think of any. It don't explain—"

"Doesn't explain. And being honest is what I'm after," she said, mollified and sweet and smiling again. "You see, Sam, the boy has intelligence; he only needs to have the school rubbish beaten out of him like dust out of a rug.

Well, the grammar book doesn't explain, Davy, because it relies on authority, which is all right and necessary within limits in such a book; if it tried to explain everything along the way it would stop being a grammar and turn into a textbook on etymology—what's etymology?"

"The—science of words?"

"Don't ask me, Brother David! I'm asking you."

"Uh—well—the science of words."

"Doesn't tell me enough. Science of what aspect of words? What thing about words?"

"Oh! Word origins."

"Had to help you on that one. Next time, snap it back at me and no nonsense. All right—that grammar is probably as good as any other on the subject, and it's also the only one I possess—of course nothing written in our day is worth a tinker's poop. Davy—English came partly from the much older language Latin, as I told you a while ago. Kay—in Latin the infinitive is a single word: you don't split it because you can't. And so, some time or other, some grammarian with an iron brain decided that the laws of Latin ought to govern English because he liked it that way—and, I'm afraid, also because that made grammar seem more mysterious and difficult to the layman, which built up the prestige of the clerical class. But language— the English language anyway—always makes mahooha out of arbitrary notions of that sort. Split 'em whenever it sounds right, love—*I* don't mind—whenever the stuffing is slight enough so that a reader can't forget the little 'to' before he gets to the verb. And what's meant by the word 'arbitrary'?"

"Decided by will or whim more than by reason."

"See, Sam? He's a good boy."

"Blows that horn good too," said my Da . . .

At that camp I did my horn practise on an open hillside some distance from the wagons. It was moderately dangerous, I suppose, and Sam generally went along, to loaf nearby and watch the part of the country that wasn't under my eyes while I played. I remember an afternoon late in April; the gang was beginning to get ready for another year's travel, and we knew the first thing would be a serious effort to relieve Seal Harbor of its loose change

231

before we turned back south. Sam had something on his mind that day. My own head was empty except for music and spring fret, and a wish that Bonnie would quit teasing and put out like Minna. She was more interested in pursuit than capture, at that time anyway; later, as I've mentioned, she married Joe Dulin, which showed a lot of good sense. When I got tired that afternoon and was finished with my work, Sam stretched and said: "Well, Jackson, I done it."

"Done what, Mister?"

"Impident. Why, yesterday, after Laura was done teaching you, I hung around like I sometimes do, and I asked her flat-out if she figured it was too late for me to pick up a mite of learning myself in my own spare time. 'What kind of learning?' she says right away, and when I told her—nay, you know, Jackson, you bein' young as all dammit and horny after the green girls, you'd never believe what a *soft* woman that Laura is, more b' token she's your teacher and such is none of your business, but it's so. 'What kind of learning, Sam?' she says, and so to make things plain I told her again about the wife I got behind me in Katskil, for I thought it might be a trouble to her mind. And that's a sad sort of a fool thing, Jackson, about my wife. Always seemed to hold it against me, my wife did, that we could never get kids—hoy, and then unbeknownst to her I went and got you by another and a better woman, anyhow we think that happened. But that wa'n't all. Year by year, seemed she felt it more and more of a duty to whittle me down, nag-nag, tell everyone'd listen the main reason I never got a master carpenter's license was I was too God-damn lazy to rise up off my ass even in a city like King-stone all bungfull of money and opportunity, only she never said God-damn of course—real saint she was—I mean, why, shit, Jackson, a man couldn't live with it . . . Ai-yah—'What kind of learning?' says Laura, and I told her—'Look,' I says, 'I can't follow along with the God-damn etymogolololy or whatever,' I says, 'account I et too much ignorance when I was young, but I had it in mind to learn about you,' I said—nay, Jackson, there's a strange shine to a woman when she's all of a sudden happy, I mean happy for true. I don't suppose a man gets to see it more'n once-twice in a lifetime—the lot of us, men and women, bein' what we are. 'About you,' I says, 'and how I'd share your bed and your nights and days, and so't of stand by, you might say, as long as I last.' And here's the thing, Jackson. After I'd said that, and was so't of shifting my feet and wondering where I'd run and hide if she was to get the wrong look onto her face—why—why, Jackson, she said: 'Then I'll teach you, Sam.' Just like that she said it—said: 'I'll teach you that, Sam, if it's all right with the boy.'"

"Merciful winds, it's all right with the boy!" I remember I was able to say that quickly, so that Sam would feel sure there were no second thoughts. And if there were any that mattered, they were buried too deep for me to know anything about them myself. I believe I was honestly happy for him and Mam Laura, who was after all the woman I would have picked for a mother if I'd had anything to say about it, and I had no feeling that she was taking him away from me.

That night, I remember, I had to have Bonnie—complaisant Minna wouldn't do, it had to be Bonnie, and never mind her quick and snippy No and her maybe-some-time. And I got her—remembering Emmia, I think. I warmed her up with kissing when I caught her behind our wagon, and followed her to her compartment after she broke away with a friendlier backward look than I was used to from her; when she would have dismissed me there at the curtains I simply went in with her and kept up the good work. When she tried to freeze me, I tickled her under the ribs and she had to laugh. When she informed me she was about to yell and scream and fetch Pa Rumley who'd give me the cowhide but good, I informed her that she probably wasn't, anyway not if she was the sweet, passionate and beautiful Spice I thought she was—in fact prettier than any quail I ever saw—and so I went on with my enterprise, warming her here and there and yonder until there wasn't really one sensible thing she could do, except beg me to wait till she got the rest of her clothes off so they wouldn't be rumpled. And I will be damned if she wasn't a virgin.

Also relieved to be one no longer, and a bit grateful—and a good wife to Joe Dulin when she got around to it—

but above all a *hell* of a musician, bless her: I've never known a better, certainly not excepting myself. I was fifteen. You can excuse me (if you like) for going rather cocky and quick-tempered and full of brag the next year or two. However, my half-comic good luck with Bonnie was only a part of the reason for it. I think everything, including the enormous discoveries of the books that Mam Laura was opening up for me, was pushing me just then in the direction of a temporary and fairly harmless toughness. I thought, like most grass-green ignoramuses, that in touching the outer fringes of learning I had swallowed it all. I thought that because a few women had been pleased to play with me, I was likely the grandest stud since Adam— (who had, you must admit, certain God-damned advantages we can't any of us duplicate). I thought that because I could see the absurdity of dreaming about buying a thirty-ton outrigger, heaving an agreeable serving-wench aboard with the rest of the furniture and taking off for the rim of the dadgandered world—why, I was mature, *mature*.

I thought those chunks of whopmagullion, yet it's all right. Humility does arrive. In fact, so fortunate is our human condition, it seems to arrive for many people early enough in life so that we can enjoy it quite a little while before we're dead.

23

We came down on Seal Harbor like a May wind; Shag Donovan and a dozen of his bully boys smacked into us like a wind out of a sewer. As I think I mentioned, three of them got rather dead, but it wasn't much of a brawl. Four of them rushed our little theater while we were putting on our souped-up version of *Romeo and Juliet*.

Minna was doing Juliet as usual; the hoodlums' idea was to drag her off into the bushes while the camp was turned upside down. But Pa had smelled trouble, a gift that seldom failed him, and we were ready. There was a personal element in it: Pa had met Shag some years before and got the worst of it; this time he took an artist's pleasure in cooling Shag off before things could get too serious. Two of the three who wound up dead had got as far as grabbing Minna and tearing her clothes—rape was fashionable up there, and I suppose they expected you to get used to it—so Tom Blaine and Sam clubbed them maybe a bit harder than they meant to; luckily Minna wasn't hurt. Third man who perished got caught in a rather unusual way by Mother Spinkton's Home Remedy. He was running fast, myself behind him at the time with my knife out and blood in my eye; he was passing through the shadow of one of our supply wagons just at the moment when four of his friends toppled it over; a full case landed on his back.

In a hazy fashion, the crowd was on our side. They had to live with Donovan's gang, however, and we didn't, so they left the fighting to us, and helped us by stealing less than you'd expect them to while we were busy. Several bottles in that case of Mother Spinkton broke, after which our guests showed a marked disinclination to hang around—you could almost say that Mother won the war. And by the way, we included the full value of those busted bottles in the bill that Pa Rumley presented next day to the Seal Harbor Town Council no less. Don't think they didn't pay it. They whimpered and said they were doing it just to get rid of us before we disturbed the peace. Pa Rumley counted the silver and tied the sack to his belt without asking the obvious question. Life in Seal Harbor had its ups and downs, that was all. A small cheerful crowd followed us to the city gates and cheered us as we departed south.

Speaking of *Romeo and Juliet,* we always did our best by that one, although since our theater was only a curtained opening in the side of a wagon we had to simplify it some. The balcony job for instance—the whole stage opening had to be the balcony, with Br'er Romeo oper-

ating from the ground, which was all right—good realism
—so long as he remembered not to get himself tangled
with a wagon-wheel in a spirited moment and set the
whole damned balcony swaying and squeaking. Billy
Truro, a romantical tenor type, was usually Romeo, and
he sometimes got a little carried away, especially when it
came to bellering that line; "Oh, wilt thou leave me so un-
satisfied?" Hung up there on that plague-take-it wagon-
wheel with Minna fading out on him, he couldn't help but
win the sympathy of the house.

As for the text, Pa used to claim it was a genuine con-
demned version; Mam Laura allowed he was right. She
didn't have it among her books, so I never read the whole
thing till I had the freedom of the Heretics' secret library
at Old City. It's true there was something slightly drastic
about our manner of tearing through the play in two fif-
teen-minute acts, with an extra sword-fight, but that was
the way the yucks liked it: we aimed to please, and what
the hell more can an artist do? As Juliet, Minna Selig was
an absolute copper-riveted whiz. I can still hear her making with "Oh, swear not by the moon, the inconstant
moon, that monthly changes in her circled orb, lest that
thy love prove likewise variable." Often she'd leave out
the line with the orb in it, for she could smell a crowd
almost as acutely as Pa Rumley, and tell whether the
yucks were the type who'd be so irritated by hearing a
word they didn't know that they might start hooting and
hell-raising. Frankly I don't know what any yuck could
do with an orb.

Hoy, little Minna in her nightgown, with her dark hair
a mist around her big eyes!—why, she *was* Juliet, the way
she looked innocent as a kitten and not much smarter, and
pretty enough to make the dullest yuck want to cry. Bonnie adored watching her perform. I remember we gave
Romeo another whirl at the very first stop we made after
leaving Seal Harbor. That was down in Vairmant, for we'd
taken the road on the eastern side of the mountains, where
Rumley's hadn't appeared for several years. Bonnie and
I watched the show out front—Bonnie was still pretty
warm for me after our little excitement in April—and she
was in ecstasies whenever Minna-Juliet sounded off, hug-

ging my arm and exclaiming over and over under her breath: "Listen at them chest notes! Aw, Davy, it's gonna make me cry—ooo-eee—ooh, *a'n't* she a pisser!"

That road east of the mountains was presently leading us down along the west bank of the lovely blue Conicut, and we took our time in that pretty country, which is full of little villages and all of them good for a pitch. Pa never would explain what old trouble it was that obliged him to keep out of Nuin: it was a question you just didn't ask. But he'd been born in Nuin and was bungfull of Nuin history, and disapproved of most of it. I remember a day on the river road when we were approaching the little city state of Holy Oak, north of Lomeda. Old Will Moon was somewhat too drunk to handle the mules—a fault he had—and Pa had taken over for him while he slept it off. Pa enjoyed driving anyway, and carried on a running grudge fight with Old Lightning, the near hind mule on the headquarters wagon. Old Lightning never seemed to pay any attention, but could generally tell from Pa's voice when it was safe to fall asleep walking, or slack off so gradually that his harness-mate never caught on to the swindle. Sam was out on the front seat with me that day, Pa slouching between us with the reins, and the splendid blue of the Conicut making a music of color under a friendly sun.

The mere name of Holy Oak had got Pa started on Nuin history, a subject that always chafed him. "This little country was part of Nuin," he told us, "in the old days of Morgan the First, Morgan the Great they call the old sumbitch. I believe it fit a war of independence after he corked off, and so did Lomeda and the other pisswilly countries this side the river—ecclesi-God-damn-astical states is what they call 'em. Morgan the Great!—gentlemen hark, it's getting so you can't believe nothing you hear no more, more b' token you never could, anyway not with Morgan the Great around. They claim you don't behold his like no more, and I say that's a good thing. Account of he was a bird. This little country, this Holy Oak, is supposed to be named for a tree that was planted by Morgan the Great. Kay, I've seen it—a'n't no great circumstance of a vegetable, it's just an oak tree, and you can say it's a purty

237

little story, but wait a minute. Let's reason it out. Let's look at what history says. You got any idea how many frigging oak trees that old man is supposed to've planted for himself? Why, gentlemen hark, it's pitiful—why, if I had as many hairs growing out of my hide as that old man is supposed to've planted oak trees, I'd be bowed down, gentlemen, I'd walk on all fours like a bear till they skinned me for a rug. You may well ask why he couldn't go and plant a cherry or a pecan or something for a change—*git* up, Old Lightning, you mis'ble petrified three-tenths of an illegitimate hoss's ass, git up, *git* up!—you may well ask, and I'll tell you. The God-durn public wouldn't let him is the reason—had to be oak or nothing and that's the royalty of it."

"Still and all," Sam said, "he called himself a president, not a king, can't get around that."

"Ayah," Pa shouted, "and there's the biggest pile of hoss-shit ever left unshoveled!" Well, Sam had said it merely to keep him perking. "President my glorious aching butt! He was a king, and that's the only excuse for him. I mean you got to make allowances for a king, the way he's got everybody after him, obliged to king it from dawn to dark—planting oak trees, laying cornerstones and maternal ancestors in sinister bars, why, balls of Abraham and Jesus H. K. Hornblower Christ, they never gave that man any *rest*—git *up,* Lightning, God blast the shiveled-up mouse-turd you got for a soul, I got to speak rough to you?—no rest at all. How'd he ever find time for kinging, 's what I want to know? Look, here's how it was, on just an average day, mind you, when this poor old sumbitch, this Morgan the Great, is trying to address the fucking Senate on a matter of life and death or anyhow a lot of money. You think he's going to get a chance to fit two sentences together end to end?—gentlemen hark! No, God butter it and the Devil futter it, *no*—and why? Because up pops the Minister for Social Contacts or whatever—'Sorry, your Majesty, we got here an urgent message concerning a bed over to Wuster that a'n't been slept in yet by no royalty, only your Majesty will have to sleep into her kind of quick, so to make it up to Lowell in time for to throw a dollar acrost the Merrimac account it says here in the book you done that on the 19th of April—more b' token, your Majesty, we just this minute got in a new shipment of oak trees—' why, goodness, gentlemen, that a'n't no way to live, not for a great man. Takes the heart out of things, don't it? How can you expect a boy to want to be President if he knows it's going to be nag, nag all day long?—you Lightning, God damn your evermore backscuttled immortal spirit, *will* you git up? . . ."

It wasn't only Nuin history that bothered Pa Rumley. He didn't actually like any part of history, nor anybody in it except Cleopatra. He used to say he knew he could have made out with her real smooth, if he could have met her in her native California when he was some younger and had more ginger in his pencil. Nothing Mam Laura said could ever convince him that Cleopatra hadn't lived in California. Sometimes he got me to wondering about that myself.

From Holy Oak we went on through the other little Low Countries into Conicut, where they were still feeling the reactions from the Rambler "strike" I told you about. Business had been very brisk, but we got there late, after too many other gangs had had the same idea. We passed on into Rhode, a dreamy small land hardly bigger than Lomeda, where coastal fishing is the main occupation and trial marriage the main entertainment—only nation where the Holy Murcan Church allows divorce by consent. The Church calls Rhode a "social testing ground"; they've been testing trial marriage there for fifty-some years now without learning anything except that almost everybody likes it. As I understand it, the Church considers this irrelevant, so they go on testing in the hope of more light. While we were there—most of the summer—I naturally did as much testing as possible: Bonnie was drifting then into her permanent attachment with Joe Dulin, and Minna (I don't like to say it) could now and then be a bore. The testing was fine, and I reached no conclusions that I couldn't duck.

Since it couldn't be Nuin, we doubled back through Conicut, and over the border into the southern tip of Levannon, wintering at Norrock where the sound of the great sea is a quieter voice, most of the time, than the one

239

I heard in later years at Old City—there at Old City, Nickie and I lived our private years within sound of the harbor and the big winds. At Norrock on clear days, we could look south from our hillside camp to a far-off blur of sandy shore, the Long Island that Jed Sever used to tell us about; and that seemed far in the past; and so did his death—and my hot-cool games with Vilet—and shafts of green-gold light remembered, slanting down into the warm stillness of Moha wilderness. Oh, the sound of ocean is the same voice wherever you hear it, and be you old or young—at Old City, or Norrock, or along the miles of achingly brilliant white sand in the loneliness of southern Katskil, or speaking of tranquillity on this beach at Neonarcheos.

The spring of 219 saw us traveling north again on the great Lowland Road of Levannon, but that time we stayed with it no further than Beckon, the Levannon harbor town across the Hudson Sea from Nuber the Holy City. Beckon is the first place where there's a reliable ferry-sailer big enough for Rambler wagons. There's another at Ryebeck, opposite Katskil's capital city Kingstone, but that would not have done for us: at Kingstone someone might recognize Sam and pass on word to his wife, who would summon the policers and clobber him with every law in the book. Even the military might get snorty about him, though by this time the pisswilly Moha-Katskil war was in the fading past. At Nuber there wasn't much risk, Sam thought. We put on a mor'l show there, pantaletted up for righteousness' sweet sake, and we cleaned up nicely with undercover selling of horny pictures to brighten the private lives of the brethren; elsewhere, selling them almost openly, we never took in half as much.

We drifted south from Nuber by slow stages. People of the Kingstone district seldom traveled in the south of Katskil. Anywhere in the country, however, there was some slight risk for Sam. He didn't work with the medicine pitch, but just lent a hand at whatever was needed—muleskinning, scene-shifting, helping Grafton at his harnessmaking—and kept more or less out of sight of the public.

He particularly enjoyed being what Mam Laura called a "noise off" during her fortune-telling. She always had a

240

small tent set up for it, with a canvas partition across the middle. In the front there'd be nothing but one little table and two chairs—no crystal or incense or such-like props. But she did love a good noise off. In the back half of the tent she kept a few gidgets—a cowbell, a drum with a crack in it that was no use to Stud Dabney any more but could still make a dismal sort of noise like a bull's intestines rumbling somewhere on a misty night. At cue words, Sam would work these objects for her, or knock something over, or sometimes heave a long horrible sigh that Mam Laura warned him not to use too often because she could hardly stand it herself. He'd build up the racket little by little until Mam Laura would holler "Hoot-mon-salaam-aleikum!" or "Peace, troubled spirit!" or something else soothing, and then quit for a while. The yuck could never be *quite* sure that the canvas panel wouldn't suddenly rise up and reveal some fearful apparition such as Asmodeus or a four-horned Giasticutus or his mother-in-law. Sam claimed that his job was good for him because it like kept him in touch with the arts but without any real God-damn responsibility. He also said now and then that he was getting old.

It should not have been true, since he was only in the fifties. But in some ways I suppose it was true.

Southern Katskil is altogether unlike the bustling northern part. A ghostly, evasive land—the big rich farms are in the central part, not the real south. Small sandy roads twist through the pine barrens as if in blind pursuit of a goal you'll never learn. If such a road comes to an apparent end, you feel sure that you must have missed some turn-off that was the road's real continuation. In many places, inland as well as close to the fine white beaches, it is deep wilderness instead of the curious pines, wilderness as profound as the semitropical jungles of Penn, which I have also glimpsed. They say that bands of the flap-eared apes have sometimes been encountered in the jungle regions of southern Katskil—the same kind that are well known in Penn, shy, wild, a little dangerous.

There are no cities in southern Katskil, unless you want to give that name to the dull harbor of Vyland in the extreme south, on the immensity of Delaware Bay; it hardly deserves it, and is hardly worth the effort it takes to reach it on the long road through the barrens and jungle and enormous swamps. Vyland was once a pirate town, headquarters of a fleet that ravaged Penn's coastal commerce with the northern nations. Katskil and Penn for once agreed on something, joining forces to clean out the raiders, as we had to do in Nuin with the Cod Islands lot. The Vyland pirates didn't have the vinegar and cussedness of the Cod Islanders, however, nor any islands for refuge; it was a massacre. Today, Vyland has nothing to show but fisheries and monasteries, which smell alike.

No proper cities there in the south of Katskil, but a good many small villages, widely separated, heavily stockaded, their people often showing a dreary distrust of strangers. We seldom had a really good pitch. I have an impression there was a good deal of hookworm and malaria, possibly other sorry conditions that held the people down through no fault of their own.

One village in that region I am compelled to remember. We came to it in the fall of 319, when we were already moving northwest with the idea of crossing over into Penn near their fine city of Filadelfia. It was late afternoon; the front and rear gates of the village were shut but not locked. We rolled down the road with our customary joyous commotion, playing and singing "I'll Go No More A-Roving," a song that usually won us a better welcome than any other. When we were drawn up before the still closed and desolate gates, I blew my golden horn to make it plainer than ever that we came in way of friendship. But no one opened to us. It made Pa angry—well, the whole summer in southern Katskil had done that. "Why," he said—"bugger me blind, we'll be going in anyhow, and ask them nicely why they won't open."

Poor things, they couldn't—the few who were there in the village were dead, and had been for months. The houses were starting to fall apart, just a little—holes in the thatched roofs where squirrels had gone through, here and there a door fallen off its hinges because the wind had banged it once too often. We went into all the twenty-odd dwellings, finding the skeletons picked clean by the carrion ants and scavenger beetles—only a few, about a dozen in all I guess; all perfectly inoffensive and dry. Most of them lay on the cord or wicker cots that they use for beds in that country; two had remnants of white hair. It was peaceful. Since the dead were all indoors, and the village gates closed against wolves and dogs, the ants and beetles had done nearly all the housekeeping; we were puzzled to notice how little the bones had been disturbed by mice and rats. Pa Rumley said that rats die from the lumpy plague, same as human beings, which I hadn't known at that time. But I had a back-of-the-neck feeling—we all had it, I think—that this could be some other kind of plague.

One man (or woman) had been left behind on the village gallows. The crows and vultures had dealt with that; the bones lay in a meek pile below the still dangling rope. At any rate the criminal was now on a level with the respectable citizens who had been hopelessly sick, or too old to travel perhaps. One body still sat in a rocking chair by a closed window, a woman by the shape of the pelvis, probably an old woman; dry cartilage still held together the spine and legs and one arm. I felt some lessening of the horror as I compelled myself to look on her tranquillity. In the world that the people of Old Time left to us, these things have happened often enough, and will again.

Penn is a land of good artisans, farmers, artists, philosophers, poets, wealth, laziness—and why shouldn't they be lazy, with nature lenient as it is, and all that smell of grape and magnolia? In some parts of the land the climate is over-sweet; the heat after a time seems to come, and mildly, from inside you, although still a gift of the sun. That illusion is strongest in the eastern part of the country, where the sea breeze drives fresh off great Delaware Bay. Filadelfia on the Bay is a fine little city quite near Old-Time ruins that are thought to be harmless—in fact they say some of the modern city is actually built over the site of the old. At Filadelfia all necessary work gets done—the streets are clean, the houses orderly—but you never see anyone, slave or free, seriously exerting himself. The citizens have much more resemblance to each other than the people of the northern countries, on the whole; maybe some of their ancestors in the Years of Confusion were exceptionally prepotent—a dark, tall people with an odd hint of Polynesian as that race appears in Old-Time pictures I have seen. I have no theory to explain that. The girls are big-bodied; deliciously lovely in youth, they stay handsome when in the thirties they begin to look old; and they are kind.

Nearly everyone in Penn seems to be kind, within the limits allowed by religion and politics. Their politics consists of defending the border, which is the Delaware River, and keeping even or ahead of the game in commercial horse-trading. This they manage with a fine fleet of small river craft and a neat army which has never been defeated and has never invaded foreign soil. Trade is assisted by a corps of ambassadors in foreign courts who must be about the most trustworthy and likable liars at large—Dion says so, and my own observation, from the time Nickie and I were with him in Nuin politics up to here, bears it out.

It is a peculiarity of Penn that except for the Delaware River between her and Katskil, and a little jag of territory north of the Delaware's headwaters that used to be a boundary with Moha, her only border is with the wilderness. I believe no one outside the confidence of the republic's government has any notion how far beyond that wilderness border Penn explorers may have penetrated. I can't think of anything more graceful than a cultured Penn citizen changing the subject when the west is mentioned. We were at Jontown in the summer of 321, as far west as any Rambler gang or other foreign group is ever allowed to go; and yet a small road does lead out of that town westerly, up into the mountains, passing right by a large sign that reads END OF TRAVEL.

As for religion, Penn people appear to take it lightly and calmly, going through the motions, putting up with the flummery in a satisfying tongue-in-cheek manner, as large sections of the population evidently did in Old Time for the sake of keeping peace with the neighbors and avoiding the bitterness of true-believing priests. It is not entirely an honest way, nor a good way in my opinion; I could never take it for my way. But it does make for good manners and a certain peacefulness, and I could blame no one very much for following it, if he has no convictions strong enough to be worth the sacrifice of good nature, or if he feels that a polite conformity with the notions of fools is a necessary protection for his adult labors.

Not that I imagine the Penn people to be a super-race operating in secret of any such fairy-tale crud. There in Penn you encounter a full supply of the old mythologies, ignorance, piety, illiteracy, barbarism. But I did sometimes feel that there might be a good deal of curious thought and ferment behind the smiling indolent surface. And I often felt in the presence of Penn people like an energetic barbarian myself, surely not from any wish of theirs to make me feel so. I think that Penn is, not excepting Nuin, the most nearly civilized of the countries we have left behind us. If one had to live somewhere away from Neonarcheos, one could do worse than dwell in Penn with one or two of the big-lipped, deep-breasted women, and grow old with just enough work and worry to enjoy the other hours of idleness or slow lovemaking in the sun. Penn is not like other lands.

My father died there.

It happened in the autumn of 321 at the town of Betlam, which is forty miles north of Filadelfia—distances are large in Penn—and not far from the Delaware. Sam was fifty-six that year, he told me. Fifty-six, full of piss and vinegar and meanness, he said—but at other times, as I've mentioned, he remarked that he was getting old.

We had gone to Jontown along the southern limits of Penn, which are marked—(so far as we're told)—by a wide twisting river called the Potomac as far as a town named Cumberland. There the only road is one that leads north. From Jontown we came back eastward by a northern route, Pa Rumley having it in mind to winter in western Katskil perhaps, or wherever we might happen to be when November arrived. (Pa didn't enjoy Penn as much as the rest of us—Mother Spinkton sold badly there, the people preferring their own yarb-women and being uncommonly healthy anyhow. Peepshows didn't do very well either, for Penn citizens are remarkably unconcerned at nakedness in spite of all the church can do to distress them about it: I've seen a Penn girl who felt a fleabite flip off her skirt on the street and go to searching with no

245

sign of embarrassment, and onlookers didn't regard her with breathless horror—they just laughed and offered bad advice.) There at Betlam a number of us fell sick with what seemed at first to be mere heavy colds, with a good deal of coughing and fever. Matters quickly grew worse.

Many of the townfolk had been troubled the same way, we learned, for several weeks. They were disturbed to think we had caught the sickness from them—a generous, decent place, where they understood music also, actually listening as crowds seldom do—and they did everything they could for us.

Pa hadn't even tried a medicine pitch there at Betlam. He snarled—around camp where no Penn ear could hear him—that they were hightoned crum-bums who didn't understand science: Mother'd be wasted on them. But he knew that was foolish talk, and his heart wasn't in it. When the sickness began to alarm us, he took Mother Spinkton himself, and grumbled that it wasn't a good vintage—maybe he'd left out some God-damn essential, getting old and incompetent, somebody'd ought to bury him if he was getting that senile—and he went about miserably among us with a bottle of her, and a lost look. No bullying, no insisting that we swallow her. Some of us missed his natural manner so much that we drank her in the hope of curing *him*. It was a bad time.

Nell Grafton's boy Jack, turned fourteen that year, was the first to die.

Sam had been sitting up with him because Rex and Nell were both quite sick. This was in my wagon. I was already nearly recovered from a light attack of whatever it was. I heard Sam call me in sudden alarm, and I got to Jack's compartment in time to see the poor kid with a blazing red face—I'd given him his last licking only two weeks before, for tormenting a stray cat—apparently choke to death on his own sputum. It happened too fast; nothing Sam or I could do. My Da sent me for Pa Rumley, and as I ran off I heard him coughing distressfully; he had been seedy for a couple of days but refused to worry about himself. I found Pa helplessly drunk, no such thing as waking him, and so I fetched Mam Laura instead. I remember how a glance was enough to tell her what had happened to Jack, and then she was staring down at Sam, who sat on a stool by Jack's bunk swaying, his eyes not quite focussing. "You'll go to bed now, Sam."

"Nay, Laura, I'm not in bad shape. Things to do here."

"We'll do them. You're to go and rest."

"Rest. Why, Laura, it's been, like, a mixed-up hard-working time, you could say. You see, being a loner by trade—"

"Sam—"

"Nay, wait. Seems I got the sickness, I want to say something while my head's clear—you seen how it goes, they get off in the head. Now—"

She wouldn't let him talk until we'd got him over to their wagon and into his bunk. I had never before seen her haunted and terrified, unequal to an emergency. Once in bed and yielding to it, Sam did not talk much after all. All I could receive from his difficult and presently rambling speech was that he wanted to thank us—Mam Laura and me—because we had known him without preventing him from being a loner by trade. At least I think that was what he tried to say.

His mind seemed remote after conveying that much to us, but his body was immensely stubborn, unwilling to yield. His battle to breathe lasted three days and part of a fourth night. The medicine priests—there were two in Betlam—came and went, helping us with Sam and three others who were sick, kindly men somewhat less ignorant than those I've met outside of Penn. We made them understand that Sam was unable to speak; he was quite conscious at that moment, sneaking me a grateful look behind their backs and the remnant of a grin when I said my father had made a true confession of faith before speech became impossible.

On the third day we thought he might win through—Nell Grafton had, and Rex, and Joe Dulin. But the decline followed. He regained a slight power of speech for an hour, and talked of his childhood in the hill country and remembered loves. After that, each breath was a separate crisis of a lost war. I am reasonably certain nowadays, from knowing the books, that Old-Time medicine might have healed him. We have no such art.

In the world that Old Time left to us, these things have happened and will again.

During even the last rasping struggles to draw air into his lungs, my father's eyes were often knowing. They would turn to me with brooding and recognition sometimes, or watch a distant thought. They were never angry, peevish, beseeching or apprehensive; once or twice I thought I saw amusement in them, mild and sarcastic, the amusement of a loner by trade. The religion inflicted on him in childhood did not return in his time of weakness, as I had feared it might, to torment him: he was truly free, and died so, a free man looking with courage on the still face of evening.

24

A few weeks later, when we were on the move northward through Katskil, I told Pa Rumley and Mam Laura that I must go away alone. I found explanation was hardly needed. "Ai-yah," Pa said—"I know it a'n't as if you was a Rambler bred and born." He didn't seem annoyed, although my horn was a valued thing at the entertainments and I had become useful in other ways.

Mam Laura said: "You're like my Sam—like your father—one of those who go where the heart leads, and they're an often-wounded tribe, no help for it."

I was thinking again, as I had done hardly at all during the Rambler years, about sailing. Not to the rim of the world: Mam Laura knew as well as Captain Barr that you can't put a rim on a lump of stardust—but maybe I would sail around the world? Others (she taught me) had done it in ancient days. Thirty-ton outriggers had no share in the fantasy now; they'd been washed away when a poor scrannel pup lifted his leg in Renslar Harbor. I didn't know how it was to be done, but Nuin, one heard, was a nation of brave enterprises. The fancy to sail around the world was certainly there in me at that time, a little while after Sam died, and is in me now, having come this far, this short way to the quiet island Neonarcheos.

"You go where the heart leads," Mam Laura said. "And the heart changes in ways you don't expect, and the vision changes, perhaps turning gray. But you go."

Pa Rumley was stone-cold sober that day. "Laura, it's a strange time for a man when his father dies." He knew that, in ways she hardly could for all her wisdom. "He's not quiet with himself for some time, Laura, no matter was his father a good man or not, no matter was he a good son to his father or a bad one." Pa Rumley knew human beings; he also knew the God-damn yuman race—yumanity—which isn't the same thing. He was already selling Mother Spinkton again, by the way, in these Katskil towns, and believing in her once more himself—or anyway expecting her to work miraculous cures, which she sometimes did. He may have guessed, out of the foggy backward regions of his own life, how I sometimes dreamed that Sam Loomis was still living. He may have guessed that in the dream I would often be wretched and confused instead of pleased, unable to greet my father in a natural way. I was impotent with Minna once or twice, and she grew bored with me. I doubt if Pa guessed that: whatever troubles he may have passed through in his rambling half-century, I can't imagine him unable to get it up. "I'm figuring," Pa said, "to cross the Hudson Sea from Kingstone, and then winter up somewheres in Bershar. Why'n't you stay with us through the winter? Then if you still be a-mind for Nuin come spring, I'll take you down as far as Lomeda and all you need do is cross the Conicut."

"Kay."

"The God-damned of it is, we'll miss you."

Maybe I said some of the right things then. I was eighteen, beginning to know what they were and why one said them.

Pa also couldn't have known how often I wished I might

249

at least have seen my mother; orphanage childhood was another thing outside his experience. His own mother was warm in his memory. She kept a dressmaking shop in Wuster, a big Nuin town. It was her death when Pa was fifteen that made him take to the roads. He wouldn't have favored that wish of mine, for he was a sensible man. Wishing for the impossible in the future is a good exercise, I think, especially for children; wishing for it in the past is surely the emptiest and saddest of occupations.

The only thing I remember with real clearness about that winter in Bershar, my last with the Ramblers, is the drill that Mam Laura gave me in polite manners. I'd encounter them in Nuin, she said, in fact I ought to do so deliberately, seeking out people who knew how to manage themselves with grace and thoughtfulness. Manners mattered, Mam Laura said, and if I didn't think so I was a damn fool. Which left me brash enough to ask why. She said: "Would you want to ride a wagon with no grease on the axles? But that isn't all. If you've got an honest heart, the outward show may become something more than that. Be pleasant to someone for any reason and you may easily wind up liking the poor sod, which does no harm."

They flung a party for me at Lomeda, Rambler style, stalling all work at the wharf and getting the ferry-sailer captain too joyously drunk to object to anything. I remember Minna telling him she'd remember him all her life, because sailors come and sailors go, but ever since she'd been old enough to belay a marlinspike she'd dreamed of seeing a live sailing captain with *balls*. I was well illuminated too when they bundled me aboard, all hollering and crying and giving good advice. I stopped singing when the ropes were cast off and I knew I was actually leaving my people, but I didn't sober up even when the captain brought her in on the Nuin side. He did so with a slam that lifted a timber off the pier, and cussed everyone in sight for building the bald-assed cotton-picking pier so that it couldn't hold up under the impact of a man with *balls*. That was fun.

To my fancy, even the air of Nuin tastes different from the air of other lands. Except for Penn, it is the oldest civilization of modern times, at least on that continent—

nay, I can't say that, either, for what do I know of the vague Misipan Empire in the far south, and who could deny the possibility of a great nation, or many of them, in the far western region that I know the continent does possess? Pity me, friends, only if I lose the awareness of my own ignorance.

Penn does not seem to have been much concerned with recording the events of its last two or three centuries—too good-natured, maybe. Nuin is loaded with history, bemused by it, sparkling with it; and shadowed by it. Dion, today still doggedly engaged in setting down whatever he can recall of that history, has never quite come out from under the shadow of it—how could he, and for that matter why should he? It was his world, until we sailed.

Oh, and sometimes I am—not weary of words, but beat-out and a little foolish from the effort, the pleasure and torment of trying to preserve a fraction of my life in the continually moving medium of words. And I think of asking this poor prince—my equal and superior, whipping-boy, cherished friend—to go on with this book if I should give up, stop short of what I set out to do and walk away from it. As I walked away from Rumley's Ramblers when there was no honest need to do so. But he couldn't do that, and with a grain of sense, I hold myself back from asking it.

When I came off the boat at Hamden, the Nuin ferry town across from Lomeda, what I first noticed was the statues. There were some modern ones, clumsy but really not too bad, of Morgan the Great and a few other well-nourished majesties, and these were shown up dreadfully by the fine sculpture of the Old-Time figures—including many bronzes that I'm certain would have been melted down for the metal anywhere except in Nuin. Hamden is proud of them—a fine, healthy, middle-sized town, clean and friendly, open to the river and neatly stockaded on the other three sides; proud of its white-painted houses too, and the pretty green, and the well-conducted market.

All the same, Old City has a flock of statues to make Hamden or any other town look sick. Most of them are of Old Time, which in Nuin is sometimes made to seem almost like yesterday, an illusion I never felt in any other place. I'm thinking at the moment of a fine seated bronze gentleman in Palace Square, who carries clear traces of ancient paint in the cracks and hollows of his patinaed garments. It's Old-Time paint, they say. Some President—Morgan II, I think—had it covered over with thick modern varnish to preserve it. It appears in patches of crimson, green, and purple; no blue. Odd to think that this unknown religious ritual must have been going on in the very last days when the Old-Time world was passing away. The inscribed name of the subject of worship is John Harvard. Nobody seems quite clear about who he was, but he sits there modestly, rather stuffily, with timeless and splendid indifference.

I wore new clothes that day at Hamden, a new shoulder-sack for my horn that Minna had sewed for me, and there was money in my belt, for the Ramblers had taken up a collection and showered me with every sort of kindness. I had still no clear aim, no plan; at eighteen, no true decision what work I would do. I knew a little carpentry, a little music; I knew the wilderness and the ways of the roads. I knew I was a loner by trade.

In the inn at Hamden I found myself in the middle of a bunch of pilgrims who were finishing the last part of what Nuin people call the Loop Journey. It means a trip from Old City up into the wild glorious mountain land of the Province of Hampsher—more people live up there in the cool hills than you'd ever suppose—then south more or less following the great Conicut River as far as Hamden or Shopee Falls, and back to Old City by southern roads. It is a secular pilgrimage. The Church approves it, and stops are made at all the holy shrines and other foci of piety along the way, but there's nothing specifically sacred about the junket itself. Anybody can play, and many do, including respectable sinners and card-sharps and musicians and prosties and all the other folk who keep life from getting dull.

Almost as soon as I entered the taproom after engaging a room for the night, a dark boy made friends with me, and I spotted him for a sinner right away because of his open kindliness and good nature. He was dressed in a Nuin style that was beginning to spread beyond that country but not enough so that I'd grown used to it—baggy knee-length britches and a loose shirt, belted in but allowed to flop out over the belt everywhere except at the knife-hilt, where it might interfere with a quick draw. About half the other pilgrims in the taproom were dressed in that style, but the boy who took it on himself to greet me and make me feel at ease was the only one who carried a rapier at his hip instead of the usual short knife. He had a knife too, I learned later, but wore it under his shirt as I used to wear mine before my Rambler days.

That rapier was a beautiful wicked thing, less than two feet long, light and delicate, scarcely half an inch at the widest point, of Penn steel so fine that it sang to a touch almost like dainty glassware. A rich man's tool, I thought, but I had learned from Mam Laura that one didn't ask about the price of such a thing unless one meant to buy, and often not then. The boy handled it like an extension of his arm. He liked to make it float almost noiselessly from the scabbard, and run his fingers airily up and down the side as if his mind weren't with it at all, which made everyone in the room extremely nervous for some reason and of course anxious not to show it. Nothing indicated how much he enjoyed this except a very light crinkling of the skin at the corners of his brown eyes, and some instinct seemed to tell him when to put it away. Instinct, or a special tone in the throat-clearings of one of the priests in charge of the group.

There were two of these, Father Bland and Father Mordan, one fat and one thin, one greasy and the other a bit dry and scurfy. Father Bland himself remarked that they represented the good bacon of religion, and everyone obligingly laughed except Father Mordan the lean one who stayed in character, that is to say grumpy. I'd hardly have taken any of the crowd for pilgrims if the landlord hadn't tipped me off, and I learned that some were really just travelers who had joined the group for safety or sociability.

"Compliments of Father Bland and Father Mordan," said the boy in greeting me, "and will you drink wid us now or a little sooner?" I hadn't heard much of the Nuin accent at that time. Nuin people don't travel very often outside their own land—Nuin has everything, they say, so what would they gain by it? I guessed the boy to be near my own age, though he acted older. There was a slightness and a delicacy about him that suggested the feminine, but without weakness. I remember in the first half-hour I knew him I wondered if his little games with the rapier might not have a practical side, as a way of discouraging anyone who might misunderstand his nature.

"Honored," I said—an item of social jazz that I happened to remember from Mam Laura's coaching. "Honored and delighted to drink anyone under the table or else join him there."

"Nay, we're a soberish crowd," he said. "Everything in moderation. Including, I insist, moderation—but that's a point I can seldom get across to my elders." He was watching me with uncanny sharpness. "I'm Michael Summers of Old City. Forgive the impudent curiosity—who are you, sir, and where from?"

"Davy—that is, David—of—well, of Moha—I mean—"

"David de Moha?"

"Oh lordy no!" I said, and noticed that everyone in the taproom had shut up, the better to enjoy our private conversation. "I just meant I come from Moha, back along. My last name's—uh—Loomis."

I'm sure he believed, for a while at least, that I was giving a false name, and he wanted to help me with it. He took me over to the others, introduced me as David Loomis with the nicest casualness, pushed me into a comfortable chair, called for fresh drinks—all as if I were somehow important, I couldn't think why.

From scraps I heard before they went quiet, I knew Father Mordan, the thin dry one, had been instructing the company concerning original sin, a regular duty which he'd pretty well wound up for the day—anyway he was ready to acknowledge Michael's presentation of me with a smile. The smile would have quickly hardened the grease on a flaming plum pudding, but he meant it kindly; some people just happen to be born with vinegar for blood and lemons for balls, that's all it is.

"Rest yourself," Michael said to me, "and look us over, man, the way you might care to travel wid us a little distance, or all the way to Old City if you're a-mind. We start

254

for there tomorrow, last part of the Loop Journey, back home to our own honest beds and beans and bosoms."

I couldn't have said no to Michael, and anyway it was what I wished. I loafed there while we talked and sang the day into night. There were two or three fair singers, and a girl with a lively guitar; with my horn, it made an evening of music, and I drank enough to help me avoid noticing how far it was from Rambler standards. Nay, it was only the drinks and Michael that kept me from going mad with homesickness—no other word; homesickness for a cubby-hole on wheels with no destination except the next village down the road.

Except for Michael and the two priests and one other, those pilgrims have become dim in my memory, and I've forgotten the name of the one other. He was a fine old gray gandyshank drink of water with droopy four inch whiskers on his upper lip that made you want to ring him like a bell, but he seemed to be a good deal of a scholar, so you let the impulse slide. When Michael introduced us he said on a soft sigh: "Mmmd." Michael told me later that this is how you say "Charmed!" in Oxfoot English, which is what the gandyshank spoke. I don't know why they call it that—there's very little real bull in it, and hardly any English.

Of course I'll always remember Michael's face winking at me, late in the evening, when we had to tear off a Murcan hymn to please Father Bland, for the wink gave me a feverish need to talk to him privately and learn whether I had met another loner of my own kind, even a heretic. Once the thought entered my head, it seemed to me that Michael had been feeling me out along that line, as subtly as a wild creature tasting the breeze, ever since we'd met.

He gave me the opportunity that night, late, slipping into my room with a candle he didn't light until he had closed the door. "May we talk, David Loomis? Something on my mind, but send me away if you're too beat and want to sleep." He was still fully dressed, I noticed, including the rapier.

I wasn't sleepy. He pulled a chair near my bed and sat straddling it, relaxed as a little cat. I was afraid of him in several ways along with a powerful affection, thinking also how slight he looked, as if a high wind would blow him away. His voice seemed more like a contralto than a tenor; he had not sung with us, claiming to be tone-deaf, and that wasn't true, but he had his reasons. "David Loomis, when I turn my face toward you I smell heresy. Nay, don't be alarmed, please. I'm hunting for it, but from the heretics' side, do you understand?—not the other." Nobody ever watched me as penetratingly as Michael did then, before he rapped out a small sharp question: "No impulse to run tell Father Mordan?"

"None," I said—"what do you take me for?"

"I had to ask," Michael said. "I've as good as told you I'm a heretic, the dangerous kind, and I had to watch for any such impulse in you. If I had seen it, I'd have had some decision to make."

I looked at the rapier. "With that?"

It seemed to distress him. He shook his head, turning his exploring gaze away. "Nay, I don't think I could do that to you. If there'd been danger of your betraying me, I suppose I'd have faded—taking you along until we'd made a safe distance. But I see no such danger. I think you're a heretic yourself. Do you believe God made the world for man?"

"For a long time," I said, "I haven't believed in God at all."

"It doesn't scare you?"

"No."

"I like you, Davy . . ." We must have talked two hours that night. My life tumbled out in words because he convinced me he wanted to know of it, convinced me it mattered to him—as a personal thing, not solely because we were like-minded and traveling the same road. In the past, only Sam and Mam Laura (and very far in the past, on a different level, little Caron who is probably dead) had made me feel what I said mattered and what I had done was in its own fashion a bit of history. Now the warmth, the reaching out and the recognition, came from one of my own age who clearly had a history of learning and manners equalling or surpassing Mam Laura's; one who was also an adventurer engaged in dangerous work that set my own ambition glowing.

I told Michael what I had dreamed about journeying,

thinking long ago that I would see the sun set afire for the day. "There are other fires to be lit," Michael said, "smaller than the sun in certain ways but not others. Fires in human minds and hearts." Yes, he was concerned with revolution in those days. Here on the island Neonarcheos I am of course never so sure of anything as I suppose we have to be sure at eighteen.

The reaching out and the recognition—why, growing up is partly a succession of recognitions. I have heard that growing old will turn out to be a series of good-byes. I think it was Captain Barr who made that remark to me, not very long ago.

Michael, that first night while the rest of the inn was snoring, did not tell me as much of his own story in return. Some things he was not ready to tell until he knew me better, others he could not have told without violating his oath to the membership of the Society of Heretics. But he was free to tell me that such a society existed in Nuin and was beginning to have a trifle of following beyond Nuin's borders. He could tell me his conviction that the Church would not rule forever, perhaps not even much longer—optimism of his own youth there, I think. And he said just before he left me that if I wished, he could very soon put me in touch with someone who would admit me to tentative membership. Probation, they called it—was I interested?

Does a fish swim? I wanted to hop out of bed and hug him, but before I could he produced a little flask from inside his shirt and handed it to me. "Virgin's milk," he said, "sometimes called cawn-squeezings—hey, go easy, you sumbitch, it's got to last us all the way to Wuster. Sleep on the talk, Davy, and come along with our gaggle of pilgrims in the morning and we'll talk again. But another time, if a heretic winks at you, don't wink back if there's a priest where he can catch the wind of your eyelashes."

"Oh!—"

"Nay, no sweat, they didn't notice anything. But be careful, friend. That's how joes like you and me stay alive."

In the morning, on the road, Father Mordan was still

concerned with original sin, and it may have prevented his insides from dealing rightly with a very good breakfast, for his discourse along the first mile or two of a dusty highway was punctuated by the sudden, uncomfortable type of burp. Father Bland endured it as long as he could and then picked on a theological point—I'm sure God alone could have appreciated it—to give Father Mordan the father and mother of an argument. Under cover of this inspiring noise and heat, Michael and I fell behind out of earshot and continued our conversation of the night.

He seemed in a more speculative frame of mind, taking me for granted a little more too. Yet there were also more unspoken things between us, in spite of the agreements and discoveries of a sudden friendship. Most of that morning's talk I remember only in bits and pieces, though all the feeling of it remains with me. "Davy—you might feel perhaps that Father Mordan is not in possession of absolute truth?"

"Well, after all—"

"Uhha. Father Bland, you know, would honestly like to see everybody safe in a comfortable heaven—no pain, no sin, just glory-glory all day long. It would bore the hell out of you or me, but he truly believes he'd like it, and so would everybody else. And that jo, Davy, gave up a rich man's existence to serve the rest of his life as a small-time priest. And in case you think there's anything trifling about him—well, a month ago he went with me into a smallpox-rotten village up in Hampsher, an escort for a wagon-load of food for any poor devils that might be still alive. The wagon-driver wouldn't go without a priest. Not a one of the other pilgrims would go, and Father Mordan felt it his duty to stay behind with them. Just Father Bland and a bond-servant driver and me—and no danger for me because I had the disease in childhood and happen to know it gives immunity, which most people won't believe—but Father Bland never had it. Is Father Bland in possession of absolute truth?"

"No."

"Why?"

In the night when he went away with his candle he had left me testing my own thoughts a while before I could

258

sleep—testing, and grappling with them to the point of suffering; but then I did sleep, profoundly and restfully. Not that I was in any sense free of confusion or uncertainty—I am not today—but what Michael was doing with me that morning was a very gentle kind of wrestling after all, demanding only that I think for myself, as Mam Laura had done in her different way. I said: "Why, Michael, I think it's because absolute truth either doesn't exist or can't be reached. A man's being brave and kindly doesn't make him wise."

We went on a time in silence, I remember, but it wasn't long before Michael took hold of my arm and said without smiling: "You are now in touch with someone who can admit you to probationary membership in the Society of Heretics. Do you still want it?"

"You yourself? You have that authority?"

He grinned then, more like a boy. "For six months, but in all that time until now I haven't found anyone who met the requirements. I didn't want to mystify you, but had to sleep on it myself. Probation only—more I can't do, but in Old City I'll guarantee you a welcome, and you'll meet others who can take you further. They'll set you things to do, some of which you won't understand right away." All I could say was a stumbling thanks, which he brushed aside.

We had halted there in the sunny road, and I noticed I could no longer even hear the pilgrims who had gone on ahead. It was a tranquil open place, where a small stream crossed the road through a culvert and wandered away into a field. The Bland-Mordan argument was less than dust on the breeze, but I said: "Should we catch up with them?"

"For my part," Michael said, "I've no more use for them. I enjoyed traveling with them, if only for the privilege of hearing 'Holy, Holy, Holy' sung in Oxfoot English with guitar accompaniment, but now I'd sooner go on to Old City with no company but yourself—if you like the thought. I have money, and a skill with this little pigsticker that makes up for my lack of brawn. I don't know the wilderness in the ways you were telling me about last night, but from here to Old City it's all roads and safe inns. How about it?"

"That's what I'd like."

He was studying the stream, and its vanishing in taller growth some distance from the road. "Those willows," he said—"away off the other side of that thicket—would they mean a pool, Davy? I'd like a dip, to wash off Mordan's original sin."

I think that was the first time I'd ever heard a priest mentioned without his title. It gave me a chill that was at first fright, then pleasure, then matter-of-fact amusement. "It should be a pool," I said, "or they wouldn't be clustered like that . . ."

I suppose there could have been some danger out in the grassland, but it seemed like safe country as we slipped through the grass, the pilgrims becoming long-ago things and then forgotten, and found the pool. I had begun to understand about Michael, but not entirely until I saw the shirt impatiently flung away from a ridiculous bandage that bound his upper chest. Then that was gone, the small woman's breasts set free.

She took off the rapier with care, but not the clumsy trousers—those she dropped and sent flying with a kick. She stood by me then all gravity and abstracted sweetness, proud of her brown slimness, hiding nothing. Seeing I was too dazed and too much in love to move, she touched the bluish tattoo on her upper arm and said: "This doesn't trouble you, does it, Davy? Aristocracy, caste—it means nothing among the Heretics."

"It doesn't trouble me. Nothing should trouble me much if I can be with you the rest of my life."

I remember she put out her golden hand against my chest and pushed me lightly, glancing at the pool, smiling for the first time since she had bared herself. "Does it look deep enough?" Nickie asked me. "Deep enough for diving?"

25

Six years ago I wrote that last episode, and laid down my pen to yawn and stretch with pleasure, remembering the pool and the hushed morning and the love we had on the sunny grass. I supposed that in a day or so I would go on writing, probably for several chapters, in spite of my feeling that I had already ended the principal part of the story I set out to tell. I thought I would go on, residing simultaneously here at Neonarcheos and at this imaginary inn of ours on the blind side of eternity or wherever you would prefer it to be—whoever you are—with many events belonging to a later time.

Particularly I had it in mind to tell of the two years that Nickie and I spent in Old City before what happened to us at that Festival of Fools. It is another book. I think I shall try to write it, after the *Morning Star* sails again and I with her, but I may not be able to. I don't know. I am thirty-five, therefore obviously not the same person who wrote you those twenty-four chapters when Nickie was no further away than a footnote and a kiss. I shall leave what I have written behind me, with Dion, when I sail.

The years in Old City after the Festival of Fools, the work with Dion in the heady, exciting, half-repellent atmosphere of high politics, the laws and councils and attempted reforms, the war we won against a pack of thieves and the war we lost against a horde of the self-righteous —all that is certainly another book, and I have a suspicion that Dion himself may be writing it, shielding himself by a dignified reticence from possible footnotes.* If I attempt that, it will not be for a long time.

---

* No, that wasn't the reason for keeping it to myself. The reason is that I have not Davy's open nature. He was able somehow to struggle for truth in autobiography even while "pursued by foot-

I laid down my pen that evening six years ago, and a few moments later I heard Nickie call me. Her voice brought me out of a hazy brown study: I think I had wandered back to the time of my father's death, and I was reflecting unoriginally how grief is likely to translate itself into philosophy, if you can wait for it, because it must.

As I see it today, my father's death appears to be a true part of the story I was first compelled to write. That story ended, not as I thought at first, when the tiger entered the village and I learned who Sam was, but with the death of Sam Loomis, a loner by trade. For that was surely the occasion when the subject of this book, less homely than a mud-turkle and well-hung, got turned loose on the world (which still turns, I think)—oh, but why now should I bother my head over what did or didn't belong in that story? There were so many stories I could never be certain which I was telling, and it doesn't matter as much as I thought it did when I was bothering you and your Aunt Cassandra about varieties of time. It may be well enough to look at the enigma, the crazy glory and murk of our living-and-dying with a pen in your hand, but try it yourself—you'll find more stories than you knew, and you'll find mirth, tragedy, dirt, splendor, ecstasy, weariness, laughter and rage and tears all so intricately dependent on each other, intertwined like copulating snakes or the busy branches of a jinny-creeper—why, don't be troubling yourself about opposites and balances but never mind, take hold of one branch and you touch them all.

I heard Nickie call me. Her pains had begun. It was the same time of evening that it is now—but this is May 20, 338—in the same tropic shelter which has held up well for

notes" and with Miranda and me looking over his shoulder most of the time. I could never attempt that. For me the struggle must be in the dark, intensely private, doubtful of outcome. This note is written in May of 339, a full year after Davy's departure with the *Morning Star*—(Barr intended to bring her back in four months). If Davy returns—(we still hope, but don't talk about it any more)—I could perhaps show him what I have written about the years of the Regency, and maybe we could talk more frankly than we ever did in the old days. I would now, of course, give anything I possess for the corniest of his footnotes.

—D.M.M.

six years, same chair and desk, same view of the quiet beach. But since everything has crept forward six long years in time, nothing at all is the same, not even the flesh of my fingers curved against a different pen. The light appears the same, a luminous red flush receding from the pallor of the sand, and a few high white clouds drifting on the eastward course that the old *Morning Star* will be taking in a few days.

The labor pains were a month premature. That alone did not alarm us too much in the first hours. Ted Marsh and Adna-Lee Jason, who know more Old-Time medicine than the rest of us, did whatever was possible. Old-Time knowledge we have, wretchedly incomplete. Old-Time drugs and equipment we have not—unattainable as the Midnight Star. Therefore diagnosis is mainly guesswork, important surgery unthinkable, and our partial possession of the ancient knowledge often a mockery.

Nickie fought the pain for eighteen hours and was at length delivered of a thing with a swollen head which was able to live an hour or two of shrieking empty existence, but the bleeding would not stop. The mue weighed twelve pounds, and she—why, at our lodgings in Old City I used to carry her up two flights of stairs for the joy of it and be hardly winded at the top of the climb. The bleeding would not stop. She had glimpsed the mue in spite of us and understood, and so could not even die with the consolation of an illusion. In the world that Old Time left to us, these things have happened and will again.

I sail before long in the *Morning Star* with Captain Barr and a small company—five women and nine other men, all of us chosen by Dion because we clearly possess what he calls a "controlled discontent." All voluntary, naturally, and me he did not exactly choose, but only asked me: "Do you want to go, Davy?" I said that I did, and he kissed my forehead in the manner of the old Nuin nobility, a thing I haven't known him to do for years, but we've said nothing more about the sailing and probably won't until the day Barr chooses.

I am thirty-five and Dion is fifty. We fought in two wars together. We tried to draw a great nation a step or two beyond the sodden ignorance of this era. We sailed together

263

into the great sea and found this island Neonarcheos. We loved the same woman. "Controlled discontent"—well, I think that appraisal was meant for me as much as for the rest. It is a compliment, but with the inevitable dark side too: we fourteen, Captain Barr and myself and the others, fitted by temperament and circumstance for the task of explorers, are to a great degree unfitted for anything else.

The explorer's task has, I'd say, very little of the splendor a boy's imagination gives it. I dreamed a multitude of fancies lying in the sun before my cave on North Mountain; but Captain Barr and I are now much more decently concerned with survival biscuits and pemmican and sauerkraut, and trying to rebuild the head of the *Morning Star* a mite further aft if you'll excuse the expression. But all that doesn't mean that the glory goes out of exploring. It is there, and the inner rewards are real enough. The sea of ignorance is vast beyond measuring, and so I, an animalcule with his dab of phosphorescence, set that light against it and find no reason to be ashamed of my pride.

In the six years we have been able to build another sailing vessel, a neat small thing the Old-Time builders would describe as a yawl. Those who remain behind can make use of the other islands while we are gone.

Our flax seed has grown well on Neonarcheos, so the *Morning Star* has good new canvas. We carry provisions for four months. Our immediate mission is to reach the mainland of what was called Europe, which should take far less time than that, learn what we can of it, and return. Our first landfall should be the coast of what was Portugal, or Spain, we suppose. But currents and winds are not as they were in Old Time.

We who sail are all childless. The women may not be sterile, but none has ever conceived, and the youngest is twenty-five. In the six years at Neonarcheos, twenty-one normal children have been born, to seven of the women. I did not father any of them. I did make Nora Servern pregnant. It was her wish, and Dion's too; they thought, and the same as told me, that they hoped it would draw me out of a black and self-destroying mood that had held me for a long time. What did draw me out of it I'll never know —just time, maybe. Sweet Nora was good to love, and that

264

part of the episode certainly helped bring me back into acceptance of daily living. But though Nora was able to bear Dion two healthy girls, the child she bore me was a mue not unlike the one for whom Nickie's life was thrown away.

Thus I am obliged to understand that the fault was not in Nickie's seed but in mine. I am not illogical enough to say that I killed her; who could live with that? But it is true that she was killed by an evil that Old Time set adrift, that came down through the generations, through Sam's body or my mother's—who could say?—to hide in that part of mine which ought to be the safest, the least corrupted. This happened, to me and to countless others, and will again.

My only children are certain thoughts I may have been able to give you. I can sometimes be tranquil in my heart about this, when I remember how much exploring there is to be done. There seems to be enough undiscovered territory, in the mind and the rest of the world—I think I could have written, in the world and the rest of the mind —so that we shall not have it all mapped before sundown, not this Wednesday.

I went down to the beach last night, because I heard the wind, and the ocean was long-voiced on the sand, and the stars were out. Before long I shall hear that music at the bows, or as a following whisper in the times when I have the wheel in my hands. I sail because I desire it; I have no children except those in your care, but may I not tell you that exploration also is an act of love?

I gave words to the breakers last night, a game I have often played, a harmless way of aiding the mind to speak to itself. You who are the earth can ask, and you who are the sea may answer, and if there is truth spoken you know the source.

I asked whether the generations could some day restore the good of Old Time without the evil, and the ocean that was a voice in my mind suggested: Maybe soon, maybe only another thousand years.

ABOUT THE AUTHOR

Edgar Pangborn was born in New York City in 1909. He attended Harvard and the New England Conservatory of Music, and he now lives and writes in upstate New York. His previous books include *West of the Sun* (1952), *A Mirror for Observers* (1953), *Wilderness of Spring* (1958), and *The Trial of Callista Blake* (1961). His short stories have appeared in numerous magazines and anthologies.

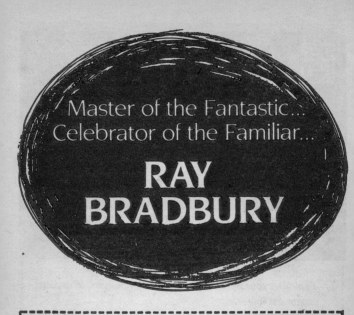

Master of the Fantastic...
Celebrator of the Familiar...

RAY BRADBURY